"LET THE DUEL BEGIN."

Incensed by Christopher Grove's insolence, Adam Vickers sprang forward like a horse released from a starting gate, slashing with the saber, a mighty stroke. The point grazed Christopher below the ribs, ripping his shirt and slicing his flesh and stinging like a thousand angry fire ants.

"No rules!" a spectator reminded the combatants, encouraging Vickers to hurl a handful of sand into Christopher's face. Momentarily blinded, Christopher staggered backward as Vickers pounced like a jungle cat, his blade biting deeply into the flesh of Christopher's sword arm. Blood gushed through Christopher's clawing fingers. Vickers pressed him, slashing with the saber again like a man possessed.

For the first time in his life Christopher stared Death in the face. Adam Vickers was going to cut him into bloody pieces. . . .

GONE TO TEXAS

① SIGNET

SAGAS OF THE AMERICAN WEST
BY JASON MANNING

☐ **GONE TO TEXAS** When Flintlock Jones and his grandson Christopher Groves come to the aid of President Andrew Jackson to aid Texas in gaining its independence from Mexico, the pair get more than they bargained for as kidnappers, river pirates, cutthroats, and bounty hunters lay in wait for them on a blood-soaked trail from Kentucky to hostile Texas territory. (185005—$4.50)

☐ **GREEN RIVER RENDEZVOUS** Zach Hannah was a legend of courage, skill, and strength ... Now he faces the most deadly native tribe in the west and the most brutal brigade of trappers ever to make the high country a killing ground. (177142—$4.50)

☐ **BATTLE OF THE TETON BASIN** Zach Hannah wants to be left alone, high in the mountains, with his Indian bride. But as long as Sean Michael Devlin lives, Zach can find no peace. Zach must track down this man— the former friend who stole his wife and left him to die at the hands of the Blackfeet. Zach and Devlin square off in a final reckoning ... that only one of them will survive. (178297—$4.50)

*Prices slightly higher in Canada

GONE TO TEXAS

by

Jason Manning

A SIGNET BOOK

SIGNET
Published by the Penguin Group
Penguin Books USA Inc., 375 Hudson Street,
New York, New York 10014, U.S.A.
Penguin Books Ltd, 27 Wrights Lane,
London W8 5TZ, England
Penguin Books Australia Ltd, Ringwood,
Victoria, Australia
Penguin Books Canada Ltd, 10 Alcorn Avenue,
Toronto, Ontario, Canada M4V 3B2
Penguin Books (N.Z.) Ltd, 182–190 Wairau Road,
Auckland 10, New Zealand

Penguin Books Ltd, Registered Offices:
Harmondsworth, Middlesex, England

First published by Signet, an imprint of Dutton Signet,
a division of Penguin Books USA Inc.

First Printing, August, 1995
10 9 8 7 6 5 4 3 2 1

PART ONE

✛

The Point

Chapter 1

The dinner hour, commencing at one o'clock in the afternoon every single day of the year, was the only time between dawn and dusk that a West Point cadet had to spend on his own pursuits. While most of his fellow cadets returned to their quarters, or gathered in small groups on the commons to indulge in idle conversation, Christopher Groves liked to walk. The serene beauty of the site of the United States Military Academy never failed to soothe his sometimes troubled soul.

Thirty-seven miles north of New York, the Academy was perched on the west bank of the Hudson River, at a place where the river bends, on a high level plain at the point of which was located the crumbling vestiges of old Fort Clinton. George Washington had described the Hudson as the "Key to the Continent" during the Revolution. It was here that a gigantic chain—like something, a romantic remarked, that had been used to bound Prometheus or some other mighty hero of Greek mythology—was stretched across the river to prevent the British from sailing upriver and cutting the rebellious colonies into two, more easily conquered, parts. Remnants of that massive chain were on display at the Academy.

West Point's fortifications were designed by Thaddeus Kosciuszko, the Pole who had volunteered his services to the cause of the American patriots. His engineering skill had proved to be of immeasurable service to that cause, his work at West Point making that stronghold virtually impregnable.

Leaving the mess hall, Christopher walked briskly along a path which led him past the post office and laboratory, then under the guns of the siege battery and to the river where the long dock jutted like a fat upside-down L into the river. The trail narrowed as it wound in serpentine fashion across steep wooded slopes to the point, above which loomed the old fort now falling into a disgraceful state of disrepair. It was nearly summer. The cool shade of the trees was a pleasure.

Gazing out at the wide blue-green expanse of the Hudson, nestled between forested heights, Christopher noticed several white-sailed skiffs on the water. He thought of his father. It never failed—he always did when he saw a sailing ship, be it skiff or schooner. Jonathan Groves had first made a name for himself as a valiant young naval officer in the war against the Barbary pirates almost thirty years ago.

Jonathan had gone on to achieve a measure of fame as the man responsible for the capture of the traitor Aaron Burr. The thought of Burr brought another traitor to Christopher's mind. Benedict Arnold. Feeling he had not received his just due from the Continental Congress as one of the heroes of the revolution, Arnold had tried to betray his fellow patriots by conspiring to hand West Point over to the British in return for twenty thousand pounds sterling and a commission in King George's redcoat army. Luckily for the patriot cause, the scheme had been exposed before any damage was done.

Jonathan's involvement in the capture of Burr, who had sought to separate the western lands from the republic and establish his own private domain—or so they said; there was no solid evidence, and Burr had been acquitted of all charges by none other than John Marshall, chief justice of the United States—had catapulted the young cadet's father into national prominence. Jona-

than had gone on to serve in the state legislature of
Kentucky and then in the Congress, resigning from the
latter institution to fight Indians in the bloody Northwest
during the War of 1812. He had been at New Orleans
with Old Hickory, and again with Jackson in the campaign against the Creeks, finally dying on the field of
battle, which had long been his desire, in the Seminole
Campaign.

Jonathan Groves' rise to national hero was the reason
Christopher was here at West Point. Two presidents had
known and relied on his father. Thomas Jefferson had
given him the mission to stop Burr. Andrew Jackson,
currently residing in the White House as the republic's
seventh chief magistrate, had considered Jonathan one
of his best lieutenants. Sam Houston, who until recently
had been governor of Tennessee, had called him friend.

A frown creased Christopher's brow. Having just
turned twenty-three, he was of medium height and slender build. Broad across the shoulders and slender at the
hips, he cut a fine figure in his uniform—regulation gray
tunic and white trousers and, of course, every cadet's
pride and joy, the bell-crowned black leather cap with
the polished leather visor and the yellow scales and eagle
which could be fastened under the chin. By anyone's
standards he was a handsome young man. His chin was
square and strong, with more than a hint of stubborn-
ness. His mouth, a testament of determination, could
flash in an easy white grin. His nose was aquiline, his
brow high. And his eyes, a startling sea green in color,
were keen and intelligent. Despite his deceptively slender build he was endowed with an agile strength. Physi-
cally he was resilient—a cadet had to be to endure the
constant drill which was a feature of the Academy. His
constitution was cast iron, which was lucky, as the worst
thing about West Point was the food. A cadet's diet was
atrociously poor. Yet Christopher thrived. Food was of
no importance to him except as fuel for the body. His

mind was a sponge that soaked up the heavy doses of French and mathematics which inundated the cadets in the Point's sand-floored "academies."

Now in his second year, Christopher was a popular member of the Corps of Cadets. Though reserved, sometimes to the point of reticence, he was amiable and reliable and eminently fair-minded. Apart from that, he was at the top of his class in horsemanship—which was little wonder considering his upbringing at Elm Tree, where some of Kentucky's most prized thoroughbreds were raised—and near the top in swordsmanship and academics. He was an accomplished dancer, and the apple of many a young belle's eye, and seldom did he have difficulty finding a dance partner for the "hops" which were all-too-infrequently arranged to break the monotony of drill and study, study and drill that distinguished life at West Point. Dancing ranked with fencing and horsemanship as an accomplishment necessary for a gentleman, and as one who excelled in all three pursuits, Christopher had already made a name for himself.

And yet he often wondered if he was not here under false pretenses. These self-doubts plagued him whenever his thoughts turned to his father. The entire nation held Jonathan Groves in high regard, but the people of the United States did not know the whole truth. In his private life Jonathan had been anything but heroic. His notorious and long-standing affair with Emily Cooper was common knowledge—and a source of unending humiliation for his son. But few knew of his penchant for strong drink, developed in his later years, when he was off on one campaign or another, fighting the British or the Indians and trying desperately to get himself killed. A suicidal alcoholic and philanderer—that was the father Christopher knew, though not at all well, since he had seldom come home to Elm Tree and his wife and son. Those few who were aware of these dark secrets—men like Jackson and Houston, to name two—kept it to themselves, out of respect, Christopher supposed, for a fallen comrade-in-arms.

To say that Christopher hated his father would be too strong a statement, yet Christopher had never been able to forgive what had been done to his beloved and long-suffering mother. Since the age of five, Christopher—and his mother, Rebecca—had seen precious little of Jonathan Groves. But it was on the strength of the hero's name that Christopher had been accepted into the Military Academy. Ironically, nearly everyone here had a higher opinion of his father than he.

Nearly everyone. Christopher knew of one exception. Adam Vickers hated the very name of Jonathan Groves, and by virtue of blood kinship, Christopher as well. Considering the circumstances, Christopher could scarcely blame him. But Vickers' hate put Christopher in an uncomfortable position of having to defend the indefensible—his father's honor.

Christopher walked on with long brisk strides, hands clasped behind his back. There was no time to dally. At precisely two o'clock there was formation, and no one wanted to be awarded the demerits which being even one minute late for that daily ritual would bring. Breaking out of the trees, he turned south along the path below the ramparts at the rim of the plateau. Straight ahead was the Battery Knox, named after the republic's first secretary of war, and beyond that the stables and riding hall, near the road which led down to the south dock. The sun beat warmly on his face, and a breeze swept up from the river carrying the fragrance of spring flowers which bloomed in profusion on the slope near the water's edge. Due west of the riding hall stood the cadet barracks, and, having timed his daily walk down to the minute, Christopher was confident he would arrive just in time to join his company for formation. He was never late.

Few were his demerits after two years. Only three cadets had a better record, and demerits were devilishly easy to acquire. There were a great many "thou shalt nots" at the Military Academy. Cadets were not permitted to drink, smoke, or play cards—nonetheless, Christopher had never seen so much tobacco use in his life, and gambling was widespread. The countryside was infested with civilians who made a good living in a brisk black market which supplied the cadets with forbidden merchandise.

A cadet was not allowed to keep in his room any novel, play, or poem. If he was going to read it had to be something akin to Farrar's translation of the *Treatise on Plane and Spherical Trigonometry* or Berard's *Lecteur Français,* and not some piece of sensational prose like James Fenimore Cooper's works, or Sir Walter Scott's Waverly novels. A cadet could not leave the Academy grounds without a pass signed by the superintendent, and it was said that getting a death certificate was easier. Still, many were lured into attempting an unauthorized nocturnal excursion to North's, where good food and strong spirits could be had.

Demerits were also received for loitering, being late for class or drill, bathing in the river, answering for another at roll call, or standing at guard duty in another's stead. Pranks and fistfights were also forbidden, which is not the same thing as saying that they did not occur on a regular basis—it was inevitable when two hundred proud, high-spirited young men were thrown together into an extremely competitive and stressful environment. Those unfortunate enough to be caught in flagrant dereliction of these commandments were often punished, but seldom court-martialed and dismissed.

The worst crime a cadet could commit—one which inevitably resulted in dismissal—was to engage in the *duello.* If a cadet so much as heard of a rendezvous with pistols or blades to settle an affair of honor, he was duty-bound to report it.

Dueling was a concept that left a bad taste in Christopher's mouth. A duel between his father and a man named Stephen Cooper had led to the disintegration of his family, for on that day his mother had miscarried, so worried was she for her husband's safety. Christopher sometimes wondered what it would be like to have a younger brother or sister. But he would never know, for his father had ignored his wife's pleas and gone through with the affair of honor, leaving her so distraught that she lost her unborn child and blamed him for it later. Jonathan had slain Cooper, and by doing so had become the object of Emily Cooper's—nee Vickers—undying obsession. Though his parents had never divorced, Christopher was painfully aware of the fact that his father had spent a great deal more time in his last years with Emily Cooper than with his mother.

Why the bad blood between his father and Stephen Cooper? Christopher had learned the details from his grandfather, Nathaniel Jones, the legendary Kentucky frontiersman they called Flintlock. His mother had been consistently adamant in her refusal to discuss the past, or at least that part of it. Apparently, Stephen Cooper and Rebecca had been sweethearts before Jonathan appeared on the scene. But a Shawnee war party had kidnapped Rebecca, and almost killed Cooper in the process. Jonathan played a role in her rescue. He and Rebecca fell in love. After lingering for months at death's door, Cooper had finally recovered—and promptly disappeared. Folks said he was never the same after the Indian attack—that there was a clearly discernible mean streak in him, and from then on he would suffer berserk fits of rage without provocation.

Cooper resurfaced some years later, having married into the Vickers family, a family of considerable wealth and influence. Daniel Vickers, Emily's father and Cadet

Vickers' uncle, owned serveral plantations and was a power to be reckoned with in the Mississippi Valley. Bent on revenge against both Jonathan and Rebecca, Cooper embarked on a campaign of terror, murdering two of the slaves who worked at Elm Tree, the Groves plantation in Madison County, Kentucky, and posing a very real threat—or so Jonathan believed—to Rebecca as well. Jonathan had felt honor-bound to call him out.

"Christopher! Christopher Groves!"

Two cadets stood on the ramparts above him, silhouetted against the bright blue afternoon sky. They had to call several times to rouse him from his brooding.

"Stay there! Wait for us!"

Christopher waved acknowledgment. He recognized them both. Gil Bryant and John O'Connor. Like Christopher, they were second-classmen, and his roommates. Of the ninety-one cadets who had entered West Point with Christopher summer before last, nineteen had dropped out before the end of the first year, and a dozen more had failed to make the grade this year. Such a high mortality rate created a strong camaraderie between the surviving classmen, and Christopher considered both Gil and O'Connor friends. Especially O'Connor. The red-headed son of an Irishman was often brash, and sometimes bold to the point of sheer recklessness. His temper was notorious. But he was an engaging, outgoing, and fiercely loyal friend. His academic marks left much to be desired, but Christopher knew that O'Connor was capable of much better. He was just the kind who exerted the minimum effort necessary to squeak by.

A hundred feet north of where the two cadets stood was a footpath which connected the ramparts with the broader path upon which Christopher was walking. The cadets negotiated this treacherous descent at breakneck speed. Christopher rocked slightly back and forth on his heels, falling prey to impatience; his keenly accurate mental clock ticked away precious seconds. He did not fancy a demerit just because Gil and O'Connor wanted to pass the time of day with him.

But it was much more than that, as Christopher soon discovered.

"The superintendent wants to see you," gasped O'Connor, breathing hard from what had been a long run from the mess hall.

"What? Now?"

"Right away. He sent us to fetch you."

"But what about formation?"

O'Connor flashed that rakehell grin of his. "There's no way out of it, bucko. When Old Silly wants you your goose is cooked."

Christopher grimaced at the butterflies in his stomach. "Old Silly" was the common barracks nickname for Sylvanus Thayer, but there was nothing even remotely humorous about the superintendent. He was a stern, austere man, a hard disciplinarian. Unlike some of his predecessors, he ran a tight ship. Christopher admired and respected him, but was also afraid, because when a cadet was summoned before Thayer it was, as O'Connor had so succinctly put it, usually the case that his goose was cooked.

"What have you done?" asked Bryant, who looked more than a little worried for his friend.

"That's what I'm wondering."

"Oh, come on," said O'Connor, with a sly wink. "You can tell us."

"I'd tell you if I knew," said Christopher, wracking his brain for the answer.

"Oh, yes, pure as the driven snow," jibed O'Connor. "I tell you what I think, Gil. It has something to do with Miss Inskilling."

"What about her?" asked Bryant, seeing that O'Connor intended to have some fun at Christopher's expense—good-natured fun—and playing his role as the Irishman's foil to the hilt.

"Well, you must be aware that Miss Greta's father and Superintendent Thayer are very good friends. You are also undoubtedly cognizant of the fact that our friend here has been seeing a great deal of the lovely lady. Maybe you've seen a bit more of her than her father thinks proper, eh, Christopher, you sly devil?"

Christopher would have taken offense at the remark and all it implied, had it come from anyone else. But he knew O'Connor meant no disrespect.

"You're just jealous, O'Connor."

"Aha! You see, Gil? He admits it."

"I don't admit anything."

"Well, you didn't deny it."

"I wouldn't dignify such an absurd statement with a denial. You're green with envy, that's all, because a young lady of Greta Inskilling's caliber wouldn't give you the time of day."

"You think not? Why, I take that as a challenge, Cadet Groves. I have made a point of not exerting my considerable charms upon the lady in question, out of respect for your tender sensibilities. But if you challenge me, as you most certainly have—and Gil here is a witness—then perhaps I ought to teach you a lesson in humility. I daresay that in a fortnight I could make Miss Inskilling forget you even exist."

"That will be the day."

O'Connor laughed heartily. His joviality was contagious, and Christopher, despite the sobering prospect of being called before Superintendent Thayer, laughed along with him.

"Come on, Johnny," said Bryant. "We'll be late for formation."

"Right." Putting on a somber face, O'Connor offered his hand to Christopher. "It's been a pleasure knowing you, Cadet Groves. I shall always treasure our friendship. Rest assured I will perform an annual pilgrimage to your final resting place.''

Christopher scoffed and slapped away the proffered hand. ''I'll dance a jig on your grave.''

It was a long-standing, if somewhat morbid, joke between the two of them.

''Let's go, Gil,'' said O'Connor, and took off running down the path in the direction of the riding hall.

Christopher watched them go, the smile born of his witty skirmish with O'Connor fading from his lips. What could Thayer want with him? Whatever it was, no doubt it meant trouble. There was but one way to find out. Christopher ascended the steep footpath to the ramparts. At the top he squared his shoulders and marched resolutely across the parade ground, making for the superintendent's house.

Chapter 2

Christopher couldn't shake the feeling that he was going to his doom. Try as he might, he could not anticipate the subject which Sylvanus Thayer had summoned him to discuss. Not that this would be a discussion, per se. A cadet did not *discuss* anything with the superintendent of the United States Military Academy as though he were an equal. The superintendent did the talking and the cadet responded with "Yes, sir" or "No, sir" at the appropriate times. Christopher was fairly certain that he had not broken the rules of West Point. That left three alternatives. Either he was going to be falsely accused of some infraction, or ordered to betray one of his fellow classmen—he was aware of plenty of infractions perpetrated by his fellow cadets. Or, it did indeed have to do with Greta Inskilling.

None of the options was especially appealing. Christopher decided that the first one would be the least difficult to endure. Although he did not approve of some of the illicit activities of his classmates, he would never rat on any one of them. Not even Adam Vickers, who hated him. And what if O'Connor was on the mark about Greta? What if this did concern her? Christopher had long ago surmised that Greta's father was less than pleased with his daughter's preference, among her many beaus, for a lowly West Point cadet.

Piet Inskilling could trace his New World roots back to the development of New Netherland as a trading post colony in 1624. Christopher was painfully aware that in those days his ancestors were still dirt-poor Welsh tenant farmers. The Dutch were never interested in colonizing New Netherland. They built a handful of forts—one of them, Fort Orange, here on the Hudson River. Dutch traders bartered with the Indians for their furs, and New Amsterdam, on Manhattan Island, became the center of the early fur trade. It also became a base for Dutch merchant ships involved in the budding Virginia tobacco trade, as well as for Dutch privateers who preyed on Spanish galleons as far away as the Caribbean. New Amsterdam became a typical sailor's town, with numerous taverns, havens for smugglers and other notorious characters, as well as a number of substantial houses owned by the money men. One of these was Piet Inskilling's great-great-great grandfather, a merchant who dabbled in everything from furs to tobacco to stolen Spanish gold.

In 1638, the States General of the Netherlands tried to encourage settlement by issuing the Charter Privileges to Patroons. Anyone who brought five hundred tenant families to New Netherland at his own expense was given a vast tract of wilderness, over which the patroon exercised manorial privileges. Soon, the most valuable land in the Hudson Valley was held in immense feudal estates—one of the grandest belonging to the Inskilling family.

But New Netherland did not prosper. It suffered poor management—a succession of autocratic governors, including the wooden-legged Peter Stuyvesant, a distant relative of Piet, who mismanaged the colony's affairs, antagonizing the Indians as well as the English colonies to the north and south. Stuyvesant persecuted the Quakers, seized the colony of New Sweden on the Delaware River, and ended the free trade policy of New Amsterdam. In naval and commercial competition with the Dutch, England finally made its move in 1664. That year a British fleet appeared off New Amsterdam and demanded a Dutch surrender. Without the means to mount a viable resistance, Stuyvesant complied, and New Netherland became New York without a shot having been fired. Most of the Dutch families—the Van Rensselaers, Van Burens, Roosevelts, and Inskillings—kept their estates and prospered under British rule.

The clannish patroons tended to guard their bloodlines rather jealously. Piet Inskilling was no exception. True, Christopher stood to inherit a Kentucky estate, but Elm Tree was inconsequential when compared to the vast wealth and holdings of the Inskillings, and it didn't really matter anyway, because Piet wanted his daughters—Greta was the youngest of three—to marry the sons of other patroons. Greta's older sisters had complied with their father's wishes, but Greta was being willfully disobedient, as was her nature, in persisting with her flirtation with Cadet Groves. Or so Piet Inskilling perceived it. Christopher sincerely hoped it was more than a flirtation, much more. He thought Greta considered it more serious than that, too, but he wasn't absolutely sure.

So maybe O'Connor was right, mused Christopher. Maybe old Inskilling had prevailed on his good friend Sylvanus Thayer to take a hand in the business. As he neared the superintendent's house, Christopher's lips thinned, a grim and obstinate expression on his face. His personal affairs were none of Thayer's business. By God he would quit the Corps of Cadets before he would allow even the superintendent to interfere in his private life.

Just shy of his destination, Christopher suddenly faltered. What was he thinking? He wasn't even sure he really loved Greta Inskilling. True, she was the most beautiful girl he had ever seen, and he was flattered by her interest, but he wasn't even sure what love was, and he had to consider whether she was worth throwing away his future, especially since it was entirely possible that her interest in him would turn out to be fleeting. He had always wanted to be a soldier. What other career path could he follow? Politics? No. Politics had corrupted his father. It had taken Jonathan Groves away from his family and forced him to compromise his values for the sake of appearances. Elm Tree? He could raise horses, but he was a poor businessman. Besides, Elm Tree enjoyed a good reputation but not much else. His mother had a difficult time keeping the place afloat financially. West Point seemed to be his only avenue, the sole means by which he could make something of himself. And he was thinking of throwing it all away for . . . what? Love? Or foolish pride?

A commotion drew his attention to the cadet barracks across the vast parade ground. His comrades were boiling out of the doors to form ranks in the bright May sun. He watched them, and longed to be among them. Formation—standing in the hot sun or the bitter cold, depending on the season, in full dress uniform—never had appealed to him as much as it did at this moment.

The door to the superintendent's small, white clapboard house opened and Sylvanus Thayer emerged. With his shock of pale hair and hooked nose and stiletto eyes he looked like a bald eagle appearing suddenly out of its aerie. He was clad, as usual, in an impeccable uniform, braid on the high stiff collar and sleeves of his tunic, epaulets on his narrow shoulders, a saber buckled around his waspish waist.

Christopher snapped to attention, a reflex action. But Thayer did not seem to notice him at first. The superintendent glowered across the parade ground at the long gray line of cadets formed in front of the gray stone barracks. If he was pleased by what he saw, his expression did not reveal it, but then he always looked stern and disapproving.

Finally his cold blue eyes flicked down at Christopher.

"Ah, Mr. Groves. Punctual, as always. Come, walk with me."

Thayer started off with long, vigorous strides, hands clasped behind his back, saber rattling against his leg. He kept his eyes on the ground in front of him, and seldom looked up. Christopher had to lengthen his own stride just to keep up.

"So, Mr. Groves, you are doing quite well this year. The President has asked about you."

Christopher was stunned. "The President? General Jackson?"

"The same. He is planning on paying us a visit in a few weeks. Prior to the arrival of the board of visitors. I suspect his interest in your progress stems from the high regard in which he held your father."

"Yes, sir."

"I was pleased to be able to inform him that your marks are quite satisfactory in every regard."

"Thank you, sir."

"Don't thank me. You have earned those marks by virtue of your hard work and dedication to duty. In mathematics you currently stand fourth in your class, with credits of one hundred and ninety-seven out of a possible two hundred. In French you are fifth, rating ninety-eight out of a possible one hundred credits. On the roll of general merit, therefore, you stand at two hundred and ninety-five out of three hundred. Very commendable. As was the case last year, I expect to see your name on the list of 'distinguished cadets.' "

"Yes, sir." Christopher's cheeks burned with the fever of pride. To be on the list of distinguished cadets—the first five in each class—was a conspicuous honor. Those five names would be certified to the secretary of war for inclusion in the army register.

"You are doing equally as well in natural philosophy and chemistry," continued Thayer, and rattled off Christopher's current marks in those two difficult disciplines. Christopher was not at all surprised to learn that Thayer knew his ratings in such detail. The superintendent had a phenomenal memory, and kept himself well-informed of the standing of both the best and the worst of his cadets. In order to be well-acquainted with the details of the Academy, he received daily reports on each cadet.

"As I recall," continued Thayer, as they passed between the Academy and the mess hall, heading down the path to the riding hall, "General Jackson wrote a letter of recommendation for your admittance into the Academy. That is quite an honor for you, I am sure. Ture, the President and I have had our differences. As you may know, I had to severely discipline two of his nephews, and on one occasion he reinstated a cadet whom I had been forced to dismiss."

"Yes, sir." Christopher studied Thayer's profile, looking for a flicker of emotion behind the superintendent's stony mask. Thayer's words were sharp with disapproval, but his features were no sterner than usual.

"Nonetheless, the President continues to evince his support for the Academy. It is well for us that he sees fit to do so, Mr. Groves. Every year, it seems, a bill to abolish this institution is introduced in Congress. I understand that this year such a bill was put forward by Davy Crockett, a representative from the President's home of Tennessee. Hmph!"

Christopher knew that sound. It meant Thayer was contemptuous of Crockett or the bill or both. But what wasn't clear was why Thayer had summoned him—and why the superintendent was telling him all of this. If Thayer's purpose was only to inform him of Andrew Jackson's interest in his progress at West Point, then what was the reason for discussing the Academy's travails? Christopher didn't have a clue. All he could do was listen and learn. Yet he could not dispel a feeling of deep anxiety. Whatever lay at the end of the path down which Thayer was leading him, Christopher was pretty certain he wasn't going to like it.

"From the beginning," said Thayer, "the Academy has had to fight for its very existence. Americans have always had an abiding distrust of the concept of a standing army. Understandable, since in the days when we were yet British colonies the redcoats garrisoned in our towns seemed to be here for the purpose of occupation and oppression, in spite of their claims that they were intended to protect our frontiers against the French and the Indians. We cherish the perception that we are a nation of farmers who will lay aside our plows, pick up our rifles, and defend our country in volunteer armies when the need arises."

"I believe it was Alexander Hamilton, sir, who said that war is a science."

"Precisely. There have always been a few farsighted individuals who understand the need for an officers' training school. But this academy would have never been established but for the possibility that officers trained here in military engineering would also be able to build roads and harbors and bridges. I believe the efforts of our graduates in that vein have proven the value of advanced scientific training a thousand times over. Still, our enemies continue to attack us. Some of them complain that this is a place of privilege, producing a military aristocracy. How quickly they forget the lessons of our recent war. Volunteer armies can triumph if well-led. The President's victory at Chalmette is a case in point. But for every triumph there were many failures, and all because our brave citizen-soldiers were commanded by imcompetents, woefully ignorant of even the most basic precepts of military strategy."

Thayer sighed, and abruptly stopped walking. He looked all about him, and his piercing gaze came finally to rest on Christopher's face. "I fear our countrymen's prejudice against professional soldiering will always be a cross for us to bear. This academy's reputation for civil engineering is all that redeems us to the popular sentiment of our times. And since there is no army to speak of, a cadet's prospects are slim, if his preference is a military career, unless of course he wishes to be posted on the frontier. What is your preference in that regard, Mr. Groves?"

"I—I'm not sure, sir. I know many of the cadets leave the Army shortly after graduation for employment as engineers or teachers."

"Is that what you have in mind for yourself?"

Christopher's reply had not satisfied Thayer. "No, sir," he said. "I want a military career."

"Our best cadets qualify for the Corps of Engineers. That is the place for young officers of vigor and ingenuity. Bearing in mind that you have some time yet to spend with us, I believe that in the end you will qualify in that respect."

"I was thinking more along the lines of the cavalry, sir."

The truth seemed to disappoint Thayer. Christopher knew as well as anyone that the cavalry was not held in high regard. The United States Light Dragoons—nicknamed the "Lazy Dogs"—was treated like the orphan stepchild of the United States Army.

"Ah yes," said the superintendent. "Your knowledge of and love for horses. And you seek adventure, no doubt."

Here it comes, thought Christopher. O'Connor was right. This *was* about Greta Inskilling. Thayer was going to tell him what he already knew—that an officer in the cavalry had no business contemplating a future shared with a young woman from the upper crust of society. What could a cavalryman expect to offer such a woman? A Spartan existence at some remote and dusty frontier outpost? An income which was scarcely sufficient for a single man to make ends meet, and a meager pension to reward a lifetime of thankless service? At least a member of the Corps of Engineers enjoyed the prospect of lucrative private practice. Christopher braced himself for what was coming next.

"I have received another letter besides the President's concerning you," said Thayer. "From a Mrs. Emily Cooper."

Caught completely off guard, Christopher was speechless. His flesh tingled, as from a thousand tiny pinpricks.

Thayer's perpetual expression of stern disapprobation seemed more severe than usual. "I assumed upon receipt of the letter that the lady intended to ask permission to visit her young cousin, Adam Vickers. So I was much surprised to find hardly a mention of Cadet Vickers. Mrs. Cooper very much wants to see you, Mr. Groves."

"Me? But why?"

"She did not share her reasons with me. I must admit that it was with some reluctance that I gave her permission."

"Yes, sir," said Christopher. He didn't know what else to say.

"I am aware of the . . . *connection* between your father and Emily Cooper. I am also aware of the animosity which exists between you and Cadet Vickers, no doubt as a direct result of that connection."

Christopher's face felt hot. "If there is animosity, it is not on my part, sir."

"Perhaps not. But it exists, and is a source of grave concern for me. This academy's reputation is a fragile thing, Mr. Groves. West Point has many enemies. The scandal which swirled around the dismissal of my predecessor, Captain Partridge, came perilously close to destroying us. Another scandal might do the trick. Do you understand what I am trying to say?"

"Yes, sir," said Christopher stiffly. There was more he wanted to say, but he was inhibited in the presence of this man who was second only to God when it came to power over Christopher's fate.

One corner of Thayer's grim mouth curled in what might have been a wintry smile. "You are wondering why I gave Mrs. Cooper permission to visit West Point if I am so concerned by what might transpire as a consequence of that visit."

"Yes, sir. As a matter of fact I was wondering precisely that."

"Two reasons. One, it is not my nature to ignore or flee from unpleasant situations. And two, I have absolute faith in your tact and your fidelity to this institution."

"Thank you, sir."

Thayer nodded. "I expect Mrs. Cooper to arrive in a matter of days. I know you will conduct yourself at all times with the best interests of the Academy in mind. Now, I intend to have my afternoon ride. That is all." He turned toward the nearby riding hall and stables, took two steps, and turned back. "Good luck to you, Mr. Groves."

"Thank you, sir."

Thayer spun on his heel and walked briskly away, head down, hands clasped behind his back.

Standing there in the hot sun, Christopher felt cold. What could Emily Cooper, née Vickers, want from him? Whatever her motives for coming to see him, he was certain that no good would come of it.

Chapter 3

Christopher tried his level best not to let the imminent visit of Emily Cooper distract him from his studies. He labored to convince himself that there was nothing to it, and that nothing would come of it. The woman had loved his father—he gave her the benefit of the doubt on that score. She must have, to have risked everything—her good name, her family's respect—to engage for so many years in what could only be described as a scandalous affair. Maybe she was coming to apologize to him, to try to explain why she had done what she'd done. And if she did ask for his forgiveness? Christopher decided he would give it. That would a gentleman's course, and bitter recriminations wouldn't alter the past.

And what would come of the visit? Right away Christopher got a taste of the changes Emily Cooper would bring about in his life. That he had been summoned by Superintendent Thayer spread like wildlife through the corps. At every opportunity his classmates beseeched him to tell the gory details. Christopher stonily refused to divulge any information to anyone. Except O'Connor. He and O'Connor shared a room with Gil Bryant and immediately after supper O'Connor found Christopher alone in their quarters.

"You were wrong," said Christopher. "As usual. It had absolutely nothing to do with Greta Inskilling."

O'Connor was surprised. "I thought for certain it did,

especially since you refuse to tell anyone what transpired between you and Old Silly."

"No. No, it's much worse."

"Worse? Good Lord." O'Connor sat down and leaned forward. "Is there anything I can do to help?"

"I doubt it. The superintendent informed me that Emily Cooper is coming here to visit with me."

He watched his friend closely. Never had the subject of his father's lurid private affairs been broached between them. They had talked about everything else under the sun, except that. O'Connor had sensed from the start that it was a sensitive subject, and avoided it out of respect for his friend's feelings. Christopher was curious now to know what O'Connor, a Tennessean, knew about the whole business. Surely he knew something. O'Connor's expression betrayed the fact that, indeed, he knew a great deal.

"Emily Cooper?" O'Connor was reading Christopher's face, as well, and could see that to be disingenuous—his first instinct—would not pass muster. "Yes, I've heard about her and your father."

"What exactly have you heard?" Christopher's tone of voice was defensive. He couldn't help it.

"It is a well-kept secret—by almost everybody."

"God," groaned Christopher, dismally.

"Look on the bright side . . ."

"I just can't fathom," said Christopher, "why she would come all this way to see me."

O'Connor brandished a pipe, packed it with tobacco, and fired it up. He sat there puffing a moment, pondering the situation, filling the room with fragrant blue smoke. Such a blatant disregard for the regulations on O'Connor's part was so commonplace that Christopher thought nothing of it.

"There is nothing to be gained by trying to understand why a woman does what she does," decided O'Connor. "There is no logic to it. I am convinced that, more often than not, they do not themselves know the reasons for their actions. 'The Heart has its reasons which Reason knoweth not.' Chateaubriand, wasn't it? Or Pascal?"

"Pascal. You're a big help, O'Connor."

O'Connor grinned. "Were I you, it's Adam Vickers I would worry about, and not her."

"Why? What do you think he'll do?"

"Well, that depends on what *she* does, and how you react. Mark my words, Vickers will be looking for any excuse to pick a fight with you."

Christopher's gesture of disdain was full of youthful bravado. "If he wants a fight all he has to do is ask for it. I'll be more than happy to oblige."

"You don't mean that. Be sensible, Christopher. You could be drummed out of the Corps."

"Words of caution from you? *That's* rich."

No longer was O'Connor grinning. The ne'er-do-well attitude was gone now, replaced by sober concern.

"Don't jeopardize your career, my friend. Not for the likes of Adam Vickers."

"You never take *my* advice, do you, O'Connor?"

"Shame on me if I don't. But I always thought you had better sense than I."

"I do."

O'Connor laughed, and Christopher laughed with him. That was one of the things Christopher liked about O'Connor. No matter how grim the situation, O'Connor could always make him laugh. Never take life too seriously. That was O'Connor's golden rule. Christopher decided he would try to live by it as he awaited Emily Cooper's visit.

Christopher tried his best to concentrate on his studies. The academic load was so he could not afford to become distracted and fall behind. It was a difficult task. He came to resent Emily Cooper for adversely affecting his life—again. Which was odd, considering that he had never met her face-to-face.

His was a full and strenuous routine. Reveille was sounded at dawn. Cadets dressed and answered roll call. Quarters had to be made immaculate, and all accoutrements cleaned and polished to perfection. A half hour after reveille, cadet officers inspected the barracks. From the sunrise gun to seven o'clock the cadets studied their lessons. Then, at seven, they formed squads and marched to the mess hall. While eating they were not permitted to indulge in idle conversation. Allowed thirty minutes for breakfast, there was guard mount at seven-thirty, parade at eight, after which they marched to the academic building, which included a chapel, the library, the chemical and physics laboratories, the engineering department, and the adjutant's office.

From eight until eleven in the morning the cadets were in classroom. The first-classmen—the "plebes"— studied mathematics, while the others tackled physics, which included calculus, analytical geometry and conic sections, drawing—which included landscape and topography—and chemistry and "natural philosophy." The latter heading was composed of instruction in mechanics, electricity, astronomy, light, heat, and magnetism, with texts which included Newton's *Principia* and Gregory's *Treatise on Mechanics*. Between eleven and noon, cadets were allowed to return to their quarters to study. From noon to one o'clock they were free. The dinner hour was at one, and at two came formation, followed by studies and recitations in French until four. The texts were *Gil Blas* and Voltaire's *Histoire de Charles XII*. From four until sunset there were military exercises. Two hours every other afternoon were devoted to artillery practice. At sunset, dress parade and roll call were followed by supper, after which the cadets retired to their quarters and wrestled with their studies until nine-thirty. Tattoo and a final roll call and inspection of quarters concluded the day. "Lights out" was at precisely ten o'clock.

Christopher customarily attacked all his studies with what amounted to grim dedication, motivated by the knowledge that in his third year at the Academy he would leave mathematics and physics behind and be introduced to the discipline he was longing to sink his teeth into, technical military training. The science of war. The course was in four parts: fortifications, artillery, grand tactics, and civil and military architecture. The topics ranged from the building of batteries and redoubts, the construction of mines, the attack and defense of fortified places, the principles of gunnery, orders of battle, laying out an encampment, the building of arches, canals and bridges. All of the mathematical and scientific study of a cadet's first two years laid a foundation for this course. Christopher could hardly wait.

In his spare time—what little he had—he did extra reading designed as preliminary forays into the realm of military training. He checked books out of the library— Machiavelli's *Art of War,* Drean's *Military Dictionary,* and Baron Gay de Vernon's *Treatise on the Science of War and Fortification.* Consuming these heavy tomes had never been a chore for him. His mind was a sponge soaking up every detail. But now, as Emily Cooper loomed ominously in his immediate future, he found it extremely difficult to concentrate.

These were crucial months for all the cadets. The board of visitors would soon make its annual visit. The board was composed of five gentlemen well-versed in military and other sciences who would be on hand for the Academy's twice-yearly examinations. They were allowed to verbally examine the cadets. Christopher wanted to excel, as he always did, in these examinations, because those whose names were placed at the top of the merit rolls received instruction from the best members of the faculty. And Christopher was determined to qualify for Alfred Thayer Mahan's class in military science. One reason was Mahan's admiration for Napoleon Bonaparte's military genius, something he shared with Christopher. Napoleon had breathed his last a few years ago, an exile on the remote South Atlantic island of St. Helena, but his reputation as one of the great captains of military history would never die.

Christopher's prized possession was a rare copy of Napoleon's *Military Maxims*. A slim printed volume bound in dun-colored leather, its full title was *A Manuscript found in the portfolio of Las Casas containing maxims and observations of Napoleon, collected during the last two years of his residence at St. Helena*. Translated from the French, it had been printed in London in 1820. Oddly enough, the volume sported a frontispiece of Wellington, of all people.

Ten days after his visit with Sylvanus Thayer, Christopher found a little time between tattoo and "lights out" to browse through the *Maxims*. Not having been entirely successful in concentrating on his studies that day, he sought inspiration from the words of the master for renewed effort on the morrow. Bryant and O'Connor were there, too, the former at his desk, plowing through Berard's *Lecteur Français*. O'Connor was sprawled on his bed, writing a letter to one of his many lady friends.

Then Adam Vickers burst into the room.

"There you are, Groves," he said curtly. "I want a word with you."

Sitting on his bed, his back to the wall, Christopher stared at the intruder, momentarily nonplussed. Vickers was a tall, brawny young man with raven black hair in a constant state of angry disarray, and blue eyes so dark they looked black at times, beneath bushy brows which met above the bridge of his nose, giving him a peculiarly predatory appearance.

O'Connor rolled out of his bunk and jumped to his feet to confront Vickers, standing toe to toe, matching Vickers' belligerence with an equal measure of his own.

"Why don't you try knocking before you enter private quarters?"

"Take care how you speak to me," sneered Vickers, and pointed to the stripes on his sleeve. He had been honored with an appointment as class staff sergeant, a position that only the best cadets of good academic standing could hope to attain. There was no denying that Vickers was an excellent student. He excelled in athletic pursuits, too. But he was not well-liked. His attitude was to blame for that.

"I wouldn't care if you wore a general's braid," said O'Connor, truculent.

Christopher rose, put a hand on O'Connor's shoulder, and spun him around. He knew O'Connor would never back down from the likes of Vickers, and he didn't want his friend to get into trouble on his account.

"Back off," he said.

O'Connor smirked at Vickers. "Well, I suppose I should only expect gentlemen to have manners."

"Why don't you and Gil leave," suggested Christopher. "I believe what Mr. Vickers wants to say to me ought to be said in private."

"You're sure?" asked O'Connor, reluctant to go.

Christopher nodded.

Once O'Connor and Bryant were gone and the door closed, Vickers said, "The Superintendent told me my cousin Emily is paying us a visit."

"So I've been told."

"He advised me not to make trouble."

"Why would you?"

"I have every reason," said Vickers, the words sharp as knives. "Your father destroyed her good name."

"My father?" Christopher barked a laugh. His ire was on the rise, and he fought to control it. "You need to get the facts straight. Your cousin pursued my father. He was a married man, and she knew it. By all accounts, she became obsessed with him after he killed her husband in a duel."

"That's a dirty lie!" roared Vickers, fists clenched, face flush with scarlet anger.

Christopher said nothing. This confrontation was teetering precariously on the brink of violence, and violence would mean disaster. Both of them would lose.

Vickers shook a finger in his face. "I don't know why Emily would come all this way to see the likes of you. But whatever her reasons, I'm warning you, Groves, you had better treat her with respect. I will defend my family's honor."

"If you've said what you came to say, get out."

"You don't tell me what to do."

"I said get out."

"You're forgetting who I am."

"Those stripes don't give you the right to remain in my quarters without my permission, unless you are conducting a formal inspection."

"You're a coward," said Vickers, eyes narrowed into slits.

He wants a fight, realized Christopher, *and the devil take the cost. 'Never do what the enemy wishes you to do, for this reason alone, that he desires it.'* Napoleon's words came to Christopher's mind as he returned Vickers' stare.

Without another word Christopher went to the door and opened it. O'Connor and Bryant were waiting just outside. They stepped into the room and watched Vickers, like a pair of trained guard dogs waiting hopefully for the word from Christopher that would loose them on the intruder.

Vickers sneered. "Three to one. Are those odds good enough for a coward like you, Groves?"

"He wouldn't need any help from us to teach you a few manners," said O'Connor.

"One day, Groves," Vickers said as he left the room. "One day we will settle what's between us."

Christopher shut the door on him.

Chapter 4

William Cozzens, West Point's mess contractor, used the upper level of the two-story mess hall as a hotel. Ten rooms were available for friends and relatives who journeyed to the Academy to visit the cadets. It was here that Emily Cooper found lodging. But as it was not acceptable that her meeting with Christopher Groves occur in her hotel room, arrangements were made, through Superintendent Thayer, for Christopher to be excused from his afternoon academics to meet with her at Kosciusko's rock garden.

The garden was near the cottage where Kosciusko had lived. A steep flight of stone steps descended from the ramparts down the wooded slope to the cottage near the river. The cottage was unoccupied now, but maintained by the Academy as a monument to one of the true heroes of the American Revolution.

Christopher was a few minutes late. From the top of the rock garden he could see a frail figure dressed in somber black near the bottom of the steps, her back to him.

Christopher hesitated. Adam Vickers' threat caused him less worry than Emily Cooper herself, for she had become a flesh-and-blood reminder of a past that Christopher was trying to overcome, if not escape. She was here because of his father, and her presence forced Christopher to confront his own mixed feelings about Jonathan Groves.

She heard him as he came near, and turned, and for an instant Christopher was shot through with supernatural awe, nape hairs crawling, because she seemed ethereal rather than solid, spirit rather than living person, a ghost in black organdy and lace that might disintegrate before his very eyes, come here to haunt him. He told himself it was just the setting, the gray sky and gray river, the exotic rock garden, the gloom-shrouded trees through which the wind whispered and moaned.

"Christopher," she said, extending a small gloved hand. "I've desired for so long to see you. Come, let me look at you."

He took the hand—it lay light as a feather in his—and inclined his upper body forward an inch or two in a stiff bow.

"At your service, ma'am."

"As gallant as your father." She spoke slowly, dreamily, and he thought she must be smiling, though he couldn't be certain, as she wore a black veil. Her face was pale and indistinct, like the moon behind a film of high, thin clouds. "You resemble him a great deal, you know. Oh, it makes me happy and sad at the same time. Does that make any sense? I miss him very much, even though he has been gone so many years."

"Yes, ma'am."

"Do you? Miss him, I mean."

"I suppose."

"You suppose? Don't you know?"

"I knew him scarcely at all. Rarely saw him. When I was very young he was in politics, often away from home, at Frankfort in the Kentucky Legislature and later the Congress. Then he was off to fight." Christopher hesitated, wondering if he should speak his mind.

She spoke it for him. "And when he wasn't off fighting he was with me."

He did not respond, out of simple courtesy.

"You must hate me," she said.

"No."

"Resent me, then. After all, when he could have come home to you and your mother he came instead to me."

"I don't blame you."

"You don't? Honestly? Others do. But I don't care what other people think."

That, thought Christopher, was stating the obvious. A woman of Emily Cooper's station would not have been content having a long-standing affair with a married man if she cared one whit for public opinion.

"Of course you aren't telling the truth, are you, Christopher?" she asked. "Surely you must blame me, if only a little. After all, I did pursue your father. They say I was obsessed with him. He saved my life, you know. Stephen was a brute. I believe he was mentally unstable. Had been, ever since that Shawnee tomahawk cracked his skull. He would fly into such terrible rages, without warning. One minute he was fine, and the next was transformed into a cruel brute. He . . . he beat me."

"I'm sorry."

"But even when he was being kind to me he was never loving, or affectionate. I don't think he was capable of affection. I believe he married me for my money. My father was, and still is, quite wealthy. Of course, I loved him, or else I would not have consented to marriage. He managed somehow to keep his darker side hidden from me until . . . until it was too late."

She looked away, in the direction of the river, where gossamer white mist clung to the wooded bluffs, and she remembered the terror and the pain of the nightmare she had lived at Hunter's Glen, the plantation her father had given her and Stephen Cooper upon their marriage.

"Worse, even, than the beatings," she said, "was his predilection for slave women. He had children by them. Your mother helped one of those poor women escape his clutches, did you know that?"

"Are you referring to Cilla?"

"Yes. Cilla. She was carrying Stephen's child when she escaped. Do you know how she is doing? Is she alive and well?"

Christopher shook his head. "I was five or six years old, I think, when that happened. I don't remember much about Cilla. I do remember Trumbull, though. He was Elm Tree's overseer. My mother told him to take Cilla as far away as possible. I believe they went to New Orleans. But I'm afraid I don't know what became of her. Or the child."

Emily sighed. "When your father killed Stephen he saved my life."

"If you were in fear for your life, why did you stay so long with him."

"I had to. It was expected of me. Your father freed me—woke me from a living nightmare. He was my savior. I had no one else to turn to."

"What about your family?"

"You wouldn't ask if you knew them. Had I run away from my husband it would have been too much of an embarrassment to the family."

"I see." Chrisopher wondered what this was all about. Emily Cooper struck him as a very lonely person. But why was she baring her soul to him in this way? It was true that divorce was not a viable option, no matter how difficult the marital situation. The stigma followed a woman forever.

"I guess you must be wondering why I have come all this way to see you," she said as though she'd read his mind.

"Yes, ma'am. I am."

"The superintendent tells me you are doing very well in your studies. You are at the top of your class. Your father would have been proud of you." She touched his arm. "I loved your father, more than you could ever know. My one regret is that I never gave him a son. But

I would like to think that had I been able, he would have turned out just like you, Christopher."

Christopher stepped back. So that was it! She was trying to stake some claim on him. She had stolen his father away from his mother, and now she was trying to take him, too.

"That would have been splendid," he said, with bitter sarcasm. "I'd be illegitimate then, wouldn't I? The bastard son."

She cringed. "I didn't mean . . ."

"I would remind you that my mother loved him, too. Did it matter to you that he had a wife and son who needed him?"

"So you *do* blame me," she said, her voice now a whisper.

"He wouldn't have left Elm Tree if he didn't have a place to go. You gave him that."

She was silent for a moment. Christopher's anger ebbed as suddenly as it had come, and he felt remorse, because he was certain that she wept silent tears behind the veil.

"I apologize," he said stiffly.

"No, no you are well within your rights to be angry with me."

Her compassion made him feel that much worse. He realized that she had been a convenient target for all the rage that had built to the breaking point inside him.

"On the other hand," he said, "my father would not have had a reason to leave had my mother not blamed him for . . ."

"Yes. The miscarriage. I know. That caused Jonathan tremendous anguish. I wish we could all stop trying to attach blame. Sometimes these things just happen. What's done is done. We all pay for our sins sooner or later, don't we?"

"I guess we do."

"I came to bring you something, Christopher. Something I'm certain your father would want you to have. I've been gravely ill of late, and entirely unable to travel, or I would have brought it to you sooner."

"What is it?"

"I'll let it be a surprise. You'll find it in your room when you return."

"And you won't tell me what it is?"

"I would like it to be a surprise. I believe it will a pleasant one."

A smattering of raindrops began to fall.

"I think we ought to be getting back," he said. "A storm is gathering."

They ascended the stone steps to the rim of the plateau, then walked along the ramparts, and neither of them spoke until they reached Cozzens'. There were few people about—most of the cadets were still in the classrooms.

"I want to apologize again," said Christopher, taking his leave of her at the door of the mess hall-hotel. "I had no right to speak to you that way."

"You've already apologized, Christopher. And you have every right to hate me. But I hope you will try not to."

"I don't."

She squeezed his hand. "I doubt that we shall meet again. Take care."

With that she turned and went inside.

Walking back to the barracks, his shoulders hunched against a cold drizzling rain, and the ground beneath his feet vibrating with the peals of thunder which rolled across a gray and angry sky, Christopher paid no attention to the fact that he was getting soaked. Going over the conversation with Emily Cooper in his mind, he realized he still wasn't sure of her purpose in coming all this way to see him. Just to deliver a gift? No, there was more to it than that. To see him one time before she died? Obviously she was ill. To explain herself? To seek exoneration?

But he did know why she was dressed in black. She was still mourning the death of his father. Even now, a dozen years later. She had loved Jonathan Groves—of this Christopher had no doubt. Loved him unconditionally. No, he did not hate her. He felt sorry for her, and sick to his stomach with remorse for having spoken so cruelly.

Arriving at his quarters, he found a bundle on his bed. Emily Cooper's surprise. Something wrapped in a carriage blanket of green wool with golden tassels.

Nestled inside the blanket was a cutlass.

Christopher recognized the blade immediately, though he had not laid eyes on it in eighteen years. It was his father's Tripolitan cutlass. Jonathan Groves had taken it from a Barbary pirate in combat, and had carried it into every subsequent conflict, including the Battle of the Thames, where Tecumseh had been vanquished, and the Battle of Horseshoe Bend, and the battle against the Seminoles in which, they said, he had died a valiant death, boldly leading his men into battle.

How had Emily Cooper come to possess the cutlass? By what right, he wondered, perturbed, had she claimed and kept it for so long? But his anger was fleeting. *Something your father would want you to have.* Christopher shook his head. He didn't pick up the cutlass, didn't touch it, but instead stood there, staring at the weapon. Finally he wrapped it again in the carriage blanket and left the bundle on the bed. He sat in a chair by the window and watched the rain fall.

"I don't want the damn thing," he told O'Connor that evening, after supper, as the young Irishman admired the cutlass.

"Why not?" asked O'Connor, perplexed. "This is a famous blade, Christopher. A fine family heirloom, I would think. If this were *my* father's I should want it to remember him by."

"I remember him well enough," said Christopher. "Every time I look into my mother's face."

"I see," said O'Connor, who could be quite perceptive at times, even though it seemed completely out of character. "Unpleasant memories."

"The past is what I'm trying to escape, not remember."

"You want the impossible, if you ask me."

"There must be a place where a person's past doesn't matter."

O'Connor shrugged. A man who lived for today, he was incapable of giving much thought to the past, or the future.

Christopher spent a restless night. He thought a lot about the cutlass, stored now in the trunk at the foot of his narrow iron bed, regretting that Emily Cooper had brought it to him. The cutlass struck him a symbol of that part of his father's life that he wished fervently had never happened. Jonathan Groves' heroic service in the war against the Barbary pirates was the main reason the people of Madison County, Kentucky, had sent him to the state legislature and, later, to the Congress of the United States. And it was as a politician that Jonathan had begun to sacrifice his principles on the altar of public opinion, which had led to his duel with Stephen Cooper, which in turn had led to Rebecca Groves' miscarriage, the subsequent separation which had driven Jonathan into a scandalous long-term affair with Emily Cooper, which had resulted in his suffering bouts of severe depression that led him to seek solace, or at least forgetfulness, in the bottle and, finally, the ultimate escape— death—on the field of battle. That was life, a chain reaction of events, one thing leading to another, beyond a person's control. Christopher despised the cutlass and everything it stood for, and gave serious thought to hurling it into the Hudson River.

He was still considering that option the next morning, as he and his roommates prepared their quarters for the first inspection of the day. Glancing up from his labors, Christopher was surprised to see a cadet named Wade Morgan standing in the doorway. Morgan's face was a stern and stony mask—and Christopher's intuition warned him that something somewhere had gone terribly wrong.

"What is it?" he asked.

He didn't know Morgan very well—just well enough to recall that the cadet hailed from Mississippi and was one of Adam Vickers' cronies.

"I have been authorized by Mr. Vickers to make the necessary arrangements," was Morgan's stilted reply.

"Arrangements?" Christopher was bewildered. "Arrangements for what?"

Morgan's eyes glittered like cold steel. "I will assume that this pretense of ignorance on your part does not stem from cowardice."

Christopher glanced at O'Connor and Bryant. The latter appeared as mystified as he, but O'Connor seemed to suddenly grasp the situation. He glowered at Morgan.

"I assure you that Mr. Groves is no coward, sir," he said coldly, "as you may have cause quite soon to discover."

Morgan showed this veiled threat the proper disdain. "Are you, then, to act as his second?"

"If asked, I will be honored to do so."

A cold chill ran up Christopher's spine. "Seconds?"

They all looked at him.

"You mean . . . a duel?"

"Of course," said Morgan.

"Vickers has challenged me to a duel?" asked Christopher, incredulous.

"That is my purpose for coming here. Mr. Vickers

has submitted to me the honor of making the necessary arrangements."

"You can go back to Mr. Vickers," said Christopher, seething with sudden anger so ferocious that he trembled in its grasp, "and tell him I will not jeopardize my position here for the likes of him."

"Christopher!" exclaimed O'Connor, aghast. "You can't back down from a challenge!"

"I can, and I do."

"Then perhaps cowardice is the explanation," said Morgan.

"This is absurd," cried Christopher, feeling trapped. "Why does Vickers want to challenge me to a duel?"

Morgan's eyes narrowed as he scanned the faces of the other three cadets. "You haven't heard the news?"

"What news?"

"Mrs. Emily Cooper is dead."

"Dead?" Christopher couldn't believe his ears. "There must be some mistake."

"She took her own life last night, in her room at Cozzens'."

Chapter 5

A few minutes prior to midnight three shadowy figures emerged from the barracks. The night was overcast, black as pitch, and though the rain had stopped an hour earlier, rumblings like distant horse-drawn caissons on the move, and the occasional piercing flash of lightning, threatened more to come.

Accompanied by O'Connor and Bryant, Christopher marched resolutely across the commons toward the riding hall. Unlike his companions, he did not look furtively this way and that. There were sentries posted at the batteries along the parapet, at the south dock, and on the road to the mainland. They were there primarily to prevent cadets from slipping away from the Academy on some illicit assignation. Christopher knew where they were—he had logged countless long hours of guard duty himself, in all kinds of weather—and he doubted any of them would spot him and his two associates as they made the relatively short walk from the barracks to the riding hall. Not that he really cared. His tenure here as a West Point cadet was almost finished anyway.

"Someone's bound to see us," whispered Bryant nervously. "We could at least stay close to the buildings and work our way around."

"No time," snapped O'Connor. "One cannot be late to an affair of honor. Or one's own funeral. Right, Christopher?"

"That's a poor attempt at misplaced humor," scolded Bryant.

"If you don't like this, go back to the room," advised O'Connor.

Christopher was aware of Gil Bryant's dilemma. He felt obliged to come along, as Christopher's friend, even though he considered the business sheer lunacy. And remaining behind would not spare him from the severe punishment which was destined to descend upon all their heads once the deed was done. He was Christopher's roommate—O'Connor's too—and the board of inquiry which would inevitably follow was not likely to believe that he was unaware of the duel which was about to take place.

Assuming Christopher survived, he would most certainly be court-martialed and dishonorably discharged from the Corps of Cadets. As for his two friends, they, too, faced dismissal, although in their case at least there was a slim chance of remaining in the corps.

The sins of the father ... Indeed, he realized now that there was no escape from the ghosts of the past. Emily Cooper had come to see him and deliver his father's cutlass and then had taken her own life—a vial of poison, arsenic or strychnine or belladonna, no one knew for certain, it seemed, and what did it matter now?

O'Connor was right. There was absolutely no way that Christopher could refuse to accept Vickers' challenge. To do so would be to label himself a coward, and in that case he would have no future in the army anyway. He was doomed, no matter which course he took.

Christopher lengthened his stride. He didn't give much thought to dying, except to the degree that it would give Adam Vickers' satisfaction if he perished, and he couldn't bear the thought of that. So he would do his damnedest to stay alive, and then try to bear the disgrace of his discharge from West Point with as much dignity as he could muster, secure at least in the knowledge that he was a victim of a malevolent fate. Cold comfort. They were right when they claimed that life was a chain reaction of events beyond a person's control. None of this was his doing. *The sins of the father...*

Ahead in the darkness loomed the bulk of the riding hall. O'Connor caught his arm and spun him around.

"Maybe Gil's right," he said in a hoarse whisper. "Maybe this *is* foolish."

"It's worse than that," opined Bryant mournfully.

"What?" rasped Christopher. "You've had a change of heart, O'Connor? You? Well, if you have, then go on. I release you from your obligation to serve as my second."

"It isn't me that I'm concerned about," said O'Connor, offended. "It's you. Vickers is an expert with the sword. You should have chosen pistols. As the challenged, it was your choice. You are an excellent shot. As good as your grandfather, I wager."

"No. I must use the cutlass."

"Why? You didn't even want the flaming thing yesterday."

"It is fitting that I use the cutlass."

"Fitting? What does that mean? You'll hack each other into bloody pieces."

"I have no intention of killing him."

O'Connor was flabbergasted. "No intention of . . . then you'll die for certain."

"Give me the cutlass and go back to the barracks."

O'Connor refused to relinquish the cutlass, wrapped in the tasseled carriage blanket, which he carried under one arm.

"No," he said grimly. "I'll see this through."

"Then come on. I mustn't be late for my own funeral, remember?"

Christopher turned for the riding hall. O'Connor and Bryan exchanged glances.

"I've never seen him like this," said Bryant, clearly worried. "What's gotten into him?"

O'Connor shrugged.

The riding hall was a cavernous stone structure with carriage doors at the north and south ends. Rows of large slanted casements ten feet from the ground along the eastern and western walls were designed to flood the interior with natural light. Sand had been dredged up in vast quantities from the river to provide a surface for the hall.

When Christopher stepped inside the hall he was assailed by the pungent aroma of horses. But the place was empty, except for Vickers and Morgan, standing in the center of the hall, a lantern at their feet emitting mustard yellow light, their cloaked figures throwing elongated shadows. As Christopher and his companions approached, Morgan took Vickers' cloak. Vickers stood there, watching Christopher, and the blade of his saber whispered and gleamed in the lantern light as he flicked his wrist, nervous or impatient or both.

"Gentlemen," said Morgan, with arctic formality. "We are ready to proceed. What rules shall apply?"

"None," said O'Connor. "Unless you are willing to accept first blood."

Morgan glanced at Vickers, who gave a curt shake of the head.

"Considering the enormity of the insult to the Vickers name and family honor, that will not suffice," said Morgan.

"Insult?" Christopher laughed, a sharp and derisive sound which darkened Vickers' face. Proper etiquette of the *code duello* required the principals to remain silent and aloof from the arrangements as made by the seconds, but tonight Christopher was in no mood to give even a moment's consideration to rules. "What insult? You bloody damned fool. If anyone should bear the blame for Emily Cooper's suicide it is you and your family, Vickers. You care so for her honor, yet you scorned her, because what she had done embarrassed you. You're a hypocrite."

"And you, sir, are a scoundrel and a liar!" cried Vickers, the words thick with rage.

Christopher shook his head and turned scornfully away, shedding his cloak and placing the garment in Bryant's keeping. O'Connor unwrapped the cutlass and tossed it to him. Christopher caught it deftly, tested its weight. The blade was heavier than the cavalry saber which he had become accustomed to.

"No rules then," said O'Connor. "We can proceed."

There was one rule, unspoken. Both O'Connor and Morgan were armed with pistols. As seconds, they would be obliged to use their weapons if one of the principals displayed cowardice. Christopher was aware that if he lost his nerve and tried to run Morgan would be within his rights to shoot him down like a dog.

But he had no intention of running. In fact, to his surprise, he found himself quite calm and clearheaded. Adrenaline surged through his veins. His throat was dry, and there was a dull, persistent ache between his shoulder blades. But his hands were steady.

"Gentlemen, if you are ready?" said Morgan.

Vickers nodded.

"I'm ready," said Christopher, his voice clear as a bell.

Morgan, O'Connor, and Bryant backed away to give the combatants plenty of room.

Vickers extended his saber, dropping into the swordsman's crouch, body turned sideways to his adversary, the stance wide apart and bent at the knees, his free hand resting lightly on his hip. Christopher batted the saber away with the flat of the cutlass blade.

"Begin," said Morgan.

Incensed by Christopher's insolence, Vickers sprang forward like a horse released from the starting gate,

slashing with the saber, a mighty downward stroke that
could have split Christopher from the skull to sternum—
except that Christopher deftly parried the blow and
stepped aside to avoid Vickers' charge. With a snarl of
rage Vickers passed him, off balance, then whirled and
struck again, this time a horizontal stroke. The point of
the saber grazed Christopher below the ribs, ripping his
shirt and slicing his flesh and stinging like a thousand
angry fire ants, but he knew the pain was worse than
the wound, which was superficial.

The two men circled. Vickers lunged again, and Christopher stepped in to meet him. Steel rang against steel.
Their blades locked at the guards, Vickers hooked a leg
behind one of Christopher's and muscled his opponent
off balance. Christopher fell and rolled to avoid the
slashing saber, coming to his feet with an agile grace in
time to parry another thrust. This left Vickers open to
a blow to the face, and Christopher's fist landed solidly
on the other's jawbone, driving him to one knee.

"No rules!" shouted O'Connor, a reminder for Morgan's benefit.

Vickers hurled a handful of sand into Christopher's
face. Momentarily blinded, Christopher staggered backward as Vickers pounced like a jungle cat, seizing the
advantage. Christopher blocked one stroke by sheer luck
and then moved sideways, under another, gasping as
Vickers' blade bit deeply into the flesh of his sword arm,
above the elbow. An exultant cry escaped Vickers' lips.
Christopher clutched at the wound as searing pain jolted
his body. Blood gushed through his clawing fingers.
Vickers pressed him, slashing with the saber again, like
a man possessed. Sparks flew as blade clashed against
blade. The two men pushed apart and circled.

Breathing hard, Christopher blinked sweat out of his
eyes. Blood had soaked his shirt and was now beginning
to drip into his hand, making his grip on the hilt of the
Tripolitan cutlass a precarious one. Distant thunder

rolled across the sky. Morgan, O'Connor, and Bryant stood by, silent and rigid spectators. Christopher could hear little else above the harsh rasp of the breath in his throat. As he and Vickers circled warily, the single lamp threw their shadows in a grotesque dance of death against the somber gray stone walls of the riding hall.

For the first time in his life Christopher stared death in the face. Until a moment ago he had considered himself invulnerable, a common delusion among youth. But now he realized he wasn't immortal. Adam Vickers was going to cut him into bloody pieces. He felt his strength ebbing as his blood made black splotches in the sand.

Vickers knew he had the upper hand, and his gloating face stirred the embers of Christopher's anger, and the anger gave him new strength, so that when Vickers lunged forward again with another mighty downward stroke of the saber, Christopher was able to overpower him, putting everything he had left into parry and counterstroke. The cutlass blade bit deeply into Vickers' sword arm, below the elbow, breaking the bone. The saber slipped from Vickers' paralyzed fingers. Vickers cried out and dropped abruptly to his knees, a bright spray of scarlet blood gushing from his wound. Christopher raised the cutlass over his head, gripping it with both hands. One stroke and he could decapitate his opponent. But then Vickers looked up and Christopher saw the fear in his eyes, and Vickers held up a hand, a feeble gesture, a plea for mercy, and Christopher came to his senses. The urge to destroy this man who had tormented him for so long passed quickly.

Christopher lowered the cutlass.

Rushing to Vickers' side, Morgan said, "It is over."

Christopher turned away as Morgan ripped Vickers' sleeve at the shoulder seam and used it as a tourniquet on the wounded man's arm, trying to staunch the profuse flow of blood. Suddenly Christopher felt dizzy, nauseated, and weak in the knees. O'Connor hurried to him, prepared to catch him should he fall, but by sheer force of will Christopher stayed on his feet, an arm laid across his friend's shoulder for support.

"You should have killed him when you had the chance," said O'Connor in a fierce whisper. "I know him. It isn't over. Not by a long shot."

Morgan approached them, spared Christopher a cold glance, and addressed O'Connor, still one second to another. "Mr. Vickers is in need of immediate medical attention."

"As is Mr. Groves."

"I predict Mr. Vickers will never again have the use of that arm."

"He's lucky to be alive," said O'Connor. "Would you rather he were dead? Whatever he has lost this night, he brought it on himself."

Glancing back at Vickers, Morgan said, "I'll bring the doctor here," and left the riding hall with long, quick strides.

Christopher started for the door.

"Where are you going?" asked O'Connor.

Christopher made no reply.

"For God's sake," said his friend, "you must remain still. You are losing a lot of blood."

Christopher kept walking. "I am going to call on the superintendent."

By the tone of his voice it was manifest to O'Connor that he would not be deterred. The Irishman nodded, with an air of resignation. "I'll go with you." He turned to Gil Bryant. "Look after Vickers."

Bryant nodded bleakly.

Outside, a night wind howled in the trees. Distant lightning illuminated the storm clouds. The smell of rain was strong and pungent. The cool, damp breeze on his face revived Christopher. He stumbled several times, but refused to fall. He dragged the cutlass, as though it were too heavy for him to lift. O'Connor stayed close, ready to help him if he should falter. But Christopher made it to the superintendent's house. Climbing the steps to the porch of the small white clapboard house took the very last of his strength. He managed to raise his fist, and let it fall against the door, leaving smears of blood on the white paint. A light appeared in a window. A latch clattered as it was thrown back. The door swung open. Thayer stood there in a nightshirt, holding a lamp aloft. Standing behind Christopher, O'Connor thought that in any other circumstance Old Silly would look quite silly indeed. But there was nothing amusing about the expression on the old soldier's face.

"What's the meaning of this?"

"I have come to report that I . . ." Christopher almost blacked out. He swayed like a tall pine in a strong wind. His words were slurred together. He struggled to get them out. "I have come to report that I have fought a duel with Cadet Vickers."

Thayer blanched. He looked at O'Connor as though he couldn't believe what he was hearing, and hoped O'Connor would tell him it wasn't so. But he saw nothing in O'Connor's grim face to encourage him to cling to that hope, and Sylvanus Thayer was not one to linger long in a state of denial.

"Why?" he snapped. "You, of all people, Cadet Groves. I thought you had better sense."

"It was a . . . a question of honor, sir."

Thayer's lips were so tightly compressed that his mouth resembled a knife slit. "Do you realize what you've done?"

"Yes, sir."

Thayer glowered at O'Connor. "And you? Why didn't you put a stop to this?"

O'Connor stood stiffly at attention. "Because Christopher is my friend."

"Were you a true friend you would have prevented this from happening."

"He had no recourse."

"No recourse," growled Thayer. He looked Christopher over from head to toe, and then noted for the first time the growing puddle of blood at Christopher's feet. "Bring him inside, O'Connor, and fetch Dr. Rhodes."

"Dr. Rhodes is at the riding hall by now, sir. Looking after Cadet Vickers."

"Vickers isn't dead?"

"No, sir."

"Well, that's something, at least." Thayer turned his attention back to Christopher. "But not enough, I fear, to save you from court-martial."

"No, sir."

Thayer stepped aside to let them enter. Christopher took one step, but the floor seemed suddenly to evaporate beneath his feet, and he pitched forward into a blackness many shades darker than the storm-swept night.

Chapter 6

"Where will you go?" asked O'Connor.

Christopher smiled at his despondent friend. "Home to Kentucky."

"But . . . but what will you do there?"

Christopher shook his head. The smile on his face was strained. He did not care to think too long and hard about the future, as it did not seem to him that he had one.

"I don't know yet," he confessed.

The last of his belongings was packed in the trunk. He closed the lid and secured the latch. O'Connor and Bryant were standing by to transport the trunk to the surrey waiting outside. Christopher was inconvenienced by his arm, which was not only tightly dressed but also immobilized in a sling. Even now, a fortnight after the duel, the slightest movement was painful.

He looked around the room, seeing it for the last time, and memories came flooding back. He remembered the last two years vividly and, now that it was over, his dreams shattered, he thought they would turn out to be the best two years of his life. The last two weeks, however, were vague, and blessedly so, because they were full of anguish, both physical and emotional. The end result was that he was out—dismissed from the United States Military Academy—and on the threshold of a long journey home, by rented surrey across the Alleghenies to a distant landing on the Ohio River, and down the river on a boat to another landing on Kentucky soil. He dreaded meeting his mother face-to-face. Not that she would be too disappointed. Rebecca Groves had never been enthusiastic about her son embarking on a military career. But Christopher wasn't looking forward to admitting failure—or his participation in an affair of honor. His mother was strongly opposed to dueling, and little wonder.

On the way to Elm Tree he would stop at Boonesboro and visit his grandfather, Nathaniel Jones, the legendary frontiersman most folks knew as Flintlock. Grandfather Nathaniel was getting on in years—he was sixty-five now. But his eye was still keen, his aim still true. Christopher looked up to him, and valued his advice. Nathaniel was a man of great wisdom, and Christopher knew that his grandfather would not judge him, but rather would give sound advice—if asked. Christopher only hoped that he would find Nathaniel at home. Now that his wife—Christopher's grandmother, Amanda—was dead, Nathaniel spent much of his time roaming the woodlands he knew and loved so well.

"Christopher?"

Lost in thought, Christopher jumped at the sound of O'Connor's voice, and turned to find his friend holding his coat of blue broadcloth. Christopher slipped his good arm into a sleeve, and O'Connor draped the coat over his other shoulder.

"You look strange out of uniform," said O'Connor, with a smile every bit as strained as Christopher's.

"At least we won't have to see how bad you look in civilian clothes."

"Yes, thanks to you."

"Amen," said Bryant.

"I simply told the board and the superintendent the truth," said Christopher, shrugging off their heartfelt gratitude.

"You told them we *both* tried to talk you out of it,"

said O'Connor. "That's only half true. If you recall, I was all for a little bloodletting."

"But you tried to talk me out of it later."

"I did?"

"Yes. I remember your exact words. You said Vickers and I would hack each other to bloody pieces." Christopher glanced ruefully at his damaged arm. "That's what happened, too."

"Still, I can't believe they didn't throw us out, and Morgan, too."

"They understand and appreciate loyalty. As do I." Christopher extended his left hand, and O'Connor clasped it tightly.

"Well," said the Irishman, "we'd better get this trunk loaded up. You have a long road ahead of you."

Christopher followed them out. It was a warm and sunny morning, but he did not have eyes to see and appreciate this—he would forever remember this day as one of the most gray and dismal of his life. He was just grateful that all the other cadets were in class. His erstwhile roommates had been given permission to see him off. Christopher thought Sylvanus Thayer had been extremely generous in his handling of the situation. Of course, he and Vickers, the principals in the duel, had to go. No question of that. But Old Silly had proved astonishingly lenient when it came to Bryant and O'Connor and Morgan.

Thoughts of Greta Inskilling intruded on Christopher's misery, and made it even more severe. He tried to banish them from his mind. He had the courage to confront Adam Vickers in an affair of honor, but not nearly enough to face Greta, now that he was ruined and disgraced, and he could only imagine how her father must be gloating over his misfortune at this very moment. Like father, like son, Piet Inskilling would tell his daughter.

Once the trunk was loaded onto the back of the surrey

the three friends parted company. Christopher did not linger over the farewell. No long goodbyes for him. As usual, O'Connor tried to be lighthearted, though Christopher could see his own unhappiness reflected in the young Irishman's eyes.

"Don't be surprised if you find my shadow on your door in a few months' time," said O'Connor. "I have a feeling Old Silly is at the end of his tether where I'm concerned. One false step and . . ."

"And you would disappoint me," was Christopher's stern reply. "As a friend, do me a favor. Obey the rules. Graduate from West Point. That way at least one of us will."

O'Connor swallowed the lump in his throat, nodded solemnly. He did not trust himself to speak.

Christopher climbed into the surrey, gathered up the leathers in his one good hand, and whipped the bay horse in the traces into motion. He didn't look back.

Less than a mile from the Point, he met a rider on the road. The horseman was heading toward the Academy, and by the looks of his horse he was in a big hurry. His uniform identified him as a dragoon. The single gold bar on the shoulder straps of his blue double-breasted frock informed Christopher that he was a lieutenant. His forage cap was adorned with an officer's badge, a gold-embroidered six-point star. He wore a red sash beneath his sword belt, which sported a Mortimer pistol as well as the regulation saber.

The dragoon slowed his lathered mount as he drew near Christopher, and Christopher became uncomfortably aware of the man's keen scrutiny. He pulled on the reins to stop the bay when the lieutenant turned his horse broadside across the road and held up a hand.

"Do you come from West Point, sir?" asked the dragoon.

"I do."

"May I inquire after your name?"

"Christopher Groves." He almost added "Cadet," but caught himself in time.

The dragoon looked him over, taking in his civilian clothes, and the bulge of the dressing and sling beneath the coat, and Christopher felt the heat in his cheeks. He imagined that by now the whole country was informed of the ignominious end to his career as a West Point cadet.

"I am Joshua Singer, Lieutenant, Second Dragoons, at your service, sir. You are the gentlemen I have been sent to find."

"For what reason?"

"To deliver this." Singer brandished an envelope from beneath his tunic.

The envelope told Christopher nothing—it bore only "Christopher Groves, Esq." and "U.S. Military Academy, West Point" in a vigorous but quite legible and distinctly masculine hand. It was sealed with crimson wax bearing the emblem of an eagle with four arrows clutched in one of its talons.

The seal of the Republic! There was no mistaking it. Official business, then. But of what nature? Perhaps a reprimand. Just what he needed, to add to his misery. But it might be something else. Christopher tried not to be a pessimist. But, considering the way his luck had been running lately, he braced himself for the worst as he opened the envelope and extracted the single folded sheet of expensive vellum contained within.

Dated three days ago, the letter read:

Dear Mr. Groves—
Genl Jackson would be obliged were you to call upon him at the President's House at your earliest convenience.
It was signed "A. J. Donelson."

Andrew Jackson Donelson was Old Hickory's nephew

and personal secretary. His brother Daniel had recently attended West Point. General Jackson had taken the orphaned brothers under his wing. In fact, the childless president had adopted a number of young men, and loved them as he would have his own sons. Apart from the Donelsons and the legally adopted Andrew, there was Andrew's cousin, Andrew Jackson Hutchings, as well as Lincoyer, the Creek Indian whom the general had saved as an infant after his soldiers killed the child's parents during the campaign against the hostiles which culminated in the Battle of Horseshoe Bend.

Christopher was stunned. "What does this mean?" he wondered aloud.

"I'm sure I don't know," said Lieutenant Singer wryly. "I am not acquainted with the contents of the letter, nor do I wish to be. I am only its deliverer. It arrived at Fort McHenry yesterday and Colonel Roberts instructed me to hand it to you and offer any assistance you might require and which is within my power to provide."

Christopher had no thought of declining an invitation from the President of the United States. In the best of circumstances he would have been apprehensive about meeting Andy Jackson in the flesh, but he was doubly so now because he could only suppose that this letter had some connection with the duel and his dismissal from the Military Academy. Otherwise he would not have come to the General's attention at all.

"Thank you, but no," he said. "I can manage."

"If you don't mind my saying so, you don't seem much enthused by the prospect of meeting the President."

"Under normal circumstances I would be. But lately, circumstances have been anything but normal."

"You wouldn't care for some assistance?"

"No, thanks."

"You appear to have had an accident. I would be happy to drive you into Washington."

"It was no accident. And I am quite capable of getting there on my own."

"I have no doubt of that. Still, I wouldn't mind."

Christopher opened his mouth to decline yet again, but then, looking hard and long at Lieutenant Singer, he realized that the man's persistence had deeper roots than simple courtesy. Singer sought an excuse to visit the capital, and now that he had one he was going to hold on to it as tenaciously as a bulldog. Obviously he was in no rush to return to his post, and after two years of virtual incarceration at West Point, Christopher could sympathize.

"I promise not to ask any untoward questions," added the dragoon with a smile.

Christopher gave in. "Well, it is a bit difficult handling this thing with one good arm."

Singer took that admission for what it was. Securing his horse to the rear of the surrey, he climbed into the seat next to Christopher, took up the reins, and whipped the bay into action.

Christopher had never been to the nation's capital, but he had preconceived notion about it—notions which stemmed primarily from some of his father's old letters. He'd been five years of age when Jonathan Groves served in the United States House of Representatives, and in writing to Rebecca, who remained behind at Elm Tree, Jonathan had shared his often less than flattering observations of Washington with his wife. He had written of bogs and marshes, avenues filled with tree stumps, roads that dwindled into cow trails, a capitol that provided the men who occupied it with precious little in the way of comfort—they were either wilting in the sweltering heat of a Potomac summer or freezing in the bitter cold of winter, and were drenched when it rained because of a ceiling that persistently leaked like a sieve. In the early years of the republic it seemed that the government itself was of too little importance to the people to deserve much attention. As a result, Washington had been neglected. For a long time it was a laughing-stock of foreign diplomats as well as the American press.

This sad state of affairs had slowly but surely begun to change after the War of 1812. The British had burned part of the city, and when it came time for rebuilding, Americans decided their capital was worthy of more attention than they had given it before. The war had been a draw, and there were many who said it had accomplished nothing, but they were wrong—it had imbued Americans with a sense of national pride which had been lacking prior to the outbreak of hostilities. Before, people had spoken of "*these* United States" and they were Vermonters and Virginians and Pennsylvanians first and foremost. Now it was "*the* United States," and people were proud to be Americans. A nation which could stand toe-to-toe with the world powers needed a capital city that didn't embarrass them, and Christopher was pleased to find rows of nice houses and clean, orderly streets. They even had street lamps adorning Pennsylvania Avenue!

In 1828, Congress had authorized a report on the condition of the President's house prior to Andrew Jackson's arrival as the newly elected seventh President of the United States. The committee report concluded that the house was too run-down for the President to occupy. Since hog and cattle theft was rampant in the city, milch cows were kept in the west wing at night. During the day they grazed along the south fence. The stables were in an unfortunate location for those who were honored with an invitation to dine at the executive mansion—directly below the windows of the state dining room. The East Room, where Abigail Adams had hung her laundry out to dry, was still an empty, unpainted cavern of a room.

As Lieutenant Singer negotiated the surrey through

the dust and traffic of Pennsylvania Avenue, Christopher gazed in wonder at the stately mansion on the hill straight ahead. The house had been painted white to conceal the scorched stone resulting from the British attempt to put the place to the torch. He recalled that there had been quite a spectacle at the mansion on Andrew Jackson's inauguration day a year and a half ago.

For months prior to the event Washington was fast filling up with supporters of Old Hickory, many from the backwoods of Tennessee and Kentucky. The city's high society looked askance at this unwashed horde, and were shocked when the new president issued an open invitation to all the people to come see him that day at the White House. In prior inaugurations only the elite had been permitted into the President's house, but Jackson had decided to demonstrate that the presidency belonged to the common man—hence the invitation to one and all. Great numbers of people pushed into the house, filling the oval saloon and drawing room. The pounding of so many feet made the floors tremble. Jackson himself was soon in danger of being crushed by the unruly well-wishers. He was seen to gasp for want of air. Jack Donelson and other aides rushed to the rescue, hustling the old general unceremoniously through a window and into a waiting carriage, which transported him to his quarters at Gadsby's Hotel. The mob continued to scramble, fight, and romp through the house until late in the day. Jackson's opponents pointed to the debacle with disdain, claiming it to be ample evidence that the election of this unlettered, unwashed barbarian backwoodsman would usher in a reign of anarchy and mob rule. But, though it took weeks to clean the White House, not a single item turned up missing.

The city quickly returned to normal after the inauguration. Jackson moved to the mansion a few days later to begin his term. His first act was to hang a portrait of his recently departed wife, Rachel, above the mantel in the presidential bedroom. Since then he had proven himself a competent president.

Christopher was surprised at the ease with which he and Lieutenant Singer gained entry into the President's house. It seemed the door was still open to anyone who happened along. They entered from the south, into a vast oval room furnished with a few settees and wing chairs lining the walls. The most striking feature of the room was the Gilbert Stuart portrait of George Washington, a beloved national treasure which Dolly Madison, with great presence of mind, had snatched up as she fled the British invasion sixteen years ago. Christopher shuddered to think of that portrait hanging on some wall in London. That would have been an unbearable national disgrace.

They were greeted by Antoine Giusta, a Frenchman who had been John Quincy Adams' faithful valet. Giusta and Adams had met in Belgium in 1814, the former having recently deserted from Napoleon's *Grande Armée,* and the latter serving as a diplomat trying to hammer out a peace treaty with the British at the quaint village of Ghent. Giusta married Mrs. Adams' maid, and the couple served as steward and housekeeper during the Adams presidency. Adams had persuaded Giusta to stay on at the executive mansion and serve under Andrew Jackson—the ex-president was no longer able to afford the Giustas now that he was retired from public service. But serving under Old Hickory was no easy task, as countless soldiers could testify. Still, Giusta endured, thanks in large measure to Emily Donelson, Jack's pretty and petite wife, the official hostess of the Jackson White House. The Giustas were devoted to Emily, as were most others who had the pleasure of her acquaintance.

There were a dozen men and several ladies in the Oval Room, some sitting, others standing or pacing, and Christopher assumed they were here for an audience with the President or one of his aides. But when Lieuten-

ant Singer informed Giusta that the General had summoned Christopher, the Frenchman whisked them off to
the East Room. He asked them to wait there for a moment, and departed with a crisp continental bow.

The two men found themselves alone in the immense
room. They gazed about them in awe. The room mea-
sured eighty feet by forty, with twenty-two-foot ceilings,
crowned by a frieze of anthemia adorned with bands of
Grecian ornamentation. Three towering windows faced
south, with three more on the north side. On the east
was the great Venetian window. Imperial-blue and
sunflower-yellow draperies fell from cornices decorated
with gilded eagles. Muslin curtains softened the sunlight.
The walls were covered with lemon yellow paper of
French pedigree, trimmed with blue velvet cloth borders.
Bracket lights and "French plate" mirrors adorned the
walls. Mantelpieces of black Egyptian marble enhanced
the fireplaces. A blue-and-yellow Brussels carpet covered the floor. The furniture—twenty-odd chairs, several
sofas, mahogany pier tables with black marble tops, and
a score of gleaming brass spittoons—added to the room's
operatic splendor. It was the most luxurious and appealing room Christopher had ever seen.

"This isn't at all what I expected," confessed Singer
in a reverent whisper.

Christopher laughed nervously. "Nor I."

"I suppose our president isn't quite so uncivilized as
they make him out to be," said the dragoon with a grin.

"Well, it's not bad for a backwoodsman, I'll say that
much."

A black man in a brass-buttoned blue swallowtail coat
and yellow breeches appeared to ask them if they would
care for anything to drink.

"I'd better not," said Singer sadly. "Not while I'm in
uniform and in the vicinity of the General."

"I could use a brandy to cut the dust," said Christopher. "I don't have to worry about that anymore."

Christopher was just finishing the brandy when Giusta returned.

"The President will see you now, M'sieu Groves," he said, his heavy accent a consequence of his previous employer's preference for using French while discussing matters with his steward. John Quincy Adams was a cosmopolitan man, fluent in many languages. On the other hand, it was said that Andrew Jackson was fluent only on the frequent occasions when he launched into one of his tirades, notorious for their astonishing invective.

"What about the lieutenant?" asked Christopher.

"I imagine he would do well to return to his regiment," replied the old ex-soldier. "It is you alone the President wishes to see, m'sieu."

Singer was crestfallen. So was Christopher. He and the dragoon had shared life stories on the long road from West Point, and in so doing became friends, and Christopher realized that in all likelihood they would never meet again. The dragoon's expression made it apparent that he felt the same way.

"Well, I guess this is it, then," said Christopher.

Singer nodded. "No help for it. Maybe we'll meet again."

"It's a big country."

"But a small world, after all."

They shook hands, and Christopher followed Giusta out of the East Room, wondering—as he had a hundred times a day during the long journey to Washington—what the President of the United States could possibly want with him.

Chapter 7

While the first floor of the President's house was open to the public, Andrew Jackson's personal and business life was confined to the second, except for the frequent levees held in the East Room, now that it was fit for something besides laundry. The upstairs rooms included the Green Room, which served as Emily Donelson's parlor—she playing the role of First Lady since Rachel Jackson was buried in the garden at The Hermitage. There was the President's sitting room, bedroom, and dressing room. The Yellow Room, located over the north door, was a guest room as well as a ladies' retiring room during the levees. The President's office suite consisted of three rooms on the south side. Since visitors like Christopher Groves had to come upstairs to see the President, glass doors bisected the central hall, separating the office end from the rooms reserved for the family. While the family enjoyed the exclusive use of the grand staircase on the west end, visitors were required to ascend via the back stairs.

Once upstairs, Giusta escorted Christopher through the "audience room" into Jackson's office. It was here that the Cabinet customarily met, seating themselves at a long table, with cabinets and bookcases along the walls. These furnishings had once belonged to Thomas Jefferson. An oilcloth, artfully painted in a tile pattern, covered the floor. The window curtains depended from glided-eagle cornices like those in the East Room which

Christopher had so admired. An iron Russian stove stood in a sandbox in front of the fireplace, which was boarded up. The stovepipe was connected to the chimney flue.

As they entered, Andrew Jackson turned from his squinting perusal of a map on the wall. The President nodded as Giusta introduced Christopher.

"Come in, come in," said Jackson. His voice was surprisingly soft. Christopher expected the legendary old warrior to be gruff and loud. "Would you like a drink?"

"No, thank you, sir," lied Christopher. His nerves were raw, crying out for another stiff brandy. But he did not want to appear dependent on strong spirits in front of the President of the United States.

"Sit down, then."

Giusta pulled out a chair, and Christopher sat down. This placed him in the middle of the long table.

"That will be all," Jackson told Giusta, and the steward vanished, closing the door soundlessly behind him.

Jackson paced the length of the table and back again, collecting his thoughts, and in that moment of silence Christopher was afforded an opportunity to garner a first impression of a living legend.

Old Hickory stood an inch over six feet in height. He was thin, weighing in at about one hundred and forty pounds. His long, pale face—framed by thick snow white hair grown long and brushed straight back—was deeply furrowed. There was that famous scar on the forehead, from the saber of a British officer whose boots a twelve-year-old Jackson had refused to polish. In his sixties now, Jackson lived in almost continual physical pain. Many a month he had spent campaigning, enduring the same hardships as his men, abusing his body, taking his health for granted. During his war years he had contracted chronic dysentery as well as a recurring inflammation of the lungs. A memento of one of his most celebrated duels, he had for many years carried a bullet in him which caused persistent pain in his shoulder and side. Only recently had it been removed. Lately, a wracking cough and blinding headaches were added to his woes. A lot of people were wondering if the old warrior would live long enough to complete a single term, and few expected him to seek reelection in 1832.

Yet, with one look, Christopher was confident that Andrew Jackson would frustrate his enemies and survive for much longer than people thought possible. His will was indomitable. No combination of ailments would stop him as long as he wanted to live Truly, Old Hickory was larger than life. He was intelligent if not well-educated, an honest and upright man. Once he determined that a course of action was the proper one, he plunged ahead with a vigor and resourcefulness that put much younger men to shame. No obstacle would keep him from his goal.

The common people adored and trusted him. Born into frontier aristocracy, he had become the spokesman for the West of the farmer and the frontiersman. He did not trust the eastern merchant and banker. The people knew he was President through no personal ambitions, for he would have preferred to spend the autumn of his life a recluse on his beloved Hermitage, an estate on the outskirts of Nashville. No, he was here to do for the people what they could not do for themselves—in short, defend them against the eastern "establishment," the banks and the tariffs and all other government-sponsored monsters which the wealthy used to keep the poor and downtrodden in their place. This, at least, was how the General perceived his mission.

"I understand you have been dismissed from the Military Academy," he said. "An affair of honor." His flinty blue eyes flicked across the dressing and sling on Christopher's arm. "Are you badly hurt?"

"No, sir."

"They say your adversary lingered for some time at death's door."

"I believe he will survive, Mr. President."

Jackson nodded, stopped suddenly, and turned to face Christopher. "I could intervene on your behalf. Perhaps have you reinstated."

'I would rather you didn't do that, sir."

"Indeed? Why not? I've done it before."

"Yes, sir. I know."

"You don't approve."

Christopher decided to be brutally honest. After the events of the past few weeks he did not think he had anything to lose by speaking his mind.

"No, sir, I don't. By doing so you have undermined Superintendent's Thayer's authority."

"I am the Commander in Chief. He works for me."

"Yes, sir. But if you trust a man with a job you should let him do it the way he sees fit."

A faint smile tugged at Jackson's taut lips. "You do remind me of your father, young man. Indeed you do. You would have made a splendid officer."

"We'll never know now, will we, Mr. President?"

Jackson heard the bitterness in Christopher's voice, and while his gaze softened with sympathy his own voice took on a more severe tone.

"There is nothing to be gained by crying over spilt milk, Mr. Groves. Forgive an old man for prying, but what compelled you to fight this duel?"

"I'd rather not say, sir. It was a . . . a personal matter."

"Hmm. Your father's good name, no doubt. Since your adversary was Adam Vickers, I presume it had something to do with Mrs. Emily Cooper."

Christopher nodded. Jackson pulled out a chair and sat down across from him, wincing as he lifted his long, spindly legs to plant his boots on the corner of the table.

"Sometimes the price of doing the right thing is high. Believe me, I know whereof I speak. But without honor, without self-respect, all of your victories in life are hollow ones. As you may know, I have engaged in one or two duels myself."

"They say you've fought a hundred duels."

"A gross exaggeration. There was that business with Charles Dickinson, of course. Some insist it sprang from a quarrel over a horse-race bet. But Dickinson's tongue became too loose when he drank a lot of whiskey, and he made the mistake of insulting my wife. He also called me—let's see, what was it? Oh yes—a scoundrel, a poltroon, and a coward. I had no choice but to obtain satisfaction. I was warned that Dickinson was the best shot in Tennessee, and I believe they were right—his bullet struck me squarely in the chest. But I managed to remain on my feet long enough to return fire and kill him." Jackson paused, his gaze far off as he remembered, and then he added, fiercely, "I would have hit him had he shot me through the brain. His bullet shattered two of my ribs and came perilously close to my heart, and the wound has caused me some little discomfort ever since. But it had to be done."

Christopher had a hunch that what Andrew Jackson described as "a little discomfort" would be sufficient to incapacitate any normal person.

"And then there was that business with the Bentons," said Jackson with a rueful smile. "I acted—reluctantly, I must add—as second for Billy Carroll, my brigade inspector during the war, in his duel with young Jesse Benton. I tried to talk them out of it, but to no avail. Both of the lads were wounded in the exchange, though not mortally, praise God. Jesse's brother, Colonel Thomas Hart Benton, took offense at my participation in the affair. To this day I am not certain why. But he made such a noise about it, attaching all manner of vile adjectives to my name in public, that I swore I would horsewhip him at the first opportunity."

Jackson suddenly began to cough violently. The attack

lasted almost a minute. When it had passed, he wiped his eyes with a trembling hand and proceeded with his narrative as though nothing had happened.

"The opportunity came a few months later, in Nashville. John Coffee and I were walking to the post office from the Old Nashville Inn when we saw Benton standing in the doorway of the City Hotel. John and I went on to the post office, collected our mail, and on our way back I noticed that Jesse Benton had joined his distinguished brother. All of us were armed, and I carried a riding whip. When Thomas Benton reached for his pistol I drew my own. He backed into the hotel, but Jesse ducked into another room, came out onto the porch through a second door, and fired at me. The bullet struck me in the arm and shoulder. I lost my balance and fell. Then Thomas Benton fired at me twice, before I could rise. Heaven only knows how he managed to miss me. John fired at Thomas, but missed, and Thomas ran. A friend of mine, Stockley Hays, happened to be in the vicinity. He wrestled Jesse to the ground and stabbed him in both arms with a knife.

"Jesse's bullet was lodged against the bone of my arm. Several physicians examined the wound, and they all advised amputation. I would have none of it, and instructed them to use a poultice of slippery elm. An old Indian remedy. It worked. The wound healed and, as you can see, the sawbones did not take my arm."

"But you and Thomas Hart Benton are friends now, aren't you?"

"Not friends so much as political allies. We have the same objectives. We shook hands ten years later, when we found ourselves sitting side by side in the United States Senate." Jackson chuckled. "I carried Jesse Benton's lead in me for many years. Only later was it removed, by a noted surgeon from a hospital in Philadelphia. Frank Blair obtained the bullet and offered it to Thomas Benton. Benton declined the gift, saying that I had acquired clear title to it in common law by twenty years' possession.''

Jackson swung his legs off the table. "Are you sure you wouldn't care to join me in a drink?"

Christopher decided it would be bad manners to refuse. "Allow me to pour them," he said, making as though to rise from his chair.

Jackson waved at him to keep his seat. He winced as he got to his feet. Old war wounds and a hard life made every movement painful for him, but in spite of it all the general was restless. Crossing the room to one of the cabinets, he poured amber liquor from a decanter into two shot glasses.

"Tennessee sour mash," said Jackson. "Best sipping whiskey on earth. Beats your Kentucky bourbon all to hell." He handed one glass to Christopher and raised his own. "To the Republic. God bless her, and damn her enemies."

Christopher stood to participate in the toast. He sipped the sour mash. Jackson knocked his back in one thirsty gulp, and gasped in satisfaction as he sat back down.

"I don't usually take so long to come to my point," said the President. "I share my war stories with you for a purpose. Though I derive no satisfaction from taking another man's life, and while those affairs of honor have caused me much physical pain, I do not regret my participation in them. You simply cannot turn your back on that kind of a challenge, son. If you do, you'll find yourself turning your back on every other kind. Then, as a man, you won't be worth a bucket of warm spit. So I am convinced that you acted properly. As I have said, sometimes the price of acting properly is exceedingly high."

Christopher finished off the sour mash. "Sir, I am honored that you have taken such an interest in my future."

"Your father was a friend of mine. I have felt a re-

sponsibility towards you since the day he died, coura-
geously leading his men into battle against the
Seminoles. I was privileged to recommend you to the
Military Academy. And I would consider it an esteemed
honor to assist you in any other way."

Christopher shook his head. "I appreciate that, Mr.
President. But there is nothing I need. I'm going home
to Kentucky."

"What will you do there?"

"Raise thoroughbred horses, I suppose."

Jackson was up again, pacing. For a moment he said
nothing, deep in thought. Then he shook his white-
maned head emphatically.

"No. Forgive me for saying so, but I believe you are
a young man with a thirst for adventure. If you are anything like your father I know I am right."

Christopher wanted to tell the old general that he had
no desire whatsoever to be even remotely like his father.
But he didn't dare. Obviously Jackson held Jonathan
Groves in high regard. It would not sit well with Old
Hickory if Christopher showed disrespect for his fa-
ther's memory.

"It will be an adventure," replied Christopher, wryly,
his tongue loosened by the sour mash, "just keeping Elm
Tree above water."

Jackson stopped pacing in front of a map. "Perhaps
what you need is a new start. May I suggest Texas?"

"Texas?"

"Yes."

"But ... but I'm an American, sir. And I would very
much like to remain one."

Jackson smiled. "There are many Americans gone to
Texas these days."

"But they have to renounce their citizenship to live
there, do they not? They must pledge allegiance to the
flag and constitution of the Republic of Mexico."

Jackson stabbed a gnarled finger at the map. "Texas

may belong to Mexico today, but that's no guarantee for tomorrow. Do you believe in destiny, son?"

"Why, yes," said Christopher.

Jackson nodded. "Guess you damn well ought to, considering what's befallen you. It wasn't your destiny to be a graduate of West Point. But that doesn't mean you can't be a soldier."

"I confess I don't follow you, Mr. President."

Jackson leaned forward, his big scarred knuckles splayed on the table. "Texas has a destiny, too. And that's to be a part of this Republic. When the time comes for that to happen she'll need brave, strong, young men who crave glory and adventure to make it happen. I think Texas needs men just like you. There's no limit to what a man can make of himself in a country like that."

Christopher realized that this was the real reason General Jackson had summoned him to the White House.

"It's the fault of John Quincy Adams"—Jackson rapped his knuckles three times on the table, once for every part of his predecessor's name—"that Texas belongs to Mexico in the first place. When I marched into Florida those powder-heads up here in Washington were scared to death the Spaniards would go to war with us. Yes, Florida was a Spanish possession, but they could not administer or defend it. Those damned Seminoles and mulatto runaways were slipping across the border at will to burn, loot, and pillage American farms and villages. The Spaniards couldn't stop them, so I did.

"I warned them, sir. I told them about the Negro fort on the banks of the Apalachicola. Fugitive slaves in that fort were inciting other slaves to flee their masters and join them. Ask any slaveowner in the South. They knew. That fort was a threat to their property, not to mention their very lives and the lives of their families. I wrote the Spanish commandant at Pensacola, told him that this would not be tolerated, and that if he didn't do something about it, we would be compelled in self-defense to do the jobs ourselves.

"I knew we had a golden opportunity to take Florida. It was right there, within our grasp, and ripe for the picking. President Monroe authorized it. Not officially, and of course he later denied knowing anything about my intentions. But I had made those intentions clear to him in a letter, and I had his permission to take the barrancas and destroy the banditti, and that's precisely what I did."

Christopher knew the story well. In addition to invading and conquering Spanish territory, Jackson had executed two British subjects, a Scots trader named Arbuthnot and a British Marine, Robert Armbrister, both of whom, Jackson claimed, were actively involved in supporting the Seminole hostiles led by Chief Billy Bowlegs. Suddenly Washington found itself on the brink of war with both Spain and Great Britain. Jackson's contention was that from the very beginning both nations were bluffing. The last thing the British wanted was another war with their American cousins, and the Spanish, though outraged, were too weak to make a fight of it. As it turned out, Jackson was right.

Nonetheless, Spain blustered and made threatening noises. Her minister to the United States, the urbane Don Luis de Onis, demanded the immediate restoration of Florida and a suitable punishment for "that freebooter" Andrew Jackson. To John Quincy Adams, President Monroe's adroit secretary of state, fell the task of dealing with Onis. Adams refused to punish Jackson, who had acted in "self-defense," and insisted that Spain must either garrison a sufficient military force in Florida to prevent future Indian outrages against innocent American settlers in the borderlands, or cede the province.

But there were Congressmen who supported the move to censure Jackson. Some were incensed that their constitutionally delegated authority to declare war had been deftly circumvented by Old Hickory. Others wanted to embarrass the Monroe administration. And still others—men like Henry Clay of Kentucky and William Crawford of Virginia, who harbored presidential aspirations of their own—saw the immensely popular general as a threat to their future plans.

"It's a shame James Monroe did not stand up to the hellish machinations of men like Henry Clay," continued Jackson. "But he was entirely too much the politician. Clay is a base hypocrite. He pretended friendship to me even as he attempted to destroy the administration through me. Your father had sound judgment, except in his admiration for Clay. I hope you do not take offense, when I speak so of a fellow Kentuckian."

"No, sir."

"But Adams—Adams should have had better sense. The dons knew they could not hold on to Florida. But Adams gave away too much in the treaty he drafted with Onís. He gave away Texas, for God's sake!"

Christopher nodded.

There had long been some question as to the western boundary of the Louisiana Purchase. Many Americans insisted that Texas was part of the Purchase. Spain insisted it was not. In exchange for ceding Florida to the United States, Spain fixed the boundary of the purchase at the Sabine, Red, and Arkansas rivers, thence westward to the Pacific Ocean along the forty-second parallel. They also got five million dollars in the bargain.

"I thought just about everyone agreed that the treaty was advantageous to us, Mr. President."

Jackson shook his head. "Why? Because it rendered in ink on paper what was inevitable. This continent belongs to us. It is our destiny to possess it. There cannot be two owners of the same house. Texas was legitimately part of the Louisiana Purchase. Adams gave it away. And for what reason? To secure Florida? I had Florida in my grasp." Jackson raised a hand and clenched it into a trembling, white-knuckled fist. "I would not have let go of it. In fact, if given free rein, I would have seized Texas from the dons, as I had done with Florida. Onis knew this. That's why he secured the boundaries in the treaty—to keep me out of Texas."

The clock on the mantelpiece chimed softly. Jackson glanced at it, and seemed to be surprised that so much time had passed.

"I'm afraid I have a diplomatic duty to attend to," he said. "I would like to talk more with you. Are you in a hurry to get back to Kentucky? Can you stay here with us for a few days?"

How did one turn down an invitation from the President of the United States? Christopher said, "Well, I . . . yes, sir."

"You will room here."

"Here?"

Jackson smiled. "Are the accommodations not to your liking?"

"No, sir. I mean—I never thought I'd sleep under *this* roof."

"I often wish I didn't. It's settled then. Tomorrow, perhaps, you would join me for my morning ride. I have some very good horses. Perhaps not as good as Elm Tree's, but they will suffice."

"I would be honored, Mr. President."

Jackson nodded curtly. On his way out of the room he paused to lay a hand on Christopher's shoulder.

"Humor an old man, son, and give some serious thought to Texas."

Christopher promised he would.

Chapter 8

Texas.

Now that Andrew Jackson had planted the seed in his mind, Texas was virtually all Christopher could think about. Old Hickory had something up his sleeve, that much was certain. He was a man accustomed to getting what he wanted, and clearly he was intent on getting Texas into the Union.

But how? An invasion? On what pretext? Unlike the case of Florida, American farms and villages were not being menaced by Indian raiders residing in the wild reaches beyond the Red and Sabine rivers. No, it struck Christopher that Jackson was keenly interested in infiltrating Texas with adventurers who, when the time was right, would rise up in revolt against Mexican rule and bring the province into the United States.

It was a rich country, Texas, long a temptation to Americans restless for a new beginning. Texas beckoned to such men with its dense, virgin forests in the east, the fecund soil of its central plains, its many natural harbors on the Gulf of Mexico, its numerous navigable rivers, its vast herds of wild horses and wilder longhorn cattle.

And yet, in three hundred years, Spain had failed in her attempts to colonize Texas. She could persuade few of her subjects to occupy that remote northern province of her vast New World holdings. The Indians were the stumbling block, from the fierce Comanches, warlords of the high plains, to the Karankawas, the cannibals of the coastal region. Apart from isolated *presidios* garrisoned by skeleton garrisons, Spain managed to settle a paltry three thousand brave souls in Texas by the year 1820.

Realizing that where American settlers ventured the American government wasn't far behind, Spain took steps to keep the Anglos out of Texas—at least at first. That was easier said than done. In the 1790s, a young horse thief named Philip Nolan made several expeditions about the border. Nolan was eventually caught and executed by a Spanish firing squad. But other freebooters poured into Texas. Their depredations became so serious that the town of Nacogdoches, located at the eastern end of the El Camino Real, with her one thousand inhabitants, was abandoned in 1820.

Finally the Spanish accepted the fact that they could not keep the Americans out forever. They allowed a carefully chosen man, Moses Austin, to become what they called an *empresario,* the proprietor of a large colony. The empresario had to guarantee that the American colonists who would settle on his land grant would pledge their loyalty to the Spanish crown and become Roman Catholics.

Moses Austin died of pneumonia while negotiating with the Spanish governor of Texas. His son, Stephen, promised to fulfill his father's dream. It was a difficult promise to keep. He found a suitable site on the Brazos River, calling it San Felipe, and more than enough applicants to fill the Spanish requirement of three hundred families, but his supply ship, the *Lively,* her hold brimming with tools and provisions for the settlers, ran aground on Galveston Island. The ship and her cargo were lost.

Still, Austin's colonists persevered. Most of them were tough, hardscrabble farmers. But one, Jared Groce, a wealthy planter from Alabama, carved a huge cotton plantation out of the wilderness and transported over a hundred slaves to work his fields. The fact that the eastern half of Texas was prime country for the kind of labor-intensive money crops which perpetuated the "peculiar institution" of slavery was causing problems for those, like Andy Jackson, who dreamed of bringing Texas into the Union. Abolitionists were adamantly opposed to adding another "slave" state. Men like William Lloyd Garrison, editor of the fiery abolitionist newspaper *The Liberator,* would stop at nothing to prevent the expansion of slavery. It was Garrison who had shredded a copy of the Constitution at a public meeting, denouncing that hallowed document as a pact with the devil, since it permitted slavery to exist.

In 1822, Mexico staged a revolution against her Spanish overlords. Austin needed every ounce of his tact and patience to persuade the Mexicans to adopt a colonization law. A few years later the Mexican policy toward colonization was liberalized, and by 1830, over twenty land grants had been made to empresarios like Austin. Speculators spread the word about Texas, and on the day that President Jackson met with Christopher Groves in the White House, there were sixteen thousand Americans in Texas, four times the number of Mexicans.

One of these empresarios, Haden Edwards, along with his brother Benjamin, almost ruined everything. The Mexicans had provided Edwards with three hundred thousand acres in east Texas, near the village of Nacogdoches, on which he settled with eight hundred families. Trouble was, there were already a number of Anglo squatters and Mexican settlers already on the land.

It was a subject that came up during Christopher's ride with Jackson the next day. The President was clad in a fine suit of cobalt blue broadcloth. He wore a white, broad-brimmed planter's hat. He seemed a much younger man in the saddle, tall and well-seated and all grace and suppleness. As they rode down the dusty length of Pennsylvania Avenue, Jackson asked Christopher what he knew of Texas, and when Christopher mentioned having heard of the Republic of Fredonia, Old Hickory's eyes lit up.

"There's what I'm talking about!" exclaimed the President with exuberance. "Americans won't live under a foreign thumb for long. Not in their nature."

"Sir?"

"The Republic of Fredonia. A glimpse of the future of Texas, my boy."

"It seemed to me a rather hopeless, quixotic scheme, when I heard of it," confessed Christopher.

Haden Edwards had threatened to confiscate the property of all the early settlers if they could not show proper title to the land they were occupying. When he proceeded to carry out his threat, the Mexican government revoked his empresario contract and ordered him out of the country. The Edwards brothers rode into Nacogdoches with thirty armed men, flying a red-and-white banner bearing the motto "Independence, Liberty and Justice." They seized the old stone fort and proclaimed the formation of the Republic of Fredonia. Six weeks later, Mexican troops marched against the rebels. Not a shot was fired. The Edwards brothers and their followers fled across the Sabine into the United States.

"It was the wrong place and the wrong time," said Jackson. "But the day will come when there won't be just thirty men, or even three hundred, but thousands, taking up arms to fight for freedom."

"But, as I recall, Mr. President, Stephen Austin sent a hundred of his colonists to help the Mexicans put down the Fredonian rebellion."

"Austin." Jackson growled the name. "The man's a traitor. He is actually serious about remaining a Mexican citizen. But what can you expect? His father preferred to live as a Spanish citizen in Missouri, back before the Louisiana Purchase. That's why the Spaniards chose him to establish the first colony in Texas."

"But Austin gave his word to the Mexican authorities."

Jackson scowled and rode on in silence for a few minutes. He was a man whose word was his bond, and Christopher's riposte had pierced his defenses.

Everyone recognized the President, and Jackson was constantly touching the brim of his hat to those who passed, be it in carriages, on horseback, or afoot. Tiring of this exercise in cordiality, Old Hickory abruptly reined his high-stepping Tennessee hunter off the avenue and plunged recklessly down a trail between scrub-covered hillocks. Christopher followed, and soon found himself on the banks of the Tiber River. This broad, turgid tributary of the Potomac was hemmed in by marsh, where cranes and herons were splotches of brilliant color among the brown and yellow reeds. To their left, near the headwaters of the brief Tiber, stood the capitol in all its splendor on a preeminent hill.

"Is that what you would do, Christopher?" asked Jackson, gazing out across the scrub and swamp. "If you went to Texas and became a Mexian citizen, would you fight your fellow Americans, men who sought only to govern themselves rather than live by the rules of elegant dons in Mexico City?"

"No, sir. I don't think I could fight against Americans."

"No. I didn't think you could. And yet I sometimes worry that one day Americans may shed the blood of other Americans over this matter of slavery."

"The abolitionists won't like the idea of annexing Texas."

"Hang the abolitionists." Jackson flashed a belated grin. "I don't mean that literally, of course. Have to make that clear, my reputation being what it is. Most sensible folks ignore them. But I doubt they'll just go away. Son, we've got to get Texas into the Union before this storm that's gathering over slavery strikes us with hurricane force."

"Yes, sir."

Jackson gave him a long, speculative look. "The fight is coming. The Mexicans are alarmed by the influx of Americans into the province of Texas. I am told by reliable sources that the Bustamente government intends to end American immigration and build a number of forts near the colonies. These forts will be garrisoned by convict soldiers who are to remain as settlers after their enlistments are up. Worse, the Mexican government refuses to give Texas its just representation in their national assembly. Fact is, Bustamente is flaunting the Mexican Constitution of 1824, and our leatherstockings, who are accustomed to exercising their God-given rights, are becoming restless.

"Yes, Christopher, the fight is coming. But those farmers and backwoodsmen are going to need leadership, if they're to have any chance against the Mexican Army. Brave young men, like you, must be in place. If your father were alive I would ask him to go, and there is no doubt in my mind that he would. Will you?"

"I will think about it, sir," promised Christopher. Seeing disappointment cross Jackson's face, he added, "If I had only myself to consider I would go without hesitation. But I have my mother to think about. I'm all she has. I could not go so far away unless she permitted it."

Jackson abruptly dropped the subject. "Come, we must go back. Unfortunately, I have my duties to perform this afternoon. Will you stay another day? We are having a levee tomorrow, and I think you would enjoy it. Are your accommodations satisfactory?"

"Satisfactory?" Christopher almost laughed. The question was absurd. He had been assigned to the Yellow Room, the guest quarters on the second floor of the White House, above the north entrance. The room, done up in yellow silk, sported handsome mahogony furniture, as well as a dressing area with a washstand and a mahogany close stool. "It is more than satisfactory, Mr. President."

Jackson grinned. "Quite a step up from the West Point barracks, eh? The work on the portico will not disturb you, I hope."

Christopher assured him it would not. Construction on the north portico, an improvement which the Committee on Public Buildings had been considering for years, had commenced a month after Jackson's inauguration. At present, workers were erecting a parapet wall with an iron railing between the foremost four columns.

They rode back to the White House, leaving their horses at the new stables, which had been built to house the President's fine thoroughbreds. Beyond the southeast gate, the stable was rather elegant itself, made of stucco-covered bricks with stone trimming on the windows, a porch with six round, graceful columns of plastered bricks, and a hayloft above the stalls. It also contained a tackroom, feed room, and accommodations for two coaches as well as quarters for the grooms and coachmen.

The President excused himself and repaired to his offices to conduct the country's business, leaving Christopher at loose ends. He roamed the grounds to have a closer look at all the work that was being done. A reservoir was being excavated near the mansion. When finished it would resemble a large pond edged with brick, and fed by water from a spring near Franklin Square, which the committee intended to purchase. The water would be piped to the reservoir in "trunks," wooden pipes made of hollowed-out logs. This would provide the President's house with running water, a convenience enjoyed by the clientele of most hotels, but which was not yet available to the Chief Executive of the United States.

Christopher met the engineer in charge of the job, a man named Robert Leckie, who was eager to share his vision. Stone pedestals would be laid in the reservoir where the pipes surfaced. The water would emerge in fountains. Here, too, were iron pumps, trimmed with brass and sheltered by ornamented wooden pump houses resembling church steeples. Pipes running from the pump houses to the mansion would be laid underground, and fitted with hand pumps which would produce sufficient pressure to carry the water to the second story. Inside the mansion, the pipes would be capped with brass cocks. Leckie informed Christopher of President Jackson's intention to install a bathing room in the east wing, which would include facilities for a shower bath and a hot bath, the latter made possible by the building of coal fires beneath large copper boilers. Christopher was impressed. Hot baths to be had by simply turning a spigot! What would they think of next?

He spent a good part of the late morning in the White House gardens. Jackson had called upon Jemmy Maher, who he had appointed Washington's public gardener, to improve the appearance of the grounds. A hard-working—and harder-drinking—Irishman who hated the British with a passion, Maher had much in common with Old Hickory, and they got along famously. Christopher counted over fifty laborers hard at work, some hacking at the earth with picks and hoes, others grading with rakes, still others pushing draymen's carts and wheelbarrows hither and yon, and all of it producing a choking pall of dust which, combined with the May heat, made working conditions less than ideal. Maher's men were transforming the north driveway into a wide horseshoe, bordered with paved footpaths. The circular road was being leveled and graded. Maher had purchased trees and shrubbery from Bloodgood & Company of New York, the nation's most prestigious nursery. Among the many trees Maher had ordered were sugar and silver leaf maples, sycamores of both the European and American varieties, lindens, oaks, and horse chestnuts, the latter highly prized for their white, wisterialike blossoms. Jackson wanted the grounds heavily planted with trees, with the exception of the two-acre flower garden. It was here that Christopher finally found blessed relief from all the dust and hubbub.

The garden was accentuated with numerous rose trellises, as well as a tunnel arbor and an orangery. The latter sported tall glass windows. It had been constructed using the shell of an old fireproof vault from the Treasury, which had been discarded after the war. Gravel walks intersected meticulously groomed stands of camelias and laurestina, and beds of hyacinth, narcissus, and tulips.

Christopher found a remote and quiet spot for his refuge, an iron bench in the welcome shade of a stately old elm, and here he sat for quite some time, thinking about Texas. He was intrigued by the idea of seeing with his own eyes this strange new land he had heard so much about. And if President Jackson was right about the destiny of Texas, then truly a young man could find all the adventure his valiant heart desired. Returning to Kentucky to live at Elm Tree had never been a very appealing prospect for him. Now it seemed even less so, when compared to Texas. In Texas he could find a new beginning, where a man's past mattered not.

He was disturbed in his ruminations by a short, round-bellied man who emerged quite unexpectedly from the arbor, carrying shears in one gloved hand and a freshly cut bouquet of roses in the other. He was clad in old, soiled dungarees and a somewhat frayed and disreputable tweed jacket. A straw hat with a hole in the brim shaded his eyes. Christopher assumed he was one of the gardeners, and ignored him. But the man came straight for him, and as he drew closer, Christopher realized that he looked vaguely familiar. His features were sharp and foxlike in a round face framed by a luxuriant set of side-whiskers.

"Might you be the young Christopher Groves I have heard so much about?" asked the man pleasantly, his mellow voice perfectly modulated, his diction precise.

Christopher stood up quickly. "Yes, sir, I am."

The man fumbled with trying to hold the roses and shears in one hand, then gave up the attempt and placed them on the bench Christopher had just vacated. Peeling off one of the heavy leather gauntlets, he extended a small, soft, white hand.

"I am very pleased to meet you at last, sir."

Christopher gripped the hand firmly and shook it. "You have me at a disadvantage, I'm afraid."

The man's eyes twinkled with merriment. "Martin Van Buren, at your service."

"Mr. Secretary!" Christopher was mortified. "I . . . I didn't recognize you!"

Van Buren chuckled good-naturedly. "And how could you, lad? I am not my usual picture of sartorial perfection, now am I? The President is kind enough to permit me to putter about in this splendid garden of his. Horticulture is a passion of mine. He, on the other hand, prefers trees to flowers. By his order they are transforming these grounds into a veritable jungle. Ah, well. There is nothing done that cannot be undone. That's my motto. Or one of them, anyway. I am fond of mottoes. My goal is to have one for every occasion. So tell me, are they treating you well?"

"Like royalty, sir."

"Good, good. I suppose the President has been trying his best to talk you into going to Texas."

"Why, yes, as a matter of fact he has been."

Van Buren nodded. "It has become something of an obsession with him. A knotty issue, Texas."

Christopher found himself completely at ease with this

man, the wily politician they called the Fox of Kinderhook. Van Buren was an extremely ambitious man, but
so disarming in his amiable charm that few could dislike
him for it. That was the key to his uncanny ability to
manipulate others into doing his will. His cherubic features and warm, genuine smile disguised a man of extraordinary intelligence and cunning.

Van Buren was a New Yorker, an "Old Republican"
and longtime foe of DeWitt Clinton. A master at political organization, he had proved instrumental in Jackson's triumph at the polls in the Northeast. He believed
in small government and free trade, and so was strongly
opposed to the "American System" of internal improve-
ments and high tariffs which defined the politics of John
Quincy Adams and Henry Clay. For this reason he had
allied himself—at first reluctantly—with Old Hickory.
They were a most unlikely pair, the rough-hewn backwoods planter and military hero, and the smooth-
tongued, urbane gentleman from the East, the warrior
and the scholar, the one preferring to settle quarrels with
pistols and swords, the other with words.

Jackson had chosen Van Buren to be his Secretary of
State, largely out of gratitude for the "Little Magician's"
invaluable support during the election of 1828. At the
time, Jackson had known precious little about Van
Buren, and what little he did know he did not particularly like, being by nature as well as experience critical
of professional politicians, especially those of the eastern
variety. But now Van Buren was Old Hickory's most
trusted confidant and loyal associate. And while the volatile John C. Calhoun of South Carolina was the vice
president, and the most obvious choice as Jackson's heir-
apparent, it was said that the General preferred Van
Buren for his successor. This was due in no small measure to the fact that Calhoun was on the wrong side of
the Peggy Eaton controversy, at least from the Presi-

dent's perspective, while the crafty Fox of Kinderhook had wisely become Peggy's champion.

"Sir, what do you think will happen with Texas?" asked Christopher.

"Oh, I do not doubt for a moment that the General will have his way. He usually does. So, you were at West Point, I understand."

Christopher nodded glumly. "I am ashamed to admit that I have been dismissed from the Military Academy."

"Well, it's not the end of the world, young man, I assure you."

"It certainly seemed so at the time."

"But already you perceive new vistas of opportunity before you. You must roll with the punches, Mr. Groves. Yes, I heard all about the events surrounding your departure from the Point."

Christopher sighed. "I guess it must be common knowledge by now."

"Ah, but I had a special source for the details. A very dear friend of mine happens to be Piet Inskilling."

"He must be gloating right about now. He said I wouldn't amount to anything."

"You shall prove him wrong. I have no doubt of that. Do not judge him too harshly. Rare indeed is the father who does not find something to criticize about his daughter's beau. To be precise, it was Greta Inskilling who wrote me a letter which provided all the details of your duel with Adam Vickers and your subsequent dismissal. She pleaded with me to intercede on your behalf, if I could. Alas, I am unable to influence Superintendent Thayer, beyond the point of presenting your case, and darling Greta's request for leniency, to the secretary of war. Which I have done, and gladly. But I have a hunch you are not the type of fellow who expects or even desires special treatment."

"Absolutely not, Mr. Secretary."

"I thought not. You were well aware of the consequences of your actions, and were willing to accept them. Frankly, I can see why Greta is so fond of you. She is a dear, sweet, beautiful child, and she has a good head on her shoulders. Surely you weren't thinking of going to Texas without at the very least saying goodbye to her."

"I'm not sure I'm going to Texas."

"Ah. Well, you and she will have an opportunity to discuss it."

"We will?"

"Oh, didn't I tell you? Greta is on her way to Washington even as we speak. I would expect her no later than tomorrow afternoon."

"Greta? Coming here? But why?"

"To see the President on your behalf. She will be staying with me. And I'm certain she'll be delighted to see you."

Chapter 9

Christopher was invited to a Jackson "family" dinner that evening. Present around the table in the White House dining room were the President, Jack Donelson, Secretary of War John Eaton and his wife Peggy, Major Andrew Lewis and his daughter Mary Ann, Martin Van Buren and Christopher. Emily Donelson, the unofficial hostess of the White House, and the wife of Jack, the President's private secretary, was ill, as she so often was these days. This did not dismay the crusty Major Lewis, a longtime associate of Jackson's, who was promoting his daughter as Emily's replacement. Mary Ann's chief rival in this instance was none other than the infamous Peggy Eaton, the pretty, brown-haired, rosy-cheeked young woman who was causing a stir in the capital's social circles these days. Jack Donelson was noticeably cool toward Peggy, because Peggy and Emily just didn't get along, but he couldn't be too cool, because Old Hickory wouldn't abide any disrespect shown the persecuted wife of his old friend, the secretary of war.

All this Christopher learned from Martin Van Buren. "It is quite an entertaining little circus," said the Fox of Kinderhook with a sly wink. The secretary of state looked altogether different in appearance from that afternoon in the flower garden. He wore an impeccable snuff-colored broadcloth coat complete with velvet collar, an apricot cravat with lace tips, a pearl-colored vest, white duck trousers, and shoes of Moroccan leather. He had arrived wearing yellow kid gloves and a broad-brimmed beaver hat. "Jedediah Smith's welcome contribution to my wardrobe," he joked, invoking the name of the famous fur trapper and mountain man.

The President prefaced dinner with a blessing. At the "Amen" the servants, clad in spotless white livery, went to work. There was one servant assigned to each diner. They carried the plates back and forth between the dining and the serving tables. The meal was a feast fit for a king, in Christopher's opinion, though the others seemed to expect nothing less. There was soup and beef bouillé, boned wild turkey, fish, roast beef, salad, canvasback duck, a variety of sweet breads and Virginia ham. The butler was continually pouring champagne, Madeira, or white sherry. Following after-dinner toasts, a servant appeared with the coffee. Mary Ann Lewis and Peggy Eaton retired to the ladies' sitting room, while the men remained at the dining room table, some smoking, to engage in a free-for-all conversation.

The discussion turned to the issue of whether the United States ought to expand its standing army—not surprisingly, since the President, Lewis, Eaton, and Donelson had all seen military service, albeit in a volunteer capacity. Jackson and Lewis shared the opinion that the army ought to be enlarged, but the others begged to differ. Jackson turned to Christopher for assistance, hoping to garner support for his position from one who until recently had been in training to become a professional soldier. But Christopher respectfully declined to get embroiled in the debate. For one thing, he did not feel qualified to address the issue, since he had been dishonorably discharged from the Corps of Cadets. For another, his thoughts were monopolized by Greta Inskilling. They had been ever since Van Buren had told him she was on her way to Washington.

"I don't think we need a large professional army,"

insisted Jack Donelson. "Tyrants and monarchs may need them, but they are unnecessary in a democracy."

"Of all the Greek nation-states, only the Spartans maintained a standing army," said Eaton. "Which doesn't mean the people of Athens couldn't fight when they were called upon to do so. The same applies to us. We are a nation of farmers who love and desire peace, but we aren't averse to taking up arms in our own defense. We've had to do so in the past, and managed quite well, thank you."

"But who did all the Greek city-states turn to when the Persians invaded their soil?" asked Van Buren, who until now had remained an amused spectator. "The Spartan Army and the Athenian Navy. Yes, John, don't forget the Athenian navy. Professionals all."

"I still say a standing army and a democracy are incompatible. A tyrant could use the army to subjugate his own people. It has happened before."

"But how could it possibly happen here?" asked Major Lewis. "Our system of government is not conducive to tyranny."

"You think not?" asked Donelson with a thin smile. "Some folks say 'King Andrew' here is a tyrant."

Jackson laughed. "They'll be saying worse than that if I have to use the army to knock some sense into damned nullifiers down in South Carolina."

"But are we really living in a democracy?" asked Eaton.

Jackson raised his bushy white brows and looked down the table at Van Buren. "I shall refer that question to our resident scholar. What about that, Martin? I must confess, I don't even know where the word came from."

"Democracy became part of the English language in the early sixteenth century, I believe," replied Van Buren. "It is borrowed from the union of two Greek roots, and refers to direct government by enfranchised citizens. In the seventeenth century it acquired a rather bad flavor in England. Those were the days of Cromwell and the Glorious Revolution, if you will recall, and the conservative element defined democracy then as government by the rabble, the worst conceivable form of government, in their opinion, bringing with it disorder and destruction of peace and property. For our ancestors, then, democracy was a fearful idea. You'll not find the word in the Declaration of Independence. Or the Constitution of the United States, for that matter. Thomas Jefferson made a point of never resorting to the word in any of his public papers.

"Common folk began after a time to call themselves democrats. They longed for a situation as was found in the Greek states, where all the citizens could vote. At the time, they could not, what with property qualifications and all of that. Only later did certain politicians adopt it. Even so, all of us here in this room are self-styled Democrat-Republicans. Of course, perhaps, I shouldn't speak for Mr. Groves."

"My God!" laughed Jackson. "You mean we might be dining with a damned republican?"

The others laughed with him. Christopher said, "I'm afraid I must admit I am not much interested in political matters."

"Smart young man," growled Jackson, and laughter again filled the room.

"We are not a democracy in the strictest sense of the word," said Major Lewis, "but rather a republic. There is a difference of no small significance."

"But you will not find that word in our Constitution, either," said Van Buren. "It, too, developed a bad odor over the centuries. Though it *has* become customary to refer to the United States as a republic. I think it's safe to say that the framers of the Constitution were all republicans in principle. But it's really a moot point. There is actually little difference between the two concepts, as we have adapted them for our own use."

"You mean our English cousins are right when they accuse us of treating the language cavalierly." Donelson smiled.

"Undoubtedly. We are certainly not a direct democracy. We are too many for that to ever work. But we are, it is safe to say, a democratic republic, which embraces certain clear elements. One, that the people are the source of all political power. Two, that through representatives chosen by the people, laws are made. Three, that all representatives must submit themselves and their actions to a review by the people. What we call elections."

"As I recall, Bonaporte was elected Emperor by the French people," said Donelson. "Who's to say such a thing couldn't happen in this country? What guarantee is there in our system of government against tyranny, against the election of a demagogue, or a gang of them, who believe they know what is best for the people, and who, in the process, end every right enjoyed by our citizens? And they could end it, believe me, gentlemen, with a large standing army."

"You are quite right," conceded the ever amiable Van Buren. "Democracy, or republicanism, does not guarantee the supremacy of constitutional government—that is to say, limited government by the people providing for the maintenance of basic rights."

"But what of the Bill of Rights?" asked Eaton.

"A crowd can be as tyrannical as a dictator," said Donelson.

"True," agreed Van Buren. "The majority can amend the Constitution, and by so doing deny the rest their rights."

"We have seen some of that at work in the Republic of Mexico," said Jackson. "They have their Constitution of 1824. But what good does it do them? Bustamente is as close to being a dictator as you're likely to find in this hemisphere—despite what the Republicans say about me."

"And in Mexico you have a perfect example of the dangers of a large professional army," said Van Buren. "There is a Mexican general down there whom my sources tell me bears watching. His name is Antonio Lopez de Santa Anna. I would not be surprised if he unseats Bustamente before too very long, and he'll have the help of the army when he does it. Then he will toss the Mexican Constitution out the window of the presidential palace, mark my words. He is a man with delusions of imperial grandeur, who thinks of himself as a kind of Latin Napoleon. He is convinced that Mexico can only be saved by a strong leader, which is what Bonaparte believed about France, was it not?"

Jackson was grim. "And he hates Americans. Then what chance will the Texas colonists have against the Mexican Army? It is far better trained and better equipped than our own."

"What chance did the world give our forefathers when they rebelled against King George?" asked Donelson.

"The outcome will hinge on leadership," said Jackson, looking straight at Christopher. "What chance would the Minutemen have had without leaders like George Washington and Daniel Morgan and Nathaniel Greene? How many battles did we lose in our most recent quarrel with the British because of poor leadership. Remember what happened in Detriot because of that incompetent General Hull?"

"Thank the Lord we had Old Hickory at Chalmette!" exclaimed Major Lewis.

"A toast to the General," said Eaton.

They all rose and lifted their cups and glasses.

Jackson pushed himself stiffly to his feet and raised his own glass. "To Texas, and the intrepid souls who will free her from the iron grasp of a tyrant."

Looking back, Christopher would remember that mo-

ment as the one during which he made his decision
about Texas.

Greta Inskilling was a beauty. To Christopher's mind
no woman could compare with her. She made Peggy
Eaton look ordinary. Full of grace, bubbling over with
the joy of life, Greta was always the focus of attention.
She was small, with an exquisite figure. Her dark curls
were piled high on top of her head. Sparkling eyes in a
heart-shaped face were as clear blue as the sky on a
sunlit spring day. Her complexion was flawless, magnolia
white, and her lips were full and red, sensuously sculptured, resembling the most perfect rose in bloom against
a field of pristine snow.

She wore a cream-colored organdy dress of the high-
waisted, low-cut Empire fashion, with delicate pink lace
rosebuds embroidered at the hem, and a pink satin sash
to accentuate her waspish waist, which was the envy of
every other woman present. All the men were captivated
by her, and that didn't endear her to the other belles,
either. She was seated in a chair by the wall, like a queen
upon her throne, attended by a dozen young beaux rendered helpless by her charm and grace and beauty, when
Christopher entered the East Room. He saw her immediately, but at first she did not see him, and he was
relieved, because he was within a hair's breadth of fleeing, and even now he considered slipping out of the
White House, to commandeer a fast horse and depart
Washington like a thief in the night.

That was a coward's way, of course, but he was afraid,
afraid to meet her face-to face, more afraid by far of
this than he had been to confront Adam Vickers at the
riding hall for their midnight duel with swords. He had
let her down by being dismissed from the Military Academy, because that had been her chief weapon in defending him against her father. Now he had next to
nothing to offer her. A struggling horse farm in Ken-

tucky? Life on the Texas frontier, fraught with peril and hardship? Not to mention the disgrace of his dismissal from the Corps of Cadets. And how was he to explain his departure from New York without even showing her the courtesy of calling upon her? The Hudson River Valley estate of Patroon Inskilling was less than a day's ride from West Point. Christopher decided he would rather fight a dozen duels than face Greta at this moment. But here he was. He could not flee. Pride prevented him. And besides, in a sense the President was watching.

The East Room was dazzling. Chandeliers blazed from the high, deeply coved ceiling, their light reflected by the French mirrors adorning the walls. At least two hundred people were present, yet the room did not appear to be overcrowded. On a dais artistically wrapped in starry bunting, a Negro orchestra in blue uniforms was gearing up for the first dance, tuning their instruments—fiddles, bull fiddles, accordions and banjos.

The glamour of the crowd made Christopher feel out of place. He was wearing his only suit of rather worn blue broadcloth. A number of the men were clad in dress uniforms—seeing them was like a knife twisting in his guts. The rest were attired in elegant suits, with boots and shoes polished to a high sheen. The women were decked out in bright lace and silk and braid, with gleaming jewels, swan's down fans, and peacock feathers dangling on velvet ribbons from dainty wrists, tea roses in little garlands in their hair, and more flowers in their sashes, many of which would end up treasured remembrances in the pockets of young men before the night was out.

Stewards passed through the crowd carrying silver service laden with glasses of champagne and sherry. And there was the President, tall and thin with that shock of white hair, clad in black, the color he always wore at public functions to let them all know he would mourn the passing of his beloved Rachel until they laid him to final rest beside her in the Hermitage garden. He passed through the crowd, stopping often to shake hands and say a few words, and he had Peggy Eaton on his arm. Christopher smiled at that. He had to admire the old general's style. Van Buren had told him there were quite a few locals who had consistently refused invitations to White House functions for no other reason than that Peggy was going to be present. And here was Jackson, forcing the saucy, coquettish wife of his friend down the throat of Washington society until it gagged.

"Grab your partners for the Virginia reel!"

This cry issued from someone in the vicinity of the dais. Suddenly the room was a kaleidoscope of color as the crowd moved closer to the walls, clearing the center of the room for those who wished to dance. Men rushed to choose their partners, bowing to the curtsy, the arms linked, the long rows being formed. Christopher looked for Greta, but he could not see her, as she was hemmed in by her suitors, all begging for the honor of the first dance. Sinking fast into a morass of melancholy, Christopher turned away from this awful spectacle and moved to a serving table where a steward handed him a glass of champagne.

The orchestra launched into the reel. Christopher didn't turn to watch. He didn't want to see Greta dancing with another man. He had not always been able to monopolize her at the West Point hops, and he'd been assailed by jealousy when she danced with other cadets. But this, this was worse, and he supposed it was because he knew he was leaving her, and soon she would find another, perhaps her future husband, perhaps even one among this particular brigade of eligible bachelors, and they would live happily ever after while he rode off into oblivion, an uncertain future on the frontier.

"Christopher?"

Heart lodged firmly in his throat, he turned to find her standing there with a smile on her lips, a sweet and somewhat querulous smile, and he had the sudden mad urge to kiss her, to taste those lips, to feel her warm breath on his face, as he had done before, in hidden places away from prying eyes. But he dared not compromise her in the presence of so many people. Besides, he wasn't sure how she felt about him now—if he had ever been sure.

"Greta," he said, and stood there, at a loss for words, and feeling like the complete fool.

"Aren't you going to get me a drink?"

"Of course. What would you like?"

"More of that punch, I think. It is absolutely divine."

Drink in hand, she said, "You were going to leave without seeing me, weren't you, you rascal?"

"Well, I . . ."

"No profit comes from making excuses," she said, but her scolding tone was gentled with a smile that made his heart contract. "You probably didn't even think about me. You probably never really cared." She pouted, looking very little-girlish.

"That's not true!" he exclaimed, horrified, and then realized she had lured him into a velvet-lined trap. "Greta, I've thought about you every waking moment. And then, when I manage to go to sleep, I see you in my dreams."

She was delighted. "See there? You can be charming when you put your mind to it. And you should know by now there is no escaping me. Oh, my poor Christopher. I know everything. I heard about your affair of honor with that perfectly horrid Adam Vickers. And that poor Emily Cooper! How tragic."

"I wish she had just stayed away from me," he said, and he could not conceal the bitterness he felt.

"She was in love," said Greta with gentle reproach. "A woman in love will risk all. Love is the most important thing in the world. Far more important than material things. And more important than honor."

"What are you trying to say?"

"Oh, you can be so dense sometimes, Christopher! Must I come straight out and say it? I love you. There. So I am not a proper lady. I don't care. I love you, I love you, I love you."

"Greta!" Christopher looked nervously about, afraid of being overheard.

"Are you ashamed of me? I don't care if the whole world hears."

"But you have your reputation to think about."

"Oh, phooey on my reputation. I love you and I am going to be with you, no matter where you go."

"You can't . . ."

"Then you don't love me. You don't want me to be with you . . ."

"That's not what I said."

"Then tell me. Tell me that you love me, and want to be with me always."

"But Greta . . ." Christopher was in sheer agony.

"Tell me."

"What about your father?"

"What about him? Surely you aren't afraid of him."

"No, not afraid . . ."

"Good. Neither am I."

"But you can't come with me. Where I'm going is no place for a young lady like you."

"You talk of Kentucky as though it were still uncivilized wilderness populated by red savages. I know better. I shall be perfectly content in Kentucky. Or don't you think I'm good enough to be your wife?"

"Good Lord, Greta, it's the other way around. You could do much better."

"I'll be the judge of that."

Christopher sighed. He looked around again, to make sure no one was listening. Then he leaned forward, and his voice was reduced to an urgent whisper.

"Greta, it isn't that I don't want to . . . to be with you.

But you just have to understand. I have nothing to offer. You won't be able to live in the . . . in the way you've become accustomed . . ."

She was fuming now. "Oh, you're simply impossible! I don't know why I am standing here trying to reason with you, especially when you insult me that way."

"Insult? Greta, I never . . ."

"Oh yes you have. You just did, you big lug. You're the one who doesn't understand. I don't care if we live in a one-room shanty with a dirt floor, as long as we're together. Now, I realize that as a man you want to be able to provide for me, but I am not *that* expensive to keep!"

Christopher was stunned. "Why, I . . . I didn't realize."

"No, of course you didn't. How could you?" Having given him a proper scolding, Greta turned suddenly and sweetly forgiving. "Besides, Elm Tree can't be all that primitive, from what you have told me about it. And I think your mother and I would get along famously, don't you?"

"I'm not going to be staying at Elm Tree for long, Greta."

"You're not?"

"I'm going to Texas."

"Texas?" Now she was stunned. "Texas?"

Christopher nodded.

"When did you make this decision?"

"Well, I'm not exactly certain. Today, I think."

"But why on earth would you want to go to Texas, of all places? Texas is . . . why, it's at the end of the world."

"There's room there, Greta. Room for a man to make something of himself, if he's got the guts to try. And in Texas it doesn't matter that much where you come from or what you've been. All that really matters is that you're willing to fight for what's rightfully yours."

"I see," she said, dubious.

He reached out and took her dainty hand, held it gently in his own big, rough paw. "Greta," he said, and swallowed hard, "Greta, I do love you. I . . . I want you to marry me. But we'll have to wait a little while. Promise me that you'll wait. Until I send for you. I'll go to Texas and make a place for us. Will you come to Texas, Greta? Will you come to me when I send for you?"

She gazed solemnly at him for a moment, and Christopher had to beat down the sudden panic rising up inside him. Tonight, for the first time, he was sure she truly loved him, that it hadn't been merely a flirtation for her, a passing fancy, and he was also sure, at the same time, that he loved her. She was willing to sacrifice everything to be with him—wasn't she? Or was Texas just too big a sacrifice for her to make? He waited, writhing with an inward agony, breathlessly waiting for her next word, the word upon which hinged his future happiness.

Then her eyes sparkled, and she stood on her tiptoes and her lips just barely brushed his, but the touch sent an electric charge through his body, and she put her other hand on his, so that his hand rested between hers, so soft and warm.

"Yes, Christopher," she breathed. "I'll wait. But I warn you, I shan't wait long."

His heart soaring, began to sink like a rock. She laughed at his crestfallen expression.

"No, I won't wait long. If you don't send for me soon, I shall be coming after you. I am not going to let you get away from me, Christopher Groves. Now come and dance. Dance with me all night long, so that I shall have something to remember you by while you are gone to Texas."

PART TWO

✛

The River

Chapter 10

Two years before, on his way to West Point, Christopher had stopped off in Boonesboro to visit his grandfather. The route he took from Elm Tree to Maysville, where he caught a boat going upriver, took him near the village. Now, two years later, his first impression was that Boonesboro had changed hardly at all. There were a few new cabins, but progress seemed largely to have passed Boonesboro by. Towns like Lexington and Frankfort were booming—they were calling Lexington the Athens of the West these days—but the same could not be said for Boonesboro. The old stockade was still standing, and for Christopher it was like stepping back in time fifty years. He could almost hear the crackle of musketry and the war cries of attacking Indians. But the Indian threat was gone now. Had been ever since the death of Tecumseh at the Battle of the Thames sixteen years ago.

Thinking about Tecumseh made Christopher eager to see his grandfather again, and he turned his horse down the road south out of Boonesboro, heading for the old cabin on the bluegrass hill where he hoped to find Nathaniel Jones. Nathaniel had been there in the thick of the fight to see Tecumseh fall, mortally wounded. As a boy, Christopher had delighted in hearing the story, over and over again. Whenever he got the chance he would pester Nathaniel to sit him on his knee and tell the tale. And, if not the story of Tecumseh's death, then one of the many exciting stories his grandfather could tell.

There was the one about his midnight ride to warn
Thomas Jefferson at Monticello about the approach of
Butcher Tarleton's Tory Legion, back in the days of the
War for Independence. Nathaniel Jones had been just a
lad then, all of sixteen years old. Christopher had particularly liked the part where a flooding creek carried away
a bridge just as Nathaniel crossed it on his hard-running
horse, Jumper, with the dragoons hot on his heels.

Then, too, there was the story of how Nathaniel had
saved his true friend, Quashquame, the Delaware, from
being burned alive at the stake. That was back in the
days of Tecumseh. The great Shawnee leader had stirred
the other tribes against the white men, even the Delawares, who had condemned Quashquame to death for
being a friend of the Long Knives. Nathaniel had arrived
at the Delaware village in the nick of time, driving the
Indians' horse herd through the teepees to scatter the
Delawares, giving himself the time to free Quashquame
from the stake. Fleeing the village with his Delaware
friend, Nathaniel had been grievously wounded, and
later captured. He was given to Tecumseh, who gave
him, in turn, to the British. Nathaniel was thrown into
the guardhouse at the redcoat outpost of Fort Malden,
but he had not lanquished long in captivity, effecting a
miraculous escape when a great earthquake caused the
guardhouse quite literally to fall down around his ears.

Nathaniel Jones—he was better known in the Trans-
Allegheny region as Flintlock—was a living legend.
Boone was gone now. Kenton, too, and Lew Wetzel.
Nathaniel was the last of his breed, mused Christopher
as he rode down the country lane on the roan horse he'd
brought at Maysville, where he had disembarked the
flatboat which had brought him down the Ohio River.
His belongings were in a durable canvas war bag lashed
behind the saddle—he'd sold his trunk to make up the
difference between the price of the roan and the money
in his pocket.

No, there weren't many men like Nathaniel Jones left these days. Of course he always made light of his exploits when he told his stories to Christopher—to hear him tell it he was just very lucky—but Christopher knew better. He was a bonafide hero, and nobody was going to convince Christopher otherwise. Yes, there were characters like Davy Crockett, whom some said was a frontiersman without peer, but Christopher was firmly of the opinion that Crockett couldn't hold a candle to Nathaniel Jones. Crockett was a great one for spinning yarns that made him come across as the greatest Indian fighter and bear killer the frontier had ever seen, but he hadn't done half the things he claimed to have done.

Nathaniel and his peers—Boone, Kenton, and that bunch of border captains—had tamed this country when it was wilderness. They had been the pathfinders, responsible for bringing civilization to "The Dark and Bloody Ground." Of course, that had not been their goal. They had come over the mountains to escape civilization, only to discover it was inescapable. Boone had moved further west long ago, across the Mississippi into Missouri, still trying to escape. And Christopher knew that his grandfather longed for the good old days when the woodlands were not filled with the ringing of axes, and one could find some place in the forest where you could not smell the smoke from a settler's chimney. Those days were long gone in Kentucky. The land was filling up.

Now that Amanda was dead, Nathaniel spent most of his time wandering the forests, going far afield in search of the solitude he longed for. As Christopher took a familiar path branching off the road and winding through a stand of trees, breaking through to the other side to gaze up the long slope of bluegrass to the cabin in the summer sunlight on the crest of a high hill, his heart sank, for he could sense that the place was empty.

The cabin was no derelict, by any means. It had been

built to last. But it had the appearance of neglect. Amanda's feminine touch had made of it a warm and comfortable home, and was obviously sorely missed. The cabin was really a home no longer. Rather, a place where, perhaps one night out of three, Nathaniel came to lay his head and tend to Amanda's grave, and Quashquame's, too. Their spirits lingered here—that was the only reason Nathaniel came back at all, and even then the memories were too strong, and the grief still too severe, for him to long endure.

The horses were gone. Nathaniel had been a hunter and explorer by nature, and ill-suited for farming. To make enough money to buy staples and a few modest luxuries to make Amanda's life a little easier he had raised horses, thoroughbreds of the bloodline traced back to Jumper, the great horse Nathaniel had ridden that storm-swept Virginia night fifty years ago to warn Thomas Jefferson. All the Elm Tree horses were of the same line, for Nathaniel and Amanda had given Christopher's parents Jumper's grandson, Gallivant, as a wedding present. Nowadays, the Elm Tree stock were much prized on the race courses so abundant in Kentucky and Tennessee. But all of Nathaniel's horses were gone. Christopher had a vivid childhood memory of admiring the sight of them grazing on this long bluegrass hill.

Riding up to the cabin, Christopher called out, but to no avail, as he had suspected. Keenly disappointed, he dismounted to loosen the roan's cinch and let it breathe. Leaning against the horse, an arm draped over the sweat-stained saddle, he gave the place a long and wistful look, wondering how long Nathaniel would be gone. He had so wanted to talk to his grandfather about Texas. Should he wait? It might be days, even weeks, before Nathaniel reappeared.

Leaving the roan to crop eagerly at the lush grass in front of the cabin, Christopher quartered the slope to the wooden slopes marking the graves of Amanda Jones and the Delaware warrior named Quashquame, yonder in the shade of a century-old hickory. Christopher had not known Quashquame very well—he'd been only eight years old when the Delaware lost his life at the Battle of the Thames, fighting at Nathaniel's side. But he had clear, fond recollections of his grandmother, who had passed away a scant two years ago. A strong yet tender woman, Amanda had been full of love and compassion. Even in her later years she had remained as slender as a willow, and as pretty as she had been when she and Nathaniel married, even though her flaxen hair had turned silver with the passing years. Always ready with a kind or encouraging word, practical, generous, and brave, Amanda's greatest pleasure had been doing for others. Christopher did not wonder that Nathaniel had loved her with unerring devotion. She had passed away quietly, in her sleep, and Nathaniel had been devastated.

"It seems like only yesterday . . ."

Christopher whirled.

Nathaniel Jones stood there, leaning on his long rifle. He had come up behind Christopher so silently that for a disconcerted instant Christopher wondered if this was an apparition before him.

". . . and yet," continued Flintlock, "the days and nights are like one eternity after another for me, now that she is gone."

"Grandpa."

Christopher went to him, embraced him.

"This is a pleasant surprise," said Nathaniel, working hard to keep strong emotion out of his voice and expression. "You are looking well."

"As are you."

Though nearly sixty-five years of age, Nathaniel Jones was still as fit as a fiddle. Tall and straight, his skin was the color and texture of old leather, his hair completely gray now, brushed straight back and long to the shoulders of his ash gray deerskin hunting shirt. Most bordermen did not live so long. Theirs was an arduous life. But Nathaniel's eyes were still bright and clear and keen. His aim was still truer than most. As a boy Christopher had thought of him as indestructible—and he realized now that he still did.

Nathaniel glanced at Amanda's grave—the final resting place of his wife of thirty-five years, and the only woman he had ever loved—and the lines about his mouth and eyes were etched more deeply than usual with a grief still keen after two years, a grief that caused him pain as sharp as a knife between the ribs.

"I'm glad you've come, Christopher," he said. "I hope you can stay a spell."

"Well, I was on my way home."

"On, I see . . ."

"But I can stay for a day or two," said Christopher, amending his plans on the spot, because he could tell that Nathaniel was deeply disappointed.

"Good! Good! It gets right lonely here sometimes, I must confess."

The admission made Christopher uncomfortable. He had never seen his grandfather like this. Vulnerable. Flintlock Jones was the kind of man you just naturally assumed was impervious to everything.

"Then why do you stay here, Grandpa?"

"Why?" Nathaniel looked querulous, as though he was surprised by the question—one whose answer was so obvious, at least to him. "Because of Amanda, of course. I made her a promise when we first came to Kentucky. By God, we were scarcely more than children then. But a promise is a promise."

"What was it?"

"That I would never leave her alone." Nathaniel's smile was rueful. "I had a difficult time keeping that promise, Christopher. Many's the time I did leave. Usually to fight Indians. Left her alone to wonder, time and time again, whether I would come back alive. I can't leave her now."

Christopher didn't know what to say.

Nathaniel put a hand on his shoulder. "Come on. I've got some venison steaks. And a little corn liquor, I think." Another rueful smile. "I'm afraid I've developed a taste for it."

"You? I can't believe that. Since when?" Christopher had never known his grandfather to touch strong spirits.

Nathaniel's eyes flicked to the grave. "Recently. Helps me sleep sometimes. And it soothes the aches and pains. I swear, boy, some mornings when I get up I can hardly move. Growing old—it hits you all at once. Creeps up on you like a Shawnee Indian. But don't fret too much about the corn liquor. It doesn't have a hold on me. And, so far as I can tell, it hasn't affected my aim. Believe me, I don't plan to end up a drunkard like Simon Girty."

Christopher nodded. Simon Girty had once been the most hated man in Kentucky. He had turned against his own kind to fight with the Indians against the encroachment of the *Shemanese*. Leading Shawnees and Mingos in numerous raids, he participated in several massacres. Kentucky mothers scared their children into staying close to home by telling bloodcurdling tales of Girty waiting in the woods to snatch unsuspecting youngsters, and the terrible fate that befell his victims. Many were the Kentucky bordermen who would have died happy if given a single opportunity to lift Simon Girty's scalp.

Though Girty managed to keep his topknot, he came to a bad end nonetheless. The Indians used him, but never accepted him completely. Spurned by the redman and despised by the white, Girty settled down in Amherstburg and began drinking heavily. Nathaniel had crossed the renegade's path during his celebrated escape from the British at Fort Malden. By that time Girty had become a hopeless alcoholic, both body and mind fading fast. He died soon after, alone and friendless, buried in an unmarked grave, his name etched in the annals of American infamy, right alongside the likes of Benedict Arnold and Aaron Burr.

They repaired to the cabin. The curtains were gone from the windows. The floor wanted sweeping. The whole place was cluttered and unclean. Two years at West Point, where he was forced to keep his quarters immaculate, had made Christopher a meticulous man, and he was shocked by the unkempt appearance of the cabin, which had once been impeccable, thanks to Amanda's loving care.

Nathaniel invited him to sit at the table. Christopher watched his grandfather rummage for a demijohn. He declined a swig, and waited while Nathaniel indulged in a good stout drink. Nathaniel gasped as the liquor exploded like liquid fire in his belly. Then, reading the expression of disapproval and dismay on Christopher's face, the old frontiersmann put the jug on the table and pushed it away as though it meant absolutely nothing to him.

"So what brings you home, Christopher? On furlough?"

"I was thrown out of the Academy." Christopher had spent much of his journey west wracking his brains to find a good way to break the news to his mother and grandfather. In the end, he decided that saying it straight out, the cold and unvarnished truth, without any shilly or shally, was his only real option. Napoleon had stated in his *Maxims* that the only true wisdom in a soldier was determined courage.

Nathaniel's features became stoic, a sun-bronzed mask. That was his way, in moments of high emotion.

"Tell me about it."

"I fought a duel."

"With who?"

"Adam Vickers."

"Vickers." Brows knit, Nathaniel tugged on his chin. "I seem to recollect . . . no, wait. Vickers. There's a family down Mississippi way by that name. There's a Dan Vickers—his daughter married Stephen Cooper."

Christopher nodded. "Dan Vickers is the one I'm thinking of. Adam Vickers is his nephew. Emily Cooper's cousin."

"Did you kill him?"

"No. But it didn't matter. I was dishonorably discharged from the Corps of Cadets."

"I assume he was the one to issue the challenge."

"Yes."

"Why did he?"

"He said it was to defend his family's honor," said Christopher dryly. "You see, Emily Cooper came to the Academy to see me. She brought me my father's cutlass. Wanted to make sure I understood that she had loved him. She also wanted to know if I hated her. I assured her that I did not. That night she took poison. Adam Vickers hated me from the day we met. His cousin's death was the excuse he was looking for."

"He *must* have hated you, to risk his life, or, at the very least, to throw away his career like that." Nathaniel glanced longingly at the jug of corn liquor, but he did not reach for it.

"Aren't you going to ask me why I accepted the challenge, and threw away my own career?"

"I reckon you felt like you had to."

"Yes. That's it exactly."

Nathaniel shook his head. "Funny, how life runs in circles. Your father fought a duel because he felt he had to, and his world was turned upside down as a result. Now the same thing has happened to you." Nathaniel paused, moodily contemplating his rough, scarred hands resting on the table. "Reckon it happened to me, too, come to think of it. When Amanda and I crossed the mountains we happened on a cabin where an old woman lived. She was crazy. She'd buried her husband under a nearby tree, and sometimes she thought she heard him calling to her from the grave, late in the night when the wind was high. Amanda was always afraid she would end up like that woman, alone out here in this cabin. Turned out to be me alone, and her buried beneath a nearby tree."

"I'm truly sorry, Grandpa. I know she meant the world to you."

"That she did." Nathaniel managed a brave smile. "Never thought I'd outlast her." He shook his head and changed the subject. "So what do you aim to do now?"

"That's what I wanted to talk to you about. I'm thinking about going to Texas."

"Texas? How'd that notion get into your head?"

"The President put it there, I guess."

"Andrew Jackson?"

Christopher nodded. "He summoned me to the White House. Told me Texas needed young men who have a hankering for adventure. Said there's going to be a fight down there pretty soon."

"That's what I hear. Some folks from around these parts have pulled up stakes and gone to Texas themselves. Land for the asking there. Lots of it. Plenty of room for everybody. Only problem is, the Mexicans are trying to shut the door so far as colonization is concerned. Of course, that hasn't come close to stopping folks from trying to get in. They say Texas is a land of milk and honey."

"Do you think there will be a fight?"

"Wouldn't surprise me. Americans are used to making their own laws as it suits them. They won't long abide by somebody else's if it doesn't suit them. If Old Hickory says there'll be a fight for Texas, I reckon it'll happen, right enough. He's usually on the mark when it comes to such matters."

"You think I should go?"

"You're old enough to make your own decisions, Christopher," was the frontiersman's solemn reply. "But I don't reckon your ma will be too happy about your going."

"No, she probably won't be," agreed Christopher, downcast. "And if she doesn't want me to go, I won't. Then I'll just stay at Elm Tree and help her run the place."

"Well, you never know about such things. Rebecca has some adventure in her soul, too."

"Maybe she'd go with me!" exclaimed Christopher. "Do you think she would, Grandpa?"

Nathaniel shrugged. "Hard to say. I stopped trying to figure out what that gal would do when she was about two years old."

Christopher leaned forward eagerly. "If she did go, would you go, too?"

Nathaniel leaned back, as though putting distance between himself and his grandson's idea. "I don't reckon," he said grimly.

"Why not? You've often said Kentucky is getting too full of folks. No elbow room anymore. And you said it yourself—Texas is a big country, with plenty of room for everybody."

Nathaniel shook his head emphatically. "I'm too old to be making a new start. And, well, I just can't leave. I promised Amanda . . ."

"I see." Christopher settled back, disappointed.

"But I will ride with you as far as Elm Tree. I haven't seen Becky in quite a while. I'll even put in a good word for you about Texas."

"You will?"

"Sure. You're a young man chock full of big dreams, and you need to carve your own niche in this world. I remember how I felt as a youngster. My pa wanted me to stay in Virginia and help him with the inn. Inherit the place from him. He'd built the place from the ground up for me. But something kept calling me over the mountains. I just had to answer that call."

Christopher nodded. "I don't know what my future holds, but I'm certain it isn't Elm Tree."

"We'll leave at daybreak," said Nathaniel.

Chapter 11

"Riders comin', Miss 'Becca."

Rebecca Groves rose from inspecting the forelegs of the tall bay thoroughbred to look at the old black man coming down the carriageway between the rows of stalls.

"Who are they, Isaac?"

The bay whickered softly at the sound of her voice, and nudged her with its velvet-soft muzzle, as though trying to recapture her attention.

"I doan rightly know, Miss 'Becca. I cain't recall ever seein' them twos befo'."

"All right." She stepped out of the stall, swung the door shut to prevent the bay from following her, which it had every intention of doing. Isaac rolled his eyes at the horse. It never ceased to amaze him, the way all the Elm Tree horses acted around Rebecca Groves. They were thoroughbreds, high-spirited and unpredictable, but they followed Rebecca like puppy dogs. They adored her, and were usually completely docile in her hands. And there were some, Isaac knew, that would kill a man if he got careless with them and they were having a bad day. Yes, Rebecca Groves had a special way with horses, reflected Isaac, who was scared to death of these big, powerful animals. He was a house servant. Always had been. Didn't know the first thing about horses and such, and he had no desire to find out. He stayed as far away from the beasts as he could.

Rebecca emerged from the stables into the hot bright

summer sunlight, and shaded her eyes with a hand to gaze across the bluegrass pasture at the lane flanked by stately oaks. Those trees, she remembered with a twinge of melancholy, had been planted as seedlings twenty-five years ago by her husband. She tried to force thoughts of Jonathan out of her mind. They were too painful still, even after all these years.

The two horsemen were approaching the house now. At this distance—a hundred yards—Rebecca could not tell much about them. Both of them were clad in long dusters, with wide-brimmed hats pulled low over their faces. Both of them carried rifles. Whoever they were, she got the distinct impression that they had not come to pay a social call. No this pair was here on business.

"They might be bounty men," she murmured.

"Yessum," agreed Isaac, apprehensive. "They sho' do look mean enough."

Rebecca sighed. Yes, that was probably the case. Those two men could very well be hunting runaway slaves. If so, their coming to Elm Tree was not surprising. She was an avowed emancipationist, and there were rumors afloat that she helped fugitive slaves escape their rightful owners. She had in fact helped only one such fugitive, the pregnant slave girl, Cilla, who had fled the wrath of Stephen Cooper twenty years ago. Trumbull, the Elm Tree overseer, had taken Cilla to New Orleans. Rebecca hadn't heard from either one since receiving a letter from Trumbull which had informed her of their safe arrival at their destination. The letter had also mentioned that Cilla had given birth to a baby girl. Stephen Cooper's child.

"Come on, Isaac," she said grimly, and started for the house. "We'd best find out what they want."

"Yessum," said Isaac. Like the thoroughbreds, he was devoted to Rebecca. He had lived and worked on Elm Tree for thirty some years now. Rebecca had freed him—and all the other Elm Tree slaves—twenty years ago. That was a decision which had caused her a great deal of grief ever since. This was tobacco and hemp county, with a lot of big plantations hereabouts, and the slaveowners of Madison County were not pleased to have an emancipationist in their midst.

Jacob followed her, but without much enthusiasm. He smelled trouble, and he was too old for it. In his younger days he would have been more aggressive. Would have used an axe handle or some other handy blunt instrument on any man, white or black, who so much as looked at Rebecca the wrong way. Oh, he would still defend Rebecca's life and honor to the death, but he no longer labored under the delusion of invincibility which had blinded him to danger as a youth.

By the time they reached the house the two men were dismounted and standing in the shade of the wraparound porch. Prissy was holding them off at the door, proclaiming in her loud shrill voice that they would violate the house with their unwashed and unwanted presence only over her dead body. She was a big woman, a substantial obstacle, her bulk filling the doorway, and she stood there with hands planted on her hips and her chin jutting out belligerently, and her eyes flashing defiance. Prissy was the undisputed boss of the house. She ruled with an iron hand, and kept all the other servants in line with a harsh word and, when harsh words were not sufficient, a rolling pin or iron skillet. Isaac was more terrified of her than he was of the thoroughbreds.

The two men were not terrified. In fact, being spoken to in such a manner by a black woman was almost more than one of them could bear.

"You better watch your tongue," he growled, "or you'll rue the day you were born, you black wench."

"Who's you callin' a wench?" shrilled Prissy. Her round cheeks got rounder, and she exhaled a gust of air through pursed lips. This was the danger sign. "Why, I oughts to punch you right in the eye."

"What's going on here?" asked Rebecca.

The two men turned to face her as she came up the steps onto the porch, and in that instant Rebecca knew they weren't bounty hunters. These two wore good broadcloth beneath their dusters. Their feet were encased in hand-tooled boots. They looked travel-worn, with gaunt cheeks darkened by beard stubble, but they weren't what Prissy would call poor white trash. Most bounty men were illiterate, rough backwoods scum. These men were born into a higher class.

"Are you Rebecca Groves?" asked one of the men.

"I am. And who might you be?"

"We're looking for your son."

"Christopher?" There was something in the way the man spoke that alarmed her. Whatever they had come for, they had not come as friends. "What do you want him for?"

"Where is he?"

"Who are you?"

"I asked you a question, lady."

"Either tell me who you are or get off my property."

They exchanged glances. Then one, the younger of the pair, said, "My name is Joshua Vickers. This is my brother, Morgan."

"Vickers? From Tennessee?"

"We have some relatives in Tennessee, yes, ma'am. But we're from Mississippi."

"What do you want with my son?"

"We intend to kill him," said Morgan, coldly, "because of what he did to our brother, Adam."

Rebecca's blood ran cold in her veins. Looking into Morgan Vickers' slate gray eyes, she did not doubt for a moment that he meant precisely what he said. She knew who these two men were now. Relatives of Emily Cooper, Stephen's widow, and the woman with whom her own husband had engaged in an illicit, ten-year affair. But that was all she knew.

"I'm afraid I don't have the slighest idea what you are talking about," she said. Though she was scared— not for herself, but for her son—she appeared remarkably calm.

Joshua glanced at his brother. "I don't think she knows. He must not be here."

"Where else would he go?" snapped Morgan, squinting distrustfully at Rebecca.

"Are you calling me a liar?" asked Rebecca frostily. "And I suppose you fancy yourself a gentleman, don't you?"

"No telling what a mother would do to protect her own son," muttered Morgan.

"I don't need to protect my son. Christopher is quite capable to taking care of himself."

"She's telling the truth," decided Joshua. "She doesn't know why we're here. If she'd seen her son, she'd know."

"You don't think she knows? Then I'll tell her." Morgan turned his hostile glare back on Rebecca. "Adam and your son fought a duel at West Point."

"Christopher? A duel? That's not possible . . ."

"They fought a duel!" rasped Morgan, with such vehemence that Rebecca shrank away from him. She was a very sound judge of people, and she had Morgan pegged as the more volatile and dangerous of the two brothers. He had a hair-trigger temper and a cruel streak. Joshua was the thinker; he was calmer, more rational, more firmly in control of his emotions. That didn't mean he was any less intent than his older brother on tracking Christopher down and killing him.

"Then your brother should have had better sense then to challenge my son," she replied coldly.

Morgan grunted. "Adam is still alive. But he's lost the use of an arm. Our purpose for coming all this long way should be abundantly clear to you now. Our family's honor is at stake."

Lost the use of an arm. The words reverberated in Rebecca's brain. How strange, the games fate played. Jonathan had lost the use of one of his arms in that celebrated duel with Stephen Cooper, on the steps of the big house at Hunter's Creek, just down the road a piece from Elm Tree. Cooper had emerged from the house with a brace of pistols, blazing away. One of his bullets had shattered the bone in Jonathan's arm. Jonathan had shot him dead an instant later. Rebecca's father, Nathaniel Jones, had slain the Hunter's Creek overseer, a man named Lewis, who tried to bushwhack them with a shotgun from an upstairs window.

Now Adam Vickers had lost the use of an arm in a duel with Christopher. Had Christopher been hurt? That was the question foremost in Rebecca's mind. Maybe these two had gotten the story wrong. Maybe Christopher had lost the duel—*maybe he was dead.* Why hadn't she heard something? She savagely beat down the panic rising within her.

"So, it's a vendetta," she said. "I wasn't aware that gentlemen engaged in such barbaric pastimes."

"There's only so much of that kind of talk I'll take from you," warned Morgan. "Even if you are a *lady.*"

Rebecca made a disdainful gesture in the direction of the front door. "Go ahead. Search the house, if you don't believe me. Prissy, let the *gentlemen* pass."

Mumbling, Prissy complied.

"Check the stables, Joshua," said Morgan. "I'll take the house."

Joshua shook his head. His intuition was better than his brother's. "We're wasting our time, Morgan. He isn't here."

"Check the stables, I said."

Joshua shrugged and left the porch. Morgan went into the house. Prissy started to follow him, but Rebecca stopped her.

"I wants to make sho' he doan steal nuttin'," explained Prissy.

"Just stay away from him."

"Hmph!" Prissy folded her arms over her prodigious chest and stood there near the door, fuming and pouting. Rebecca moved to the edge of the porch and pretended to watch Joshua crossing to the stables. But she wasn't paying attention. Her mind was racing. What would the Vickers brothers do when they failed to find Christopher on the premises? Wait for him to come home? If he had dueled at the Military Academy then he must have been discharged from the Corps of Cadets. If he was on his way home, and the Vickers brothers waited for him here, then somehow she had to warn him before he arrived.

On the other hand, these two might vent their rage on her, or on her help, or on Elm Tree. Morgan certainly seemed to be capable of such an act. She didn't care at all about her own safety, but if they meant to do harm to her home or her horses or Prissy or Isaac or the other servants they would have to go through her to get the job done.

"What's we gwine do?" whispered Isaac, standing close behind her.

"I don't know, Isaac," she admitted. "But don't worry. We'll think of something."

"If you wuz any kind of man at all, Isaac, you'd throw dem two offen this property, dat's what you'd do," said Prissy, who liked nothing better than to chide and chastise the old man.

"Hush, Prissy," said Rebecca sternly.

"Hmph!"

Morgan Vickers emerged from the house, scowling. Rebecca gave him an I-told-you-so look. He glowered back at her, and moved to the corner of the porch where he could watch the stables. His brother appeared a moment later and began walking back toward the house. Morgan cursed under his breath.

"So you see, Mr. Vickers," said Rebecca, "you've come all this way for nothing. Christopher isn't here, and if he has been dismissed from the Military Academy for dueling I very much doubt that he would dare show his face here. He would not care to have to explain his disgraceful behavior to me."

Skeptical, Morgan grunted again. "Oh, you're a clever specimen," he said. "But I don't believe you. He's coming home. And when he gets here, we'll be waiting for him." He turned his dark and hostile gaze upon Isaac. "Old man, you take care of our horses."

"Oh, nossuh. Please, Ah doan like horses . . ."

"Do what I say," snapped Morgan, raising his rifle as though to strike Isaac.

"I'll tend to your horses," said Rebecca.

"No. He will. You might just get it into your head to jump into the saddle and ride off to try and find your son and warn him. Well, I'm warning you. Anybody tries to leave this place, I'll kill him. Or her. And then I'll burn Elm Tree to the ground. Do you understand?"

"Isaac, tend to the horses."

"Miss 'Becca, Ah . . ."

"Do it."

"Yassum," sighed Jacob, and shuffled off the porch like a man resigned to meeting his end.

Morgan put his hand on his chest, smiling coldly. "I and my brother have traveled a long road. We're hungry. You, Mrs. Groves, and your smart-mouthed nigger, will prepare a meal for us."

Prissy shrilled, "Who you callin' a smart-mouthed nigger, you . . ."

"Prissy!" barked Rebecca. "Let's do what he says. We don't need to be poor hosts just because we have poor guests."

Mumbling something about poor white trash, Prissy preceded Rebecca and Morgan Vickers into the house.

*　　*　　*

Watching them eat, Rebecca had to give the Vickers boys some credit. Though they consumed the food put before them like they hadn't enjoyed a decent meal in a month of Sundays, at least they demonstrated some good manners. They used their napkins and utensils like men of good breeding. Each had several helpings of smoked ham, beans, collard greens, corn bread, and coffee. Rebecca sat at the other end of the long dining room table from them, trying to develop a plan of action.

Prissy carried the food in from the kitchen. Isaac helped her. The other four blacks who worked at Elm Tree stood with their backs to the wall—three men and a woman. Rebecca had summoned them, on Morgan's orders. They hadn't been told anything about what was going on, but they could sense that something was amiss. Both the Vickers brothers kept their rifles close at hand, leaning against the table, and Morgan had placed a pistol beside his plate. While he ate, Morgan kept a wary eye on the servants, as though he expected one of the men to make a hostile move, or try to escape. There was not the slightest doubt in Rebecca's mind that he would shoot to kill, without hesitation or remorse.

"You set a fine table, ma'am," complimented Joshua as he pushed his plate away.

"Thank you," said Rebecca, barely civil. "Now that you've eaten your fill, I think you should be on your way."

Morgan's laugh had an ugly ring to it. "On our way where?"

"Home."

"We'll go home—when your son is dead and buried. And not before. We gave our solemn word."

"To who? Your father? I can't believe a father would send his sons on such a fool's errand."

"He didn't send us," said Joshua. "He doesn't know."

"Shut up," growled Morgan. "He'll be right proud of us when he finds out what we've done."

"I doubt it," said Rebecca. "I think you should go, now. You see, you're just not very bright. I'm afraid the two of you are the ones who will be killed."

Morgan scowled. "I'm bright enough to pull a trigger."

"No. For instance, that food could have been poisoned. Did you ever think of that?"

The expressions on their faces told her that they had not. Joshua blanched, looking from his plate to Rebecca and then to Prissy.

Smirking, Prissy said, "Lordy, Ah wish Ah'd thought of that."

"Fetch some more coffee," snapped Morgan.

Prissy departed for the kitchen. Morgan turned to his brother. "I think we should lock them all up in the smokehouse. Then we'll take turns standing guard."

"Even Mrs. Groves?"

"Why not? She won't mind. She loves niggers. Don't you, ma'am? Set them all free. Pays them a wage for their work."

"I would much prefer being locked in the smokehouse with them to staying in this house with the likes of you," she declared.

Prissy returned with the coffeepot, holding it with both hands and using her apron to keep from burning herself on the handle. She filled Morgan's cup, then Joshua's, and came to Rebecca just as Isaac appeared to place another cup on the table.

"I don't care for any, Prissy."

"It's mighty good coffee, Miss 'Becca."

"No thank you."

"Now, you come on and try a little of dis coffee."

"No, Prissy."

"Miss 'Becca, you gots to try some of dis . . ."

Isaac had taken the empty plates from in front of the brothers. As he turned away from the table, one of the plates slipped from his gnarled fingers and shattered on the floor. Rebecca's nerves were on edge; she nearly jumped out of her skin. Morgan stood up so suddenly that he overturned his chair. He snatched his pistol up from the table. Seeing that both Vickers boys were looking in Isaac's direction, Prissy let the horse pistol she had kept concealed beneath the apron drop into Rebecca's lap. Rebecca was so startled that she nearly let the pistol fall to the floor. She caught it between her knees. Prissy beamed at her and moved away, to descend on Isaac like an avenging angel.

"You clumsy fool. I shoulda knowed better than to let you handle the china. Now jis' look at what you's done. Go get the broom and clean up dis here mess. Land's sakes!"

Completely cowed, Isaac ducked out of the room, Morgan righted his chair, belted his pistol, and sat down, disgusted, glowering at them all, as though daring anyone to indicate by the slighest change of expression that they were amused by his show of nerves.

The horse pistol lay heavy in Rebecca's lap. It had belonged to Jonathan, but she'd kept it anyway, in a wardrobe in her bedroom. She had never had occasion to use it, and she was reluctant to do so now. But maybe Prissy had the right idea. Maybe this was the only way to save Christopher's life. Prissy was watching her— Rebecca could feel her eyes, but she kept her own gaze fixed on Morgan Vickers at the other end of the table. She could shoot one of them, and with any luck the three hands standing over against that wall would see their chance and jump the other. One word from Prissy and they would jump.

"Where did that old man go?" asked Morgan.

Rebecca glanced at Prissy, and Prissy's eyes were pleading with her to act.

What was Prissy up to?

The sound of a horse cantering past the house . . .

Suddenly Rebecca understood. Prissy and Isaac had

devised a scheme of their own. At some point, when she was supposed to be in the kitchen, Prissy had slipped up to Rebecca's bedroom to get the pistol. Isaac had dropped the plate as a diversion, to give Prissy the opportunity to hand Rebecca the weapon. And now that courageous old man, in spite of his fear of horses, was riding for help. And Prissy—Prissy expected her to use that pistol. Now.

Both the Vickers boys were on their feet at the sound of the horse. Rebecca was up, too, the horse pistol held in both hands. She aimed it at Morgan.

"That black bastard!" said Morgan, snatching up his rifle, not looking at Rebecca, unaware that she was armed. "I'll kill him!"

"You'll do nothing of the sort," she said, quite calmly.

Chapter 12

Morgan Vickers saw the pistol then—and froze. But Joshua kept his wits about him. Joshua—the calm and rational one, thinking on his feet, quick to act, so quick that before Rebecca knew what was happening he had grabbed Prissy. Prissy was the nearest. He locked an arm around her throat and put his own pistol to her head.

"Please drop it, ma'am," he said in the same tone of voice he would have used to ask her to pass the bread.

How ludicrous, thought Rebecca, for him to be so well-mannered at a moment like this. Please and ma'am! The whole scene struck her as so unreal that she wondered if she was dreaming.

"Doan you do it, Miss 'Becca," said Prissy. "You go ahead and shoot, and doan you fret none about me."

"Don't make me shoot her," said Joshua.

Rebecca threw the pistol onto the table.

With a growl Morgan bolted from the room. Joshua shoved Prissy away, grabbed the horse pistol from the table, and collected his own rifle, before following his brother.

Rebecca couldn't move. She was frozen in place by the horror of what she had done. Prissy was standing across the room, raising her arms to the ceiling, her face upturned, and she was beseeching the Lord Almighty in a hoarse whisper, asking God to deliver Isaac, and Rebecca knew only a miracle could save the old man now.

God helped those who helped themselves, anyway—
Rebecca was overwhelmed with guilt.

"What we gwine do, Miss 'Becca?" asked one of the
hands.

"Run," she said dully. "They'll kill us all. Run. Out
the back way. Run and don't ever come back. There
won't be anything to come back to."

"But Miss 'Becca . . ."

"Go! Now!"

They ran—all except Prissy, who watched Rebecca
sink heavily into a chair.

"Go on, Prissy."

"Ah ain't gwine, lessen you come, too."

"I'm staying here. This is my home."

"Mine, too. So Ah's stayin' with you."

A rifle spoke. The sound lanced through Rebecca's
heart like a knife, causing her such pain that she twisted
in the chair, as thought she could feel the bullet tearing
through her body, just as it was tearing through poor
Isaac's.

"I'm sorry," she sobbed, knowing Isaac was dead,
knowing it as surely as she knew she was to blame for
his death. For if she had done what had been expected
of her . . . "I'm sorry."

The Vickers boys returned. Morgan looked downright
smug. The smell of gunpowder and death clung to him.
When he saw Rebecca he remembered what she had
done and his features contorted in a sudden hot rage
and he struck her, the back of his hand across her face,
and the impact of the blow rocked her back in the chair.
Prissy flew at him, hitting him like a freight train with
her considerable bulk, and almost knocked him off his
feet. But he recovered his balance and struck back, vi-
ciously, this time with a clenched fist, and Prissy went
down. He raised his rifle, wanting to crack her skull open
with the stock, but Rebecca was out of her chair, throw-

ing herself across the fallen Prissy, shielding her, before he could deliver the blow.

"Don't do it," said Joshua.

It was his brother's voice that stayed Morgan's hand, not Rebecca's intervention. The elder Vickers would have killed them both in his blinding wrath.

"I won't be a party to killing a woman, Morgan," said Joshua. "So why don't you just lay down that rifle."

Morgan lowered the rifle. Then he grabbed Rebecca roughly by the arm, his grip so tight that it would leave bruises, and hauled her to her feet.

"I won't kill you," he sneered. "No, you'll live to stand over your son's grave."

"No," she said, and it was as if the hate flowed out of him and into her, as though it were some kind of contagious disease that she contracted just by his touching her, because now, suddenly, she could understand what was going through him, and the desire for blood vengeance stirred her own blood.

"No," she said softly, her eyes blazing. "It's your grave I'll stand over, Morgan Vickers."

He laughed, a little nervous all of a sudden, and a little shaken by something only he could detect lurking deep in her eyes.

"The others," said Joshua. "They've bolted."

"Doesn't matter."

"It does matter. They'll fetch the sheriff."

"To hell with the sheriff."

"Groves won't come here now."

"Yes he will," said Morgan. "He'll come on her account." He nodded at Rebecca, and he sounded very confident.

"Let's get out of here, Morgan. This isn't working out. They'll hang us."

"For what? For shooting a nigger in the back? Hang a Vickers for *that*? Not likely."

"Let's go. We'll get Groves some other time."

"No!" barked Morgan, tired of arguing. "Go on. Run, if you're of a mind to. I didn't know you were a coward. But if you are, then I don't need you."

"You know better than that."

"Do I? You're sure talking like a yellow coward."

A muscle worked in Joshua's jaw, but he maintained his composure. "I'll stay," he muttered.

Morgan leered at Rebecca. "Since all your bucks ran out on you, lady, I guess you'll have to be the one to bury that old man. He's out yonder, lying in the road. But that's only fair, come to think of it, since you're to blame for his getting killed. That was a stupid thing to do. I warned you. But you just wouldn't listen, would you?"

"Let go of me."

He let her go. She turned away and helped Prissy to her feet. Prissy's lip was cut and bleeding.

"I'm sorry, Prissy," she said. "I . . . I just froze. I guess I wasn't prepared to kill a man." She looked coldly at Morgan. "But I am now."

Morgan laughed. Joshua didn't join him. He watched Rebecca solemnly, warily, sensing that hers was no idle threat.

Sundown caught Christopher and Nathaniel some miles shy of Elm Tree. They decided to push on. Christopher was so sick and tired of worrying about how his mother would react to the news of the duel and his dismissal from the Military Academy and to his ideas about Texas that he just wanted to get it over with.

They heard the galloping horse before they saw the rider, emerging from the indigo gloom of fast-falling night as he charged hell-bent for election up the road toward them.

"I didn't think we had a problem with Indians in Kentucky anymore," said Nathaniel. "But that feller sure looks like he's being chased by a passel of hostile Shawnees."

"Something's wrong," said Christopher. "He's burning the tallow off that horse."

They checked their mounts and waited for the rider to reach them. He turned out to be just a lad, not yet old enough to grow side-whiskers. Pulling rein so hard that his lathered horse sat down on its haunches in a pale cloud of drifting dust, he gaped at Christopher and Nathaniel with wild eyes.

"One of you be Christopher Groves?"

"I am."

"Lordy, I'm right glad I found you. We figured you'd be coming down this here road."

"We? Who are you?"

"Billy Steptoe's the name. The Madison County sher-. iff sent me to find you. He said to ride all the way to Maysville if I had to."

"But how did you know I was coming? What's the matter? My mother—has something happened to my mother?"

"I don't rightly know . . ."

"What do you mean you don't know?" snapped Christopher.

"Settle down, boy," said Nathaniel. "Billy, why don't you tell us what you *do* know?"

"Yessir. The sheriff and six or seven men rode out to Elm Tree a couple hours ago. They were armed to the teeth. I dunno why. The sheriff just told me to tell you, Mr. Groves, that one of your ma's hands showed up at his place this afternoon with a story about two men with rifles holding everybody prisoner at Elm Tree."

"Two men? What two men? Why?"

"We won't find out here," said Nathaniel. "Let's go."

By the time they reached the vicinity of Elm Tree the old leatherstocking and his grandson had left Billy Steptoe behind. The boy's horse had bottomed out.

They spotted a campfire up ahead, beneath the trees, close by the road. A black shape separated suddenly from the night shadows and loomed in their path, blocking the narrow road, appearing so abruptly that Christopher let out a shout of alarm and groped for the pistol in his belt.

"Who goes there?" boomed the big shape.

"Easy, Christopher," said Nathaniel, and Christopher had a hunch his grandfather had known this man was lurking in the brush even before he had stepped out into the road. Though the night was clear and the stars were out and a three-quarter moon was just now beginning to rise above the horizon, it was black as pitch here on the tree-shaded lane, and Christopher could scarcely see the ground, much less distinguish anything about the man blocking their path. But Flintlock Jones still had the eyes of a cat.

"I'm Nathaniel Jones," said the frontiersman. "This is Christopher Groves. We're looking for the sheriff. So take a deep breath and ease your finger off that trigger."

"Sorry, Mr. Jones." The man was contrite. "Reckon I'm a little nervous."

"Well, young Billy Steptoe's about a quarter of a mile behind us. Whatever you do, don't shoot him when he gets here."

"No, sir. I sure won't. Pardon me, sir, but aren't you the feller folks call Flintlock?"

"I am. It's a name I don't cotton to, I must admit. But there's not much I can do about it."

"I'm right glad you're with us, Mr. Jones."

"Under the circumstances," said Nathaniel grimly, "I wouldn't want to be anywhere else."

"The sheriff's over by the fire."

They rode on. Six men stood or sat around the crackling fire. From here they could look across the lane, past the fence marking the boundary of Elm Tree, under the sweeping limbs of an ancient pecan tree, and across a field of excellent graze to the house on a slight rise about three hundred yards away. Lamplight gleamed in some of the windows.

It was all Christopher could do to refrain from kicking the weary roan horse into a gallop and making straight for the house and his mother. But he didn't. If he did something stupid like that somebody could get killed. There was a fine line between audacity and foolish impetuosity, and the difference in this case might be his mother's life or death.

A man approached them as they dismounted. At the very edge of the firelight, Christopher could distinguish this man's spare frame and angular features. He looked worried, which did nothing for Christopher's own peace of mind.

"I'm Sheriff Ainsley. Might you be Christopher Groves?"

"I am. And this is my grandfather, Nathaniel Jones."

"*The* Nathaniel Jones. *Flintlock* Jones?" The man's ear-to-ear grin expressed vast relief. "My father talked quite a lot about you, Mr. Jones."

"Your father was sheriff before you, wasn't he?"

"That he was. Sheriff of Madison County for nigh on thirty years. Died a few years back. Guess the folks gave me the job on account of him. Of course, I could never fill his shoes. Never had cause to rue the job—until now."

"I take that to mean you don't have much experience in such matters," said Christopher.

"I'll be the first to admit it. The country's pretty settled now. We don't have too many problems anymore. Oh, an occasional horse stealing. Had a highwayman prowling these roads about a year ago, but some of the folks caught him and left his carcass hanging from a rope. This business here—" Ainsley shook his head. "Beats all I ever seen."

Christopher grimaced. Sheriff Ainsley did not inspire much confidence.

"Who are the two men?" asked Nathaniel.

"The boy who came and told me about it said he thought their name was Vickers."

"Vickers!" exclaimed Christopher.

"They ain't from around these parts," said Ainsley. "Ain't no Vickers here in Madison County, unless you count Emily Cooper. As I recollect, that was her maiden name."

Nathaniel nodded. "They're related. By the way, Emily Cooper's dead."

"Dead? How? When? I knew she'd been gone from Hunter's Creek for a spell, but I . . . dead, you say? How did it happen?"

"It's a long story. I'll tell you later." Nathaniel nodded at the five men near the fire. "Is that all the help you could get?"

"I'll be honest with you, Mr. Jones. That's all would come."

"What do you mean?"

"I mean Rebecca Groves ain't the most popular person in Madison County. She done stirred up a lot of hard feelings when she went and freed those slaves of hers. Most folks around here just don't think she ought to have done such a thing."

"What do you think about it, Sheriff?" asked Christopher, his tone less than cordial.

"I'm here, ain't I? It's my job to be here."

"But would you be here if it wasn't?"

"That's enough, Christopher."

"They might as well go on home, Grandpa. We can't go charging up there and start a shooting spree."

"I don't rightly know what to do," confessed Ainsley. "I rode up there this afternoon to try to talk them into giving themselves up."

"How did that work out?" asked Nathaniel.

"They said they were waiting for Mr. Groves here. Then they fired a shot over my head."

"Well, there it is," said Christopher. "There's only one thing to do. I'll go in alone and give myself up to them, if they'll release my mother in exchange."

"There's bound to be a better way," said Nathaniel, gazing thoughtfully across the road and the field at the distant house.

"The boys and I have been discussing it all evening," said Ainsley. "We were thinking we might could sneak up there under cover of darkness and get a good shot at the two of them. But they're dangerous men. The boy told me they done killed one of the servants. An old man. Don't recall his name . . ."

"Must be Isaac," said Christopher, and a chill shot down his spine. "If they'll shoot a harmless old man they'll shoot a woman. I've got to go, Grandpa. There's no other way."

"They'd kill you, son," said Ainsley.

"Better me than her."

"You're forgetting one thing," said Nathaniel. "Your mother would never walk away if you were in danger, Christopher. They'd have to kill her first." He shook his head. "No. I can't let you do it."

"We've got to do something!"

"We will. I've got an idea. Might just work." He put a hand on Christopher's shoulder. "But it will require a cool head and steady nerves. Can I rely on you?"

"Yes."

"Good. This is what we'll do . . ."

It proved to be one of the longest nights of Christopher's life. He had to wait until a couple of hours before daybreak, when the moon had set, to make his move, according to Nathaniel's plan. The frontiersman suggested that he get some sleep. Ainsley and his men were rolled up in their blankets for some shut-eye, leaving a single sentry to watch the road as well as the house. Nathaniel slept, too, and Christopher envied his grandfather the ability to do so. The plan was a risky one—especially for Nathaniel—yet that didn't seem to bother him, at least not enough to keep him awake. And Christopher knew that Nathaniel was just as concerned for his mother's well-being as he was. Still, Nathaniel slept. He had taught himself to do so, even in moments of crisis, a habit developed from many years in the forest stalking Indians, or being stalked by them. He awoke right on time, just as the moon descended and the darkness deepened.

They reviewed the plan once more before Christopher set out on foot, knife and pistol in his belt, rifle in hand. He crossed the road and clambered over the wooden fence and started off across the field. The distant house was still ablaze with lamplight. A hundred yards from his destination he got down on his belly and crawled the rest of the way. Reaching the north side of the house, he found the doors to the root cellar closed, but without a padlock. The doors had never been locked to his knowledge, but it had occurred to him that if the doors *were* secured for some reason, the whole plan would go up in smoke.

He tried to be careful opening one of the big wooden doors, but the iron hinges were old and rusted, and made such a loud, screeching complaint that the hair on the back of his neck stood on end. He froze, certain that the whole of Madison Country had heard the sound. There was a window just to the right of the cellar doors, one of the dining room windows, and he watched it for a moment, expecting one of the Vickers boys to appear there. But no one did. There was no sign of life in the house. No sound at all. That worried him. Maybe they had slipped away in the night. Maybe they had taken his mother with them as a hostage. Or maybe . . . maybe she was dead.

He cursed himself silently, and tried to put a short rein on his imagination.

Negotiating the steep wooden steps, he decided to leave the door open, rather than risk making more noise by trying to shut it behind him. At the bottom of the steps he crouched for a moment, giving his eyes time to adjust to the darkness underneath the house. The pungent aroma of old wood and older earth filled his nostrils. Straight ahead, if he remembered correctly, was one of the big piers which supported the house, a ten-foot length of hickory tree trunk buried four feet into the ground, so big that he could have just reached all the way around it with both arms. Locating the pier, he groped for and found a lantern hanging from a stout peg. He thanked the good Lord it was there, as it had been for as long as he could remember. But he could not take these things for granted—the cellar door being unlocked, the lantern being on the peg—not tonight, with so much at stake.

Taking the lantern from the leg, he jostled it. Yes! It was at least half full of coal oil. Christopher used a sulphur match he had gotten from Sheriff Ainsley and lighted the lantern. Keeping it turned down low, he proceeded further under the house. In the vicinity of another wooden staircase, this one located at the center of the house, he found a broken chair, an old armoire with one door missing, several small casks, a rack containing a half-dozen bottles of wine. He climbed halfway up the stairs. The hatch opened into the center hall of the house. He listened hard, hoping to hear something which would tell him where in the house his mother and the Vickers brothers were located. But still there was no sound. He fought the urge to go through the hatch. Anxiety was tying his insides into knots, souring his stomach, parching his throat. Waiting—that was the hardest part. Still, he *had* to wait. Nathaniel would make his move at daybreak. That was less than an hour away.

Sitting on the steps, rifles across his knees, Christopher put the lantern out, fearing that its light might be seen leaking around the edges of the hatch. There he remained, head in hands, in the black womb of the cellar, wishing for the dawn.

Chapter 13

It was just after dawn when the Vickers boys heard an odd sound coming from somewhere in front of the house. They were in the front parlor, and Rebecca was with them. Morgan and Joshua had taken turns standing guard. Joshua had slept when given the chance, stretched out on the horsehair sofa. But Morgan hadn't been able to sleep. He spent most of the night pacing the floor, and when he got tired of pacing he sat in a wingback chair and glowered at Rebecca, or stared out the windows. Rebecca sat in another chair all night, almost afraid to move, tired but too worried to sleep. Worried for Christopher's sake. As for Prissy, Morgan had locked her in the smokehouse. He didn't need two women to keep an eye on. Neither did he need two hostages.

The odd sound was a creaking noise, and though both brothers rushed to the window and peered cautiously out, they could see nothing that would explain it. Finally, Morgan turned abruptly and crossed the room to where Rebecca was sitting, his rifle leveled at her.

"Come on," he said hoarsely.

She stood, haughtily ignoring the rifle. He motioned to the door to the hall and she preceded them out of the room and to the front door. Morgan jabbed the barrel of the rifle into the small of her back.

"Don't do anything foolish," he warned.

"I would give you the same advice," she said, "except it's too late."

She opened the door and stepped out onto the porch. Morgan followed right behind her, while Joshua remained just inside the doorway, rifle held at the ready.

Nathaniel's long frame was draped in a rocking chair at the end of the porch. Morgan made a funny sound and swung his rifle around to aim it at the old leatherstocking.

"Who the hell are you?"

Nathaniel didn't stop rocking. "Nathaniel Jones is the name. That happens to be my daughter you're hiding behind."

Smelling a trap, Morgan swept a suspicious glance about him.

"I'm all alone," said Nathaniel. "And unarmed."

"It's a trick," said Joshua from the doorway.

"No tricks. I just want to talk."

"You know who he is?" Joshua asked his brother. "He's the one they call Flintlock."

"Flintlock Jones?" Morgan's smile resembled the snarl of a wolf.

"He's as dangerous as a sack full of cottonmouths," declared Joshua.

"This old man?" scoffed Morgan.

"Don't underestimate him."

"Stop telling me what to do. I'm sick and tired of you telling me what to do, Joshua!"

"Your nerves are in poor shape," was Nathaniel's amiable observation. "Must've passed a restless night."

"Get up," growled Morgan.

Nathaniel did as he was told.

"Hold your arms out away from your sides and turn around. Move slow, old-timer, like molasses in wintertime."

Nathaniel complied. Morgan looked for a pistol or a knife secreted in the back of the frontierman's leather belt. But Nathaniel had told the truth. He was unarmed.

"This snake's got no teeth," said Morgan, chuckling.

He felt a lot better about things now. All night he'd been worried about the Madison County men camped across the road, figuring that at dawn they would raid the house in an attempt to rescue Rebecca Groves. Instead, here was this old man, and without any weapons, to boot!

Nathaniel smiled reassuringly at Rebecca. "Are you well, Becky? Have they hurt you?"

"No, I'm fine."

"What were you going to do if we *had* hurt her?" sneered Morgan.

"You don't want to know."

Morgan laughed. He thought this old leatherstocking was just all bluff and bluster. He didn't hear the steel menace in Nathaniel's soft-spoken reply.

"They killed Isaac, Father," said Rebecca, and just the mention of Isaac's name brought tears welling up in her eyes. "Prissy and I buried him."

"Killing old men and hiding behind a woman's skirts." Nathaniel shook his head. "Not what I'd expect to see from brave men."

"I don't cotton to standing out here in the open," said Morgan. "You want to talk, come on inside. Of course, I won't guarantee you'll come out again."

"Don't require guarantees," said Nathaniel, and went into the house.

Once in the hallway with the door closed, Morgan allowed Rebecca to go to her father, who put a comforting arm around her shoulders. Morgan kept them covered while Joshua stayed by the door, looking outside. He was thinking that maybe Nathaniel had been sent in to distract them, giving the Madison County sheriff and his *posse comitatus* the opportunity to slip in unseen.

Having logged first impressions of the Vickers brothers, Nathaniel decided that Joshua was the more dangerous of the two. He used his head, while Morgan was ruled by emotion, which meant Morgan could make mistakes in the heat of the moment. Nathaniel was counting on it.

He was also counting on Christopher being ready to act, waiting beneath the hatch to the cellar, twenty feet down the hall. But he dared not even glance in that direction.

"You wanted to talk," said Morgan gruffly. "Then say what you came to say."

"I hear tell you're waiting for Christopher."

"He's going to die. He's the reason our cousin Emily took her own life. And he turned our brother Adam into a cripple."

"That was a fair fight. But I didn't come here to argue the point. I came to tell you that if you want Christopher you'll have to go to Texas."

Morgan was stunned. Joshua looked around from the door, sparing his brother a quick glance, then fastening his gaze on Nathaniel, searching the frontiersman's craggy, weathered face—looking for the truth.

"Texas!" exclaimed Morgan. "I don't believe you."

"It's true. He stopped off at Boonesboro a few days ago and told me Texas was where he's bound. He's on his way down the Natchez Trace by now."

"You're lying," declared Morgan hotly. "If he was as close as Boonesboro he would have come here to see his mother."

"No. He was too ashamed to face you, Becky. Ashamed of being thrown out of West Point. Which is why I'm here. He asked me to tell you. He said he knew it was the coward's way, but he couldn't help it. He could face a hundred Adam Vickers, but he couldn't face you."

Morgan stared at the frontiersman, befuddled by this unexpected turn of events, and trying to think it through. Nathaniel plunged ahead, sensing that he had a slight advantage, and not wanting to give either one of them much time for thinking. He was beginning to wonder if there wasn't a chance of getting out of this without bloodshed.

"So you can see you're in a bad spot, boys. You might as well give yourselves up."

"Not a chance," said Morgan.

"What are you worried about?" asked Nathaniel. "All you've done so far is kill an old Negro."

"Father!" exclaimed Rebecca, aghast and affronted by the offhanded way Nathaniel had referred to Isaac's murder.

The frontiersman studiously ignored her. "You boys come from an important family. You can buy justice. I doubt if you'd wind up paying for that crime."

"Maybe he's right," Joshua told his brother. He had been predisposed since yesterday to leave, and he was just as willing to go now.

"Of course, all bets will be off if you kill a white man—or woman," continued Nathaniel. "What other choice do you have?"

"We'll just ride away," said Morgan, by way of testing the waters.

Nathaniel shook his head. "Those Madison County men out there won't let that happen, I'm afraid. They came here for a fight."

"They'll let us go if we've got your daughter for a hostage."

Nathaniel's smile was deceptive. There was steel resolve behind it. Morgan didn't see it, but Joshua did.

"You'll have to kill me first," said the old leatherstocking quietly.

"I can handle that," promised Morgan. He felt trapped, and was ready to strike out, regardless of the consequences.

"*Tripoli!*" shouted Nathaniel.

He threw Rebecca to the floor and draped his body over hers, a human shield.

In that instant Christopher burst out of the cellar,

throwing the hatch back. Morgan swung his rifle around and triggered it from hip level. Christopher fired at the same time, only halfway out of the hatch. Morgan's bullet cracked as it passed, missing him by inches. Christopher's aim was marginally better. His bullet struck Morgan in the thigh. The impact kicked the leg out from under Morgan. He toppled like a cut tree. Cursing, he dispensed with the empty rifle and yanked a pistol from his belt. Nathaniel was near enough to kick it out of his hand. The pistol skittered across the floor.

As he cleared the root cellar hatchway, Christopher discarded his own rifle and brandished a pistol. Now that Morgan was down and disarmed, he turned his attention to Joshua. But Joshua had already made up his mind to flee. He was out the front door before Christopher could line up a shot. Nathaniel leaped to his feet and gave chase.

Seeing his brother turn tail and run brought a roar of rage from Morgan as he struggled to get up. He drew a knife from its belt sheath and started toward Christopher, dragging his wounded leg, leaving smears of bright scarlet blood on the floor.

Christopher was astonished. Was Morgan Vickers mad? Didn't he see the pistol in Christopher's hand?

"Drop the knife."

Morgan kept coming.

"Drop it or I'll shoot."

"This is for my brother," rasped Morgan, coming on.

"Shoot him, Christopher!" cried Rebecca.

"You're a fool, Vickers," said Christopher, taking careful aim, arm fully extended, body turned slightly, the pistol rock steady in his hand.

"Go on and shoot, you coward!" snarled Morgan.

Still, Christopher hesitated.

Rebecca lunged for the pistol Nathaniel had kicked out of Morgan's hand. She whirled and aimed it at Morgan, pulling the trigger at almost point-blank range.

The hammer fell into the pan. Powder flashed, but the pistol did not discharge. Suddenly Morgan had turned on her, raising the knife.

Christopher lowered the pistol a few degrees off the horizontal and squeezed the trigger. The pistol spoke, spewing flame. Morgan cried out as the bullet struck his good leg. He lurched forward, falling on his face. Screaming incoherently now, mad with rage, he started to crawl, making for Christopher again. Christopher stepped forward and kicked the knife out of his hand. Morgan tried to grab his leg, but Christopher eluded him, stepping back, and Morgan let out a roar of frustration that shook the rafters before he lost consciousness.

Outside, Joshua leaped off the porch and headed for the stables and his horse. He looked back once, and was alarmed to see Nathaniel in hot pursuit, astonished by the speed and agility of the old leatherstocking. In a glance he could tell he wasn't going to reach the stables, so he turned, bringing his rifle to bear. Already Nathaniel was close enough to knock the barrel aside just as Joshua triggered the rifle. Nathaniel plowed into him at full speed, driving a forearm into Joshua's face. Joshua lost his grip on the rifle as he went down. He hit the ground hard, and Nathaniel landed on top of him, planting a knee in his sternum, and Joshua would have cried out in pain as a rib cracked, except that his mouth was filled with blood, and all the air had been punched out of his lungs. Nathaniel hit him in the face again, this time with a fist that fell with the force of an anvil, and Joshua passed out, strangling on his own blood and teeth.

Nathaniel rolled the unconscious man over on his belly after plucking a pistol from his belt. Then he turned and raced back to the house. As he reached the porch, Rebecca and Christopher emerged. Nathaniel let out a gusting sigh of relief to see them unscathed. The distant drumbeat of horses at the gallop drew his attention to the lane. Ainsley and his boys were charging through the gate. In no time at all they were checking their horses in front of the house, and Nathaniel climbed up onto the porch to join his daughter and grandson— and to avoid the drifting dust churned up by the iron-shod hooves of the seven ponies.

Ainsley spared Joshua a quick glance. "Has he crossed the river?"

"No," said Nathaniel.

"Where's the other one?"

"Inside."

"What about him? Is he dead?"

"He's alive," said Christopher.

Ainsley dismounted. On his way across the porch to enter the house he paused to give Christopher a funny look.

"Ordinarily, I'm not one to encourage killing," remarked the Madison Country sheriff. "But in the case of these Vickers boys, you might do better to just finish 'em off."

He went inside, followed by several of his men—the other three crossed the yard to collect Joshua.

Christopher glanced solemnly at Nathaniel.

"You know," he said, "I think he might be right. I had the chance. That one in there came to me with a knife. I could have shot him through the heart."

"Why didn't you?"

Christopher shook his head. "I just couldn't. All he had was a knife. But I have a feeling I'll live to regret it."

They laid the Vickers boys out on the parlor floor. Ainsley sent one of his men to fetch the doctor—old Doc Mattson, who had delivered Christopher, as he had almost every other child born in Madison County since the turn of the century. Before turning his attention to

the two wounded men, Mattson gave Rebecca a once-
over and sternly ordered her to bed.

"Ah's been tryin' to tell her she needs rest," said
Prissy, vindicated. She had been fussing over Rebecca
ever since her release from the smokehouse. "But she's
sho' mule-headed."

"I'm fine," insisted Rebecca.

"You're not," said Mattson. "I don't want to see her
on her feet until tomorrow afternoon at the earliest," he
told Christopher.

"You can count on me, sir."

With a curt nod, Mattson entered the parlor. Prissy
and Christopher escorted Rebecca to her room. She
protested all the way. Nathaniel stepped out onto the
porch. His horse, along with Christopher's roan, had
been retrieved from the woods across the road, and
the frontiersman rummaged through his belongings,
contained in a gunnysack tied to the threadbare saddle, for his pipe and tobacco. Finding them, he repaired to the rocking chair on the porch, where he
packed his pipe, fired it up, and rocked gently, sa-
voring the bite of the pungent tobacco and letting the
tension drain from his body.

Christopher came outside to join him a little while
later.

"I told her about Texas."

"You might have waited a day or two. She's been
through a lot."

"I just couldnt' wait any longer, Grandpa. I had to get
it off my chest."

"How did she take it?"

"Better than I expected. She was disappointed in
me for fighting the duel and getting thrown out of
West Point, of course. But not too disappointed. I
don't think she ever really wanted me to become a
soldier."

Nathaniel rocked and puffed, puffed and rocked, and

eventually said, "You acquitted yourself well today, Christopher."

Christopher was pleased. Praise from his legendary grandfather meant more to him than almost anything.

"I reckon Texas will be lucky to have you," added the frontiersman.

"I wish you'd come along."

"You know, I've been thinking I just might."

Christopher was flabbergasted. He couldn't believe his ears. "Do you mean it?"

"I said it, didn't I?"

Christopher couldn't restrain a whoop of pure elation.

"When I was but a lad," said Nathaniel, gazing off into the western sky, "I always had this hankering to see what lay on the other side of the mountains. I was born and raised in Virginia, but the Old Dominion never felt like home to me. When I first laid eyes on Kentucky I knew in my bones I had found my true home. But it just isn't the same anymore, with Amanda gone. And now, out of the blue, I've got that urge to see new country again. First time in nigh on fifty years I've had this feeling."

"She'd be glad you're going with me."

"Well, I think she'd want me to look out for her only grandchild, that's for sure."

Dr. Mattson emerged from the house, carrying a pan of bloody water, which he emptied off the side of the porch.

"How are they, Doc?" asked Christopher.

"Was it you shot that man in the legs?"

"Yes, sir."

Mattson grimaced. "My God, boy, you would have done him a favor by shooting him right between the eyes."

"I thought about it. But all he had was a knife."

Mattson heaved a deep sigh. "I may be able to save one of the legs. I doubt it, but there's a chance. I understand you fought a duel with another of the Vickers clan."

"Yes, sir."

"Didn't kill him either, did you?"

"No, sir," said Christopher, sheepishly.

"You had better pray that there are only three of them. If there are any more brothers they will be coming for you, my boy."

"I'm going to Texas. If any more show up here, send them on."

Mattson grunted. "Texas, eh? Well, if you pass through the state of Mississippi to get to Texas I suggest you keep your eyes peeled and your head down. The Vickers family has a great deal of influence down there, and in Tennessee, too. It wouldn't surprise me if they put a bounty on your head."

"A bounty! I've broken no laws."

"Are you that naive? Men like Daniel Vickers write their own laws, and they have the money to pay for its enforcement." Mattson shook his head. "Fighting duels and such. You're becoming more and more like your father."

"I am *not* like him," protested Christopher.

"No?" Mattson relented. "Excuse me, Christopher. I have become a crotchety old man. If I scold you as a father would his son it is only because I feel as though you and all the other young men and women I have delivered *are* my children. And I must confess to a particular attachment to your mother. She is a brave, kind, wonderful woman. One of a kind. Your father caused her considerable grief, if I do say so."

"I realize that."

"I know you do. And I know you don't want to cause her any more grief by your own actions. There. I have said my piece. Now I think I will go make sure she is following her doctor's orders."

When Mattson tapped on the door to Rebecca's bedroom Prissy let him in.

"Ah sho' is glad to see you, Doctor," sighed Prissy.

"What's the matter?"

"Landsakes! Ah jis' hope you can talk some sense into her."

Rebecca was sitting up in bed, arms folded, an expression of stubborn resolve on her face. Mattson knew that look. It meant Rebecca Groves had made up her mind about something. When that happened, there was no hope of persuading her otherwise.

"What's the meaning of this?" asked Mattson. "I told you to get some rest, young lady."

"I'm not tired," said Rebecca. "I know that tone of voice. Don't waste your time trying to bully me, Doc."

Mattson ruthlessly suppressed a fond smile. "What have you been saying to Prissy that's got her so upset?"

"I told her I'm going to Texas."

"What?"

"Oh mercy," whispered the distraught Prissy.

"Texas. T-E-X-A-S. I am going there with my son."

"But ... but ..." Mattson was stunned to the point of speechlessness.

Rebecca smiled, sensing that she had the upper hand. "Are you afflicted, Doc? I've never known you to be at a loss for words."

"But you can't go to Texas, Rebecca."

"Why can't I?"

"Well, because—because it's no place for a lady."

"I'm no lady. I was born in a little log cabin and my father is a hunter."

"But what about Elm Tree?"

"I would like to leave it to you to sell for me. Of course, I would expect to pay you a commission."

"Sell Elm Tree?"

"Yes, Doctor. Sell. S-E-L-L."

"I do wish you would stop spelling out words for me," said Mattson crossly. "You're just trying to aggravate me—and you are succeeding admirably. You can be so infuriating sometimes, Rebecca."

"Only when I'm not getting my way."

"Oh, does that ever happen?"

"Will you do me that favor? Will you see to the selling of Elm Tree? Or must I rely on someone else."

Mattson threw up his hands. "If you're absolutely certain it's what you want, yes. But what about Prissy, and the others? What about your thoroughbreds?"

"I honestly don't think any of the others will be coming back, after what happened here. As for Prissy, she is free to do what she wants. Personally, I hope she will consent to accompany me."

"To Texas?" cried Prissy. "Oh mercy me! Snakes and scorpions and . . . and wild Indians and such? Texas is a wild country, Miss 'Becca."

"Then we had better waste no time in taming it."

"And the horses?" asked Mattson.

"I'll take a few with me. Jumper and a couple of mares. Sell the rest for a grubstake."

Mattson shook his head, and felt compelled to make one last, feeble attempt to dissuade her. "I can't believe you're serious. I wish you would take some time and think this through, Rebecca. Don't act on the spur of the moment. When people do that they inevitably regret it. Elm Tree is your home, and has been for twenty-five years . . ."

"It has many bad memories, Doc."

"But there are some good memories, too, aren't there? Your son was born here . . ."

"And I don't want to see him die here. You know how powerful the Vickers clan is. Do you think it was finished here today—this . . . this blood feud?"

"No," admitted Mattson. "I was just telling Christopher the same thing."

"There you are. Perhaps he will be beyond their reach in Texas."

"Perhaps," said Mattson dubiously.

"Texas is where he is bound," said Rebecca. "And if my son is going to Texas, then so am I."

"Oh mercy," whispered Prissy.

Chapter 14

Sheriff Ainsley had a wagon brought in to transport Morgan and Joshua Vickers back to town. Doc Mattson was preparing to remove one of Morgan's legs as soon as possible. Christopher's bullet had shattered the bone and was lodged among the fragments, and within a day's time Morgan had contracted a high fever as infection set in. Apart from a cracked rib, Joshua was unhurt. Ainsley promised Nathaniel he would try to keep the Vickers under lock and key at least as long as it took him—and Rebecca and Christopher—to get out of Madison County.

"You reckon they'll stand trial for Isaac's murder?" asked the frontiersman. He had a pretty good idea himself, but wanted to hear the sheriff's views on the subject.

"Want a straight answer, Mr. Jones?"

"I'd rather you didn't lie to me."

The Madison County sheriff tugged on a earlobe as he thought it over. Then he shook his head.

"I doubt it. If Judge Dunston was still around he'd give it a shot. But them being Vickerses and all . . ."

Nathaniel nodded. "Well, just try to hold on to them for as long as you can."

The next morning, Rebecca was up and around, in violation of doctor's orders, and seeming none the worse for her experiences. Nathaniel was almighty proud of the way she was bearing up. She had plenty of grit, just like her mother. He was glad she had decided to go with them to Texas. That made leaving a lot easier on him. He was sure that were Amanda alive she would want him to go, to look after their daughter and grandson. Of course, he was getting a little long in the tooth, which left him wondering who would be looking after whom. Not that he intended to be a burden to his kin. If it got to the point that he could no longer take care of himself, he had resolved to make one last trek into the wilderness—a trek from which he would not return. No headstone over a hole in the ground for him. He wanted to die looking up at the stars.

In a way Nathaniel was sorry to leave Kentucky. He had spent the best years of his life here. He had many acquaintances. Not many friends, though. Being by nature a man who kept to himself, he hadn't made a lot of lasting friendships. There was Daniel Boone, and the Delaware warrior, Quashquame. But they were gone now. Gone, too, was the Kentucky he had loved with a passion exceeded only by his feelings for his family. Gone was the virgin wilderness, where a man could travel for days on end without coming across another living soul. Gone were the great herds of bison, the great flights of passenger pigeons—so many that they could blot out the sun for hours as they winged overhead. The deer and bear were even getting scarce, and the beaver were all but wiped out. Seemed there was a cabin perched on every hilltop, a cultivated field in every clearing. Nathaniel was hoping he would find the true wilderness again in Texas. That was where he wanted to spend his remaining days.

Rebecca asked for a fortnight to settle her affairs. She placed a notice in Madison County's weekly newspaper, announcing that the Elm Tree thoroughbreds were up for sale. This brought a horde of prospective buyers to her doorstep. Christopher helped her make the transactions. In short order nineteen horses were purchased at top dollar. Rebecca kept the stallion Jumper and the two best-looking mares. It saddened her to see the others go, but she refused to entertain second thoughts about pulling up roots and going to Texas.

The stallion reminded Nathaniel of the horse by that very name which had carried him on the now legendary midnight run to warn Thomas Jefferson, then Virginia's governor, of the approach of Bonastre Tarleton's notorious Tory Legion. This Jumper had similar markings, the same splendid lines, the same indomitable spirit. If Nathaniel hadn't known better he would have thought it the same horse. The mares, Clio and Delilah, were nothing to sneeze at either. "They'll be the finest horses in Texas," declared Christopher, and Nathaniel didn't doubt the truth of that statement.

They spent several days discussing the best means of travel. There were two options. One was by boat, down the Mississippi to New Orleans. The other was overland, on the Natchez Trace. From New Orleans they could head due west and be across the Sabine and into Texas in no time at all.

"I went down the Trace twenty-five years ago with Jonathan," said Nathaniel. "Back when we were on Aaron Burr's trail. The Trace was infested with robbers even then, and from everything I've heard, it's worse today."

"We could probably find other folks to travel with," said Christopher. "There is strength in numbers. And there are robbers on the river, too."

Nathaniel nodded. "That's true. Morrell's gang."

John Morrell, known as the Reverend Devil, was the most notorious outlaw of the era. His proclivity for traveling in the disguise of an itinerant preacher had earned him his legendary nom de plume. He and his river pirates were the scourge of the Mississippi River. Rumor was that Morrell had over five hundred cutthroats at his beck and call. His headquarters were located somewhere in the Arkansas canebrakes, a barracoon of thieves and murderers, complete with women and children, ruled by Morrell the way Jean Lafitte had reigned at Campeche. For years Morrell and his henchmen had preyed on the flatboats carrying goods and people down the river to Natchez and New Orleans. But even the big steamboats which plied the Mississippi these days were not safe. It had gotten so bad that a detachment of dragoons had recently been dispatched by the government to find Morrell's hideout and destroy it. But Morrell's pirates had ambushed the dragoons, torn them to bloody shreds, and sent them packing. The law couldn't touch the Reverend Devil.

"We would be easy pickings for Morrell on the river," said Christopher.

"What do you think, Becky?" asked Nathaniel.

"Can we transport the horses on the river?"

"Of course."

"Which way would be the quicker?"

"Barring anything unforeseen," said Christopher, "I suppose we would make better time on the river. But it would not be the safer of the two. Even if we suppose that Morrell will give us no trouble, there are natural hazards to consider."

"It will be a hazardous journey, regardless," said Rebecca. "I say we go by the river."

"May I ask your reasons, Mother?"

"The Natchez Trace passes through Mississippi, doesn't it?"

"Why yes, but . . ."

"Then we'll take our chances on the river."

"If it's because of Dan Vickers . . ."

"That's precisely the reason," said Rebecca sternly.

"Your mother's right," said Nathaniel. "I reckon there will be some men out looking for you, Christopher. By taking the river we may be able to outflank them."

"We'll need a good boat," said Rebecca. "Can you find one for us, Nathaniel?"

"I can. The only problem, Becky, is that we could use a couple more men with strong arms and stout hearts."

"First things first," said Rebecca. She was still hoping against hope that the three hands who had fled would eventually show up again at Elm Tree, even though Prissy was firmly of the opinion that they were long gone.

"Dey's still runnin' skeered," she had told Rebecca. "Dey's prob'ly halfways to Canada by now."

"Oh, I hope not, Prissy. They have no documents to prove they're free. What if they run into bounty hunters?"

"Dey can take care of demselves, Miss 'Becca. Doan you fear none 'bout dat."

"I'll miss them terribly if they don't come back."

"Dem worthless field hands? Hmph!"

"Prissy! That's an awful thing to say. And you don't mean it. I know you don't. You miss them, too, but you just won't admit it."

"Miss 'Becca, was dey to come back dey'd jis' run off again after you tol' dem you was gwine to Texas."

Rebecca smiled. "You don't have to go if you don't want to."

"Ah'm gwine," said Prissy grimly. "Ah'm gwine to Texas if you is, Miss 'Becca, and dat's dat. Somebody's gots to look out for you and dat headstrong boy of yours."

Rebecca knew that Prissy was as devoted to Christopher as she was. In fact, Prissy thought of Christopher as her own son, in a way. And why not? She had spent just as much time and effort as Rebecca in nursing, bathing, feeding, and clothing Christopher during his childhood years. She still fussed over him like he was ten years old.

*   *   *

Christopher stayed behind at Elm Tree when Nathaniel left to purchase the boat. Now that the thoroughbreds were sold, Rebecca set about arranging for an auction as a means to dispense with most of the furnishings. Nathaniel had warned her that she could take no more personal belongings than would fit in a wagon. The decision was a difficult one for her. She had spent twenty-five years selecting the pieces which filled the rooms at Elm Tree, and there was precious little that she wasn't reluctant to part with. Finally she decided on her four-poster bed, an escritoire, the dining room table and chairs, a rocking chair her mother had given her, a trunk full of her clothes and a few mementos. And then there were the books—another trunk filled with books. She had done a lot of reading in the past few years, and had the idea that perhaps she could teach school in Texas.

Everything else was earmarked to be sold. The auction was a rousing success. It seemed to her as though the entire population of Madison County was present for the occasion. Rebecca saw quite a lot of people who had once called themselves her friends—before she had so offended southern sensibilities by emancipating the Elm Tree slaves.

"I'm glad to see they haven't permitted personal feelings to get in their way of acquiring quality furniture at rock-bottom prices," she told Christopher sarcastically.

"Maybe they're just glad we're leaving, and this is their way of donating funds to meet our travel expenses."

In what little spare time he had, Christopher struggled ferociously with a letter to Greta Inskilling—a letter which took him a fortnight to write. She had made him promise to write her when he reached home. He was to address the letter to one of her friends—evidently she feared that any letter sent directly to her might be intercepted by her father. Christopher knew the fate which would befall any correspondence from him to Greta if it fell into the hands of Piet Inskilling.

Christopher was a mediocre letter writer in the best of circumstances. In this instance, as he tried to put his innermost feelings into words, he had an awful time of it. Ever since the levee at the White House his thoughts had been of her. Only then had he been certain of her love for him. She *had* to love him, to be willing, as she clearly was, to defy her father, risk her reputation, and brave the perils of Texas just to be at his side. Christopher still had a hard time believing he had been so blessed, and he certainly did not feel worthy of her affection. But there it was. Undeniably, Greta truly loved him. And once he was settled somewhere in Texas all he had to do was send word and she would come to him, by ship, down the Atlantic coast, around the tip of Florida, and across the Gulf of Mexico. Calculating the months ahead during which they would be apart made Christopher wretchedly heartsick.

In the letter, he told Greta that both his mother and grandfather were accompanying him to Texas. He described the sale of the horses and the auction, while leaving out altogether the business with the Vickers brothers. Sharing his expectations of their arriving in Texas and getting settled before winter, he concluded with the fervent wish that come the following spring she would make the long journey to join him.

The following spring! Writing those words produced a cold empty place inside him. It was all he could do to keep from tearing up the letter and starting a new one, in which he would beg her to come to him without delay. But it wouldn't do to put Greta at risk by asking her to make the journey down the river with him. No, it was entirely too dangerous. He had to put aside his own selfish wishes and do what was best for her. By next spring he would have a cabin erected somewhere in Texas—the least a man could do for his future bride was to have a home she could live in. As for being apart from her for such a long time, well, he would just have to endure.

Nathaniel returned in eleven days. He had found a boat, a broadhorn, down at Cully's Landing on the Cumberland. Built by masters at the trade, it was available because some unspecified tragedy had struck the family for which it had been built, and Nathaniel had bought it for a very fair price.

"Problem is," said the frontiersman, "she's more boat than Christopher and I can safely handle. We need at least two more men, and I have found none so far. Perhaps somewhere along the way we could pick up an experienced keelboat man."

Rebecca had reservations about hiring a couple of river rats. They had a reputation for being crude, rough men, heavy drinkers, inveterate brawlers, profane and reckless fellows.

"Can such men be trusted?" she asked. "From what I've heard, they would think nothing of cutting our throats as we slept just to steal our belongings."

Nathaniel laughed. "I've met some of them, those that ply their trade on the Ohio River. They are a rough-hewn lot, but the vast majority are honest, hardworking men. And we could use someone who knows the river."

By this time Rebecca had all but given up hope of the Elm Tree hands returning. But the very next day their problem was at least partially solved by the unexpected arrival of Christopher's erstwhile West Point roommate and true friend, John O'Connor.

"I told you not to be surprised to find me at your doorstep," said O'Connor.

"What did you do to get thrown out?"

"Oh, what does it matter? It was inevitable, Christopher, old bean. Just a matter of time. I'm only glad I made it before you took off for Texas."

"How did you know I was going to Texas?"

"Greta told me." O'Connor laughed at the expression on Christopher's face. "Now, don't go flying off the handle. I'm not trying to trespass on your territory. Of course, if I did try I *could* steal her away from you, and not even raise a sweat doing the deed. But no, I wouldn't do such a thing to a friend of mine. I went to see her before I left New York, to tell her I was coming to Kentucky, in case she had a message for you."

"Did she?"

"No."

Christopher was crestfallen.

O'Connor snapped his fingers. "Oh, I forgot. She did ask me to tell you that she loved you with all her heart, and that she would wait forever if she had to." He shook his head. "What a waste."

"I ought to punch you in the nose."

"How is that arm?"

"Good enough to teach you some manners."

"I doubt that. So you are off to Texas. Want some company?"

"*You* want to go to Texas?"

O'Connor shrugged. "Why not? Where else am I to go? I have no desire to return home to Boston and spend several years before the mast on some flaming whaler or merchantman. I'm strictly a landlubber, though I come from a long line of sailors."

Christopher smiled. "Then I've got some bad news for you. We're going by boat, down the Mississippi."

"Oh well. How bad can that be? It's just a river, isn't it?"

"Just a river?" Christopher laughed. "You've never seen the Mississippi, have you?"

"My friend, this is my first time west of the Alleghenies."

"What do you think you might do in Texas?"

O'Connor shrugged again. "What do you plan to do?"

"I don't know yet."

"Well now, I've heard there's a fight brewing down there. I don't want to miss it. So when do we leave?"

O'Connor had a strong back and wasn't afraid of work, so they made quick progress preparing to depart from Elm Tree. Nathaniel took an immediate liking to him, and so did Rebecca, who despite her best efforts to resist, fell prey to O'Connor's charm. He paid her profuse compliments at every turn, and she was flattered, even though she knew it was good old-fashioned blarney, for the most part.

With the furniture, Rebecca's personal belongings, and all the provisions they had room for, they managed to fill two wagons to the weight limit. Oxen proved hard to come by, so Rebecca bought six mules, to go with the two she already owned, and a four-mule hitch was put on each wagon. It was decided that Christopher and Rebecca would ride in one wagon, while O'Connor drove the second, with Prissy for company. Nathaniel would ride horseback, leading the three thoroughbreds.

On the morning of the date set to leave Elm Tree, Christopher awoke feeling oddly listless. The prospect of the long journey ahead exhausted him before he had taken the first step. Suddenly his excitement had waned. He could no longer hear the exotic siren song Texas had been singing to lure him thither. Over breakfast, Nathaniel took one look at him and intuitively knew something was bothering him, and when they rose from the table to go outside and hitch up the mules, the old frontiersman asked his grandson what was bothering him. Christopher told him how he felt.

"Don't worry," said Nathaniel. "You're just homesick."

"I am?"

"Sure. Now that it's time to leave Elm Tree, you're suddenly not sure you want to go."

Christopher looked about him—at the house and stables, the pastures and fields bright in the morning light, and that distant line of trees marking the creek, from which he had derived so much pleasure during boyhood explorations.

"You're right," he said, surprised. "I'm not even gone yet, and I miss it."

"This is the only home you've ever known. What you're feeling at this moment is perfectly natural."

Christopher figured that, as bad as he felt, his mother must feel far worse. But if she did, Rebecca didn't show it. She was very businesslike as they made their final preparations. As for Christopher, he felt almost like crying as he drove the lead wagon down the lane to the country road. How ridiculous, he told himself, especially for a twenty-five-year-old. He made the mistake of looking back, once.

Sitting beside her son, with her eyes on the road ahead, Rebecca did not see his stricken expression, but somehow she sensed his anguish, and said, "Don't ever look back, Christopher."

"Yes, ma'am," he said, and whipped up the mules.

Rebecca took her own advice, but she couldn't avoid thinking back, to all the events which had occurred in that house, all the laughter, all the tears, and all the years. Yet she kept her sorrow to herself. She had become skilled at doing so.

Chapter 15

Cully's Landing had become a place of some renown on the Cumberland River. Starting out as a small inn, in a few short years it had grown into a thriving community, with a wharf and boatyard, tavern, and about twenty cabins. Its sixty full-time residents made a living cutting timber or building boats—flatboats, keelboats, and broadhorns, canoes, pirogues, and barges—and enjoyed a brisk business. Boats of all description were in great demand, as the commerce of the rivers was booming as never before. Timber, coal, hemp, cotton, tobacco, livestock was floated down the rivers in great quantities. Tons of goods were moved down the mighty Mississippi each year. The vast majority of it was bound for the great port of New Orleans, and much of it began the long journey to the Crescent City on one of the tributaries of the Father of Waters—the Ohio, the Missouri, the Tennessee, or the Cumberland.

When Christopher and his party arrived at Cully's Landing, the place was bustling with activity. Another keelboat was being built, while men were loading a brand new flatboat with a cargo of tobacco and pigs. The pigs were being difficult. They refused to board the vessel of their own free will, and had broken loose, to scatter throughout the town. It appeared as though the entire population was engaged in trying to round them up. Pigs and people were scurrying hither and yon, the pigs grunting and squealing, the people cursing or laughing. Christopher safely maneuvered his wagon through this melee without running over anybody, and climbed the harness leather in front of the inn, where a burly, redheaded man was standing in the doorway, hands on hips, and shaking his head as he watched the goings-on with a jaundiced eye.

"Looks like great sport," remarked Christopher.

"Aye, that it be," agreed the man. He spoke with a heavy Scottish brogue. Squinting up at Christopher, he asked, "And who might you be, laddie?"

"My grandson," said Nathaniel, arriving with the three Elm Tree thoroughbreds in tow. "Christopher Groves. Christopher, this is Angus Culloden."

"Flintlock Jones! I've been expecting you." The innkeeper turned back to Christopher. "Friends call me Cully. I canna tell you what my enemies call me, not in the presence of a lady." As he reached up to shake Christopher's hand he smiled at Rebecca. "And who might this be, young Christopher? Your younger sister?"

"My mother."

Nathaniel chuckled. "Watch out for this one, Becky. He can charm the rattles off a rattlesnake. I don't know which one is worse—him or O'Connor."

"O'Connor!" exclaimed Cully. "Now don't be tellin' me you brought a bloody Irishman along!"

Nathaniel performed the introductions all around.

Cully sighed. "Good God, Flintlock. And I suppose you'll be wantin' me to let your Irish friend under my roof next."

"I'm sure the women could use a room. And while I cannot speak for these young men"—Nathaniel's gaze flicked guiltily in Rebecca's direction—"I could do with some of your ale."

"Ale, yes," said O'Connor enthusiastically. "Or something stronger, if you've got it."

They all dismounted. Nathaniel started for the first wagon to help Rebecca down, but Cully beat him to it.

O'Connor managed to transport Prissy, for all her bulk, from the seat of the other wagon to the ground.

"Just one room?" asked Rebecca. "What about you and the boys?"

"We'll load up the boat today and sleep on it tonight. Leave at daybreak."

"Then I will sleep on the boat, as well." She looked past him, at the broadhorn moored to the nearby wharf.

Seeing the look on her face made Nathaniel crack a smile.

"She's a well-built craft, Becky. About sixty feet in the beam, eighteen feet amidships, and she only draws four feet. That cargo box in the middle is large enough to store all the furniture, with room enough to spare for you and Prissy. We'll secure the horses in the steerage. The boys and I will make do bedding down on deck."

"You sound like an old mariner, Father, like you know all about boats."

"I don't know much," confessed the frontiersman. "And though I am old, I'm quick to learn."

"But I don't require the luxury of a room."

"Won't be much luxury in a Scottish inn," joked O'Connor, who had overheard.

"Becky," said Nathaniel, "enjoy your last night on solid ground in Cully's inn. By morning the boys and I will have everything in place on the boat. I can vouch for Cully's rooms. They're clean, and the beds are comfortable."

After two whole days in a wagon, Rebecca's body was a solid mass of aches and pains. She gave in to his persistence with a rueful smile. "I have to admit, a nice comfortable bed sounds wonderful. I must be getting old."

Nathaniel laughed. "You're still a very attractive woman, Daughter. I can see I'm going to have to beat the men off you with a stick. I've already got Cully and O'Connor to watch for."

"Don't be silly. O'Connor's just a boy. And it's all idle flattery, anyway."

"You'll see. Especially when we get to Texas. From what I hear, there aren't enough women to go around down there."

Rebecca shook her head. "I'll never marry again," she said, and sounded quite adamant.

Nathaniel dropped the subject and took her inside.

Cully's inn was a two-story log building, built to last, with the first floor given over to Cully's quarters and the common room. The latter reminded Nathaniel of his father's inn at Louisa, Virginia. The sights and sounds and smells triggered boyhood memories.

They were provided with a good meal—ham, stew, spoonbread, and fresh summer vegetables. Cully was a widower. His wife and two sons had perished eight years ago, victims of a cholera epidemic. He employed a young woman to cook and clean.

After dinner, Nathaniel sold the wagons and mules to Cully, who counted on turning a quick profit by selling the lot to the lumber crews. Business concluded, the Scotsman broke out his bagpipes and regaled the women with some lively tunes from his homeland, while Nathaniel, Christopher, and O'Connor went to work transferring the furniture and provisions from the wagons to the broadhorn. They took the horses aboard, too, the three Elm Tree thoroughbreds as well as Nathaniel's.

"There is no shortage of thieves in these parts, I'm sorry to say," the Scotsman told them, "and those splendid animals of yours will draw many a covetous eye. I would strongly suggest you take turns standing guard—and continue to do so until you reach New Orleans."

"Will it be any better there?" wondered Nathaniel, who thought of big cities as cesspools of iniquity.

"You have a point, Flintlock. Probably worse."

Leaving O'Connor to watch the boat and their belongings, Nathaniel and Christopher returned to the inn.

Night was falling, and purple shadows had gathered beneath the trees. The town of Cully's Landing was quiet. The boat builders and lumberjacks had called it a day. The errant pigs had been rounded up. And Cully was no longer playing his bagpipe.

They found that Rebecca and Prissy had already gone upstairs to their room. Christopher went up to say good night. Nathaniel purchased a jug of corn liquor from Cully. He and Christopher were about to return to the broadhorn when a sudden commotion in the street drew their attention. Before they could go to investigate, a man burst into the common room, his face flush with excitement.

"Klesko stole a pig, Cully, and now they're talkin' about hangin' him for it!"

With that he was gone.

"Good God," breathed Cully. He reached for a rifle hanging above the fireplace and turned to Nathaniel and Christopher. "If you're of a mind to, I could use your help to save a man's life."

He did not linger long for an answer, disappearing into the night.

There were people out in the street, all of them running in the direction of the river, mostly men, with a few women and children among them, dogs yapping at heels, some of the men carrying lanterns to light their way. A babble of excitement rose from this stream of humanity. Cully plunged into the stream, wearing an expression of grim resolve. Nathaniel and Christopher followed him.

Down near the wharf, a crowd had collected, and Cully shouldered his way through the press toward the water's edge, where angry voices were raised. Emerging from the crowd in the wake of the innkeeper, Christopher paused to take in the scene.

Three men were holding one of the biggest characters

he had ever seen. One was gripping the Goliath's left arm, another his right, and the third had an arm locked around his neck from behind. Christopher assumed their prisoner was the pig stealer named Klesko. Klesko wasn't fat, just big. Barrel-chested, bull-necked, his arms bulged with muscles, his legs as stout as the trunks of full-grown oak trees, and just about as solid. His hands were the size of hams. He wore a torn and dirty linsey-woolsey shirt and ragged dungarees that ended in tatters at the knees. His feet and head were bare; his hair was long and matted and black as the ace of spades, like his beard, which so covered his face that Christopher could see little else besides a bulbous nose, obviously broken more than once, and blazing blue eyes so dark they looked black.

He wasn't trying to escape, exactly—had he tried he would have tossed his three captors around as though they were rag dolls. Of this Christopher had no doubt. But he was standing rigidly, legs braced apart, head raised in a defiant pose, and shouting at the top of his lungs. Christopher wondered if he was drunk. Yet his stentorian voice was quite clear, the words not the least bit slurred.

"Cast your eyes on me, boys! You know who I am? I'm the original, brass-mounted, copper-bellied corpse-maker of the Cumberland!"

"You're a windbag and a thief," said someone in the crowd.

The Goliath seemed not to hear. "I'm the bloodiest son of a wildcat you'll ever see," he declared. "My mama was an earthquake and my papa was a hurricane. I'll have a dozen alligators and a barrel of corn liquor for breakfast—and that's when I'm not hungry."

"I'll believe the corn liquor part," said another, and the crowd laughed.

"Stand back! Stand back and give me some elbow

room. Blood's my favorite drink and the wails of the dyin' is my favorite music."

As he spoke, the Goliath shook his head and glowered fiercely about him, and moved his arms up and down, seeming unaware of the fact that two strong men were attached to those limbs.

"Better get some rope and tie him up," growled the man who had Klesko by the throat.

"Rope hell!" gasped the man clinging for dear life to Klesko's right arm. "Somebody fetch some iron chain!"

"Bow your heads and say a prayer if you know one!" boomed Klesko. "The massacre of entire communities is my favorite pastime."

"Next to stealing pigs," said someone with a laugh.

"Where's the pig?" cried a man who stood facing Klesko, his face congested with anger, his fists clenched.

"Klesko cooked it," said the man dangling from Klesko's left arm. "He'd already done et most of it by the time we seen his campfire back up in them woods yonder and found him."

"Ate it!" cried the man. "That was one of my best sows. You know how much I could have got for that sow down in New Orleans? You damned thief!" he snarled at Klesko. "I say hang him. Hang the thief!"

Klesko just glared at him. He didn't seem to comprehend what was happening. "My heart's as hard as petrified wood. My bowels are made from boiler iron. I'm a child of calamity, and when I raise my voice I still the thunder. I comb my hair with bolts of lightning, and I've been known to drink large rivers dry when I've worked up a thirst."

"Hang him and be done with it," someone said.

"Hold on," said Cully, stepping into the center of the circle. "You canna hang a man for stealing a pig."

"You'd hang him for stealing a horse, wouldn't you?" asked the owner of the dead sow. "What's the difference?"

"No, I wouldna hang him for stealing a flaming horse, either. I wouldna take a man's life unless he was a murderer."

"He murdered this feller's pig," said one of the wits in the crowd, and several men laughed.

"This is no laughing matter," scolded Cully.

"Klesko stole my axe."

"Yeah, and he stole some of my chickens."

"My dog turned up missing a fortnight ago. I'd bet Klesko stole him and ate him. I declare, he'll eat anything that ain't been dead too long."

"A lot of things have turned up missing since he started hanging around here. He's a no-good thief."

"This is a bloody nonsense," said Cully. "You canna hang a man like this, without a fair trial, not in this country. That's the kind of rough justice many of us sailed across the flamin' ocean to escape."

"Why are you defending Klesko, Cully?"

"Yeah. Klesko don't mean nothing to you."

"No, by God, I hardly know the beggar from Adam. But he's an American, and he deserves a trial by a jury of his peers. He's guaranteed as much by the bloody Bill of Rights, isn't he?"

Christopher admired Cully's determination to stand up for what he thought was right. Clearly he was the last person who would want Cully's Landing to get a reputation as a den of cutthroats and thieves. A reputation like that could destroy a town, and could easily be created by a relatively harmless man like Klesko. The Scotsman's argument seemed to work on some of the spectators, but the majority still cried out for Klesko's blood.

It was then that Nathaniel intervened. He stepped forward, placing himself shoulder-to-shoulder with Cully.

"There'll be no hanging today," he said.

"Who are you?"

"What gives you the right . . . ?"

"This is Flintlock Jones," said Cully.

The effect of the name on the crowd was instantaneous. Everyone fell silent, as though struck dumb by an act of God. Christopher was astonished. He scanned the faces by the light of the lanterns some of the men held aloft. They looked to him as he imagined the people of ancient Greece might have when they chanced to gaze upon Zeus or Apollo or some other deity down from Olympus. They looked at the rifle in Nathaniel's hands, too, knowing what wonders he had wrought with the weapon. Here was a living legend, standing up for Klesko, and none of them were willing to go against him.

"Take him to the inn and lock him in the cellar," Cully told the men who were holding Klesko.

"This is an outrage!" cried the owner of the dead sow. "What about my losses?"

"Well," said Cully, with a smile. "You could stay here with us for a spell, Mr. Krueger, until the circuit judge comes around. I'm certain he'll make some kind of arrangement for restitution. Of course, it might be weeks before we see the gentleman again."

"Weeks? I can't wait weeks. My boat is loaded. My son and I have got to get down the river."

"Then perhaps you will be so kind as to tell me where I could send the money, if restitution is ordered."

"If? Is there any question? Wasn't that my sow? Isn't it dead?"

Unruffled, Cully said, "Fine. *When* restitution is made. Does that sound better to your ear?"

Krueger snorted. "And I'm to trust you? This whole town is a nest of thieves, if you ask me."

Christopher thought he could actually hear Cully's teeth grinding together as the Scotsman, by an astonishing act of will, kept his temper in check. "Perhaps it would be better if you got started on your journey right away, Mr. Krueger," he said, frosty with cordiality.

Krueger glowered at the innkeeper, then looked to

Nathaniel. His expression changed when he saw the old leatherstocking. He turned abruptly and stalked away.

Klesko's three captors were hustling their prisoner to the inn, and the crowd began to disperse. Watching them go, Cully mournfully shook his head.

"They're not bad people, Flintlock. But even good people, when they become a mob, seem to lose their common sense. They might have hanged Klesko in the heat of the moment. As a lark, you might say. And when they woke in the morning they would have felt flamin' bad aboot it."

"You saved them from themselves, Cully."

"I think you had a lot to do with it. Your name carries a lot of clout in these parts."

"What will become of Klesko?" asked Christopher.

"He's rough around the edges, and, yes, a bit light-fingered. A river rat. Can't seem to hold a job. Been in these parts for several months. Lives by himself in the woods. He's not a bad sort, really. Down on his luck, is all."

"Will he get a fair trial?"

"I doot it," said the Scotsman. "He's not well-liked here, as you might have noticed. I'm sure he's stolen a few things, though not half of what he's been accused of stealing. But he's an outsider, a loner. He won't hang, but I wager he'll spend a good bit of time languishing under lock and key once the circuit judge gets through with him."

"Does he know the river?" asked Christopher.

"Aye. He's an old keelboat man, I'm told."

"We could take him with us, Grandpa. We could use another man, especially one who knows the river."

"I'm not sure your mother would approve."

"I'll take care of that. What do you think?"

Nathaniel shrugged, turned to Cully. "Do you think he would agree to come with us?"

Cully grinned. He thought Christopher's solution to

the problem was an excellent one. "I'll see to it. Leave everything to me. After all, what are his options?"

The next morning they got under way early, in the pearl gray light of dawn. Nathaniel took the helm, while O'Connor and Christopher used the long poles to guide the broadhorn into the deep channel. In a little while Rebecca and Prissy emerged from the cargo box and moved forward, planning to sit there in the cool of the morning and take in the scenery. Both of them were captured by the novelty of traveling on a river. There was no place to sit aft of the cargo box, for there the four horses were secured. Having spent the night on board, the horses were quick to accustom themselves to the pitch and roll of the boat. But when Prissy let out a shriek, the animals spooked, and if they hadn't been firmly tethered Nathaniel figured they would have gone right over the side.

Lashing the rudder in place, the frontiersman moved forward. O'Connor and Christopher were already there, trying not to laugh. Most of their provisions were lashed down in the front of the broadhorn and covered by canvas tarpaulins stripped from the wagons they had sold to Cully. Prissy had settled her considerable bulk on what she assumed were some sacks of grain for the horses. But it was Klesko, not grain sacks, and he was struggling to crawl out from under the canvas—no easy task with his hands tied behind his back. Though gagged, he managed to growl like a bear rudely awakened from its winter hibernation. Eyes wide as saucers, Prissy cast about for something with which to defend herself. She discovered a tree axe, and advanced on Klesko, weapon raised. Christopher was the first to reach her. He wrestled the axe away from her before any damage was done.

"Don't kill him, Prissy," he said, laughing. "We went to a lot of trouble to smuggle him aboard without the folks back at Cully's Landing knowing."

"Who is he?" asked Rebecca.

Christopher told her the whole story, explaining how in the night they had taken Klesko from Cully's cellar and secreted him aboard the broadhorn. The Scots innkeeper had been their willing accomplice.

"And why didn't you inform me this morning?" asked Rebecca.

Christopher wasn't laughing any longer. "Well, to tell you the truth, Mother, we weren't sure you would approve. I was going to tell you, after we'd gone a few miles."

"A few miles too far to turn back."

"Something like that," he said sheepishly.

Nathaniel helped Klesko to his feet and used a hunting knife to cut the rope which bound the river man at ankles and wrist. They had deemed it the wiser course to leave him in that condition until they were well under way. Nathaniel stepped back, wary, not knowing what to expect from Klesko, now that he was untied. But Klesko just sat there, pulling the gag away from his mouth, and squinting at each of them in turn. His gaze finally came to rest on Nathaniel.

"I've been shanghaied," he said.

"Better than getting hanged, don't you think?"

"Where are we going?"

"We're bound for Texas."

"They got any rivers in Texas?"

"That's what I hear."

Klesko simply nodded.

"But you can go your own way once we reach New Orleans."

"What if I don't want to go to New Orleans?"

"Do you remember anything from last night?"

Klesko scratched his jaw, digging under the tangled mat of his rust-colored beard. "Not much."

"Had too much to drink, didn't you?"

Klesko grunted. "A man cain't never have too much to drink."

"Well, they were going to hang you. You stole another man's pig, and ate it. If you don't want to go to New Orleans, we'll just take you back to Cully's Landing, and your comeuppance."

Klesko looked the frontiersman over, then studied O'Connor and Christopher, and Nathaniel began to think the riverman was going to try all three of them on for size. But Klesko didn't make a move.

"Reckon you folks did me a good turn," he said. "So I'll go along. But only as far as Natchez."

"Fair enough."

Klesko turned his dark gaze on Rebecca. "Who's she?"

"My mother," said Christopher.

"And my daughter," added Nathaniel.

Klesko grunted again. He stood up. Rebecca had to crane her neck to look up at him. She decided he had to stand at least six feet six. He was the biggest man she had ever seen.

"River's no place for a woman," he muttered.

Taking a pole from O'Connor, he went to work.

Chapter 16

They were all quite impressed by the Cumberland—it seemed to them a mighty and magnificent stream—all except Klesko, who laughed at them as they expressed admiration for the river. He told them it didn't hold a candle to the Mississippi, but they couldn't imagine how a river could be any wider or deeper or faster. So they were in for a rude awakening when, eight days later, they reached the Father of Waters.

Christopher was truly amazed. The Mississippi was a mile wide where the Cumberland emptied into her. He assumed this to be an abnormality, but in the days to come he would discover that the river *averaged* a mile width at high water until one got much closer to the Gulf of Mexico, where, strangely enough, she became more narrow.

He had read all about this river during his sojourn at West Point. He had learned that she was over four thousand miles long, the longest river in the world. It discharged three hundred times more water than the Thames River, of which the British were so proud. The area of its drainage basin was so immense that the countries of Turkey, Portugal, Spain, Italy, France, Austria, Germany, Ireland, Scotland, Wales, and England could be fitted into that space with room to spare.

The Mississippi was notorious for changing its course, cutting through necks of land almost at whim, to the point that geographers now claimed the entire thirteen hundred miles of the river explored by La Salle a hundred and fifty years ago was today dry land. More than once a town built on the east bank of the Mississippi awoke one morning to find itself on the west side, or a mile away from the river.

It had been known by many names. Indians called it Sasseguola, Tamalisen, Chuagua, Meast Chassipi, depending on the tribe. From the Chippewa's Mescesipi came its current name. The Spaniards knew it as the Río Escondido—the Hidden River—or the River of the Holy Ghost. The French had labeled it the River of the Immaculate Conception on their maps. Then, too, folks called it Old Man River sometimes, or the Devil of Rivers, if they happened to meet with some mishap because of it.

They were not alone on the river—there was tremendous commerce, much of it in keelboats and broadhorns. In the old days the keelboat men had carried cargo down to New Orleans—the goods produced by settlers from Ohio and Kentucky and Tennessee—and poled back up the river with manufactured products in high demand on the frontier: fabrics, furniture, sugar, and other luxuries. In those days, men like Klesko had ruled the river.

In 1807, when Robert Fulton designed the first steamboat, life on the river was drastically changed. Four years later, the paddlewheeler *New Orleans* made her first trip down the Mississippi. In spite of the great earthquake of that year, which occurred during the maiden voyage, and which demolished the river town of New Madrid and completely altered the course of the river, the trip was a tremendous success. In 1814, the *Enterprise* became the first steam-powered vessel to make an *upstream* trip. Several other boats had tried it, and failed because they lacked sufficient power to overcome the mighty currents. Two years later, a radically new steamboat design was made reality with the launching of the *Washington*. This vessel sported two independent steam engines and had a very shallow draft. The reign of the keelboat was almost over. Nowadays, keelboats were still sometimes used to transport goods downriver. Men like Krueger would sell their pigs and tobacco in New Orleans, and then sell their boats, too, for scrap lumber, before catching the next steamboat bound upriver.

Christopher got a good look at some of these "floating palaces." They were spectacular. Long and trim and gleaming with paint, two tall chimneys with crowns of metal plumes, fancy pilothouse atop the texas deck, a picture or gilded sun rays embellishing the vessel's name on the paddle boxes, all three decks—the texas, the boiler, and the hurricane—adorned with whitewashed ornamental railings and garnished with elegant wood filigree.

Men like Krueger journeyed upriver with their pockets full of money, having sold their goods in New Orleans for top dollar, and the steamboat owners were dedicated to the proposition that such men should part with some, if not all, of that money. In their saloons one could dine on the finest china, with the light from crystal chandeliers gleaming off the best silver service money could buy. (Rumor had it that on some of the steamboats the china was never washed; used once, it was tossed over the side.) One could sample the finest liquors, or try one's luck at the gaming tables. Many were the poor souls who succumbed to such gilded temptations, only to arrive home without two coins to rub together, wiser if poorer, having spent the money needed for seed or flour or curtains on the windows or the wife's new dress.

Christopher got the chance to tour one of the steamboats. While the broadhorn was tied up at the wharf of some sleepy nameless village on the Missouri side of the river, the cry "Steamboat a-comin'!" pierced the sultry summer somnolence of the place. From every home and business establishment emerged the locals, to rush down the river, coming from every quarter to crowd the wharf, from whence they could watch the show.

And what a show it was! The steamboat's engineers tossed pitch pine into the boiler furnaces to produce dense black smoke, which rose in great pillars from the chimneys. Up on the texas deck the pilot's cub rang the ship's big brass bell for all he was worth, while the pilot tugged on a rope, and steam shrieked as it escaped the gauge cocks. Upon the captain's orders the wheels were thrown into reverse, and the river foamed as the vessel slid neatly into place alongside the dock. As the crowd of spectators cheered, deckhands ran out the gangplanks, down which cavorted a minstrel group, clad in red-and-white jackets and straw hats and playing a merry tune on banjo and accordian and French harp. When the number was over, the captain invited one and all to come aboard and see with their own eyes the splendor of his ship. Christopher and O'Connor and Rebecca seized the opportunity, while Nathaniel stayed aboard the broadhorn with Klesko and Prissy.

Christopher marveled at the opulence of the saloons, with their velvet draperies and velvet-upholstered furnishings, Persian rugs underfoot, brocaded walls adorned with mirrors in ornate gilded frames. The cabins were cocoons of elegance, with soft carpet wall to wall, goosedown pillows and mattresses on the narrow bunks, oil paintings on the walls, and porcelain knobs on the doors.

"If this boat is bound for New Orleans, I think you should book passage on it," Christopher told his mother. "We can afford it."

"We most certainly cannot."

"But, Mother, all the money you got for the thoroughbreds, and your furniture . . ."

"We will need every bit of it once we reach Texas."

"They say that the five hundred miles of river between here and Natchez are the most dangerous of all."

"Steamboats are dangerous, too. Klesko says their boilers are always exploding. A month doesn't go by that one of them doesn't blow up and send all its passengers to the bottom."

"Klesko! He's an old keelboat man, with a keelboat man's prejudices."

"Nonetheless, I refuse to do as you suggest. If the rest of my family is going to New Orleans on a broadhorn, than I will, too."

Christopher didn't waste his breath arguing. He recognized his mother's tone of voice only too well. It meant the discussion was over, and her mind was made up.

To attend to the steamboats, carrying the fuel the packets required, great coal barges and timber rafts plied the river. Christopher lost track of all the boats he saw, from pirogues to paddlewheel steamers. They numbered in the scores during his eleven hundred miles on the Mississippi. Still, the river always seemed serenely empty.

Klesko proved to be worth his weight in gold. He knew the river, knew it like the back of his hand, knew it despite the fact that the river was continually changing, moving its main channel, throwing up new hazards, and disguising them so cleverly one might wonder whether the river had a diabolical mind of its own. But the river couldn't fool Klesko, try as it might. He would gaze at the water up ahead and read the river like a scholar reads a book.

He was happy to share his knowledge with Christopher, who had a young man's eagerness to learn something new. Where someone unversed in the wiles of the river saw only a long slanting line on the sparkling surface, Christopher was taught to identify the line as the telltale mark betraying the presence of a bluff reef, a solid sandbar which could easily "kill" a boat. The head of the reef, where a crossing could be made safely, was identifiable by locating in the line the place where the water took on a ruffled look. Where the surface was boiling, Christopher learned that a dissolving reef lurked, and the river was in the process of altering its channel. Where the surface was very smooth and covered with radiating circles, a potentially dangerous shoal was fast developing.

"You must know the banks of the river," said Klesko. "They will tell you how to run your boat further downstream. For instance, how high would you judge the western bank yonder to be?"

"How do I know?" asked Christopher. "It's a half mile away, if it's an inch."

Klesko shook his head. "You're a tad young to be needin' spectacles."

"I don't need spectacles! There's nothing wrong with my eyesight."

"Must be something wrong, because you cain't tell how high yonder bank stands above the danged river."

"And you can?"

"Course I can. That's a six-foot bank. Last year about this time it was nine feet high. Now what does that tell you?"

"The river is running high for this time of year."

"Is she rising or falling?"

"Rising. There's a lot of driftwood about."

Klesko nodded. "The river has risen, on account of that rain we had last week. But you'll see driftwood awhile after the river's stopped risin'. She's fallin' now. You can see the high watermark on the bank."

"I can scarcely *see* the bank," said Christopher, thoroughly disgusted, and squinting so hard his eyes hurt.

"Surely you can see that point up ahead. See the cypress on the tip? The water is just over the knees. Make a note of that, boy. That's mighty all-fired important. It tells me there's eight feet of water in the chute down yonder at Cat Island."

"Cat Island?" Christopher saw no island downriver. "Where is that?"

"We'll pass it in the morning."

"You mean to tell me that by looking at those cypress trees you can calculate how much water there is in a chute thirty miles downstream?"

"Now you're gettin' the hang of it," said Klesko, pleased with his pupil's progress. "You don't ordinarily run chutes with the river fallin' unless you're just plain tired of livin'. But we'll have just enough water to do her in the morning."

"I see," said Christopher dubiously.

"Good. You must know the river, boy. You got to learn to read the banks. There'll be half a hundred chutes twixt us and New Orleans, and if the river rises a foot from where it is now we'll be able to run ten of 'em. Rises another foot, and we'll take another ten without breakin' a sweat. But if she falls another foot, there aren't six we'll be able to take, and you've got to know, and be dead certain of your facts, on account of that once you start through a chute there ain't no turnin' back, and if you get caught you might as well start clearin' and plowin' right there, 'cause you could be stuck there till winter."

The river's beauty did not fail to impress Christopher. On both sides the river was hemmed in by unbroken forest, with an occasional opening where some hardy soul had carved out a clearing for his cabin. In the mornings a dense fog often clung to the river like cotton, dissipating slowly as the sun rose. But dusk was his favorite time, when the river turned blood red, then gold in the middle distance, and finally indigo blue at its furthest reaches.

They did not travel at night, opting instead to secure the broadhorn to shore in a likely looking place. The river was entirely too perilous at night. Many a small craft had been rammed and sunk by steamboats, and of

course not even Klesko could "read" the river in the
dark. The horses were taken ashore and allowed to graze
on a long tether. If there was some daylight yet lingering,
Nathaniel would go hunting. Sometimes Christopher or
O'Connor would accompany him. Shortly after dinner
everyone would turn in, exhausted from a long day's
labors, and knowing that at first light they would be
riding the river again.

As their twelfth day on the Mississippi drew to a close,
they put to shore on the near side of a wooded point.
After supper, Christopher checked on the horses. He
was shocked to discover that one of the thoroughbred
mares had slipped its tether, and he hurried back to
camp to inform the others.

"I'll find her," he promised, taking up his rifle.

"You ought not to go alone into these woods after
dark," admonished Rebecca.

"I'll go with you," said O'Connor, rising from his
place at the campfire.

"It's my fault she's gone," said Christopher. He was
upset with himself, and spoke brusquely. "I tethered the
horses. Napoleon said that for every major defeat there
is a major culprit, and in this case it's me. She can't have
wandered far. I don't need any help."

Rebecca threw a worried glance at Nathaniel.

"He'll be fine," said the frontiersman, adding another
chunk of wood to the blaze. "He knows to fire a shot if
he gets into trouble."

Christopher realized early on in his search that he
would have to rely on his ears to lead him to the errant
thoroughbred. Moonrise was an hour away, and it was
so dark in the woods he could scarcely see his hand in
front of his face. The underbrush was devilishly thick,
and he couldn't help but make a lot of noise passing
through it. But he figured that applied to the mare, too.

Before long he thought he heard the horse, and

worked his way in the direction of the sound, pausing often to listen for another so as to get his bearings. But he didn't hear anything else for a while except for the sawing of the locusts and the murmur of the great river. When he reached what he thought was the general vicinity of that first sound he waited for a long time, thoroughly frustrated, before hearing another—a rustling sound, a large creature blundering through the brush— and now it was far off to his left. *This is impossible,* he thought, but he refused to turn back, to give up. He had told the others in no uncertain terms that he didn't need help in finding the wayward horse, and by God he was going to do it himself if the task took all night.

So, swearing under his breath, he struggled to make his way through the brush that tore at his clothes, stumbling over exposed roots and into holes, making for the sound, and when he got there he heard something crashing through the brush straight ahead, so close it startled him, but still he couldn't see anything. Resigned by now to chasing the damned invisible horse through the woods until dawn, he plunged ahead. It occurred to him, belatedly, that maybe it wasn't the mare he was chasing, but a bear or panther. He could still hear the river to his left, and took some consolation from the knowledge that at least he would be able to find his way back to the broadhorn as long as he knew where the river was. *Of course, I might be halfway to Natchez by daybreak.*

A little while later he saw the flicker of torches up ahead through the trees and, very faintly, voices raised. Curious, he moved closer, assuming that other river travelers had camped on the western bank. He calculated that he was well south of the wooded point, which explained why these torches were not visible from the spot where the broadhorn was moored. How far had he come from his own camp? At least half a mile, perhaps more.

As he drew nearer he saw a flatboat run up on shore in a shallow inlet ringed by cypress trees festooned with

Spanish moss. One of the trees was festooned with something else—a man, hanging upside down, tied at the ankles. He was stripped naked, and two men were torturing him, jabbing at his face, groin, buttocks, and feet with their torches. All the hair had been singed off the man's face, which was transformed into a charred, grotesque mask. The man writhed each time the flames seared his flesh. Terrible grunting sounds emerged from his ruined mouth.

A hideous scream set every one of Christopher's already frayed nerve endings aflame. Looking in the direction of the sound, he saw another pair of men, one holding a pig, the other cutting the animal's throat. Here and there lay several more pigs, each being butchered by another man. And there—there on the bank near the flatboat, lay a young boy, dead.

Christopher realized then that the man being tortured had to be Krueger, the farmer he had met at Cully's Landing, the one who was taking a cargo of tobacco and pigs downriver to sell. Yes, it was Krueger, though even his own mother wouldn't recognize him now. And the dead boy was his son, age fifteen.

River pirates!

Christopher's blood ran cold. His first, almost overwhelming impulse was to run. He had to warn the others. Yet he hesitated—feeling as though it was wrong to leave Krueger like this. But what could he do? He counted eleven pirates—there were others on the flatboat, looking for loot. They were a rough-looking lot, too. Bearded, filthy, armed to the teeth. Human vultures. Sadistic bastards. Why were they torturing Krueger? Why didn't they just kill him and be done with it? Christopher looked at the rifle in his hands. One shot, an act of mercy, and then he could run for it. The pirates would never find him in the night-shrouded woods. But he was scared. He had never been so scared in his life. The sheer brutality of these men shook him to the core.

One of the pirates left the flatboat and approached the two who were taking such delight in torturing Krueger.

"We can't find anything on the boat," he said. "Has he told you anything?"

"I don't think he's got no gold or bank notes stashed, Mr. Morrell."

Morrell. The name sent electric jolts of fear through Christopher. The King of the River Pirates himself. The Reverend Devil in the flesh!

Morrell squatted in front of Krueger and studied what was left of the man's face.

"You've ruined his mouth. He couldn't tell you anything if he wanted to."

"He was cussin' us," said one of the torturers. "So Frenchy stuck the torch in his mouth."

"You're a damned idiot, Frenchy," said Morrell. He rose and turned away, saying, "Kill him."

The one named Frenchy took a cane knife from his belt and cut Krueger open from scrotum to sternum.

Christopher shut his eyes to the grisly scene.

Something came crashing through the brush behind him. With a strangled cry, Christopher rolled over and triggered the rifle, shooting blindly. He glimpsed one of Krueger's pigs in the muzzle flash. The pig shrieked and fell, shot through the head.

Christopher scrambled to his feet and ran for his life.

Over the rasping of the breath in his throat and the pounding of blood in his ears he heard the shouts of the river pirates. Plunging through the woods, he didn't look back, running for all he was worth, falling several times, and the last time he fell twisting his ankle on a root, so that when he stood and tried to put his weight on the ankle it gave way, and he went down again, despair clutching at his heart. He listened hard, trying to subdue his own hard breathing so that he could hear something.

But there was nothing to hear. The woods were quiet. Christopher dared to hope that the river pirates had given up the pursuit. In fact, he couldn't be certain they had come after him at all. Maybe the rifle shot had sent them packing.

Christopher tenderly felt his ankle. It was already swelling. He lurched to his feet and tried to use his rifle as a crutch. He hobbled a few more yards, then realized he could no longer hear the murmur of the river. Panic gripped him. He was lost! Why was the night so dark? A moment later, for the first time, he heard thunder, distant rolling thunder, and he knew there would be no moon tonight. Which way to go? If he chose wrongly . . .

But he couldn't stay put and wait for dawn. He had to warn the others. Had they heard the rifle shot? If so, they were probably out looking for him. What if they ran into the pirates instead? No, he couldn't sit still and wait out the night. He had to keep moving.

He had gone another fifty yards, slow and painful going, when he heard something rustling in the brush. Another one of Krueger's pigs? That damned mare? Nathaniel? One of Morrell's cutthroats? Christopher froze, waiting with bated breath, straining his eyes in a futile attempt to see in the pitch black night.

The shadows seemed to move—he saw the movement out of the corner of his eye, and turned just as something very hard and heavy hit him in the back of the head. White light exploded behind his eyes and he fell. Semiconscious, he groped for the pistol in his belt. Then he caught a glimpse of a leering, bearded face with yellow teeth, saw the club rise and fall, and in another bright flash of pain he was gone.

Chapter 17

When he came to, Christopher did not understand at first what had happened to him. A moment passed before his vision cleared, and the first thing he saw was the chest and forelegs of a horse—upside down. It took him a moment to come to the realization that he was the one who was upside down, not the horse. Lifting his head, he saw that his hands and feet were bound, wrists and ankles lashed so tightly that he had lost all feeling in his extremities. He was tied to a pole which was secured at either end to the saddles of two men on horseback. His last conscious thought was that it was morning—then he passed out again.

Regaining consciousness a second time, he found himself bound to a stout pole, his hands tied to an iron ring at the top of the post. It was early in the afternoon—the sun was blazing down from a burnished sky. His head felt as though it were going to explode. He was naked, and his flesh was not only painfully scorched by the sun, but further tormented by the bite of ants and the sting of mosquitoes.

A village stood before him—a collection of ramshackle hovels, erected in no apparent order. There were no streets, no rhyme or reason to the place at all. A few scraggly trees, and beyond the shacks lay the canebrake, an impenetrable wall of cane standing ten feet high, and seeming to stretch on into infinity. The trees marked the progress of a turgid stream. He assumed that this water source was one of the main reasons the village had been located here.

As for the denizens of this filthy, desolate, godforsaken place—they were everywhere. Christopher had never in his life seen such a motley crew. Dirty, naked children played in the dirt between the shanties. Women washed clothes in the stream, or toiled over cookfires built out in front of their hovels. Twenty or so men were collected in the space between two shacks. By the sound of it, a game of chance was under way. Suddenly, voices soared in anger, curses were flung, and the crowd parted as two men locked in hand-to-hand combat, knives flashing in the sunlight, rolled across the hardpack. No one attempted to intervene. On the contrary, the others cheered the combatants on, and hasty wagers were made as to the eventual winner of the struggle.

The fight was of short duration. A blade struck deep. Blood spewed in a scarlet geyser from a slashed throat and the dying man's bootheels drummed against the earth. The victor rose and spat upon his victim before returning to the game. Another man nudged the corpse experimentally with the toe of his boot. Apparently satisfied that no life remained, he proceeded to relieve the dead man of his boots. Several more men took their cue and descended like vultures on their recently departed colleague. In a matter of minutes the corpse had been stripped clean. The carcass was left to lie in the dust. A yellow cur dog wandered over to sniff it, then went on its way.

Staring at the corpse, Christopher was struck by the enormity of his predicament. He was a prisoner of river pirates in their lair, and if there was such a place as a hell on earth this must surely be it. Here he would die. Of that he was already firmly convinced. It was just a matter of time, in a place where life was so cheap. He would never see his mother or Nathaniel—or Greta—again.

Two questions plagued him. Why was he still alive? And had his mother and the rest of his party escaped the clutches of these fiends?

It struck him as singularly odd that no one was paying him the slightest attention—and just as this occurred to him he let out a hoarse yowl of pain as he was stuck from behind without warning, the sharpened end of a stick thrust into his back near the kidney, hard enough to pierce his flesh and draw blood. A grimy-faced boy of ten or eleven years danced around the post, yipping in delight, brandishing the stick. When he jabbed at Christopher's groin, Christopher lashed out with a foot and kicked him head over heels into the dust. The boy got up and ran away, screaming as though he had been scalped.

Suddenly it seemed as though everyone in the village had stopped what they were doing to stare at him—and Christopher didn't like at all the *way* they were staring.

A woman appeared out of nowhere, running at him, yelling at the top of her lungs in Spanish. Christopher was intimately acquainted with French, thanks to his exhaustive study of that language while at West Point, but when it came to Spanish he was woefully ignorant. But he surmised that the woman was furious, and when she paused thirty feet away to pick up a stone and hurl it at him he knew who she was mad at. He assumed that the boy he had kicked belonged to her. The stone glanced off the point of his shoulder. She looked around for another weapon. Seeing a pile of firewood, she snatched up a piece as big around as Christopher's forearm and started for him.

In no mood to endure more pain, Christopher yelled at her to keep her distance. But she didn't understand, or wouldn't listen, and kept coming. He kicked at her— his only defense—but she was quick, agile, and she eluded him, managed to hit him just above the knee with the stick. She circled around behind the post and landed a few more blows. A crowd was gathering, moving in closer to form a ring around the post to which Christopher was helplessly lashed, and they thought it was great sport, and cheered the woman on.

A blow to the head sent bright lights dancing across Christopher's eys, and he sagged, head lolling forward on his chest. He wasn't unconscious, but pretended to be, hoping that by playing possum he would escape further punishment. But the wrathful woman wasn't satisfied. She came around in front of him and raised the stick. He lashed out in desperation with a foot and kicked her squarely in the face, and she went down. The crowd cheered, thinking he had been intentionally devious, concocting a ruse to lure her into range, and they appreciated cunning subterfuge. Stunned, the woman lay in the dirt, drooling blood. When she raised her head to look up at Christopher there was such naked malice in her eyes that he knew she was going to kill him if she could.

Pouncing to her feet, she spat a mouthful of blood at Christopher. Then she grabbed a knife from the belt of a man who stood nearby, acting so swiftly that he had no chance to stop her. Turning on Christopher, she muttered something that he was certain was no compliment. The crowd fell silent, smiles frozen in place. Christopher thought, *She's going to cut me open, like these pirates did to Krueger. What a way to die. What a place to die.*

And, oddly, he wondered what Greta Inskilling was doing at this moment—the last moment of his life . . .

A man and a woman emerged from the crowd as Christopher's tormentor advanced on him, brandishing the long, wicked blade. The man lunged forward and tripped her by sticking the cane he was carrying between her legs. She fell, bounced to her feet, and whirled, still holding the knife, but when she recognized the man she shrank away, terrified, and dropped the knife as though it were hot and singed her fingers.

Christopher took a closer look at the man. It was Morrell. He hadn't recognized him at first. Down at the river Morrell had been virtually indistinguishable from the rest of the pirate crew. But today he was dressed like a real gentleman, green claw hammer coat, broad-brimmed white planter's hat, doeskin trousers tucked into high black boots. Christopher wondered what dead man Morrell had taken those clothes from.

Morrell spoke curtly to the woman in fluent Spanish. She answered him, her anger flashing again as she gestured curtly at Christopher. The man they called the Reverend Devil barked back at her, and she sulked away. Morrell scanned the press of onlookers with cold blue eyes.

"Go about your business," he said brusquely.

The crowd despersed.

Christopher got his first good look at the man who was the terror of the Mississippi River Valley. Morrell had a muscular build and stood nearly six feet tall. His hair was black and unruly. Long side-whiskers framed a square-cut face. He would not be considered handsome by even the most generous of standards—his features were too fleshy, and the nose was crooked like that of a bird of prey, and the cold blue eyes were set too close together beneath bushy black brows which formed a solid line, meeting across the bridge of the nose. There was an animal grace to his movements, and an aura of brutality. Christopher figured Morrell had to be a ruthless and violent individual to keep such a cutthroat band as this in line. He could see that they feared him, and jumped to do his bidding.

"So," said Morrell, looking Christopher over with dark amusement, "you have got some fight left in you, I see."

"Cut me loose and I'll show you."

Morrell threw back his head and laughed heartily. "Wagh! What do you think of that, Noelle?"

The woman smiled. "I think he is very brave."

"Yes, and brave men deserve to die well, don't they?"

Christopher scarcely heard Morrell's last remark. He was suddenly mesmerized by the woman named Noelle. She was striking. Tall and willowy, her flawless skin was a fetching café au lait color. She was mulatto, half-Negro and half-white, and she had been blessed with the best physical attributes of both races. Her curly hair, black as a raven's wing, was loose and unbound and fell to her shoulders. Her hazel eyes were sultry, eyes that, as the poets said, a man could drown in. Her nose was aquiline, her lips full and finely sculptured, slightly parted to reveal a glimmer of white teeth. She wore a pale yellow chemise and a layered skirt of white muslin. Her feet were bare. She wore a peculiar talisman around her neck, fashioned from pure silver, of a serpent entwined in a human skull.

She was, Christopher decided, quite simply the most beautiful and alluring woman he had ever seen—next to Greta—and the most sensuous bar none.

He was embarrassed by his nakedness. But there was nothing he could do about that, and he tried to put it out of his mind. His helplessness infuriated him. He was past the point of being scared. There wasn't a doubt in his mind that he was going to die. Once a man is resigned to his fate he can master his fear. Morrell, studying him with the curious detachment of a scientest examining a specimen, could discern this.

"What is your name, my brave friend?"

"Christopher Groves." He saw no reason to keep his identity a secret.

"Groves?" This was Noelle. "Are you from Kentucky?"

"I am."

"Do you know this man?" Morrell asked, and there was a lurid light in his eye which informed Christopher that he was jealously possessive of Noelle.

"No. But I have heard of the Groves of Kentucky. Haven't you?"

"Enlighten me, my dear."

"They are a family of wealth and influence."

"Are they indeed."

"You have me confused with someone else," said Christopher.

Morrell was watching Noelle like a hawk. "Are you suggesting that I might ransom this young man?"

Noelle shrugged, seemingly indifferent. "What you do with him is up to you. But why have you kept him alive if you did not think he might be worth something to you?"

Christopher had been wondering the same thing himself.

Morrell chuckled, cupping Noelle's chin in his hand. "You are as intelligent as you are beautiful, sweet Noelle. I like to know what a man is worth before I kill him. All this young fellow had was a rifle, a pistol, and the clothes on his back. Rather ordinary clothes, too, though the boots were handsomely made, I must say."

"Speaking of clothes," said Christopher, "I'd like mine returned."

"Unfortunately, they have found new owners." Morrell gestured at the crowd of men gathered between two shacks, where the game of chance was apparently still going on. He paid no attention to the body of the dead man fifty feet away.

"We found no money, though," continued Morrell, as though he were scolding Christopher for his empty pockets.

"Sorry to disappoint you."

"So tell me, what were you doing in the woods last night, Christopher Groves?"

He wasn't sure why, but Christopher glanced at Noelle before answering. *I have heard of the Groves of Kentucky. . . . They are a family of wealth and influence.* He was certain that there were no other Groves in Kentucky, especially influential ones. Was she merely mistaken? Or was she playing some kind of a game? She was watching him intently, but her expression was unfathomable.

It was becoming clear to him that Morrell and his river pirates were unaware of the existence of his mother and Nathaniel and the others. That was a tremendous relief to Christopher, and he was determined to keep it that way.

"I was out hunting," he said, "and got lost. By the time I got back to where my boat had been moored, they were gone."

"They?"

"The people I was with."

"How many of them are there?"

"Twenty-two," said Christopher, picking a number out of thin air.

"And they just left you behind?"

"I was more than twenty-four hours overdue. I'm sure they sent out search parties. When they couldn't find me they pushed on."

"And what were you and these men doing on the river?"

"We were going to Texas. Looking for adventure." Christopher managed a convincingly rueful smile. "We had heard there was going to be a fight down there."

"Looking for adventure," murmured Morrell. "I'd say you have found more adventure than you bargained for, Mr. Groves. Maybe you should have stayed home. So tell me. What are you worth? What would your family pay to have you back safe and more or less sound?"

Again Christopher glanced at Noelle, and again he could not read her expression.

"Nothing," he replied, "to the likes of you, Morrell."

Morrell's grin was not a pretty sigh. "We will see

about that," he snapped, and turned abruptly on his heel. "Come, Noelle."

Walking away, her arm in Morrell's, Noelle glanced over her shoulder at Christopher, an engimatic glance that left him thoroughly mystified.

He was left to hang there throughout the remainder of the day, tormented to the brink of madness by the flies, ants, and mosquitoes. When, finally, the sun went down—blessed relief for Christopher's blistered flesh— an old hag brought him a plate of food. At least he thought it was food—a thin and bitter gruel. She spoon-fed him, and said not a word during the entire process, chewing methodically on a mouthful of shag tobacco instead, occasionally expectorating a stream of yellowish brown juice. Christopher considered himself fortunate that she didn't spit on him.

It was well into the evening before the village quieted down. There was a shot fired, drunken voices raised, dogs howling, a woman's scream, several scuffles. Under cover of darkness someone came and wept over the body of the dead man fifty feet away, and then another shadowy figure appeared, and the two dragged the corpse away. Christopher had no way of marking the passage of the hours, as clouds had rolled in to blot out the stars. He told God that he could have used those clouds during the heat of the afternoon. But he didn't really think God was listening to him anymore—understandable skepticism from a man in his predicament. Eventually it began to rain, a drizzle at first, strengthening into a good strong downpour, soothing his tortured body, quenching his thirst. Christopher didn't mind it at first, as it also kept the insects away, but the rain was cold, and before very long he was shivering uncontrollably.

He did not see or even hear her approach. But suddenly and quite unexpectedly he was falling, and only as

he lay facedown in the viscous, sour-tasting mud did he
realize that he was no longer lashed to the post. He tried
to stand, but he could not push himself to his feet because his arms were numb from shoulder points to fin-
gertips, and completely useless until the circulation was
restored to them.

A cloaked figure loomed above him, then knelt to
help him up into a sitting position. Strong, limber fingers
removed the rope from his raw, blood-caked hands.

"Who are you?" gasped Christopher. A hood concealed his benefactor's face.

She looked up at him, so that he could see her
features.

Noelle!

"Why?" Christopher was too stunned by this unexpected succor to think of anything else to say.

"No time for talking now. Come. We must hurry. Can
you walk?"

"I'll do better than walk," he said, comprehending.
"I'll run."

"Here." She draped a soggy blanket around his shoulders. "It is all I could find. And this."

She handed him a pistol. Although he was fairly sure
that the powder was soaking wet by now, Christopher
did feel better with a weapon in his hand.

"I have a horse waiting. Come on."

She helped him to his feet. The blood was coursing
through his arms now, and the pain was excruciating,
but he ignored it. Clutching the blanket around him, he
followed Noelle, stumbling in the muck as they slipped
past several darkened shanties, thinking that whatever
happened he would not be taken back to that hellish
post alive. He could not endure another hour strung up
there like a side of beef.

They reached the horse. It was bridled, but there was
no saddle. Christopher took the reins and crawled onto
its back, then held out a hand to help hoist Noelle on

behind him. He knew the Mississippi had to lie to the east, and he knew which way to go now to make for the river, having marked the agonizingly slow passage of the sun across yesterday's sky.

"How far to the river?" he asked her.

"About ten miles. We mustn't waste time. Morrell will be after us with every man and dog he has. His dogs are manhunters. They have been used to track runaway slaves."

"He'll want you back more than he wants me, I'll wager."

"Yes. He has told me that he would kill me if I ever tried to leave him."

"Then why . . ."

"Later. We must go."

He kicked the horse into motion, and they plunged into the dark and dripping canebrake, following a narrow footpath. An hour later Christopher began to wonder if there was an end to the cane. Eventually they reached a strip of forest. Beyond that was a marsh. The horse could not carry them both through the bog. Christopher dismounted. The blanket tied around his waist now, he led the horse, wading through stinking black water that sometimes reached hip level. He was exhausted, weakened by his ordeal on the post, but he pressed on, reaching down deep to find the strength to go on.

Dawn's early light found them emerging from the swamp into a hilly stretch of pine barrens. Christopher listened in vain for the murmur of the river, which lay somewhere up ahead—and for the sound of pursuit from the direction whence they had come. He heard neither.

At Noelle's insistence they paused for a few minutes. She could tell he desperately needed rest, although he refused to concede as much. Hard ground had never felt so good to him. He stretched out under a tree and watched low gray wisps of cloud drifting like smoke through the tops of the pines.

Dozing off, he woke with a start and was alarmed to find that the sun was out, shooting golden shafts of light through the trees. Noelle was sitting beside him, leaning back against the trunk of the tree.

"How long did I sleep?"

"Not long. About an hour."

"An hour! Why didn't you wake me?"

"You need the rest. How do you feel?"

In fact, Christopher felt awful. His body ached from head to toe. His eyes burned, and he was light-headed.

"I feel fine," he lied.

She shook her head, her smile one of gentle reproof. "We must always be truthful with each other."

"We'd better get moving. The river can't be far now."

"And when we get there? What then?"

"I lied about those twenty men. I'm traveling with my mother and grandfather. A friend of mine named O'Connor. Then there's Klesko and Prissy."

"Your mother. That would be Rebecca Groves, wouldn't it?"

"Why, yes." Christopher was astonished. "How did you know?"

"She saved my own mother's life."

"I don't . . ."

"My mother's name was Cilla. She was a slave at a plantation called Hunter's Creek. Her master was a cruel man named Cooper. He was also my father."

Chapter 18

"Good Lord!" exclaimed Christopher.

"Now you know who I am."

"Yes. I remember your mother. I was about five years old at the time, but I remember. She was pregnant with you when she came to Elm Tree, trying to escape from Stephen Cooper."

"And your mother helped her escape. Gave her money, and told Trumbull to take her to New Orleans. Do you remember Trumbull?"

"Indeed I do." The thing Christopher remembered most of all about the Elm Tree overseer was being carried around on the big man's shoulders. In those days his father had been absent from home for months at a time, first as a representative in the Kentucky General Assembly and then as a member of the United States Congress, and Trumbull had filled a void in Christopher's early years.

"Trumbull was like a father to me," said Noelle. "He was devoted to me and to my mother. They were never lovers, but he was always there when she needed him."

"Is he still alive?"

She shook her head, and Christopher could tell she missed Trumbull terribly.

"He lost his life in a fight. A fight over me."

"I'm sorry."

"Men in the Vieux Carre naturally assume that

women such as I are ... available to become their mistresses. You have heard of the quadroons?"

Christopher confessed that he had not.

"Mothers bring their daughters to quadroon balls, to dance with young gentlemen, who are expected to make an 'arrangement' to provide for a girl if he takes a liking to her. The arrangement includes her family. He must keep her in a nice house, and he must buy her nice clothes and jewels, and see to her education. Sometimes, when he marries a white girl, he will give up his quadroon mistress. If he does, he must make a 'settlement' with her, to provide for her future. But sometimes a gentleman will keep his mistress even when he is married." Noelle gave Christopher a long, enigmatic look. "I am not quadroon, but I have the color."

And the looks to make all the young gentlemen of New Orleans seek an arrangement, thought Christopher, but he dared not say it.

"My mother decided it would be a good idea for me to try to find a young gentleman. There is no shame in it. On the contrary, it is considered very desirable to make such an arrangement. But Trumbull was opposed to the idea. When he was killed I blamed myself."

"How did you become involved with Morrell?"

"An arrangement had been made, but after Trumbull's death I could not bring myself to remain in the situation. The young gentleman was very possessive. He said that if he could not have me, no one else would. Just what Morrell said, later. He made another arrangement—this time with a 'soul driver.'"

"Soul driver?"

"A slave merchant. I was sold on the auction block."

"Sold into slavery?" Christopher was shocked. "But you were born free, weren't you?"

"Yes. Trumbull bought papers which proved my mother was free. They were counterfeit documents, of course, but no one knew any different. Yes, I was free, but that doesn't matter to soul drivers. A man named Fletcher bought me. He was a very wicked man. And then I met John Morrell.

"You know, Morrell dabbles in much more than merely robbing boats on the river. He is a horse thief, a counterfeiter, a stealer of slaves. He will entice a slave to run away from his master, and make a deal with the slave to sell him to another. No sooner is the transaction closed than the slave, as prearranged, runs away from his new master, with Morrell's help. He receives a portion of the money Morrell was paid for him. Some slaves are sold in this way three or four times. But always, in the end, Morrell will murder the slave and dispose of the body in the Mississippi. After so many escapes a slave becomes a liability to Morrell. Slaveowners circulate descriptions of runaways, and sometimes offer rewards. Morrell could not afford to have one of those slaves caught and turned into a witness against him."

"He made such a deal with you?"

Noelle nodded. "But he never sold me. He wanted to keep me for himself from the very beginning."

"You're free of him now, at least."

"Am I? When we reach the river, what will we do then?"

Christopher gave that a long moment of thought. He had been away from the broadhorn for two nights now. They had searched for him—but how long would they search? If they had discovered the bodies of Krueger and his son, Nathaniel would find himself in a position where he would have to weigh his daughter's safety against remaining in an area that was obviously an unhealthy one for travelers in order to continue looking for his grandson. What would he do? Christopher decided that Nathaniel would probably take his mother to safety and then return to continue the search. But his mother would not leave of her own accord. In a clash of wills, who would prevail? Christopher figured Nathaniel's word would be law.

"Will your people still be there?" asked Noelle.

"I honestly don't know. But it doesn't matter, in the long run. You're not going back. I won't let Morrell get his hands on you again."

She smiled at that, and he realized how silly he must sound—battered and naked and weak as a kitten, armed with only a pistol which he was certain would not fire. How did he propose to protect her if the river pirates caught up with them?

But a second glance at her smile revealed that Noelle wasn't amused by his bravado. She didn't think him silly at all. In fact, the way she looked at him made him feel suddenly quite uncomfortable. At the White House levee a couple of months ago Greta had looked at him in this very same way, a look of fond wonder, mixed with that wisdom about such things that only women possess, when they know they will have the man they have set their sights on, that he will belong to her and to no other, and, further, that he will have nothing to say in the matter; he will no longer have a will of his own, or be the master of his own fate.

Thoughts of Greta propelled Christopher to his feet.

"Come on," he said. "We'd better keep moving."

He did not see how Morrell and his cutthroats could catch them now. The best dogs in the world could not track a man through a blackwater swamp, and Christopher figured they had crossed a couple of miles of bog at least.

An hour later he heard the river, and a short time after that they were standing on the western bank of the mighty Mississippi, gazing out across a mile of sun-silvered water. Christopher didn't recognize this stretch, but he realized that as a novice in reading rivers he could just as easily be upstream from the place he had left

Nathaniel and the others as downstream. There was no sign of life, not so much as a pirogue.

He turned to Noelle. "I don't know where we are, exactly. Do you?"

She shook her head. She was looking at him in that funny way again, and she didn't appear to be the least bit worried about their predicament. Her eyes said *I trust you to take care of me, as you promised you would.*

"We'll go downriver," he said, and turned the horse in a southerly direction.

They had traveled for at least two hours when Christopher saw a man emerge from the forest into their path. He seemed to materialize out of thin air, and gave Christopher a start—until he recognized Nathaniel and let loose with a whoop of joy and vast relief.

"Grandpa!" he cried out, jumping off the horse.

Nathaniel greeted him by clamping a hand firmly over his mouth.

"Keep the noise down, boy," said the frontiersman, a fierce whisper. His keen blue-gray eyes scanned the shadowy green depths of the forest. "There are men about, and they're up to no good. Come, we must hurry. The boat is not far. Leave the horse. We'll go the rest of the way afoot."

When they reached the broadhorn Rebecca wept tears of joy as she embraced her son, and Prissy dabbled at her own eyes, even as she proceeded to scold Christopher for going astray and causing everybody to worry so.

"Oh dear Lord!" gasped Rebecca, seeing the cuts and bruises which covered Christopher's body. "What has happened to you?"

"John Morrell and his gang. I stumbled upon them as they were killing Mr. Krueger."

"We found what was left of Krueger and his son," said O'Connor grimly.

"They captured me. Took me to their camp. Noelle

helped me escape. Mother, Noelle is Cilla's daughter. You remember Cilla . . ."

Rebecca's hand flew to her throat as she stared at Noelle.

"It is a small world, Mrs. Groves," said Noelle. "You saved my mother's life. I had the opportunity to return the favor."

"God works in mysterious and wonderful ways," said Rebecca, clasping Noelle's hands tightly in her own. "How can I ever repay you?"

"We must make certain she never falls into Morrell's hands again," said Christopher.

"We'd better get going, before we all do," warned Nathaniel. "Klesko, cast off the bow line."

"You found Clio, I see," said Christopher, noticing that the errant thoroughbred mare was back on board.

"She came back on her own," said Nathaniel as he headed aft to take the rudder. "O'Connor, grab a pole."

O'Connor clapped a hand on Christopher's shoulder. "I was beginning to think we had lost you."

"Not a chance. I'm going to dance a jig on your grave, remember?"

O'Connor laughed and moved on to brandish the starboard pole. Klesko took the other side, and in moments they were well away from the bank, and none too soon, for suddenly men appeared on the point of land downstream from where the broadhorn had been moored. Christopher saw a muzzle flash, a puff of smoke, and a bullet splintered a board on the cargo box.

"Get down!" he yelled, pushing his mother to the deck, whirling to find that Prissy was already seeking cover. Yet Noelle stood there, staring intently at the men on shore, and Christopher knew intuitively that she was seeking John Morrell, her expression once again unfathomable. Most of the river pirates were shooting now, and Christopher winced at the loud crack! each of the bullets made as they burned the air around them. He lunged forward, grabbing Noelle and bearing her down to the deck.

Wondering if they would clear the point, Christopher dared to raise his head to look, in spite of the hail of bullets. The shore along the point resembled a solid sheet of flame—twenty, maybe thirty men shooting at them. O'Connor and Klesko had to drop their poles and seek cover. Christopher looked around for a rifle or a pistol, even though he knew there was no hope of winning this fight. The odds were lopsided.

But then he saw that indeed they *would* clear the point. He could feel the broadhorn pick up speed as the current caught it and swept it along—in moments the craft was moving faster than a man could run.

The river—the river would save them, would carry them out of John Morrell's bloody grasp.

Christopher felt like giving a cheer. Yet, suddenly, his head began to spin, and he tried to get up, but fell down instead, and dimly he heard his mother's voice, full of alarm—"Is he shot?"—and then he felt Noelle's cool touch, her hand on his forehead. He heard the word *fever* as he slipped into oblivion.

A few days later they put in at a landing on the Arkansas shore, a nameless collection of squalid shanties with a ramshackle wharf. Noelle left Christopher's side for the first time, hastening ashore on some mysterious errand. Prissy took this opportunity to speak her mind to Rebecca.

"You best keep that high-colored gal away from yo' son, Miss 'Becca," she warned.

"But why? She's clearly devoted to him. Surely she means him no harm."

"You done seen dat talisman round her neck, ain't you? Dat's a voodoo talisman."

"Oh, Prissy! Really now!"

"Dat's the gospel truth, Miss 'Becca. She's a voodoo princess."

"There's good voodoo and bad, isn't there? Well, I don't care what she does, as long as Christopher recovers, and I am certain she would never do anything to hurt him."

There was, of course, no physician available in the town. The only thing they could do was try to break the fever that had Christopher in its deadly grasp.

"It's swamp fever," was Klesko's somber diagnosis. When asked what could be done by way of a cure, the riverman grimly shook his head. "Not much you can do, 'cept pray. It's a cryin' shame. He was a bright young feller."

"My son is not going to die," snapped Rebecca.

Klesko recoiled from her flashing eyes. "Whatever you say, ma'am," he mumbled contritely, and beat a hasty retreat.

Hours passed before Noelle returned. She was carrying a muslin pouch which emitted the most awful, nauseating odor—a poultice, she said, which she applied liberally to Christopher's chest. Rebecca and Prissy stood just inside the cargo box doorway, watching. Prissy held a handkerchief to her nose, which muffled her continuous muttering. "Oh Lordy. She gwine steal his soul with dat black magic. Oh Lordy."

Noelle ignored her, but there was only so much Rebecca could take. "Be quiet, Prissy," she said sternly. The sight of Christopher, bundled up in the four-poster bed which took up the majority of the space in the cargo box tore at her heart. He was so pale! His face was covered with sweat. His eyes seemed sunken in their sockets. His cheeks were hollow. One minute he was shaking like a leaf, and the next thrashing weakly under the covers and mumbling incoherently. Horrified, Prissy could stand it no longer, and took her leave.

When Noelle was finished applying the poultice she

resumed her vigil, seated in a chair beside the bed, wetting a strip of cloth in a basin of water and dabbing at Christopher's cheek and forehead. Rebecca put a hand on her shoulder.

"You are exhausted, dear. You should try to rest, if you can."

"I will rest later, when he is well."

"Will he ... be well?" Rebecca's voice quavered with emotion.

"Yes. Do you trust me, Mrs. Groves?"

Rebecca looked deep into Noelle's hazel eyes, and nodded.

"I don't believe in coincidence. I see the Master's hand in this. Your mother came to me for help, and I was able to do something for her. Now, in my son's hour of need, you appear. I feel sorry for anyone who would be so blind as to think this was all luck and happenstance."

"You knew my father. Was he ... an evil man?"

"He was a good and decent man, but there was great misfortune in his life, and he let that turn him into an angry, bitter, and vindictive person. He was tested, and he failed the test."

"Sometimes we all fail."

"Of course we do, sometimes." Rebecca glanced at Christopher. "But even in the face of misfortune we must learn to carry on somehow."

Noelle placed her hand on top of Rebecca's. "Don't worry, Mrs. Groves. Your son will not die."

Just as they were about to cast off from the landing, a commotion on shore captured Nathaniel's attention. Three Indians had emerged from the forest. By their garb the frontiersman pegged them as Cherokees. The warrior in the lead towered over his companions. He stood six feet six in his moccasins. He did not stoop, as did many tall men who are ashamed of their height, but rather stood straight and proud. His hair was plaited in a long queue down his back. His face was covered with a chestnut beard. That made Nathaniel take a closer look.

Klesko appeared at his shoulder. "What do you reckon them savages are up to?"

"They're not savages," corrected the old leatherstocking. "They're Cherokee. And the tall one is Sam Houston, unless I'm very much mistaken."

Houston's long strides brought him straight to the broadhorn. He wore a white doeskin shirt, elaborately worked with beads and dyed porcupine quills, yellow leather leggins, and a blue breechclout. The feather of a turkey jutted from his turban of yellow silk. A brightly hued blanket was draped over a shoulder.

Nathaniel met him on the dock. They shook hands and introduced themselves.

"I am called The Raven by my Cherokee brethren," said Houston. His firm-set mouth twitched in a wry smile. "Though there are some who prefer to call me Big Drunk, a consequence of my reputed fondness for strong spirits. We have not met before, have we?"

"No, but I've heard a lot about you."

"And I, you, Flintlock Jones. I have a favor to ask."

"Ask away."

"My brothers and I must cross to the other side. Can you accommodate us?"

"Of course."

"Good. Perhaps we can share a pipe. Cuss and discuss, as they say."

"I have a jug we could share, too."

Houston's eyes flashed with delight. "Now you're talking my language! Where are you and yours headed, by the way?"

"Texas."

"Texas!" Houston said it as one might speak his lover's name. "Then we really must have ourselves a good long talk."

*   *   *

Sam Houson was pleasantly surprised to learn that the legendary frontiersman's daughter was Jonathan Groves' widow. He and Jonathan, he said, had fought many a battle together under General Jackson's command, and Houston had deeply mourned his death. If he had ever known that Flintlock Jones was Jonathan's father-in-law he had forgotten it in the passage of the years. He looked in on Christopher and he expressed most fervent wishes for the young man's quick and complete recovery. It was peculiar, mused Nathaniel, to hear a man clad in such garb to speak English with such fluid and gentlemanly grace.

While Klesko steered the broadhorn across the mile-wide river, Houston's Cherokee companions manned the poles. This left Houston and Nathaniel free to palaver. They invited O'Connor, who was at loose ends, to sit with them in the bow of the broadhorn.

"I came down this river about a year ago," said Houston, gazing pensively at the green water slapping against the hull. "That was shortly after I resigned from the governorship of Tennessee. *Sic transit gloria mundi.* I turned my back on civilization. I swore never to wear the white man's clothes again, or speak the English language. Of course, I do speak it when the occasion requires. But I was firmly committed to living out the rest of my days in self-imposed exile among my Cherokee brethren."

Nathaniel knew better than to ask for the reason Houston had abandoned politics at the height of his career. Who did not know the story of Houston's ill-fated marriage to Eliza Allen? The mystery of their much-publicized divorce had been put to scandalous use by Houston's political enemies.

"I'd spent the happiest years of my childhood among the Cherokees," continued Houston after a long pull on the jug of corn liquor. "They accepted me into the tribe unconditionally. Chief Oo-loo-te-ka—He Puts the Drum

Away—adopted me. It was he who christened me Co-
lon-neh. The Raven. The young braves taught me the
green corn dance, the hoop and pole game. I spent many
a day wandering along the banks of streams, side by side
with some Indian maiden, sheltered by the deep woods,
making love and reading Homer's *Iliad*. I swore to return to that life and never leave it."

"What has changed your mind?" asked Nathaniel.

Houston flashed a big, loose grin. "You're a sharp
one, Flintlock. A couple of things happened to me on
that downriver journey from Tennessee. I admit, I drank
myself into an agony of despair, and there was a time
or two when I was strongly tempted to leap overboard
and end my worthless life. But then came the first omen.
An eagle swooped down near my head, and then, soaring aloft with a wild scream, was lost in the rays of the
setting sun. I knew somehow that a great destiny awaited
me in the West."

Houston indulged in another drink before relinquishing
the jug to Nathaniel. "But where in the West? The answer came later, when I happened to meet Jim Bowie.
Do you know of him?"

Nathaniel admitted that he did not.

"Ever since that chance meeting my mind has been a
blur of dreams and dark fancies of Texas. Bowie was
settled there. Married the daughter of a Mexican *hacien-
dero*. They say she is one of the loveliest women in all
of Mexico, and one of the richest. Bowie told me all
about Texas. He spun golden tales of great riches. 'Texas
is a fine field for enterprise,' he said. 'It is a matter of
time before she fights for her independence. The future
of those who fight for her will be assured.'"

"I heard rumors that you intended to engage in an
expedition against Texas," said O'Connor. "That you
planned to conquer Mexico, too, and crown yourself emperor and be worth two million in two years."

Houston laughed harshly. "The rumor-mongers never

seem to have enough of me. Do I look like an emperor? I confess, I live like a king among the Cherokees. That's why I'm still here, and not in Texas with Bowie. Now there's a man who deserves his legend. He grew up on the bayous of Louisiana, riding alligators for sport. It's true! He is the greatest knife fighter in the country. He showed me a most remarkable knife, one of his own design, made to stab like a dagger and slice like a razor. Did you hear about that big shivaree on the sandbar off Natchez three years back? Two pistol duellists were determined to settle a grudge, but a fight broke out between the ten men who were present as witnesses. One of them was Bowie. He was shot twice, and stabbed once in the chest. Yet he managed to kill one man and slashed another to ribbons. What a free-for-all that must have been!

"I am told he has recently fought another duel, this one down in Texas. A man hired three assassins to ambush him. Bowie decapitated one, disemboweled another, and split the third's skull to the shoulders with a single blow of his big knife. But don't go getting the wrong idea about the man. He loves peace, and he is a true gentleman. I am told that on a stagecoach in Louisiana some obnoxious fool ignored a lady's request that he extinguish his pipe—and the next instant he found himself thrown to the floor by Bowie, and Bowie's knife at his throat."

"I bet he put out his pipe," said O'Connor.

"They say the man has never indulged in tobacco since," exclaimed Houston, and they all laughed.

"Are you bound for Texas, sir?" asked O'Connor.

"No, no. Not yet. My Cherokee friends still need me. I am going to Washington, to lodge a formal complaint with the Secretary of War, John Eaton, about those damnably dishonest Indian agents at Three Forks. They sell flour and beef at outrageously high prices, and pocket much of the profit. They introduce strong spirits,

knowing it will make my brothers foolish in the head.
I'm not sure why, but Indians just can't seem to handle
liquor. Maybe it's because they haven't built up a toler-
ance for it, like we have." He took the jug and indulged
in another massive dose of tongue oil. "Worst of all, the
government promised the Five Civilized Tribes a bounty
for giving up their ancestral lands and relocating in the
West. To date that bounty has not been paid, and I
intend to know the reason why."

"Do you think the President will listen to you?" asked
Nathaniel. "After all, he played a large part in forcing
the Indians to move West."

"He'll listen to me. We go back a long way, the General and I. And listen, he knew that moving West was
the only way to protect the Indians. The land they eke
out a living on now is land the white man will never
covet."

They reached the other side of the river a moment
later. Houston took one more long swig for the road
before disembarking with his Cherokee companions. He
bowed with a continental flourish to Rebecca, shook
O'Connor's hand, and then Nathaniel's.

"Whereabouts do you intend to settle once you reach
Texas, Flintlock?"

"I have no idea. I've heard the Mexicans are trying
to discourage new immigrants, so we may meet with
some trouble."

"Their *presidios* are widely scattered and badly un-
dermanned. I suggest you settle near other Anglos.
There is strength in numbers. Nacogdoches, perhaps. Or
Anahuac. And if you need a few strings pulled, seek out
my friend Jim Bowie. You can usually find him in San
Antonio de Bexar, down on the Camino de Real. He is
not without connections. Tell him Big Drunk sent you."

Houston started to turn away, had a thought, and
added with a cryptic smile, "I will see you all one day
in Texas. Until then."

With that he was gone. He and the two Cherokees were quickly swallowed up by the forest.

They continued on their way downstream. At Natchez, Nathaniel invited Klesko to take his leave. The riverman had indicated that Natchez was as far as he would go, a condition Nathaniel had readily accepted, without questions. He didn't know if Klesko had a good reason for avoiding New Orleans, or if he was merely intent on partaking of the notorious pleasures offered by the infamous dens of iniquity located in the section of town known up and down the river as Under the Hill.

But when the time came, Klesko surprised the frontiersman by expressing a desire to stay with them.

"You said there are rivers in Texas. I've got a hankering to see them for myself."

Nathaniel surmised there was more to Klesko's change of plans. He had caught the riverman watching Rebecca. He had never shown her anything less than the utmost civility—in fact, he seemed quite shy and almost awestruck in her presence. Nathaniel knew he did not mean her any harm. On the contrary, Klesko worshipped the ground his daughter walked on.

"We'd be glad to have you along," said Nathaniel, and they shook hands on it.

The next day, Christopher's fever broke. He demonstrated a hearty appetite, and was quick to recover his strength, so that by the time they arrived at New Orleans, in the first week of September, he was on his feet again.

PART THREE

✛

The Storm

Chapter 19

The decision was made to remain in New Orleans for a few days. There was much business to attend to. The broadhorn had to be sold. Wagons and mules had to be purchased for the last leg of their journey, overland to the Sabine River. Nathaniel wanted to find out as much as he could about current conditions in Texas. There were people in New Orleans who had that sort of information. The Crescent City was the jumping-off point for the majority of those who were bound for Texas.

He was immediately aware of a difference of opinion among these experts regarding the best route to take to get to his destination. Some were staunch proponents of going overland. Wagons were available which could be floated across the Sabine like a raft—there were no fords to speak of. With such a wagon a person could cross anywhere, or at least anywhere there weren't Mexican border patrols. Then there were the proponents of the sea route. Numerous were the coastal vessels—schooners, sloops, and brigantines—which plied the offshore waters between the mouth of the Mississippi River and Galveston Island or Matagorda Bay. The advantage of the latter was time saved—with favorable trade winds a vessel could make the passage to Matagorda Bay in four days. Besides, these ships were of such shallow draft that they could put in at almost any of the dozens of secluded inlets that dotted the Texas coast. Something else to consider: Lafitte and his freebooters were all cleared out of

Galveston now, and the Karankawa cannibals who had once infested the coast, making life miserable for early explorers, had been all but exterminated.

Nathaniel made the acquaintance of Sterling C. Robertson, who had obtained a colony grant from the Mexican government four years earlier. He was in New Orleans arranging for a shipment of much-needed supplies for his one hundred families.

Robertson took the frontiersman to the pharmacy of Antoine Peychaud, who happened to be the inventor of a drink Americans were calling the "cocktail." On previous visits, the Texas empresario had developed a strong affection for Peychaud's concoction. Served in a French egg cup called a coquetier, the drink was a savory mix of brandy and a blend of bitters.

Nathaniel liked the taste of this new drink. He liked even more what Robertson had to tell him about Texas. Not to worry about the Mexicans, said the empresario. There weren't enough of them to drive the Anglos out. Too late for that. Either the Mexicans learned how to live with the Texans, as the Anglo settlers were calling themselves, or *they* could vacate the premises. Robertson and his people weren't going anywhere.

Texas was pure paradise—or as close to paradise as a man could get on this earth. So said Robertson. In glowing terms he described the land: good black soil ideal for farming in the bottomlands. Why, he had seen with his own two eyes corn grown ten feet tall. An abundance of game, wild horses, and cattle, and more buffalo, deer, and antelope than a man would believe. The woods were thick with bee trees—a man could have honey on his biscuits every morning if he was of a mind to—as well as wild grapes, cherries, plums, and persimmons, walnuts and pecans. The climate was so mild a man did not really need a house, or very many clothes.

Robertson waxed eloquent about the many virtues of Texas, but remained discreetly quiet regarding the ever-increasing danger from the Indians, whose traditional hunting grounds were being invaded by the settlers. Nathaniel had already been made aware of this growing problem by others, and he figured these tribes, the Comanches and the Kiowas, might put up a harder fight than the Mexicans when the time came.

The empresario invited Nathaniel to bring his party to the colony and settle there. He pointed out that he had recruited most of his colonists from Kentucky. "Best pioneer stock around," he said. "No doubt they will all know you, Mr. Jones, and be glad to have a man of your reputation living among them."

Nathaniel didn't bother trying to explain to Robertson why settling in a colony sounded so unattractive to him. He was hankering after the wide open spaces, where a man could travel for days on end and not see, hear, or smell another living soul. But he did express interest in taking up Robertson on his offer of embarking for Texas on the brigantine the empresario had chartered to transport the supplies he had come to New Orleans to purchase. There would be a fortnight's wait, but once under way the journey would have a swift conclusion. The frontiersman assured Robertson that he would talk it over with his traveling companions. Robertson said he was staying at the Hotel de la Marine, down on the riverfront, an old hangout for Baratarian smugglers.

Discussing it with the others that night, Nathaniel found Robertson the following day—not at the hotel, but at Peychaud's, indulging his appetite for the cocktail. He informed the empresario that they would be pleased to take him up on the offer. Robertson was delighted. As for the thoroughbreds, the Texan convinced Nathaniel that it would be best for him to bring the horses overland. There would be no room for them on the ship; besides, such fine animals would be too great a temptation for Mexican soldiers, if any were met along the way. "They wouldn't dare take them from me," said Robertson, "but they might try to steal them from you. That's the kind of trouble you won't need." Nathaniel agreed. His instincts told him he could trust this man.

As it would require Robertson at least ten days to purchase the supplies needed by his colony and have them loaded into the holds of the brigantine *Liberty,* Christopher found himself with a lot of idle time on his hands. His only responsibility was to go once daily to the livery on Iberville Street, located a few blocks from the hotel where they were staying, where the thorough-breds were being kept. So he was happy to accept Noelle's offer to give him a tour of this exotic and romantic city.

She knew it well, having been born and raised in the Vieux Carré, the Old Quarter, living there for twenty years. It was here that the French explorer, Jean Baptiste leMagne, Sieur de Bienville, had founded La Nouvelle Orleans. Thirty-six years earlier, in 1682, La Salle had claimed all the lands along the Mississippi River for France, calling this vast new territory Louisiana in honor of his king, and Bienville's vision was to create a capital city to secure that claim. A strange blend of settlers came to populate what began as a collection of squalid huts surrounded by swamps, battered by hurricanes, and beset by perennial floods and fevers. There were a few aristocrats among them, some entrepreneurs, and a large number of undesirables from the prisons of Paris. And, too, there came the "casket girls," poor young women willing to brave the perils of the New World in order to find husbands. There were the Ursuline Nuns, who took it upon themselves to bring some order and decency to the community. Later, Acadian trappers and fishermen, driven out of Canada by the British, settled the surrounding countryside.

In 1762, Louis XV gave Louisiana to his cousin, Charles III of Spain. Alexander O'Reilly arrived in New

Orleans with three thousand Spanish troops to occupy the town. Some of the residents, rendered unhappy by the prospect of Spanish rule, talked about revolt and independence. The Spanish commandant became known as Bloody O'Reilly when he nipped this talk in the bud by executing a number of French patriots.

Eventually New Orleans adjusted to being part of New Spain. Spanish and French families intermarried. Children born of such unions became known as Creoles, a name which was soon applied to an entire culture, as well as the cuisine of the community.

In 1803, when Spain gave Louisiana back to France and Napoleon Bonaparte sold the territory to the United States for funds he desperately needed to continue his war with Great Britain, the Creoles of New Orleans again found themselves under a new flag and subject to new laws. They considered the Americans to be barbarians, and it is little wonder, since the only Americans with whom they were acquainted until then were the rough and rowdy rivermen. Unwelcomed by Creole society, the Americans established their own community on the other side of the Canal. It took a common peril—a British invasion fleet in 1814—to bring these disparate halves of the city together. Yankee, Creole, slave, and pirate set aside their prejudices and differences and fought side by side at Chalmette, under the dynamic leadership of Andrew Jackson, to save the city from the redcoats.

At the same time, the success of an experiment in granulating sugar created the extremely profitable sugarcane industry. This, coupled with the advent of the steamboat on the Mississippi, heralded a golden age for New Orleans. By 1830 the city had become the fastest growing and richest commercial port in the United States. The Yankees made their fortunes as brokers or shippers, while the Creole aristocrats monopolized the sugar trade. The Yankees built their mansions on St.

Charles Avenue, while the well-to-do Creoles built their townhomes along the cobbled streets of the Vieux Carré. Gambling houses flourished in the Old Quarter. There was French opera and the theater, duels and fencing masters, opulent balls and banquets, slave dances and the Mardi Gras. Built on the foundation of the slave trade and river commerce, New Orleans prospered.

Christopher's tour of the Old Quarter began at The Square, the Plâce d'Armes, a rather barren piece of ground near the levee, encompassed by a low fence of wrought iron. Nearby stood the St. Louis Cathedral, with its Spanish-style bell-shaped towers. To one side of the cathedral was the Cabildo, the old Spanish government house, now the city hall. It was here, Noelle told him, that the documents of the Louisiana Purchase had been signed.

Between the Cabildo and the cathedral was Pirates' Alley. Noelle wasn't sure where the name had come from. This narrow street was bordered on one side by a row of two-story townhomes and on the other by the beautiful garden which had been kept by Père Antoine, the priest who, since 1779, had performed the baptisms, weddings, and funerals for almost all the Old Quarter families.

Pirates' Alley emptied into Royal Street. Most of the homes here were built around courtyards luxuriant with oleander, bougainvillea, jasmine and azaleas. Porte cocheres allowed horse and carriage to pass from the street into the courtyards; these entryways were usually secured with heavy double doors of age-blackened timber or gates of ornate wrought iron. Every house sported wide galleries on the second and third floors, with tall shuttered French windows. Most of the buildings were constructed in the style known as brick-between-post, and covered with a layer of stucco for protection against the elements.

Turning north along Exchange Alley, Noelle pointed

out that many of the buildings along this side street housed the *salle d'armes* of the city's fencing masters. Such men were in great demand in New Orleans, where the *affair d'honneur* flourished as it did nowhere else. Denis Prieur, the current mayor of the city, was a duellist of some repute, who had recently slain a man over a disagreement about the merits of the two political parties. Bernard Marigny, an old Creole with an infamously volatile temper, had fought fifteen successful duels. William Claiborne, the first American governor of Louisiana, had fought the first duel in New Orleans under the American flag. Many a headstone in the local cemeteries bore the inscription "fell on the field of honor." Though forbidden by law and the Church, dueling was commonplace, and every young gentleman profited from learning the use of the rapier.

This innocent commentary opened the floodgates for unpleasant memories which intruded upon Christopher's contentment. Noticing his troubled expression, the perceptive Noelle asked him if he had ever fought a duel.

He told her grimly that he had. "And it ruined my life."

"You are an accomplished swordsman?"

"I used a cutlass. My adversary used a saber. We hacked away to one another for a little while. I was thrown out of West Point as a consequence."

"You attended West Point? There is so much you have kept from me, Christopher," she said with mock reproach, and then, with a lilting little laugh, put her arm through his.

Thinking about the Military Academy brought Greta Inskilling to Christopher's mind, and he experienced a twinge of guilt as they walked on, arm in arm.

Christopher was astonished by the sheer number of street vendors who plied their wares in Vieux Carré. Men offered sun-dried Spanish moss, ideal for mattress and pillow stuffing, palmetto fronds perfect for the cleaning of chimneys, and clothes displayed on long poles. Women balanced wicker baskets on their heads, singing out the identity and price of the baskets' contents—vegetables, blackberries, pralines, and delicious hot rice fritters called *callas*. Fruit, oysters, fish, and lamp oil were sold from two-wheeled carts and horse-drawn wagons.

Of particular interest to Christopher was the Salle d'Orleans, next door to the popular Théâtre d'Orleans. It was here at the Salle that the quadroon balls were held. Nearby, in a small garden called the Dueling Ground, was the place where arguments were settled and insults repaid at the point of a sword. Noelle did not say so, but Christopher could surmise from the look on her lovely face that it was here in this garden that Trumbull, the Elm Tree overseer, had died because he objected so strongly to Noelle becoming the mistress of some young gentleman.

At the end of Orleans Street, just beyond the Ramparts, was Congo Square. Noelle took him there on a Sunday afternoon to watch the slaves dance. Over a thousand slaves congregated that day to cavort to the sometime sensuous, sometimes frenzied rhythm of the drums, while hustlers and vendors worked the crowds, and soldiers on horseback discreetly patrolled the perimeter. At dusk a cannon was fired in the Plâce d'Armes, the signal for all the slaves to return to their quarters.

Noelle showed him the blacksmith shop on Bourbon Street which had served as a front for Jean Lafitte's smuggling business. Importing slaves into the United States had been outlawed in 1807. This was done, in part, to keep out slaves from the Caribbean islands, where numerous bloody servile insurrections had occurred, and for fear that this troublesome island breed would encourage the more docile American-born slaves to rise up against their masters. Then, too, whites in the South were becoming alarmed by the fact that in so many areas they were greatly outnumbers by blacks.

But the law had never concerned the pirate Lafitte, who made a fortune taking slaves off foreign ships and smuggling them into New Orleans to sell to the sugar and cotton planters. Frustrated in his attempts to apprehend Lafitte, Governor Claiborne resorted to offering a five-hundred-dollar reward to the man who delivered Lafitte to the sheriff. Not long after that, Lafitte mockingly posted his own reward: fifteen hundred dollars in pirate gold for the delivery of the governor to Barataria, his stronghold.

Christopher marveled at the cemeteries in the Old Quarter, at the tombs made of stone and wrought iron, some of them quite elaborate, like palaces and cathedrals in miniature. Noelle took him with her when she visited her mother's grave. Cilla's final resting place was marked only by a small stone, inscribed CILLA TRUMBULL, BELOVED MOTHER.

"She never had a last name," said Noelle, "so she took Trumbull's. They weren't lovers, though. There was a bond between them much stronger than that. He was pleased when she asked him if she could use his name. She did it, not so much for herself, but for me. I prefer Trumbull to Cooper."

"Considering the circumstances, that's understandable."

As they were leaving the cemetery Christopher noticed something odd lying on the threshold of an iron gate which accessed an above-ground tomb. He leaned closer to get a better look in the gloom of twilight. It was a feather tied to a bone.

"What is this?" he asked Noelle.

"Gris-gris."

"What?"

"Gris-gris. An object which can cast a spell over someone. It can bring good luck or bad. It can be used to make someone fall in love with you. Or you can use it to bring harm down upon your enemies. It might be a bone, or salt poured in the shape of an X, a powder of brick dust, yellow ochre, and cayenne pepper."

Christopher straightened. He felt a sudden chill in his bones. "Voodoo."

She nodded. "It is practiced here, though prohibited by law."

"Just like dueling. You folks don't pay much attention to the laws down here."

"Even respectable, churchgoing people sometimes seek the help or advice of one who practices voodoo. You have perhaps heard of Marie Laveau?"

He shook his head.

"She is a voodoo Queen, and she has great power. Some say she is evil. Her name is much maligned. But this is because people fear what they do not understand. Voodoo is a religion. It originated in Africa. Among the tribes there, the god Voodoo is an all-powerful being. Everything that happens is his doing. Often he can be malicious. His symbol is the snake. One who practices voodoo is able to communicate with this god. Like a priest. Only, in voodoo, one can ask for a curse as well as a blessing. The god Voodoo will always answer a true believer.

"No one has more powerful magic than Marie Laveau. Despite what you might hear to the contrary, I have never known her powers to be used for anything other than the good of others. For instance, a few years ago, a wealthy young man was accused of a murder which had been committed by someone else, someone he knew. This acquaintance was very clever, and planted such convincing evidence pointing at the innocent young man that everyone was certain he would be convicted of the crime and executed. In desperation his father turned to Marie Laveau as a last resort. He offered her a king's ransom if only she would somehow save his son. On the day of the trial, Marie Laveau entered the cathedral. She placed three Guinea peppers in her mouth as she knelt at the altar rail. She stayed there for hours without moving. Then she proceeded to the Cabildo, where the trial was to be held, and placed the three peppers beneath the judge's chair before the proceedings got under way. The trial did not last long. The evidence against the young man seemed overwhelming. To everyone's amazement, the judge declared the young man to be innocent.

"Some weeks later, the father of the young man returned to Marie Laveau. He had another problem. It seems the city as a whole believed he had bribed the judge. Not only was the reputation of the judge endangered, but also the livelihood of the father, for he was a prominent businessman whose success depended on the trust of others. He asked Marie Laveau if she could pry a confession out of the man who had committed the murder. Again he offered to pay her a fortune in gold. Marie Laveau told him to give the gold to the poor. She learned from her informants that the murderer visited a certain saloon every night. She arranged for a potion to be slipped into his drink. When the potion took effect, the man began to talk about the crime. He had never, of course, dared utter a word about it before, but now he gave every grisly detail. He tried to stop himself, but was powerless to do so. He could not control his own tongue. Imagine his horror as the truth spilled out of him. He was arrested, confessed, and was hanged."

"I never knew much about voodoo," said Christopher. "I thought it was all black magic and devil worship."

"The god Voodoo is no more a devil than our own God."

"*Our* God? Then you don't believe in voodoo yourself."

"I didn't say I don't believe. I have seen too many strange and wondrous things not to believe there is something to it."

"Prissy says she thinks you are a voodoo princess. She

was afraid the poultice you made for me when I had the fever would steal my soul."

"Would you love me any less if I *was* a voodoo princess?"

"Love?" Christopher was taken aback. "I never said . . ."

Suddenly she was standing very close to him. Her eyes were ablaze with the flame of passion. Her lips, slightly parted, glistened in the darkness, beckoning to him.

"You don't have to say it. I know." She put her hands on his shoulders. "If I could have made a voodoo potion it would have been to steal your heart, Christopher Groves. Not your soul."

"Noelle, I don't think . . ."

She kissed him, lightly, but the touch of her lips, warm and soft and wet on his sent an electric charge through his body.

"Don't think," she said, her voice as sultry as the night. "Do you believe in destiny? I do. I believe we were meant to be together. How else can you explain what has happened? Don't think, Christopher. Listen to your heart, not your head."

He took her in his arms and kissed her. An image of Greta flashed across his mind, but only fleetingly, and the heat of Noelle's body enveloped him, and he couldn't resist her, wondering if maybe Prissy was right after all, and he *was* in the grip of some kind of magic. Noelle slipped to the ground, pulling him down on top of her, and he knew it was wrong, knew he would live to regret it even as he made love to her, there on the cold gravestones, and her cries of ecstasy were answered by the raucous call of a crow somewhere across the night-shrouded cemetery.

Chapter 20

Nathaniel slipped easily into the habit of visiting daily the pharmacy of Antoine Peychaud for the purpose of indulging in the proprietor's "cocktails." He tried to time it so that he arrived while Sterling Robertson was there. The Texas empresario usually made an appearance at about one o'clock in the afternoon, and Nathaniel found him to be nearly as regular as clockwork in that regard. The frontiersman liked Robertson. The man was straightforward in his speech and seemed as honest and fair-minded as one could hope for in a successful businessman. And Nathaniel never tired of hearing about the wonders of Texas, the bountiful game, the verdant forests, the sweeping plains. The prospect of acquainting himself with this new land, of learning its many secrets, made Nathaniel feel young again.

One day, as he and Robertson were talking, three men stormed into the pharmacy from the street. By their attire it was manifest that they were young gentlemen, scions of well-to-do Creole families. It was clear, as well, by the expressions on their faces, that they were here on some grim purpose. They scanned the men seated at the little tables Peychaud had arranged along one wall for the ease and comfort of his cocktail-drinking clientele. Then one of the young Creoles pointed an accusing finger across the room and cried out in an agitated voice, pitched high with nervous excitement, "You! There! Yes, you, M'sieu Laird!"

A man rose slowly from the table furthest from the door. He had been conversing with a portly man clad in a hand-tailored blue suit, whose black hair and olive complexion indicated a Spanish heritage. The man who stood was tall and thin and white-haired, but in spite of his obvious age—Nathaniel figured he had to be close to seventy—he was in splendid shape, straight and lithe. His features were sharply angular, set off by a prominent scar above one eye. He was well-dressed and carried a malacca cane with a silver ferrule and a silver grip fashioned into the shape of a lion rampant.

Robertson did not fail to notice the way Nathaniel was staring at this man. It was as though the frontiersman were seeing a ghost.

"Do you know Peter Laird, Mr. Jones?" asked the Texan.

"Laird?"

"Yes. By all accounts, one of the city's foremost sword masters. Don't let his age fool you. He is a dangerous fellow. And still quite a hand with the ladies, I understand. He has an insatiable appetite for the young belles, and the younger the better. I wouldn't be at all surprised if this concerns a lady of tender years whose reputation has been compromised."

Peter Laird? Nathaniel's smile was cold and enigmatic. Peter McLeod was the name by which he knew this man.

McLeod—who had ridden with Tarleton's Tory Legion in Virginia, on a campaign of terror which included a plot to capture Thomas Jefferson, and during which Nathaniel's own father had been killed by one of the Tory Rangers. This was the same McLeod who had turned up next with the traitor Aaron Burr, and who had come very close to killing Nathaniel as he tried to prevent the frontiersman and Jonathan Groves from capturing Burr. And they had met again almost ten years later; Nathaniel had been captured by Tecumseh's Indians and turned over to the British, and McLeod had been there, a redcoat officer. Though American-born he had remained loyal to the Crown, and Nathaniel wondered if his burning hatred for the United States had cooled at all in the passing of the years.

As the trio of young gentlemen approached McLeod he watched them with frosty disdain. Not a trace of anxiety was to be detected on his hawkish face. He had abundant courage—Nathaniel was willing to give him that, and figured it might be his sole virtue.

"You, m'sieu," said the Creole who had identified McLeod as Laird, "are an unprincipled scoundrel. You have polluted my sister with your vile touch."

"An *insulte majeure,* as they call it here," Robertson whispered across the table to Nathaniel. "I fear there may be some blood shed."

The portly man who had been sharing McLeod's table got to his feet. "Malot, you are a fool to challenge this man."

"My sister's honor demands it."

McLeod looked at Malot with an icy grayness. "I am at your service," he murmured. "Name the time and the place and I will most assuredly be there."

"Here! Now! I am ready."

"My good friend Peychaud would not appreciate the spilling of your hot Creole blood on his clean floor."

"In the alley, then."

McLeod nodded curtly. "As I am the one who has been challenged, I own the privilege of choosing the weapons. Naturally, I choose blades."

"Naturally," sneered Malot. "I have brought mine."

"As have I." McLeod raised the malacca cane.

Malot turned on his heel and stalked out of Peychaud's pharmacy, followed by his two friends.

McLeod turned with an apologetic smile to the portly Spaniard. "Will you consent to stand as my second in this affair, Ramirez? I assure you, it will be of short duration, and then we will be free to continue our conversation."

"I?" Ramirez broke into a sweat and began to dab at his pockmarked cheeks with a monogrammed handkerchief. "I want no part of this, Señor Laird."

"Hmm." Unperturbed, McLeod scanned the room. His gaze came to rest on Nathaniel. *Surely he must recognize me,* thought the frontiersman. *But his expression betrays nothing.* McLeod approached the table where Nathaniel and Robertson were seated.

"Will you serve as my second, sir?" McLeod asked Nathaniel. "All I ask for is a fair fight. Malot's two friends are impetuous Creoles. They may forget their manners."

"You have a lot of gall," said Nathaniel.

"Ah, so you know me."

"Well, I am a believer in fair fights," admitted Nathaniel. He was intrigued by the irony of this game McLeod was playing. He rose, smiling at the shocked expression on Robertson's face. "I'm sorry, but this is an offer I can't refuse. Excuse me for a moment."

Nathaniel followed McLeod out of the pharmacy and around to a pair of wrought-iron gates which opened into a cobblestoned alley wide enough for the passage of a dray wagon. Malot was waiting, with his two seconds and a white-haired black man in blue-and-yellow livery—obviously a house servant. Malot had a rapier in his hand now, and Nathaniel surmised that it had been in the servant's keeping while the Creole and his companions entered Peychaud to, so to speak, beard the lion in his den. The servant now held Malot's coat.

As he shed his own coat, McLeod said, "Allow me, gentlemen, to introduce Nathaniel Jones, of Kentucky, who has generously consented to act as my second. I assure you, he is a man of impeccable integrity." He made to hand his hat and coat to Nathaniel, thought

better of it, and hung them on the gate. "As you gentlemen can see, Mr. Jones is armed." With a brief gesture
he indicated the pistol and knife wedged under the frontiersman's belt.

"As are we," said one of Malot's companions. He
opened his exquisitely tailored, plum-colored coat to reveal a pistol of his own, accompanied by a French
dagger.

"My, my!" McLeod was amused. "Armed for bear,
aren't we?" His tone was mocking.

"Let's get on with it," rasped Malot.

Nathaniel noticed the young man was sweating, more
profusely than the sultry heat of the September afternoon warranted. In contrast, McLeod appeared thoroughly cool and confident.

"By all means," said McLeod, his voice smooth as
silk. "I have a busy schedule today, Malot, and precious
little time to waste on the likes of you."

Twisting the head of the malacca cane, he drew the
concealed blade. He tossed the cane to Nathaniel and
advanced, free hand behind his back, extending the rapier. Malot crossed the blade with his own. Then
McLeod stepped back and lowered his weapon, his posture taunting by its very openness. With a strangled
sound Malot lunged forward.

"En garde!" McLeod laughed, as with disdainful
ease—a riposte so swift and deftly executed that the eye
could not follow—he parried Malot's thrust. A flick of
the wrist and Malot cried out and jumped back. Nathaniel saw the blossom of blood on his white shirt.

"Touché!" exclaimed McLeod. "But really, Malot,
you do not possess the artistry to make a good
swordsman."

He lunged, perfectly balanced, torso erect, knee bent,
leg extended, and Malot frantically beat his blade away
with a clumsy, desperate parry.

"Tsk, tsk," said McLeod, circling Malot. "You bent the elbow. Keep the arm rigid. What deplorable form."

Malot cursed him savagely and thrust again—and again. McLeod scarcely seemed to move. With cold perfection he neatly deflected each lunge. His blade sang in a lethal whisper. Then, with contemptuous ease, he pricked Malot again, and the Creole reeled away, gasping, his face twisted into a rictus of anguish.

"There," said McLeod. "Are you not satisfied, Malot? Go home. You have done what was expected of you. Now leave, while you are still able."

With that, McLeod turned his back on his adversary. Malot leaped forward. One of his colleagues shouted, "No, Malot!" But it was too late. Malot did not realize that he had been lured into a deadly trap. His companion saw it. So did Nathaniel. But Malot was blinded by his rage, and McLeod whirled, struck aside the Creole's blade, and ran his own completely through the foolish young man. Malot stood rigidly impaled on McLeod's rapier for a breathless instant, his face very white, his eyes seeming to bulge from their sockets. Suddenly he dropped to his knees. His own rapier clattered on the cobblestones. McLeod withdrew the blade and made a final gesture of disdain, stepping away as Malot flopped forward on his face. Taking the cane from Nathaniel, he sheathed the bloody blade.

Malot's companions rushed to his side, gently turning him over. His shirt, once snowy white, was soaked with blood.

"Find a doctor!" one of the Creoles snapped at the black servant.

The servant did not move. He looked at Malot with stony impassivity, but strong emotion lurked behind his hooded eyes, and intuitively Nathaniel knew that the slave hated Malot and was glad he was dying.

"Do as I say!" roared the Creole.

Nathaniel distinctly heard the death rattle in Malot's throat.

"It's too late," he said.

And so it was. Malot's body convulsed and then went limp. As McLeod put on his coat, one of the Creoles snatched Malot's coat from the old servant and covered the dead man from the waist up. Without a word—and without so much as a glance at the body of the young man he had slain—McLeod departed the alley, pushing through a group of onlookers who had gathered in the street. Nathaniel was startled by their presence. He had not noticed them before, so engrossed was he in the bizarre dance of death performed by McLeod and Malot.

Robertson was among the spectators. He clutched Nathaniel's arm as the frontiersman pushed through the people in pursuit of McLeod.

"What happened?" asked the empresario.

"Somebody died," replied Nathaniel, extricating himself from the Texan's grasp.

McLeod was proceeding along the *banquette* of Royal Street with brisk strides. Nathaniel caught up with him and waited until he was right behind him before speaking.

"McLeod."

McLeod whirled, eyes blazing. Nathaniel thought for a moment that he was going to draw the concealed blade and run him through with it. But then McLeod composed himself. His eyes flicked furtively along the street, and he realized that no one had been near enough to hear Nathaniel use his real name. He even managed a rather chilly half-smile.

"If you wish to speak to me it will have to be privately."

"Lead on."

McLeod turned on his heel and walked with long strides, turning left off of Royal Street onto Conti, then half a block to Exchange Alley. The frontiersman stayed right with him, passing through an iron gate and down a narrow cobbled passage to a secluded courtyard, then up a flight of wooden steps sagging with age to a gallery and then through a heavy wooden door.

Nathaniel found himself in a large room, with French windows arrayed at the far end, presumably overlooking Exchange. Several bare wooden pews lined the unadorned walls, where in places the plaster had fallen in chunks from the bricks. There was a large brick hearth, a rack containing a half-dozen épées, and in the far corner a wooden screen partitioning McLeod's austere living quarters—a narrow iron bed, a trunk, a porcelain washbasin and pitcher on a rickety stand—from the rest of the *salle d'armes.*

Doffing his hat and tossing it negligently onto the nearest pew, McLeod turned on Nathaniel.

"So, we meet again. Tell me, why didn't you shout my name out there on the street? You realize that if my true identity became known New Orleans would be, shall we say, untenable for me."

"I can always go to the authorities."

"Can you? I could kill you here and now."

"You probably could. But you would have the devil of a time trying to explain that."

"I suppose so. What do you intend? Blackmail, perhaps?"

Nathaniel laughed. "You misjudge me."

McLeod turned away, moving restlessly about the salle, swinging the sword cane as a farmer would a scythe.

"I remember thinking that indeed I had done so on the occasion when you were my prisoner, in the guardhouse at Fort Malden. You kept hurling yourself at the cell door. Even though you knew there was no escape. Day and night you threw your body against that unyielding door. You quite unnerved my men, as I recall."

"What are you doing here, McLeod? I would have thought you'd be living in Europe somewhere."

"I gave England a try, after the war. It came as something of a shock to me that in spite of all my service and sacrifice for the sake of the Crown, all the blood I had shed for the good of the British Empire, I was treated like a colonial." McLeod's laugh was edged with bitterness. "Many doors were closed to me. I was a second-class citizen. So I returned. This city proved to be most suitable. It is, as you may have noticed, very cosmopolitan. Americans are actually in the minority here. And, too, the women are very beautiful. And generally very willing. It must be the climate. I parlayed my skill with the sword into a lucrative profession." He raised his arms in a gesture to indicate the Spartan chamber. "You might not think it so lucrative by the appearance of my humble abode, but I assure you, I live quite comfortably. So many foolish young gentlemen, like Malot, whose idiotic notions of honor oblige them to become familiar with the use of the blade. They pay well. I, in turn, spend every bit of my earnings on wine, women, and song. Why should I die rich? I have no one to leave a fortune to. No, I learned long ago to live for today, not plan for the future."

"No family?"

"Oh, you didn't know? Of course you didn't. We've met only twice, and both times we were too busy trying to kill each other to get acquainted. No, I have no family. I used to. But your damned American rebels— excuse me, *patriots*—murdered them."

"Is that why you've hated this country?"

"Precisely," snarled McLeod. "It is a country of hypocrites. Holier-than-thou Americans, who murder and steal and rape with the worst of us. I shall hate this country and everything it stands for until the day I die. That is why I have done everything in my power to destroy it. I rode with Butcher Tarleton. I conspired with

Aaron Burr. I gave aid to Tecumseh. I fought with the British in two wars. But then I came to realize that I was, in effect, hurling my body against an unyielding door. I still hate your damned United States of America, but I am too old to fight it any longer."

"My God, McLeod. You should have been killed a long time ago."

McLeod laughed harshly. "Only the good die young. Haven't you heard? So now you know my little secret. What do you intend to do about it?"

"I don't know."

"You could put an advertisement in the local paper. Then I would have to flee, or face incarceration."

"You're a dangerous man. You enjoy killing."

"What? Do you mean that business with Malot? That was self-defense."

"You leave dead bodies and wrecked lives behind you."

"How poetic." McLeod made a gesture indicating his indifference to Nathaniel's decision. "Do as you will."

"You're not going to try to stop me?"

"I knew back at Fort Malden that I could not kill you, Jones. In fact, if the truth be known, I admire you. I admire your spirit. You have lived your life with honor. Which is more than I can say. Strange, isn't it? Well, very little about life makes any sense."

Nathaniel turned to go.

"You're bound for Texas, aren't you?"

The frontiersman was startled. "How did you know?"

"Deductive reasoning. There will be a war in Texas soon. Not soon enough for me, though, I'm afraid."

"I don't have to ask which side you would fight on."

McLeod laughed again. "Of course not. I could have a commission in the Mexican Army if I wanted it. There are a number of mercenaries in the service of Mexico already. But I am too old for another campaign. Pity. Watch out for that fellow Santa Anna. He's made quite a name for himself butchering those rebel Indians down in the southern provinces. A man after my own heart."

Without another word, Nathaniel left the salle.

Should he expose McLeod? Then the man would finally answer for his crimes. Or should he adopt a policy of live and let live? McLeod had spent a lifetime fighting and conspiring against the United States, opposed to the very things which Nathaniel had risked his life for time and again. But if what he had said about his family was true, perhaps his hatred, if not justified, was comprehensible. Nathaniel mulled the problem over in his mind all the way back to the hotel, and still he could not decide.

Chapter 21

Sterling Robertson came to Peychaud's three days later with the news Nathaniel had been waiting for. The *Liberty* was loaded and ready to embark on the morrow for Texas. The Texan apologized for the wait. They had been delayed by a very special shipment overdue from France.

"Tonight you must board her," said the empresario. "I have told the skipper to expect you. Quarters have been arranged. They may be a little cramped, but then, a brigantine is not built for luxury, is she?"

Nathaniel told the others—Rebecca, Prissy, Klesko, and O'Connor. Rebecca was excited by the prospect. The novelty of New Orleans had worn off, and she was tired of waiting, ready for the journey to end, eager to begin a new life in a new land. Prissy, on the other hand, was leery of the idea of a sea voyage. Klesko and O'Connor were ready to go. They had spent a lot of time together, with the riverman giving O'Connor a tour of the bars and bawdy houses he knew so well, and they had managed to exhaust the young Irishman's limited funds in the process. Like Prissy, Klesko was less than enthusiastic over the prospect of putting to sea. A river was one thing, the high seas another. But wherever Rebecca went he was bound and determined to follow.

The frontiersman found Christopher in the room he shared with O'Connor—Nathaniel and Klesko roomed together, and the womenfolk had a third room. Christopher was agonizing over a letter. Nathaniel knew about Greta Inskilling. Christopher hadn't said much about her, but that in itself educated the frontiersman to the fact that his grandson's feelings for the young woman ran deep, and Nathaniel assumed the letter was for her.

Christopher received the news of their imminent departure with an ambivalence which surprised Nathaniel. Putting down his quill, he sighed and slumped back in his chair.

"Will there be room for Noelle on the ship?"

"I didn't realize she was going along. But yes, we will make room for her."

"I suppose she's going."

"Don't you want her to?"

"She can't very well stay here. It isn't safe for her, after she betrayed Morrell."

"That didn't exactly answer my question."

Christopher gave the frontiersman a long, anguished look, and Nathaniel surmised that his grandson had something he very much wanted to talk about, a tormenting quandary concerning which he desperately needed advice, and yet, because of its intensely personal nature, something he could not quite bring himself to discuss. Obviously it had something to do with Noelle. But it wasn't in Nathaniel's nature to pry.

The old leatherstocking put a hand on Christopher's shoulder. "If there is anything I can do to help you, just let me know."

"Thanks."

"I'll go let them know there'll be one more passenger for the *Liberty.*"

He was at the door before Christopher spoke.

"I've made a terrible mistake, Grandpa."

"Noelle?"

Christopher nodded. "I don't love her, though. At least, I don't think I do. It's not the same feeling as I have for Greta. Oh, I don't know. I'm so confused. Can you love two women at the same time?"

"I'm no expert on affairs on the heart," said Nathaniel. "But I reckon there can be a difference between the woman you'd like to spend some time with today, and the one you want to spend the rest of your life with. Of course, Amanda and I grew up together. I always knew she was the one for me. Don't recall ever looking at another woman."

"Noelle is . . . bewitching. I sometimes think she's cast a spell on me."

"Women can do that." Nathaniel smiled. "But don't let Prissy hear you say such things."

"Don't get me wrong. Noelle is a good person."

"Of course she is. She saved your bacon, didn't she?"

"But I can't seem to think straight when she's around."

"The two of you had quite an adventure together, getting away from those river pirates. That kind of thing creates a strong bond between folks. And she's a very pretty lass, too."

"Very." Christopher sighed. "She says we were meant to be together."

"Maybe she really believes that. But for it to work, you have to think so, too."

"That's just it. I don't know what to think. In a way I wish she wouldn't go to Texas with us. But then I . . . I like being with her."

"I reckon she should go," said Nathaniel, "if her life is endangered by staying. But her going with us shouldn't prevent you from writing that letter."

"I don't know what to write. I feel as though I ought to tell Greta the truth. About Noelle."

"I wouldn't, were I you."

Christopher was surprised. "You mean lie? I can't believe you would recommend that course, Grandpa. Not you. You've never told a lie in your entire life."

"How did you come by that notion? Where women are concerned, what they don't know won't hurt you. If not telling is the same as lying, so be it. There's the little matter of your own survival to keep in mind. Now, I don't know much at all about women, but I do know that much."

"You're right, of course. But I . . . I feel guilty."

"You probably ought to. Still, I wouldn't cut my own throat just to atone for a mistake."

Christopher smiled. "I see your point."

"Write the letter, boy. Don't fret over this business with Noelle. I wouldn't be at all surprised if it just kind of works itself out before you know it."

Christopher bent to the task at hand as soon as Nathaniel had left the room. The words flowed as fast as he could scribble them down. He informed Greta of their safe arrival in New Orleans, and their imminent departure on the *Liberty*, bound for Texas. He omitted any mention of the river pirates. He did not want her to worry. And he didn't mention Noelle, either. As he closed, telling Greta how much he loved her, and how terribly he missed her, he prayed fervently that his grandfather was right, and that this thing with Noelle would resolve itself before Greta came to Texas to join him.

Christopher was finishing up with his packing when Noelle arrived. O'Connor was getting his belongings together, too, and offered to leave the room, giving Christopher a sly wink. Christopher was not amused. He told his friend to stay.

Something was troubling Noelle—that much was clear at a glance. Christopher was afraid it had something to do with the two of them, and what had transpired a few nights ago in the cemetery. Thinking about that night, and standing so close to Noelle now, stirred the embers of his longing for her into a white hot flame, and this desire made him ashamed, as not an hour before he had written Greta to tell her how much he loved her.

"Three men are searching the Old Quarter for you, my love," she said.

"Three men? Morrell's?"

She shook her head. "Is there a bounty on your head?"

"Bounty men." Christopher glanced at O'Connor. "Good God. I never really believed it. I never thought Vickers would do it."

"Who is Vickers?" asked Noelle.

"It's a long and sordid story. But, how did you find out about these men?"

"I have many acquaintances in the Vieux Carré."

"Yes, but why would they tell you . . ."

"We have been seen together quite a lot these past weeks. Word gets around."

"They must have trailed you as far as Cully's Landing," surmised O'Connor. "And someone there told them where we were bound."

Christopher nodded, a sinking feeling in the pit of his stomach. "They will check all the hotels, of course. Shouldn't take them long to find me."

"Then we'll just have to fight them," said the Irishman. "With Klesko and your grandfather, the odds are on our side."

"Damn!" Christopher angrily paced the room. "This is utter madness! Emily Cooper committed suicide and it had nothing to do with me. Why can't they accept that? Why must more people be hurt?"

"It has very little to do with her suicide," said O'Connor. "Haven't you realized that yet? This is about your father and his affair with Emily Cooper, and the Vickers family honor."

"Can a person never put the past behind him?"

"You can't run away from it. But sometimes you can

bury it. We will deal with these bounty men and be on our way to Texas."

"No. I won't have the lives of my family and friends put at risk." Christopher turned to Noelle. "Can you arrange to have a message delivered to these bounty men?"

"I know people who will kill them for you."

"Absolutely not. I won't hire assassins. Can you arrange the message or not?"

"I can."

"Then I will meet them, an hour after sundown. But where? The Dueling Ground, behind the Salle d'Orleans. Yes, that's an appropriate place for the kind of business we will be conducting."

"Alone?" queried O'Connor.

"Yes."

"Are you insane? I can't let you go alone, Christopher."

"You will. And I will have your word that you won't breathe a word of this to my grandfather. Or, God forbid, my mother."

"I can't give it!" exclaimed O'Connor.

"You must."

"I cannot. I will not. At least let me go with you."

"And if I let you, you will swear not to tell the others?"

"Then I will swear it."

"All right. Noelle?"

"I will see that they get your message."

Christopher turned to his trunk. With sharp, angry motions he threw it open, dug beneath his neatly folded clothes, and extracted the Tripolitan cutlass which had once belonged to his father.

"It's only fitting, I suppose," he said bitterly, "that I carry this tonight."

It was not far from the riverfront hotel to the Salle d'Orleans, on the corner of Orleans and Royal streets.

Nonetheless, Christopher left early, half an hour after sundown.

"We mustn't be late," he told O'Connor. "A gentleman isn't late for his own funeral."

But the Irishman had lost his usually indomitable sense of humor, and the morbid joke failed to elicit even a weak smile from him.

With the cutlass and a pistol concealed under his long cloak of pilot cloth—O'Connor was armed with a dagger and a brace of pistols—Christopher walked with quick strides past the Plâce d'Armes, thence up Pirates' Alley, with the cathedral looming on his right hand. The night was humid; a mist had crept in from the river and seemed to cling to the buildings in the Old Quarter. The streets of the Vieux Carré were still bristling with vendors, carriages, and pedestrians. Christopher knew it would have been better to meet the bounty men at midnight, when there would be fewer witnesses. But, on the off chance that he survived, he was to be aboard the *Liberty* at that hour.

His thoughts flew back to that fateful night, months ago, at West Point, when he had met Adam Vickers at midnight in the riding hall, the senseless duel which had triggered a chain of events which brought him now to the gate of the little garden behind the cathedral, the Dueling Ground, where the soil had drunk the blood of so many men, including Trumbull. And maybe tonight it would drink his blood. One way or the other, this feud with the Vickers family had to be resolved, here and now, tonight, for good. It was unfinished business, and he was determined to write the final chapter before he embarked for Texas and a new beginning. He just didn't know how the chapter would end.

It was dark and quiet at the little iron gate near the end of Pirates' Alley. People and carriages passed to and fro on Royal Street a stone's throw away. Peering through the wrought iron into the garden, Christopher

could see precious little in the gloom of night—a stretch
of cobbled walkway, luxuriant tropical growth which had
once been tended with such loving care by Père Antoine,
now somewhat overgrown. But they were there—Christopher could sense them. There was a funny, tingling
sensation at the base of his spine. Yet his heart beat
calmly in his chest, his palms were dry, his hand steady
as he reached for the gate's latch.

A rustle of cloth, the whispered warning of O'Connor
behind him, made him turn away from the gate, to see
a cloaked figure separate from the shadows in a deeply
recessed doorway across the alley. A pistol materialized
in O'Connor's hand. Christopher struck it down, recog-
nizing Noelle an instant before she was in his arms, em-
bracing him and trying at the same time to pull him
away from the gate.

"Don't go in there, my love!"

"I must."

"You are early," she said, distraught. "You mustn't
pass through that gate."

"What are you talking about?" asked Christopher,
exasperated.

The sound of a scuffle, followed by a sharp, abbrevi-
ated cry of pain came suddenly from the darkness of the
garden. A pistol spoke, steel range against steel, a muttered curse. Christopher lunged for the gate. Noelle tried
to stop him, but he broke free of her grasp, threw open
the gate, and rushed into the darkness, brandishing the
cutlass from beneath his cloak.

Coming to a turn in the walkway, Christopher almost
collided with a man running the other way. In the darkness Christopher could discern very little about the man.
But he did get a quick glimpse of the man's face—and
saw terror etched there. The man stumbled backward,
raised his pistol. Then O'Connor's pistol roared. The
Irishman was right behind Christopher, and Christopher
flinched at the muzzle flash, the barrel so close to his

face that he thought he felt the burn of several powder grains on his cheek. The man reeled and fell. His ears ringing from the pistol shot, Christopher hurtled the body and pushed on.

The walkway led to a circular patio in the center of the garden. Reaching the edge of this open space, Christopher stopped, frozen in his tracks by the sight that met his eyes.

Three black men were hacking someone to pieces with cane knives. Horrified, Christopher watched the blades rise and fall in geysers of blood. Another black rose from a second victim—this one had already been decapitated and dismembered.

"Look out!" yelled O'Connor.

A fifth black man appeared out of the verdant foliage to launch himself at Christopher, who blocked the stroke of the man's cane knife with his cutlass. Sparks flew as the blades met. Christopher yanked the pistol out of his belt with his free hand, jabbed the barrel into his assailant's midsection and pulled the trigger. The impact of the bullet shoved the man backward. He jackknifed and pitched forward to sprawl, dying, at Christopher's feet.

Christopher whirled as two more of the blacks advanced. O'Connor appeared at his shoulder, aiming his second pistol. The pistol did not seem to deter the blacks. They kept coming. But before the Irishman could shoot, Noelle appeared to throw herself into his line of fire.

Seeing her, the blacks lowered their cane knives, rose out of menacing crouches into a posture of harmless subservience, and as she snapped at them in Creole, they shrank away, as though her words stung like a master's lash, flaying their ebony skin. She spoke again, her tone imperious. Two of them picked up their dead accomplice, and then the whole lot vanished into the darkness like ghosts.

On the other side of the stone wall separating the

garden from Royal Street came the sound of people running, voices raised in alarm. The pistol shots were attracting a crowd. Any moment and they would invade the garden itself.

"Come," said Noelle urgently. "We must leave this place at once."

Christopher grabbed her roughly by the arm. "My God, Noelle. What have you done?"

She wrenched free of his grasp. "This is not the time or the place to discuss it," she said curtly, and walked away.

"What's wrong with you, Christopher?" asked O'Connor.

"This . . ." Christopher gestured at the grisly remains of the two men who had fallen beneath the cane knives of the blacks. He knew who they were. The bounty men. O'Connor had killed the third. "This is her doing."

"Of course it is. She probably saved our lives. And yet you're angry with her."

"You used to talk a lot about honor. Well, where is the honor in this?"

"Come on. If we're caught here we may never get to Texas."

Christopher followed him. With Noelle in the lead, they left the garden by a small wooden door located near the rear wall of the Cathedral, escaping undetected in the dark shadows of Pirates' Alley. In the Plâce d'Armes Christopher stopped Noelle. This time, as she tried to free herself, he held on to her arm.

"You're hurting me, Christopher."

"You ambushed those bounty men, didn't you?"

"They would have killed you."

"That's not the point."

"Yes. I arranged an ambush. You said you would be in the garden an hour after sundown. I told them a half hour after sundown. It would have been finished before you arrived—except that you came early. And almost got yourself killed."

"Who were those men with the knives?"

"You don't need to know. Or want to know."

"I asked, so I *do* want to know, and you're going to tell me."

"I don't know what's gotten into you, Christopher," said O'Connor. "Why don't you just drop it?"

"Stay out of this. Tell me the truth, Noelle. Who were those men? Why were they so afraid of you?"

"They are just ordinary men."

"Who would do anything you asked of them. Isn't that so?"

"Yes."

"Why?"

She held the talisman for him to see, the one that ordinarily lay between her breasts, dangling from a silver chain. He stared at the silver snake entwined about a human skull.

"This is why," she said, defiant.

"Voodoo."

"Are you satisfied now?"

"You shouldn't have done it, Noelle. It was my fight."

"But I did it for you, Christopher." She stepped closer, and the sweet fragrance and soft warmth of her filled his senses, and she put her hands lightly on his chest. Even under these circumstances she managed to excite him. Again Christopher wondered if she had somehow worked a spell on him.

"You don't understand," he said.

"I understand this: After what happened to those bounty men, no one will want to try to collect the reward that man Vickers has offered."

"She's got a point," said O'Connor.

"They would have killed you," she said. "I did what I had to do to save the life of the man I love. I am glad

I did it, even if you hate me for it. If you do hate me, say so, and you will never see me again."

Christopher didn't know what to say. Here was his chance. He could tell her now that he did not want her to accompany him to Texas. But was that what he really wanted? Did he really want to be rid of her? What about Greta? He stared at Noelle, at that beautiful dusky up-turned face, drowned in those dark eyes, was tantalized by her lips, slightly parted, so close he could feel her warm, sweet breath on his face.

"No," he said hoarsely. "No, I don't hate you."

She turned away and left him standing there, and he watched her go, wondering if she would be on the *Liberty* when the brigantine sailed at dawn. Wrapped in the black hooded cloak, she was soon swallowed up by the night.

"An extraordinary woman," murmured O'Connor. "You have all the luck, Christopher."

Glancing at his friend, Christopher could see that O'Connor, too, was thoroughly bewitched.

Chapter 22

Christopher had spent a frivolous afternoon in a small boat on the Hudson River with Greta Inskilling—and that was the sum total of his naval experience prior to walking up the gangplank to board the brigantine *Liberty*, bound for Texas. He wasn't sure how he would like going to sea. The first day out was pleasant enough. The fresh air and salty spray were invigorating after two weeks breathing the stench of the city. The sun was bright yellow in a sky the delicate blue of a robin's egg. The sea was a translucent green except where it foamed white beneath the bow of the ship. The *Liberty* was skimming along nicely with her sails billowing full, and with none of that clumsy pitch and roll which Christopher had expected from a ship with its hold so full. Which only demonstrated, he mused, how ignorant he was of nautical matters.

He didn't become seasick at all, which was more than some of the others could say. O'Connor and his mother looked rather green around the gills, while Klesko, wretchedly ill, spent most of that first day bent over the bulwarks and heaving into the sea. Prissy remained in the captain's cabin, which she and Rebecca shared, and by all accounts was calling upon the Lord to go on ahead and bring her to His bosom, lest she suffer any longer. Nathaniel, on the other hand, seemed to take this new environment in stride.

"You must have inherited your father's sea legs," the frontiersman told Christopher.

And, thought Christopher, *his knack for becoming involved with the wrong woman.*

Noelle was not aboard. The last he had seen of her was in the Plâce d'Armes, walking away from him without a word, disappearing into the night. That image, seared into his memory, nourished his guilt—and O'Connor didn't make him feel any better about it. The Irishman had wanted to mount a full-scale search for her, even if it meant delay in the departure of the *Liberty.* Christopher pointed out how ludicrous that idea was. What chance would they have of finding her in the Vieux Carré? Especially if she did not want to be found.

"But what if Morrell caught up with her?" asked O'Connor.

"Then I would have to say, God help Morrell."

O'Connor didn't look the least bit amused. In fact, when it came to Noelle, he had apparently misplaced his well-developed sense of humor altogether. Christopher fondly remembered the old O'Connor, from their West Point days together, a happy-go-lucky character who never let himself become too serious about anything.

"You're an ungrateful wretch," said O'Connor bitterly. "Twice she saved your life. And this is how you repay her. She loved you."

"I don't think so."

"Then you are a fool."

Christopher didn't bother to respond. He remained carefully impassive in the face of O'Connor's harangue.

"I will sail with you to Texas," said O'Connor. "But as soon as we get there I'm coming back to find Noelle."

That was his final word on the subject. For the rest of the day, and the day after, his attitude was decidedly cool.

Christopher's heart ached for missing Noelle. He was willing to concede that he had done wrong by her. But he consoled himself with thoughts of Greta. And, to his surprise, he found that as the day wore on he began to feel better about things. The memory of Noelle gave his heart a sharp twinge along about sunset. He countered this bit of unpleasantness by writing another letter to Greta. Elaborating on how much he missed her, pouring out his heart as he had never done before, informing her that in a matter of days he would be settled somewhere in Texas, and then he could send for her. Greta was a tonic which eased the misery of his longing for Noelle. He went to his bed hopeful that by tomorrow Noelle would have faded from his thoughts, that as the distance between them grew the hold she had on him would weaken. Yet she came to him in his dreams, haunting him with her hot, silky, café-au-lait skin against the cold graveyard stone—and then he saw the cane knives, flashing in the moonlight, dripping blood, and he woke up in a cold sweat.

The morning dawned gray and blustery. The sea had become violent overnight. The brigantine clawed her way westward, a strong southerly wind laying her over and howling in the rigging. Massive gray foam-crested waves smashed against the ship. The port bow of the *Liberty* received the brunt of this brutal assault, and the impact would send the bowsprit leaping toward the sky, and the brigantine began to heave slowly over, with the bowsprit rising, rising, rising ever more steeply, until she rolled and slid down the far side of the wave, and the ship would settle for a moment on an even keel, heeling into the wind as the wave passed beneath the stern and lifted it. Then the next wave came, hard on the heels of the one before it, and the bowsprit leaped for the sky again, and she would begin to heave slowly over ... Pitch, roll, heave, roll—in this way the *Liberty* gamely corkscrewed her way through the heavy seas, with the waves crashing over the bulwarks and sweeping the deck.

Even Christopher felt a little nauseated now. He went aft from his forecastle berth to check on his mother and Prissy. Rebecca was trying to console Prissy—a futile attempt.

"We all gwine drown!" screeched Prissy, quite beside herself.

"Don't be ridiculous," said Christopher. "We'll be fine."

"Dere's a big storm a-comin'," said Prissy. "The cap'n done tol' us to stay below. You mark my words, we all gwine drown."

Christopher asked his mother how she was bearing up.

"I'm fine," was Rebecca's stoic reply. "But keep an eye on Mr. Klesko, Christopher. I dont think he's doing too well."

Christopher didn't tell her he had just left Klesko, swaying in his canvas hammock and looking like he would have to get better to die.

Leaving the captain's cabin, he went up a companion-way to the deck, and was thoroughly drenched by a cascade of seawater as he threw open the hatch. He didn't care. It was preferable to staying below, where the sound of the sea hammering against the hull trying to get in, mingled with the creak and groan of the ship timbers as they tried to keep the sea out, and the stench of the lower deck, and the grim, anxious faces of that portion of the crew not on watch all combined to create an oppressive atmosphere.

He saw Nathaniel and the captain on the quarterdeck, and started across the waist to join them. A thirty-foot wave rose up out of the sea and crashed over the port bow. He felt the deck shudder beneath his feet, and lost his balance just as the wave struck him and threw him into the starboard scuppers. The brigantine heeled over and before Christopher could get a grip on anything the water collecting against the bulwark lifted him off the deck. Gripped by sudden panic, he realized that he was about to be swept overboard, and knew he wouldn't last five minutes in such rough seas. He grabbed a handful of rigging and held on for dear life until the *Liberty* settled on its keel. Making it to the quarterdeck, he saw by the expression on Nathaniel's face that the old leatherstocking had witnessed his brush with death.

"You better get below," said Nathaniel, shouting to be heard above the harping of the wind.

"No thanks. As bad as it is up here, it's worse below."

Nathaniel nodded, and turned to look at the captain as the latter yelled to the helmsman to turn her a few points into the wind.

"We'll have to take in another reef," the *Liberty*'s skipper told his first mate, shouting even though the man stood at his shoulder. "There's nothing for it."

"Aye, sir," agreed the mate. "We'll lose canvas if we don't. The wind is picking up." He cast a worried glance aloft.

"And the sea is becoming steeper." The captain glanced grimly at Nathaniel. "No ordinary squall, I fear, Mr. Jones. We are in the very teeth of a hurricane."

"Call all hands, Mr. Wells," said the captain.

Leaning over the poop rail, the *Liberty*'s brass-throated first mate passed the word along. A seaman threw open the forecastle hatch and yelled to the men below.

"All hands! All hands to reef topsails!"

They came pouring out of the hatch, scattering to their stations. Christopher watched them go to work with great admiration for their prowess as well as their nerve. The brigantine pitched and rolled violently. Steep waves crashed down upon the decks. Yet the crew was an experienced lot. They manned the halliards and reef tackles, and Christopher could scarcely believe that any man would have the guts to venture aloft under such conditons. But these men scampered up the rigging, agile as monkeys.

"Haul away!" bellowed Mr. Wells, and his stentorian voice seemed to pierce the banshee wailing of the wind. "Bear those backstays! Hands to the weather braces! Haul in the weather main brace! Haul away, boys!"

In moments he was able to turn to the captain and report that the sails had their reef.

"Bring the men down," replied the captain, well-satisfied with the conduct of his crew. "But have them stand by."

Nathaniel noticed that the *Liberty*'s skipper was continually searching the gray gloom of storm and sea off the starboard side, and the frontiersman had a hunch he knew what the man was looking for. Of course there was nothing to see but driving sheets of rain and towering waves. But there, somewhere near, was the coast—a coast notorious for its treacherous sand reefs.

"Give her a turn into the wind," said the captain.

The helmsman responded. As the brigantine swung to port, Christopher happened to glance up and saw a line of white separate sea and sky. For an instant his horrified mind refused to register what he was seeing—a wave, a wave as tall as the *Liberty*'s mainmast, or so it seemed to him.

"Good God," he breathed.

Wells saw it next. "Grab hold of something and hang on!" cried the first mate.

And then the monstrous wave came down upon them.

Gripping the poop rail for all he was worth, Christopher was slammed against the deck by the impact of tons of descending seawater. He felt the ship shudder and tilt precariously beneath him, and thought, *She's going to break apart. This wave will smash her into so much kindling.* But the ship emerged, popping up to crest like a cork, and reeling down the back side of the wave. As he gasped for breath Christopher heard a rending crash, the screams of men being swept overboard, and looked up to see the mainmast falling, toppling sideways to starboard. The captain was yelling, but Christopher couldn't make out the words. Looking about the quarterdeck, he saw that the helmsman was gone, and the wheel was spinning madly. Mr. Wells lunged for it, and tried to hold on, but it was turning with such velocity that it struck him down, and he went sliding across the deck.

The next wave, as tall as the one before, was instantly upon them. The *Liberty,* helmless, pivoted, and the comber caught her broadside. She tilted sharply to port as the wave crested and descended to strike her so savagely that the impact shook Christopher loose from the rail. The brigantine convulsed, lurched sickeningly, rolled, and then struck with a deafening crash, the rending of timbers. The stump of the mainmast was swept against the quarterdeck, shattering the poop rail. Christopher was hurled into a tangle of rigging, to which he clung for dear life as yet another comber smashed down upon the mortally wounded ship and almost drowned him.

"Christopher!"

He dimly heard his grandfather's voice, and answered with a weak "Here!" An instant later, Nathaniel appeared, struggling to reach him through the tangle of shrouds and ratlines.

"She's run aground," said the frontiersman.

Christopher was too shaken to respond. The ship was dying. He could hear it. It was as though the *Liberty* were a living creature, cracking and shrieking and groaning as the relentless sea crashed against her and mercilessly ripped her to pieces. He had never heard such a terrible sound.

"We must find your mother."

Nathaniel's voice was calm and sane and it pierced the mad chaos of noise and destruction to reach Christopher and wrench him free of that strange, deadening apathy which had overwhelmed him.

"Yes," he mumbled, feeling new life pulse through his frozen limbs. "Yes, we've got to find her."

With Nathaniel's help he managed to untangle himself from the rigging. The ship's deck was no longer pitching and heaving. That was something, at least. But every time a comber smacked into her the deck shuddered so violently that he was certain she would disintegrate into splinters. They descended the ladder to the waist, which was littered with the debris of the foremast. The door to the captain's cabin, located beneath the quarterdeck, was blocked by the trunk of the mainmast. Several members of the crew stumbled out of the hatch. Christopher grabbed one of them.

"We need your help."

The seadog stared at him, like a man in a trance, uncomprehending.

"We must get into the captain's cabin!"

Still the man did not speak.

"What's it like below?" asked Nathaniel.

Queried on the subject of the ship and the sea the man seemed to come to life.

"Can't you hear it?" he rasped. "She's broke deep. The sea's in her belly now, and she's coming apart at the seams." He began to struggle to free himself from Christopher's grasp.

"We need help," said Christopher, holding on.

"Help yourself," cried the crewman, becoming frantic. "Get off the ship. Get off and try to make it to shore. It's your only chance."

"Let him go," said Nathaniel, realizing they would get no help from this one.

Christopher complied. The man stumbled away across the deck, vanishing behind a gray curtain of rain and sea.

"Stay here," said Nathaniel. "I'll be back."

The frontiersman returned in a matter of minutes— minutes that crept by like hours for Christopher as he clung to the rigging of the fallen mast and tried to catch his breath between the overwhelming waves. Brandishing an axe, Nathaniel hacked his way through a snarl of tangled rope and canvas until, crouched beneath the shattered trunk of the mast, he was able to reach the door. There was room for only one man, and precious little room at that for wielding an axe against the door, so Christopher had to stand helplessly by, pummeled by the waves that swept across the *Liberty*'s waist, feeling the deck tremble and shift beneath his feet, as the sea surged through great jagged holes in the hull below him and tore at the guts of the doomed vessel.

It seemed like an eternity before Nathaniel called out that he had cut a hole in the door. Christopher scrambled into the captain's cabin, squirming through the hole on his grandfather's heels. He was shocked by the wreckage which filled the cabin. Gaping gashes had been torn out of the flanks of the brigantine, through which the battering sea rushed in with every wave. He called out, in a panic, and was relieved to hear Rebecca's voice in the darkness. Clambering over and under shattered timbers, he and Nathaniel reached her side.

Rebecca was kneeling in the water which sloshed too and fro across the deck, cradling Prissy's head in her lap. A heavy beam lay across Prissy's chest—too heavy for them to budge. Nathaniel attacked it with the axe, but the wood was old and seasoned and nearly as hard as iron, and the frontiersman was quick to realize that it would take hours to cut through. They didn't have hours. The groan of the ship was loud in their ears. At any moment the *Liberty* would surrender to the sea and break apart. It was as inevitable as death.

"We've got to get you out of here," he told Rebecca.

"I won't go. Prissy's still alive."

Christopher felt the flutter of a pulse in Prissy's wrist. She was unconscious, and blood leaked out of the corner of her mouth.

"He's right, Mother. There is nothing we can do for her. The ship is breaking apart . . ."

"I won't leave her while she lives!" cried Rebecca.

Christopher tried to lift her, hooking his arms beneath hers. She fought him. "Prissy!" she wailed. He got a better hold around her waist and pulled her away, but then another wave struck the brigantine, spewing through the gaps in the cabin wall, and with a tremendous wrenching sound the deck shifted violently and he fell. When he looked up the fallen beam was gone and so was Prissy, and there was a jagged hole where half of the cabin floor had collapsed. A geyser of water spewed up through the hole, temporarily blinding him. The *Liberty* was moving again, lurching soggily sideways, then tilting at a sickening angle to starboard.

Another wave struck, hurling the wreck against the reef, and part of the quarterdeck gave way, raining debris down upon them. Above the din Christopher heard Nathaniel shouting, saw the frontiersman silhouetted for an instant against the white foam of another incoming comber, legs braced wide apart on the disintegrating deck, swinging the axe with all his might, and knocking out the remnant of the cabin wall on the starboard side. Christopher struggled to his feet, shouldering aside the wreckage of the quarterdeck, his arm still locked around Rebecca's waist.

"Jump!" yelled Nathaniel.

Christopher half-fell, half-jumped through the hole, holding on to his mother, plunging feet first into the sea, and the sea clutched greedily at him with powerful undercurrents, wrenching Rebecca out of his grasp. He flailed frantically, his lungs bursting. Bobbing to the surface, he was struck a stinging blow across the shoulders by a timber. Clutching at it, he saw Rebecca, and reached out his hand, and she took it. He pulled her to the timber. Above them, the stern half of the *Liberty* disappeared beneath a breaking wave, and the wave descended upon them and drove them underwater. Christopher was slammed against the sandy flank of the reef, an impact so severe that it knocked the wind out of him, and he choked on the seawater pouring into his mouth. Then the sea lifted him up and carried him across the reef, into calmer waters; having almost killed him it now delivered him. Rebecca was still clinging to the timber. The thundering waves spent themselves against the reef, and the gentler surf deposited them on wet Texas sand littered with the debris from the wreck of the brigantine *Liberty*.

Chapter 23

All day the storm raged, tearing the wreck apart, dragging some of it down into the deep, hurling the rest across the reef, where the surf took it and deposited it on the beach. Broken in two, the brigantine's stern portion sank into deep water. The bow, tilted at a forty-five-degree angle, the bowsprit pointing like an accusing finger at the gray and sullen sky, clung fast to the seaward side of the sand reef, a monument to the helpless inconsequence of man when confronted by the cataclysmic power of nature.

But there is one thing nature cannot conquer—the indomitable will of man.

Washed up on the beach, like so much flotsam, half-drowned and exhausted, trembling uncontrollably from the cold and the shock of the disaster he had but narrowly survived, Christopher wanted nothing more than to lie there in the wet sand and close his eyes and sleep. Instead, he forced himself to his feet and went to work. Helping Rebecca to the meager shelter from the howling wind and driving rain provided by low sand dunes which began fifty yards from the edge of the sea, and which extended inland as far as the eye could see, Christopher returned to the beach to search for more survivors. Seeing a body floating in the surf, he waded out to it, a prayer on his lips. It wasn't Nathaniel, or O'Connor, or Klesko, but rather a member of the ill-fated *Liberty*'s crew, dead, his skull crushed, his face a bloody mask.

He found Nathaniel next. The frontiersman was struggling to get ashore. His arm was broken. The captain's cabin had disintegrated an instant after Christopher and Rebecca had abandoned ship. A falling beam had struck Nathaniel, breaking bone and hurling him, half-conscious, into the sea. Christopher pronounced him lucky to be alive, and helped him to the place in the dunes where Rebecca was waiting out the storm. Now that she had something to do, someone to care for, Rebecca came to life. She promptly set Nathaniel's arm, using shattered pieces of wood from the *Liberty* for splints, and tearing the hem out of her skirt for strips of cloth with which she secured the splints to her father's arm.

Christopher continued to patrol the beach, all but oblivious now to the gale force wind that tried to knock him off his feet, as well as to the rain that fell so hard it stung. He could scarcely remember a dry and sunny world. Debris from the wreck was strewn for more than a mile in either direction. He found five men alive, and took each one back to Rebecca and Nathaniel. One of them was Wells, the first mate. He insisted on helping Christopher with his rescue and salvage work. The other men, two of them injured, huddled in the dunes, dazed and listless.

As time went on, Christopher despaired of finding O'Connor and Klesko. He came across four more bodies—all crew members. These were retrieved from the sea and left on the beach for proper burial later. He kept telling himself there was hope for his friends, but he knew that in all likelihood their bodies, like poor Prissy's, had been claimed by the sea.

With the first mate's help, he salvaged some timbers, rope, and a tattered portion of sail, and managed to fashion a makeshift shelter for Rebecca and the others with this material. By now he was staggering from sheer exhaustion. Rebecca begged him to rest, but he refused, staying on his feet until the long and terrible day drew to a close, and the gray cocoon of the storm darkened with the coming of night. In the falling light he made two significant discoveries. One was a crate of oranges. Robertson had made a point of shipping some fresh fruit to his colonists. His people were faring well enough with their crops of corn and other vegetables, and they had planted fruit trees, but these would take a few years to mature and produce. Christopher's last discovery of the day was his own trunk. He couldn't believe his luck. All the trunk's contents—clothes, a few books, including his prized possession, Napoleon's *Maxims,* and his father's Tripolitan cutlass, were as dry as bone.

Seeing Christopher's trunk, Rebecca thought of her own belongings—the four-poster bed, the rocking chair, her books, and most importantly, the box in which she had kept the money, their stake, under lock and key. Thinking of the future, she despaired.

"Don't fret, Becky," said Nathaniel. "We've got our lives. We'll make out just fine."

"Thank God we placed the thoroughbreds in Mr. Robertson's charge," she said, trying to look on the bright side.

Christopher ate an orange and then curled up in the wet sand and went immediately to sleep, the canvas overhead cracking like a whip in the wind.

He was awakened in the middle of the night by the first mate's stentorian voice, opened his bleary, salt-encrusted eyes to see a man, his clothes in tatters, stumbling toward the shelter. The night was pitch black, and he could not see who it was until the man tripped over his legs and fell across him.

"O'Connor!"

The Irishman was too weak to move. Lying where he fell, his eyes fluttering closed, O'Connor managed a wan smile. "Jig on your grave . . ." he mumbled, and passed out.

*   *   *

When Christopher awoke he could not tell if it was morning or afternoon. Rain was still pouring out of an overcast sky. The sea was still rough, the combers booming as they spent their fury against the reef.

He and Wells continued their salvage work. They found little of value until, some hours later, the first mate spotted a crate half-buried in the sand some yards offshore. With the surf foaming around their waists, they tried to carry the crate ashore, but could hardly budge it. Returning to camp, they enlisted the aid of O'Connor and one of the crew members. The others were in no condition to walk, much less work. Gathering up some rope, the four men managed to drag the crate up onto the beach. Intent on acquainting themselves with its contents, they broke open the lid.

Inside, nestled in straw, was the barrel of a cannon.

"What the hell is that?" asked Wells.

"Six-pounder," said Christopher. "Brass-mounted, of French manufacture."

"Cannon?" Wells was dumbfounded. "This couldn't be from the ship. We carried no cannon."

"None that you knew of," said O'Connor. "It had to have been on the *Liberty*. Did you handle the manifest?"

"Why no. The captain did. But ..." The first mate's denial died stillborn. Staring at the cannon, and realizing that O'Connor was right—it must have come from the brigantine's cargo hold—he comprehended the truth of the matter.

"Interesting supplies Mr. Robertson was sending to his people," remarked Christopher. "Somewhat more lethal than the usual coffee and tobacco."

"Coffee and tobacco are contraband," said Wells. "The Mexicans reserve for themselves the right to sell those commodities."

"Yet we had coffee and tobacoo aboard."

"Yes. Usually, a bribe is sufficient to persuade a customs officer to turn a blind eye."

"I doubt if he would turn a blind eye to this."

"I wonder if there was powder and shot?" murmured O'Connor.

"One thing is certain," said Wells. "If the Mexicans find this it will go badly for us."

They decided to conceal the crated gun in the sand dunes, burying it in a shallow grave which Christopher marked with two shattered timbers from the wrecked ship.

Later in the day the wind and rain slackened, and they caught their first glimpse of the sun as it set in a blaze of orange glory behind strips of purple clouds. Christopher had never been so happy to see anything in his whole life. The next day dawned warm and clear. No one ventured far from camp that day. Everyone lay about in the sun, drying out, eating oranges, drinking rainwater which had collected in the canvas of their makeshift shelter. Rebecca tended to the two wounded sailors as best she could. One had a broken leg, which she set, and several crushed ribs, which she could do nothing about. He was bleeding internally, and she feared he would not survive. The other had a hole in his side, having been impaled on a jagged piece of spar.

"Someone has got to go for help," Nathaniel told Christopher. "We can't stay here forever, and those two men need a doctor's care. I'll leave in the morning."

"I'll go. You're in no condition with that arm. Stay here, Grandpa, and keep everybody alive until I get back."

"Fresh water's the problem," said the frontiersman. "Or it will be before long. We may have to move inland to find a creek or something. If so, I'll leave plenty of sign, so you can find us."

Before sunrise the next morning, Christopher was ready to go. Using a rope for a sling, he carried the Tripolitan cutlass on his back. He also had a makeshift pouch containing several oranges.

"You might be mistaken for a pirate," said O'Connor, only half-joking.

Christopher had to agree. He was barefoot, his trousers ending in tatters at his ankles, and one leg torn to the knee. His shirt wasn't in much better condition. His trunk had contained several shirts and an extra pair of pants, but he had given O'Connor one of his shirts—the Irishman had been without one—and another had been sacrificed to make bandages for the wounded, leaving him a single change of clothes. He wasn't going to ruin them on an excursion like this one. He had tried to fit into his extra pair of boots, but to no avail. His feet were too swollen. On his head, as protection against the sun, he wore a strip of cloth tied in a knot at the back.

"All I lack is a ring in my ear," he said.

"I ought to be going with you," said O'Connor.

"No. I'd feel better knowing you were here to look after my folks."

"Look out for them?" The Irishman laughed. "It's your grandfather who will be taking care of the rest of us, I'm sure. He's a pretty remarkable fellow."

"He is that," agreed Christopher.

He said his goodbyes to the others. Rebecca put on a brave front, but he saw right through it. He told her not to worry, and promised to return with help within a fortnight.

Striking out due north, he crossed more than a mile of sand dunes before coming to a large body of water. Tasting it, he found it to be seawater. He turned west, and traveled several more miles before coming to a point of land from whence he could see breakers foaming over a hidden reef and, beyond, the limitless blue-green expanse of the Gulf of Mexico.

The truth was apparent to him then. They had been shipwrecked on an island.

Retracing his steps, Christopher returned to the place where the inland waterway was at its most narrow, some two hundred yards. He swam it without difficulty, and it wasn't until he was on the other shore, sitting down to rest for a moment and eat an orange, that he saw the fins of the sharks cleaving the water right where he had made the crossing. He shuddered, forced himself to finish the orange, and moved on.

Heading north again, he soon found himself in the blessed shade of a hardwood forest. He was cheered just to see a tree again. The woodlands opened up here and there to meadows of lush grass and an occasional salt marsh. He spotted wild turkey and quail in abundance, as well as several white-tailed deer. His mouth watered and his stomach clenched at the thought of venison steak or a nice juicy turkey leg roasting over a fire, and he wished fervently that he had a rifle. The cutlass was less than worthless under these circumstances.

Christopher didn't care if he ever saw the open sea again, and he was reluctant to leave the forest, but he realized that his wisest course would be to return to the coast and follow it until he came to either the mouth of a navigable river or—the best case—a town. Wells had told him that there were several villages along the coast, and all the colonies he had ever heard of were located on one of the rivers: the Trinity, the Neches, the Brazos, or the Colorado. With this in mind, he turned back. Reaching the coast, he headed west, a sun brown scarecrow in tattered clothes leaving lonely footprints in the wet sand of a beach that curved off into a hazy infinity.

He slept that night among the dunes, and awoke to the eternal roar of the surf and the raucous cries of seagulls. The sun was already high and hot, bleeding the blue out of the Texas sky. Christopher lay there a moment, wincing at the cramps in his empty stomach. The inside of his mouth was dry as old leather, and he knew he would have to detour inland and find a freshwater source before the day was out. He did not relish taking another step. But the thought of Nathaniel and his mother and the rest motivated him, and he picked himself up with a groan. They were depending on him, and he would not let them down.

Then he saw the row of lances, beyond the next dune, and heard the creak of saddles, the jingle of bit chains, and then someone barking a harsh command—in Spanish.

Christopher threw himself to the ground. Heart racing, he crawled to the crest of the next dune and dared to raise his head for a look down at the beach.

They were Mexican troops—lancers, with their weapons held at the vertical, couched in stirrup cups. They rode by twos, and the lances of the first pair were adorned with red-and-green pennants. In front of the column rode an officer, and in front of him by a good twenty paces was an Indian, jogging to keep ahead of the horsemen, his head constantly swiveling back and forth as he scanned the sand for sign, raising his eyes now and again to check the horizon. The Indian wore a breechclout and headband. He was short and stocky, nothing like the tall, slender, handsome Indians of the eastern forests that Christopher was accustomed to.

The lancers wore straight-brimmed black hats, green *chaquetas,* and black pants tucked into cavalry boots. In addition to the lance, each was armed with a pistol and a short saber. The officer was similarly attired, distinguishable from his men by the shoulder tabs on his jacket. He, too, carried pistol and saber, but was without a lance.

Christopher took a quick head count. Sixteen lancers, not counting the officer. Two of them were in charge of four pack horses. One of the packhorses was carrying a brass-mounted French six-pounder barrel identical to the one he and Wells had found among the wreckage of the *Liberty.*

Behind the packhorse trudged four men. Their hands were pinioned behind their backs, and a long rope was

looped around their necks. The end of the rope was
secured to a heavy ship's timber in such a way that the
prisoners were forced to drag the timber along behind
them. The timber laid a deep furrow in the sand, and
the men were straining to make headway. The sheer
brutality of this sadistic arrangement turned Christopher's blood to ice. With the rope around their necks
all four men were slowly but surely choking to death.
They were guarded by two lancers, and when one of the
captives faltered, a guard would prod him with his lance.

Klesko was one of the prisoners.

Christopher recognized the others as members of the
Liberty's crew. No doubt they had washed ashore further
along the coast, and fallen into the hands of the patrol.
And Christopher was willing to bet that the six-pounder
had come ashore with them. That would explain why
they were being treated like criminals.

He was happy to see Klesko alive, but under these
circumstances he had to wonder how long the riverman
could survive. Because of his size and strength he was
faring better than his three companions. They looked
half-dead. When the man in line behind Klesko, who
was in the lead spot, stumbled and fell to his knees,
Klesko turned to lift him bodily to his feet. When Klesko
stopped the whole line came to a standstill, and that
angered the guards. Their orders were to keep up with
the rest of the column. One of the lancers spurred his
horse forward, lowered his lance, and drove the point
into Klesko's shoulder. Christopher winced as he saw
the spray of blood. Klesko staggered under the blow, yet
somehow managed to keep to his feet. Christopher was
astonished. So was the lancer. Klesko glowered at his
tormentor, then turned and plodded after the column,
leaning against the rope, his whole mighty frame shud-
dering with the strain.

"I'm a child of calamity!" cried Klesko, a wheezing
roar. Christopher couldn't believe he could even whisper

with that timber-anchored rope around his neck. "I'm the bloodiest son of a wildcat that ever lived. They call me Sudden Death and General Desolation. Blood's my natural drink. When I'm cold I boil the Gulf of Mexico and take a bath. When I'm hot I call down the winter storm from up Canada way. When I'm hungry and thirsty, famine and drought are found across the land wherever I've been. With one look I can freeze the blood in your veins, and with my bare hands I can grind your bones into dust. Whoop! Don't look at me with the naked eye! Beware. The massacre of whole communities is my favorite pastime."

The guards exchanged bewildered glances.

Hidden in the dunes, Christopher had to smile. God bless Klesko and his unbreakable will! One had to wonder if maybe this bearded Goliath could haul that ship's timber all the way to Louisiana on his own.

Still, it was almost unbearable to stand by and watch Klesko and the three crewmen being tortured so. If this was any indication of how the Mexicans behaved, little wonder the Texans were talking independence. It was one thing to arrest a man suspected of trying to smuggle contraband—and the cannon was most assuredly that—but to murder him by inches like this was depraved.

Yet what could he do against seventeen soldiers? It didn't take a Napoleon Bonaparte to figure out that this was a battle he could not possibly win.

The fact that the column was headed east was another concern. Their course would take them to the island where Nathaniel and the others were camped. Clearly the Mexicans were searching for the wreck. It was reasonable to assume they would scout the island. Christopher could not bear to think of his grandfather being treated like Klesko and the three men from the *Liberty*. And heaven only knew what these sadists would do to his mother.

Resigned to the fact that there was nothing he could

do for Klesko at present, Christopher made up his mind to warn Nathaniel and his mother.

Saying a silent prayer for Klesko and the crewmen, Christopher crawled deeper into the dunes. When he was certain that he was far enough from the beach to remain undetected, he got to his feet and started running. In no time at all he was exhausted. He could imagine nothing more difficult than running in deep sand. But he had to go on as far as he could in the dunes to put sufficient distance between himself and the Mexican lancers so that when he emerged onto the beach, where he could make much better time, he would not be seen.

He ran until he thought his heart would burst, until his legs felt like chunks of lead, until his muscles burned like red hot flame—until he simply could not run anymore. Somehow he made two miles—he had no way of calculating the distance, but it seemed to him to be at least twenty miles—before stumbling out onto the beach at a spot where the waves reached the base of the dunes. A quick glance to the west—he could not see the column. With a grateful sob he staggered into the surf and collapsed.

The wash of the waves over his body revived him. Not much, but enough to push, groaning, to his feet. Tried to run, but he seemed to have lost control of his legs. He reeled and staggered like a drunken man, arms flopping uselessly against his sides. He still had sufficient wits about him to keep to the surf. The waves would wash away all trace of his passage, so that not even the Indian scout would know he had passed this way.

Yes, it was easier to run on firm, wet sand than in the dunes, but it was too late for that to matter. He couldn't make it. Lack of food and water had taken its toll on him. An incoherent cry of dismay escaped him, and an instant later he passed out on his feet and fell into the shallow surf. . . .

Someone was shaking him.

He came to, sputtering in the wash of saltwater, and his heart lurched in his chest as he remembered the Mexican lancers, and he struck out blindly, thinking they had found him.

But the man bending over him was a red-faced, blond-bearded Anglo in grime-blackened buckskin pants and linsey-woolsey shirt, and he carried no lance, but rather a double-barreled Fox shotgun.

"Take it easy, mister," grumbled the man. "Kin you walk, or do I have to carry you?"

"I can walk," gasped Christopher.

"Good. Then let's get the hell off this beach. Them Mexcans are a-comin'."

Chapter 24

Five men on horseback were waiting back in the dunes. Four of them were clad in buckskin or homespun. The fifth was dressed quite differently. He wore a blue clawhammer coat, red pantaloons, and a white planter's hat cocked rakishly on his head. A brace of fancy pistols were stuck in his belt.

"He's alive, Will," said the man who had gone out to fetch Christopher. He addressed the man in the red pantaloons. "Looks about half-drowned and three-quarters starved, though."

"Identify yourself," said the man named Will.

"Christopher Groves. My family and I were aboard the *Liberty*. She was wrecked a few days ago, just up the coast from here."

"How many survivors?"

"I'm not sure. Counting myself and the four men who have been captured by the Mexican lancers, I know of thirteen. There might be more. Who are you, anyway?"

"William Barrett Travis, at your service. These men and I are from Anahuac. It was to Anahuac that the *Liberty* was bound. We heard a rumor that disaster had struck, and came to investigate. So did Captain Piedras." Travis grimaced. "Unfortunately, he recovered one of the cannons."

"We have the other," said Christopher.

Travis leaned forward in the saddle. "We?"

"My mother and grandfather and six others are encamped on an island a few miles east of here. We pulled one of the six-pounders from the sea."

"East of here, you say," murmured Travis. "Then Captain Piedras will no doubt find them."

"Two of the sailors are in bad shape."

"They'll all be in bad shape when Piedras finds 'em with that other cannon," opined the blond-bearded man.

"Precisely," said Travis.

For a moment the others watched Travis in grim silence, and it was apparent that he was the one they looked to for leadership.

"Tucker, do you think you and Lucas can hold Piedras up for a while?"

"How long?" asked the blond-bearded man.

"At least a few hours. Preferably until sundown."

Tucker scratched his beard. "I reckon so. How 'bout it, Lucas?"

"Suits me."

"You mustn't be caught," warned Travis. "It would go hard for all who lived in Anahuac if you were."

"We'll take a few shots at 'em from the dunes," said Tucker, smiling as he warmed to the idea. "Piedras will come boilin' after us, and we'll lead 'em a merry chase. Won't we, Lucas?"

"Sounds good," was the laconic reply.

"Meanwhile, we will get those people, and that cannon, safely off the island," said Travis.

"Wait just a minute," said Christopher. "What about the four prisoners?"

"What about them?"

"You can't leave them in the hands of those sadists."

"This is neither the time nor the place to start a shooting war, Mr. Groves."

"Isn't that what those cannon are for?"

"The cannon are to be used to protect ourselves from the Indians who have a bad habit of sweeping down from the high plains to raid our farms and village. The

Mexican soldiers are too busy trying to catch smugglers to fight Comanches, it seems. Speaking of Indians, Tucker, be sure to kill that Tonkawa son of a bitch who's scouting for Piedras.''

Tucker grinned from ear to ear. "Be my pleasure, Will.''

"Mr. Groves, you may ride double with me.''

"On of those four prisoners is a friend of mine. I will not abandon him.''

"Loyalty is a commendable virtue. But there is nothing you can do for your friend at present. If he gets back to the presidio alive then, perhaps, we can save him.''

"You're a heckuva lawyer, Will,'' said Tucker, "but you're not that good. Piedras will like as not chop his head off and stick it on a pole as a warning to other smugglers.''

"My friend is not a smuggler,'' protested Christopher. "We had no idea those cannon were aboard.''

"Of course not,'' said Travis. "Only the captain knew. I believe it was Benjamin Franklin who said that three men can keep a secret—if two of them are dead.''

"How is it that you know?''

Travis smiled. "Robertson has my assurance that I will take good care of those six-pounders.''

"I'm not going with you,'' said Christopher.

The smile vanished. Travis' eyes flashed cold blue flame. "We are not playing a game, Groves. More lives than just those four hang in the balance.''

"What if I could get that cannon back for you?''

Travis stared at him.

"If Tucker and Lucas can draw most of those lancers off into the dunes, that Captain Piedras will order the prisoners and packhorses to remain under guard on the beach. If he leaves only a couple of guards, I can take care of them, free the prisoners, and take that six-pounder back.''

Travis thought it over. A slow smile crept across his angular face. "A clever strategy," he conceded.

"It gets better. I'm a stranger to the Mexicans. If they catch me, there's no way they can connect me with Anahuac."

"You ought to be a lawyer, Groves. You make a compelling case. But can you handle two lancers?"

"Give me a rifle or a pistol, and I will."

"I don't like it," said Tucker. "He'll git hisself kilt for sartin."

"If he does," said Travis tersely, looking straight at Christopher, "they'll take him for a smuggler. He's right about that. Then we'll be off the hook."

"Until they find us with the other cannon," said one of the Texans.

"When that happens it will be too late."

Christopher thought that was an intriguing and cryptic answer, but now was not the time to ask Travis to clarify it.

"Here they come!" said Lucas, who had positioned himself atop a nearby dune from whence he could watch the beach.

"How about it?" pressed Christopher.

Again the Texans looked to Travis, waiting for his decision. It was not long in coming. Travis was not an indecisive man.

"Very well, then." He drew one of the pistols from his belt, handed it to Christopher. "As you can see, this is a matched set. I would like to have it back when you are done with it."

"Believe me, I'd like to be able to return it."

Travis laughed. "Good luck. Come on, men."

He reined his horse sharply about and kicked it into motion. Followed by three of the Texans, he rode deeper into the dunes.

Christopher turned to find Tucker looking at him with a positively morose expression on his face.

"You don't think I'm going to make it, do you?" asked Christopher.

"Well," drawled Tucker, "I don't think I'll ever see an elephant fly, either—but I wouldn't mind being wrong." The Texan mounted up. "We'll move on down a ways, so's the column will pass you by. Mebbe you kin Injun-up on 'em from behind."

He and Lucus rode on. Christopher crawled to the top of a dune on his belly. Looking west, along the curve of the shoreline, he saw the column of lancers approaching. Suddenly he felt very much alone. But he was resolved to rescue Klesko, or perish in the attempt.

The column had just passed Christopher's position when the first shot was fired. A pink mist suddenly appeared around the head of the Indian scout loping in advance of the lancers. The Indian pitched sideways, twitched once, and lay dead in the sand.

An instant later Tucker's shotgun roared. With a shrill scream the horse of one of the lead lancers went down. The lancer's left leg was shredded by the buckshot. His right leg was pinned beneath the thrashing horse.

The column was thrown into turmoil—shouting men, pivoting horses. Captain Piedras spun his horse around, barking orders, trying to bring order out of confusion. Another shot—Christopher knew it came from the rifle of the Texan named Lucas. A lancer somersaulted over the haunches of his horse to lay sprawled and lifeless.

Christopher realized that the lancers, while they had a forbidding and very martial appearance, were not well-suited for the kind of fighting they would see against these Texans. They would do all right in a set piece battle, in a charge against a line of infantry, for instance. But unless they could close with their enemy, their lances were practically worthless.

Piedras was a professional. He kept his wits about him. His well-trained troops responded, recovering quickly from their initial surprise. With lances lowered they charged into the dunes. Piedras lingered a moment to order the two men responsible for the packhorses to watch the four prisoners. Everyone else went into the dunes, and the captain was hot on their heels, the blade of his drawn sword flashing in the sun.

So far so good, thought Christopher. Only two men left behind for him to deal with. There was no reason for Piedras to leave more. The prisoners would not take much watching. All three of the crewmen collapsed, exhausted, into the sand, scarcely conscious of events around them. Klesko, on the other hand, remained standing, watching the lancers disappear into the dunes in pursuit of their ambushers. But there was little the burly riverman could do to trouble the two guards, with his hands bound and anchored to the heavy timber by the rope around his neck.

Christopher heard Tuck's shotgun boom again, farther away this time. The chase was on. The two Texans were going to lead Piedras and his lancers on a merry chase. Christopher wished them luck—and made his move.

While one of the lancers left behind took charge of the packhorses, his colleague dismounted and rushed to the aid of the man who was pinned beneath his dying horse. The former was watching the dunes, where the rest of the patrol had gone. He did not see Christopher coming up from behind until it was too late. His shout of alarm was cut short by the crack! of Christopher's pistol. Christopher waited until the last possible moment to shoot, so that when he did finally squeeze the trigger it was at very close range. The bullet struck the lancer squarely in the chest and knocked him out of the saddle. The reins of the packhorses slipped from his dead hand. The animals scattered. Christopher gave no thought at the moment to the cannon. Laden as they were, the packhorses would not stray far. Time enough later, if he survived, to retrieve the six-pounder.

He had the Tripolitan cutlass drawn. A single stroke, and he cut the rope from the timber. Klesko roared with delight as the razor-sharp blade sliced the rope which bound his wrists together. Christopher moved on, leaving Klesko to deal with the rope around his neck.

The second guard had drawn his pistol. Dismounted, he stood in the duellist's stance and drew a bead on Christopher. A packhorse darted between them. This bought Christopher valuable seconds. The lance of the Mexican he had shot lay in the sand at his feet. Christopher discarded the cutlass, scooped up the twelve-foot weapon, and charged. The lancer's pistol spit yellow flame and white powder smoke. The bullet made a disconcertingly loud cracking sound as it missed Christopher by inches. An instant later Christopher drove the lance through the Mexican. As the man fell, Christopher saw that the lancer pinned beneath his horse also had a pistol in his hand. The pistol spoke. Christopher felt the burn of the bullet. He reeled, dropping to one knee, and clutched his arm. The blood was hot and sticky between his fingers. Just a flesh wound—nonetheless, he felt suddenly light-headed and nauseated. Looking up, he saw Klesko lumber past him. The riverman had extricated himself from the rope and picked up the cutlass and now he fell upon the helpless lancer with a vengeance. Christopher turned his head away as the cutlass rose and fell, rose and fell.

A moment later Klesko was kneeling before him, grinning. His face and clothes were splattered with the lancer's blood.

"Damn it all, Christopher, you're a sight for sore eyes! You bad hurt?"

"Just a scratch."

"Your ma. Is she . . . ?"

"She's alive."

"I reckon I'm gonna have to get religion. I told the Almighty I'd go to church if He'd just make certain she came through in one piece. I didn't think He'd listen to the likes of me, but I guess I was wrong. How 'bout the others?"

"Prissy's dead. The others are well. We've got to get out of here before the lancers come back."

"Let 'em come," growled Klesko. "I've got a score to settle with those buzzards."

"Settle it later. We're getting out of here. Catch that horse with the cannon on it."

Christopher picked himself up and listened for a moment to the sound of distant gunfire. He could only hope that Piedras and the rest of the lancers had not heard the shooting on the beach. Apparently Tucker and Lucas were doing their job.

Looking about him at the dead soldiers, it occurred to Christopher that this was a hell of way to make a new beginning in Texas.

Klesko managed to catch two of the packhorses, while one of the dead lancer's mounts stood passively by and let Christopher collect its reins. The packhorse that wasn't carrying the six-pounder had its burden of provisions removed and a new burden, one of the crewmen, put on its back. A second crewman was helped into the saddle of the lancer's mount. Neither man looked able to take another step. The third member of the *Liberty*'s crew, who identified himself as John Barnwell, had held up better than his two colleagues. He was a squinty-eyed old seadog, twice the age of the others, but obviously twice as durable.

"You ought to be riding, too," he told Christopher, with a glance at the younger man's bloody sleeve.

"I'll make it."

"Where do we go?" asked Klesko.

"Anahuac. It's somewhere up the coast. I'm not sure how far. But we'd better swing inland. Those lancers will be looking for us."

"I know this coast like the back of my hand," said Barnwell. "Anahuac's about thirty miles from here."

"Thirty miles!" Christopher grimaced. "Well, I guess we'd better get started."

"Just a minute." Barnwell collected the pistols and the shot pouches of the dead men. "In case we run into them bastards again."

Christopher didn't bother telling him that if Piedras caught up with them they were as good as dead.

They moved a couple of miles inland before turning west, keeping as much as possible to the heavily wooded areas. There was plenty of good cover, but it made for slow going. Christopher, Klesko, and Barnwell each led a horse. It was all that Barnwell's shipmates could do to stay in their saddles.

It was a day of unending misery for Christopher, one he thought would never end. Apart from his wound, and the anxiety of being a fugitive on the run, he worried constantly about his mother and Nathaniel. Had Travis managed to rescue them from that island?

Finally the sun dipped below the horizon, and they found a good place to camp for the night, in a clearing deep in the heart of a thicket. Klesko used one of the pistols to bag a wild turkey while Barnwell built a small fire. Christopher was of the opinion that neither the shot nor the fire was a good idea, but Klesko would not heed his warnings.

"We've got a long way to go, and we need food," said the riverman.

While the turkey, impaled on a stick, sizzled over the flames, Klesko took a more careful look at Christopher's wound. He shook his head.

"You've lost a lot of blood."

"It's just a scratch. Don't worry about it."

"I'm worried about it plenty. If I let anything happen to you your ma will skin me alive."

Klesko used gunpowder to cauterize the wound, pouring it from a flask into the wound and setting it ablaze with the burning end of a stick plucked from the campfire. That just about finished Christopher off. Though he was starving he scarcely found the strength to eat. Had anyone asked him what he desired most from life at that moment it would have been a month flat on his back in the heavenly luxury of a feather bed. Even the hard ground felt good. His stomach full, he slipped into a deep and exhausted sleep.

When Barnwell shook him awake it was daylight. Christopher sat up quickly—and groaned. He was stiff as a board, his whole body a solid mass of pain. Barnwell put a finger to his lips.

"Riders," he whispered. "Klesko's gone to see."

Christopher was sure it had to be Piedras and his lancers. But when Klesko returned to the clearing he had Travis and Nathaniel with him. Christopher was so relieved to see them he didn't know whether to laugh or cry. He asked about his mother. Nathaniel assured him that Rebecca was fine. They all were, thanks to Travis and his Texans.

"What about Tucker and Lucas?"

Travis nodded. "Worked like a charm. Piedras is running in circles." Spotting the cannon, his eyes flashed with delight. "So you pulled it off, Mr. Groves. Splendid piece of work. We'll bury both cannon, somewhere conveniently close to Anahuac, until the time comes."

"The time for what?" asked Klesko.

"Why, to win our independence, of course."

Klesko felt his neck where the rope had rubbed it raw. "I'm ready for that fight," he growled.

"I hope all of you will see fit to settle near Anahuac," said Travis.

"The Mexicans will be looking for us," said Barnwell.

"We'll find a safe place to hide the four of you, until such time as we can make arrangements to get you safely back to the United States." Trvais looked at Nathaniel and Christopher. "As for the rest of you, there will be some questions asked, but none we can't answer. Piedras won't be able to connect you with the *Liberty*."

"I don't want to go back," said Klesko, crestfallen. The thought of being so far away from Rebecca Groves made him sick to his stomach.

"Don't worry," Nathaniel told him. "We've come too far together to split up now."

"His staying will not be without risk," warned Travis. "Piedras knows his face."

Christopher laughed. It struck him as absurdly funny to be weighing risk after everything they had been through. As far as he was concerned, Klesko stayed, and the devil could take the hindmost.

Chapter 25

Anahuac had been established in 1821, when a Spanish presidio was constructed at the mouth of the Trinity River and made a port of entry for American colonists. Erected on the eastern shore of Galveston Bay, the town consisted of about sixty homes and a dozen businesses. The streets were well-ordered, the buildings stoutly made of timber harvested from the abundant forests in the vicinity. Farms prospered on the fertile black bottomland.

The first order of business upon their arrival in Anahuac was the concealment of the two French six-pounders. They were buried at the edge of a swamp two miles south of town. Almost everyone knew the location, but that was no cause for concern. Christopher soon learned that the Anglo settlers were a tightly knit group. They had their share of internecine squabbles—they were hardheaded individualists, these colonists—but when it came to deceiving the Mexicans they were all of one mind.

The swamp was a place where a Mexican soldier was unlikely to venture. The area swarmed with mosquitoes and poisonous cottonmouth snakes. But the swamp's most fearsome denizen was the alligator. In the gloom of night, when they emerged from their nests to forage for food, their bellowing was a bloodcurdling sound, and a warning heeded by the prudent. In the ten-year history of Anahuac, several people had fallen prey to these beasts.

Travis assured Christopher that the garrison at the presidio, located some miles away at the northern tip of the bay, had a particularly good reason for avoiding the swamp. Two summers ago, a patrol out searching for a deserter had camped in the area. That night, several alligators invaded the camp, crawling boldly into the tents to seize their victims by leg or arm, then making for the blackwater nearby. One of the creatures succeeded in dragging a soldier into the swamp—the alligator killed its victim by drowning. A booted foot was all that was ever found of the unfortunate man. The other alligators were slain, but one soldier lost a leg and died from the loss of blood, while another lost an arm, an alligator's mighty jaws having snapped the limb off at the elbow. No soldier had ventured near the swamp since. It was the safest place to cache the cannon.

The four men who had been Captain Piedras's prisoners also had to be hidden. A farmer named Dale Strom agreed to hide them on his farm. There was an old, long-abandoned dugout in a secluded corner of his property, which Strom had occupied while he cleared his land and built the comfortable cabin he now lived in with his wife and three strapping sons. Klesko and the three sailors could stay in the dugout until other arrangements were made. Strom's wife would take food to them every day, after sundown, and Strom's sons promised to keep a sharp lookout for soldiers.

Anahuac was a major Texas port, a depot for the supplies brought by ship for inland settlements. A coastal schooner arrived from New Orleans a day after the arrival of Christopher and the others. The vessel was due to depart on the following day, and the skipper agreed to carry Wells, Blackburn, and the other seamen back to Louisiana. One of the sailors, however, was in poor shape, and died the night before. He was buried in the

Anahuac cemetery. The rest of the survivors of the ill-fated *Liberty* departed as planned—only hours prior to the arrival of Captain Piedras and his lancers. That solved a problem for Travis and the other residents of Anahuac. There was no mistaking those seadogs for settlers.

"Piedras is no idiot," Travis told Christopher. "He was bound to suspect those fellows as having some connection with the wrecked ship. You and your family, on the other hand, will pass muster. As long as everyone gets their stories straight."

It was decided that, when asked, they would say they had come overland by wagon, and lost all of their belongings in a rough river crossing. An old man named Fulshear, one of Anahuac's founders, agreed to vouch for Nathaniel as his cousin. O'Connor would masquerade as Christopher's brother. Fulshear possessed a head-right, and according to the immigration law, was within his rights to bring family into Texas.

Christopher admired the courage and compassion shown by the Stroms and the other Texans. They were all putting themselves at risk for the sake of strangers. But such generosity and self-sacrifice seemed to be commonplace among these people. They accepted Christopher and the others into their homes with open arms, and freely shared what little they possessed.

Wild game harvested from the forests and the corn they grew themselves were the main components of the settlers' diet. The corn was boiled or fried or roasted. Christopher preferred corn buried, husk and all, in hot ashes. Ears were scraped on graters fashioned from old tinware, and the corn was then pounded into meal, mixed with water, and baked into a rich, sweet bread. Real flour cost ten dollars a barrel after the Mexicans had imposed their tariff, and few of the settlers possessed that kind of money. Pelts were the principal medium of exchange. Domestic animals were almost as scarce as coin of the realm. Those who owned a few hogs or a milch cow were considered fortunate indeed. As a result, milk and butter were also in short supply. Christopher didn't mind. During those first few days in Anahuac he stuffed himself with venison and corn bread. Never had food tasted so good to him.

They were invited to stay in an empty two-room cabin at the edge of town, built by a colonist whose wife had died back in Alabama while waiting for her husband to send for her. The man had departed and never returned. These were fairly comfortable quarters, and they wanted for nothing thanks to the generosity of their neighbors.

Travis mustered all the persuasive powers of an accomplished lawyer in trying to convince Christopher that Anahuac was a good place for him and his family to put down roots. He had taken a liking to Christopher, and was doubly impressed when he learned, through O'Connor, that he had a pair of West Pointers on his hands.

"We'll need good men in the fight that's coming," he told Christopher. "You proved you could handle yourself back there on the coast."

"We're grateful to you and the other folks here for taking us in. But we're just not sure yet where we want to settle. This is a big country. My grandfather and I were talking about taking a trip upriver to have a look around."

"Go ahead. But you won't find a better place than Anahuac, or better people."

"Probably not," conceded Christopher.

"When we have our independence, there will be abundant opportunity for a young man with your background. For my part, I hope to play an active role in creating a republic we can all be proud of. Are you interested in politics?"

"I don't know. I might be."

"We'll have to keep an army," said Travis, warming to his theme. "After we whip the Mexicans we'll have the Indians to deal with. As a graduate of the United States Military Academy I am certain you could have a commission."

"I didn't graduate."

"What? But I thought . . ."

"Evidently O'Connor didn't tell you the whole story." Christopher proceeded to do just that.

"I see," said Travis, and smiled. "I, too, came to Texas to escape an unhappy past."

In the privacy of his cramped one-room law office on the main street of town, as they shared a bottle of rum, Travis told his story, and Christopher came to realize that this man was typical of so many others who had come to Texas to seek a new beginning.

Born in South Carolina in 1809, Travis had moved to Alabama with the rest of his family at the age of nine. While studying the law he taught school to make ends meet. In 1828 he married one of his pupils, Rosanna Cato, the daughter of a prosperous farmer. Travis passed the bar and became the proud father of a strapping baby boy. Then his world was shattered. His young wife was unfaithful to him. They say he killed the other man. He would not confirm or deny this to Christopher. To Texas he had come, hanging his shingle in Anahuac, listing himself on the Mexican census as a widower. As far as he was concerned, Rosanna *was* dead. He resided at Peyton's boardinghouse, down by the docks. He drank a little, gambled a lot, and, as a handsome young bachelor, vigorously engaged in casual affairs, including one with the wife of a lieutenant posted at the Anahuac presidio.

"You like taking risks," said Christopher.

"It adds spice to an otherwise bland existence. I am sick unto death of writing wills and settling petty squabbles over property. Thus far my most spectacular case has been fighting the sale of a blind horse. My best fee has been a yoke of oxen."

He was a well-read man. Christopher discerned this

by his conversation, and confirmed it with a look at a shelf on the wall behind Travis' desk. The shelf was laden with the works of Steele and Shakespeare, Homer and Herodotus. He was also vain, temperamental, supercilious at times, and most assuredly ambitious to a fault. In the beginning of their acquaintance Christopher wondered if Travis wanted war with the Mexicans because he was genuinely committed to winning freedom and justice for all Texans, or if he merely wanted to create an environment in which he could wield power. In the months to come Christopher would meet other men—men who were destined to become leaders in the fight for Texas independence—whom he had no doubt were motivated by a lust for power. But he became convinced in time, and never swerved from that conviction, that Travis, a romantic at heart, wanted the fight for all the right reasons.

When Captain Piedras and his dusty, trail-sore lancers returned to Anahuac they did not enter the town, but rode directly to the presidio. That surprised Travis, who had expected the Mexicans to search every house for cannon or smugglers or both. Several days later, Piedras appeared at the town's meetinghouse, a one-room log structure furnished with split log pews. This building also served as the community's church and dance hall and court of law. The captain summoned Travis, whom he knew to be the town's spokesman. Travis appeared at the borrowed cabin a little while later. The lawyer looked positively grim as he told Christopher, Nathaniel, and Rebecca about his meeting with Piedras.

"I had expected him to turn this town upside down," said Travis. "But he's a clever fellow. Nothing quite so predictable. I expect he would make a worthy opponent in a game of chess."

"He suspects the truth?" asked Nathaniel.

"Of course. He is by nature a suspicious man. That is

not an issue, really. He can't prove anything unless he finds those cannon. Or your friend Klesko. Somehow, though, he knows about the three of you."

"How is that possible?" asked Christopher. "I haven't seen a single soldier."

"Perhaps one of our Mexican civilians. Or maybe more than one. The captain's eyes and ears."

Christopher nodded. He had seen a handful of Mexican women about town, and a number of Mexican men worked as common laborers on the busy docks.

"He wants to talk to you and your grandfather," Travis told Christopher. "And O'Connor, as well. Where is O'Connor, anyway?"

"On his way back to Louisiana. Borrowed a horse and left this morning."

"Louisiana? What for? Is he coming back?"

"I don't know. He's gone to find someone."

"Just as well. There's nothing to worry about. Just stick to the story we've devised. Only be careful what you say. Piedras is a sly fox."

"Why doesn't he want to question me?" asked Rebecca.

"The captain has a rather low opinion of women. He doesn't think they are worth interrogating, I suppose. He can't imagine that you would know anything of value."

Rebecca's eyes flashed with resentment. "If that's his attitude, it's lucky for him he *doesn't* want to talk to me."

Christopher volunteered to go first. Travis walked with him as far as the door to the meetinghouse. Captain Piedras' escort, four lancers, sat their horses in the hot sun, their lances couched, their dark eyes beneath the visors of their shakos regarding the pair of Anglos with nerve-wracking impassity. It seemed to Christopher that somehow they knew he had slain two of their comrades. Of course there was no way they *could* know, unless Travis or Tucker or one of the other Texans who had been on the coast that day had talked. That was inconceivable.

"Keep your wits about you," said Travis, with a final word of advice. "Offer no information unless asked. Say as little as possible."

"Thanks, Counselor."

Travis smiled. "You've got some good nerves, Mr. Groves."

"If you only knew," said Christopher, and went inside.

Captain Piedras sat behind a table at the far end of the room. To one side of him stood a young, slender, scowling lieutenant. The captain rose from his chair as Christopher approached. He was short and stocky, with a square-jawed face and hair graying at the temples. His uniform was impeccable. Christopher sized him up as a stickler for rules and regulations, a man who expected the utmost from his men, a demanding taskmaster who never indulged in leniency. In the field he would be bold and aggressive, perhaps overly so.

Clicking the heels of his high-polished boots together, Piedras bent almost imperceptibly at the waist, a stiff and entirely minimal bow. A faint and meaningless smile touched one corner of his mouth, barely noticeable beneath the bold sweep of a cavalryman's mustache.

"Señor Christopher Groves, I presume."

"Yes." Christopher was surprised by the captain's excellent grasp of the English language.

"Let me welcome you to Anahuac, señor. I hope your voyage was a pleasant one."

"My voyage? I'm afraid I don't understand. I came overland, by wagon."

"Indeed?" Piedras cocked an eyebrow and glanced at the lieutenant, who was glowering at Christopher as though at a common criminal. "Then I am puzzled, señor. You see, my men found a trunk on the beach near the site of the wreck of the brigantine *Liberty*. Your initials were inscribed on that trunk."

A chill of apprehension seized Christopher. His mother had brought his belongings off the island, but under the circumstances it had not been possible to carry off the trunk itself. He had forgotten all about the initials he'd carved on the lid of the trunk on the day of their departure from Elm Tree.

"They may have been my initials," he said, "but that wasn't my trunk. I . . ."

"Yes?"

Offer no information unless asked. "Must be a coincidence."

"Perhaps. Where are you from, Señor Groves?"

"Kentucky."

"What are you doing in the Republic of Mexico?"

"Looking to make a new start."

"Are you a farmer?"

"No."

"What is your occupation?"

"My mother and I raised horses in Kentucky."

"Thoroughbreds? I am told they raise the most excellent horses in Kentucky."

"We like to think so."

"But you brought none of these thoroughbreds with you?"

"No." On the verge of telling Piedras that Sterling Robertson was bringing the three Elm Tree thoroughbreds to Texas with him, Christopher caught himself just in the nick of time. The captain likely knew that there was a connection between Robertson and the *Liberty*.

"So what do you intend to do, señor?"

"I haven't made up my mind. I had heard there were many opportunities in Texas."

"I see. Not really. You are related to Samuel Fulshear?"

"That's right. A distant relative."

"We were not aware that Señor Fulshear had any distant relatives."

"He probably just forgot to mention it."

Piedras gave him a strange look. Christopher cursed himself for a fool. The captain hadn't asked a question, so why the blazes was he talking?

"Well," said Piedras, with a throw-away gesture. "Señor Fulshear is an old man, isn't he? Old men tend to be forgetful."

He glanced expectantly at Christopher, who said nothing.

"Are you aware, Señor Groves, that if you intend to stay you must renounce your United States citizenship and swear an oath of loyalty to the Republic of Mexico?"

"Yes, so I've heard."

"You are willing to do this thing?"

Christopher hesitated. He couldn't help himself. Having spent two years at West Point preparing for a life in the service of the United States of America, he was loath to even pretend to forsake his country. He had known all along that such an oath was required of American settlers in Texas, but he had not given it a moment's thought during the long trip from Kentucky. Or perhaps, he told himself, he simply hadn't wanted to think about it.

"You hesitate," observed Piedras.

"As a soldier you must realize how difficult it would be to turn your back on your country."

"I myself would not do it. Are you a soldier, Señor Groves?"

"No. No, I'm not."

"Perhaps you should return to your country if you love it so much."

"I think I'll stay."

"Ultimately it is I who will decide whether you stay or go. We are no longer encouraging immigration."

"I noticed," said Christopher, becoming exasperated by the captain's imperious tone.

"The problem is that so many of your countrymen have proved to be troublemakers. For instance, are you aware that several suspected smugglers were seen in this vicinity only a few days ago?"

"I wasn't aware of that."

"Of course not," said Piedras sardonically. It was manifestly clear that he thought Christopher was lying. "You are not aware of much at all, are you, señor? You aren't aware of two cannon which were smuggled ashore from the *Liberty*. And neither are you aware of the killing of several of my soldiers a few days ago."

"I'm sorry to hear it."

"I am confident that you are also not aware of Señor Fulshear's age."

Christopher didn't miss a beat. "Afraid not. Like I said, he's a very distant relative. Ever since I can remember folks have said he was as old as dirt. But you might ask my grandfather."

"Oh, I am sure your grandfather will be able to tell me by the time he gets here." Piedras sat back down, put both booted feet on the table, and rocked back in his chair, piercing Christopher with a dark and unblinking gaze. Christopher stared right back at him. Finally, Piedras broke eye contact. He made a curt, dismissive gesture. "That is all. Thank you for your cooperation, Señor Groves. You are free to go."

"What about that oath? Don't you want me to take it?"

"You are young and brash. I think you might be a troublemaker. So I have not yet made up my mind on whether you are staying."

Oh, I'm staying, thought Christopher, but he was prudent enough not to say it out loud. Instead, he turned on his heel and left the meetinghouse.

"How did it go?" asked Travis.

Christopher glanced at the nearby lancers, who were watching him like vultures. He swallowed his anger.

"I think he got the better of me," he replied.

Chapter 26

After their interrogation at the hands of Captain Piedras, Christopher and Nathaniel both were inclined to think the wiser course might be to leave Anahuac for good. Travis tried his level best to dissuade them. Piedras might be suspicious, but he had no proof, and without proof he would not act. By fleeing, they would only confirm the captain's suspicions. Better, said Travis, to sit tight and see the bluff through to the end.

After discussing the matter with Rebecca, Christopher and his grandfather decided to take a trip up the Trinity to Sterling Robertson's colony. Rebecca would stay in Anahuac, and Klesko would remain in hiding. They would retrieve the thoroughbreds and study the lay of the land. Travis gave them his word that he would look out for Rebecca. Rebecca was quite certain she could look after herself. She did not like Travis, and Nathaniel surmised the reason: the Anahuac lawyer was a dashing, ambitious, and somewhat impetuous man—in these and other ways he bore a striking resemblance to one Jonathan Groves.

Old Sam Fulshear bestowed upon Nathaniel the gift of a rifle, a Kentucky flintlock, with powder and shot to go with it. Nathaniel was reluctant to accept the rifle, but Fulshear insisted. He couldn't see well enough anymore to use the weapon—in his own words he couldn't hit the broadside of a barn from the inside. If Nathaniel got around to it he could bring some venison steaks every now and again.

On the morning of their departure they had barely left the outskirts of Anahuac behind them when a pair of Mexican lancers stopped them on the road. One was the grim-faced lieutenant who had been present during the questioning. He fired questions at them in Spanish and was aggravated by their inability to comprehend. Switching to broken English, he insisted on knowing where they were bound. Nathaniel replied that they were heading upriver to visit a friend. Again, no mention was made of Sterling Robertson. They would be back in a couple of weeks. Christopher thought the lieutenant was going to forbid them to go. Instead, they were allowed to pass.

"Little wonder these Texicans want their liberty," said Christopher when they were well out of earshot of the lancers. "Those soldiers treat our people like dirt. Is that how the redcoats treated us in the old days, Grandpa?"

"Well, I was only a lad then, in a backwater town. I didn't see too many redcoats. I reckon some were good and some were bad. Same with these Mexican troops. And there are some Mexican civilians around here who don't like the soldiers any more than the Americans do."

"That lieutenant would like nothing better than to shoot the lot of us."

"He does seem to have a chip on his shoulder."

Christopher wondered aloud if it was the wife of that particular lieutenant who was having an affair with Travis.

"I'll tell you one thing," said the frontiersman. "When the time comes, those Mexicans will put up one heck of a fight."

They took passage on one of the sidewheelers that plied the Trinity, transporting the supplies which arrived in Anahuac to the colonists located inland. This rickety craft was a far cry from the floating palaces Christopher had seen on the Mississippi River. But then, these Texans seemed to have a knack for making more out of less. Throughout the journey Christopher didn't see a single iron plow. The colonists' plows were forked limbs; one prong turned the earth, another was the handle, and the third the tongue, which was lashed to the yoke on a pair of oxen—or the horns of the beasts if a yoke was lacking. Carts balanced on a single axle with two big solid wheels seemed to be the most common conveyance, and the river craft Christopher saw most often were made of cowhides sewn together and stretched over a framework of poles. There were one or two genuine flatboats. Seeing these made Christopher think of Klesko, hidden away in that secluded dugout on the Strom farm, like a rabbit in its hole.

"We should have brought Klesko with us," he told Nathaniel.

"He's probably better off laying low for a spell. Besides, I doubt that he would have come along."

"Why not? He said he wanted to see these Texas rivers."

"That man's not ever going to stray too very far from Becky if he can help it."

"You think he's in love with my mother?"

"Pretty certain that's the case." Nathaniel gave Christopher a sidelong look. "How does that sit with you?"

Christopher was silent for a moment, thinking it over.

"I think it's about time she found a man who won't stray."

Nathaniel laughed. "I agree. Your father and I were two of the strayingest men ever born. And I don't think you're much different. But I wish you wouldn't sell your father short. He was a decent man. Just made some mistakes that he couldn't live with."

"After what happened with Noelle, I see things a lot differently, Grandpa."

"I'm glad to hear it."

"But you're wrong about me. I'm going to put down roots, as soon as Greta gets here."

"Did you get that letter written?"

"And a couple since. Mr. Wells took the last one back to New Orleans with him. He said I could count on him to send it on."

"I reckon we'd better get you a cabin built before she arrives. Never met a woman yet who didn't like having her own roof over her head."

"Question is, where do we build that cabin?"

"You'll know the place when you see it."

It was Rebecca's nature to want to be useful at all times. The people of Anahuac had gone out of their way to help her and her family, and she very much desired to repay their kindness. When she asked Travis if Anahuac might be in need of a schoolteacher, he was enthusiastic. Being the most educated member of the community, and the only one with any books other than the Bible, Travis had been burdened with the task himself. The fact that he had been a schoolteacher back in Alabama had also been a factor. He was more than happy to turn it over to Rebecca, and offered her the use of his library.

Classes were held in the meetinghouse. On Rebecca's first day only five children showed up. The next day there were seven, but only four on the third. Not a single pupil managed to attend for more than three consecutive days. Rebecca did not make an issue out of this poor attendance. She understood that these were the children of farmers who worked very hard just to survive, and the youngsters were often required to labor in the fields from dawn to dusk side by side with their parents. Book learning was a luxury few could afford on a full-time basis.

The man named Tucker sat in during her second day of class, and on the day after he was joined by another buckskin-clad character. By the end of her first week there were half a dozen men in the meetinghouse. When she told Travis about this he laughed.

"Those are Anahuac's eligible bachelors, Mrs. Groves. They're not interested in learning the classics—they're interested in you."

Cheeks burning, Rebecca said, "I wish they would attend to their own business. It's rather disconcerting. They sit against the back wall and grin at me all day long."

"None of them are farmers. Take Tucker for instance. He makes a living hunting game and trading in furs. But you have done us all a great service by attracting his interest. I've been here for more than a year now, and last week was to my knowledge the first time Tucker ever bathed."

"Well, if they are not seeking an education, they don't need to attend school."

"Wild horses couldn't drag them away, ma'am."

"Oh, I shall rout them," promised Rebecca.

The next school day she began her campaign by asking Tucker to solve a ciphering problem, and imposing on another man to read a passage from Shakespeare's *Hamlet*. From then on not a single man appeared at the meetinghouse while school was in session.

Rebecca found that she still had time on her hands, and took up spinning. She had done a little darning and quilting as the mistress of Elm Tree, though she had much preferred working outside in her garden or with the thoroughbreds to staying inside. But what she was familiar with was nothing compared to weaving in the Mexican style. An old woman, Dona Petra, who lived and worked alone in a small dirt-floored shack on the edge of town, agreed to teach her. They worked without benefit of card, wheel, or loom. The wool or cotton was dyed, then picked out by hand. A piece of wool was attached to a spindle which was placed in a bowl and

spun between thumb and finger. The thread was drawn
out while the spindle turned. This was slow and tedious
work, and weeks were required to spin enough thread
for a blanket. The warp was then stretched on a frame.
The filling of unspun wool was worked in and out of the
warp by hand, secured with the use of a board which
was passed over and under the threads to pack the filling tightly.

Rebecca found that she still had some idle time, and
in those moments with nothing to do her thoughts
turned to Klesko. She wanted to visit him, now that Nathaniel was away. She knew her father would have objected strenuously had she attempted anything so rash
while he was present. Klesko was a fugitive, and she
would endanger herself as well as the riverman. She
tried to talk herself out of it, but failed. When she
broached the subject with Travis, it was the lawyer's turn
to try and dissuade her.

"You forget," he said, "that Captain Piedras has eyes
and ears in Anahuac. Someone is informing him of everything that goes on here. Under those circumstances
it is an entirely too hazardous venture."

"Nonetheless," she said, "I am going to see him. He's
been buried in that dugout for weeks now, and I am
certain he would appreciate a little company."

Travis kept trying to talk her out of it, to no avail. The
next day, a Sunday, Rebecca accompanied the Stroms to
their farm after church service. She spent the rest of the
day with them. Late that night, when the farmer's wife
took some bread and rabbit stew out to Klesko, Rebecca
went along.

The night was dark and the journey long—a half-mile
jaunt through thicket, across field, and over a babbling
brook. The wind had picked up, thrashing the top of
the trees about, and the woods were filled with moving
shadows. Rebecca was tortured with second thoughts,
and so keyed up that she saw a Mexican lancer behind

every tree. Why was she putting Klesko and the Stroms in jeopardy like this? She was on the verge of telling Mrs. Strom that she wanted to turn back when the farmer's wife whispered, "It is just ahead." The dugout was built into the side of a hill, deep in a thicket, and Rebecca couldn't make it out until she was right up on it. Mrs. Strom tapped lightly on the door. Klesko opened up immediately. When he saw the two women he sheepishly lowered the pistol he was holding.

"You have a visitor, Mr. Klesko," said Mrs. Strom as she handed him the bread and the bowl of stew. "Should I wait for you, Mrs. Groves?"

"Thank you, but there's no need for you to do that. I can find my way back."

Mrs. Strom smiled and disappeared into the night.

"You shouldn't have come, ma'am."

"Perhaps not. But here I am. Aren't you going to let me in?"

"It don't look right," protested Klesko. "You being out here with me like this."

"Well, the damage is done now, isn't it? They can think what they want. I'm here, and I would prefer not to stand outside."

The dugout was black as the womb until Klesko lit a candle. The Spartan furnishings consisted of a rough-hewn table, a couple of empty casks for sitting on, and a rope-slat bed. Blankets over a single window kept any telltale light from escaping.

"It ain't much," said Klesko. "But it's better than some places I've stayed. And it sure beats a Mexican jail."

"Mr. Klesko! You've shaved off your beard!"

Embarrassed, he ran a hand over his face. "Yes, ma'am. Not that it would fool them soldiers."

"You have a strong, handsome face."

Klesko blushed furiously. A woman had never talked

to him like that. "Shoot, ma'am, I'm as ugly as warmed-over sin, beard or no beard."

"You really must call me Rebecca. 'Ma'am' makes me feel even older than I am."

"You ain't old, ma'am—I mean, Rebecca."

She smiled, realizing that she had been fishing for a compliment. She ordered him to sit down and eat, and he offered to share the meal with her, even though he was famished. She declined the offer. They sat on the casks, at the rickety table, and she made small talk while he ate, bringing him up-to-date, telling him about her adventures as a schoolmarm, and how she had learned to weave in the Mexican style, and how Nathaniel and Christopher had gone north for a few weeks. He asked about O'Connor, and she informed him that the young Irishman had gone back to New Orleans, quite unexpectedly, without giving any indication whether he intended to return.

"I reckon he's gone back for that gal Noelle," said Klesko solemnly.

"Whatever happened between Christopher and that girl? He hasn't spoken a word about her since we left New Orleans. I thought they were getting along famously."

Klesko shook his head and shoveled more stew into his mouth. Rebecca had a hunch he knew more about the matter than he was letting on. But she didn't press the issue.

"Why didn't you go back to Louisiana with the others, Mr. Klesko?"

Klesko almost choked on the bread he was chewing. The question rendered him momentarily speechless.

"I mean," continued Rebecca, "you must know how dangerous it is for you here."

"Yes, ma'am," he mumbled.

"I would . . . I would truly hate to see anything happen to you, Mr. Klesko."

Klesko swallowed hard and smiled tentatively.

"I know you said you wanted to see the rivers of Texas," continued Rebecca, plunging nervously ahead. "But, really, is a river worth your life?"

"I'm goin' where you're goin,' ma'am ... Rebecca. And hang the risk."

Now it was her turn to blush. "I'm flattered, Mr. Klesko, really I am. But I simply can't have you risking your life on my account. I ... I want you to go back to the United States, where you will be safe from harm."

Her words knocked the breath out of him. He gasped, crestfallen.

Somehow Rebecca managed to keep smiling. "I wouldn't want that on my conscience, you see."

"I see," he muttered.

Rebecca stood up. "I had best be on my way. I shall see what I can do to make arrangements for you to leave on the next available ship."

Klesko rose as she turned for the door. "Rebecca ..."

She stopped, but did not turn to face him. "Yes?"

His voice was anguished. "My given name is John."

"Very well, then. John, I want you to know that I ... I hold you in very high regard."

Before he could say anything in response she was gone, escaping into the night, into the darkness, where no one could see her tears.

A few days downriver from the colony of Sterling Robertson, Nathaniel and Christopher disembarked the sidewheeler at a town called Arcadia, which was built on a bluff overlooking the Trinity River. Here they met a Colonel Hosea Ingram, late of Kentucky, who recognized Nathaniel and greeted him effusively. Ingram had been a lieutenant in Richard Mentor Johnson's mounted regiment during the campaign against Tecumseh and the British, a campaign which culminated in 1814 in the Battle of the Thames, a smashing victory for the American cause. Nathaniel had served as a scout for the American Army on that campaign.

Ingram invited the frontiersman and his grandson to stay the night at his home. Nathaniel was glad to accept. He learned that Ingram was now the proprietor of a trading post at Arcadia. In spite of the heavy duties the Mexican government required on most manufactured goods, he fared well in his enterprise. He lived with his wife and two young children in a cabin on the outskirts of town, located in a clearing where a handsome crop of corn was growing. His wife was a cordial and self-effacing woman, the two children well-mannered.

At supper they all sat around a clapboard table on stools. They ate from wooden platters, with forks made from joints of sugarcane, and cups fashioned from wild cymlings, scraped and scoured until they were white. The fare was simple, but nourishing. Christopher enjoyed himself immensely. The talk was stimulating, and the Ingrams made him feel right at home.

"A brick house will stand here someday," vowed Ingram. "My dear wife deserves that much."

"I am quite content with what we have," said Mrs. Ingram as she offered Christopher more bread, yams, and venison.

"Of course you are. But you'll have that brick house. I made you a promise and I shall keep my word. All it will take is our getting out from under the Mexican heel." Ingram scowled. "As a trader I can tell you, Nathaniel, that we can't endure this much longer. The Mexican government has levied a high tariff on everything we colonists need. I'm not talking about luxuries like coffee and tobacco and"—he picked up his sugarcane fork and dropped it on the table with a look of disgust on his face—"silverware, but the staples, like flour. You have seen, no doubt, the primitive conditions of our homes. We have to make virtually everything we use from scratch. I tell you, they are intending to strangle the life out of us."

"But once they wanted you here," said Nathaniel.

"Yes. To fight the damned Indians."

"Hosea! Watch your language in front of the children."

"Sorry, dear."

"What are they afraid of?" asked Nathaniel.

Ingram smiled grimly. "They fear the inevitable."

"You mean revolution."

Ingram nodded. "That is exactly what I mean, old friend. The British made the same mistake with our forefathers, who were taxed for everything under the sun, and yet possessed no rights, no representation in Parliament so that they might have some say in how those tax revenues were expended. The Mexicans—and the Spaniards before them—used us to tame this wilderness. We've given of our blood and our sweat to do the job, and learned to love this promised land with a passion that might surprise you. Yet we have no voice in how we are governed. We thought this was a republic similar to our own, with a constitution like ours which guaranteed basic and inalienable rights. It's bad enough now, but it will get worse. There is this fellow Santa Anna. Have you heard of him? One day he will seize power. I'm as certain of that as I am of the turning of the earth. And when that day comes it will be a dark day indeed for us. We will have to fight to survive."

Word had quickly spread throughout Arcadia that the legendary Flintlock Jones was in town, and several people dropped by the Ingram cabin that evening to welcome the visitors. More than once Nathaniel and Christopher were invited to stay for a few more days. Tomorrow there would be a wedding—always a huge social event on the frontier, with a big feast and a dance to follow. Everyone would be there. The frontiersman was inclined to stay, and so was Christopher. There was something neither could define that appealed to them about Arcadia.

Attending the wedding on the following day was a bittersweet experience for Christopher. Greta Inskilling was foremost in his thoughts. He wondered if she had received any of his letters. And would she come to join him in Texas? Perhaps she had changed her mind. That was a woman's prerogative, wasn't it? Or maybe she had found someone else she cared for more than him. Or maybe she was already en route. And even if she did come, how would she adapt to the primitive living conditions here? Would she be content to eat out of wooden bowls and use sugarcane forks and walk on dirt floors— she, who was accustomed to the very finest that money could buy in every regard? Such doubts preyed on Christopher's mind as he watched two of Arcadia's young people promise to love and cherish each other until death parted them.

On the heels of the wedding came the supper, and all of Arcadia showed up at the town's meetinghouse for the occasion. When the supper was cleared away the dance promptly began. The Arcadians made the splinters fly. They "shuffled" and "wired" and "cut the pigeon's wing." Three black men provided the music. One played the fiddle, another the clevis, and the third scraped a hoe with a clasp knife. Several of the young ladies of Arcadia cut their eyes at the tall, young stranger who had come up the river with the legendary Flintlock, wishing he would ask them to dance. But Christopher was too heartsick to participate in the festivities. With all these people around having a good time, he felt as lonesome as he had ever felt. He stood with his back against a wall and watched the others do-si-do. Managed to put on a good front, even though he was perfectly miserable, and nobody but his sharp-eyed and perceptive grandfather could see through his brave facade.

*　　*　　*

Next morning they bade Arcadia farewell and continued upriver. The sidewheeler had gone on without them the day before, but they hailed a passing flatboat and caught a ride. Three more days on the river were required before they reached their destination. The rivermen were glad to have a hunter of Nathaniel's prowess along. He bagged squirrels, wild turkeys, and a doe, and kept their bellies full.

Sterling Robertson had arrived home from Louisiana a week earlier. He was thrilled to see Nathaniel and Christopher, having already learned of the disaster which had befallen the *Liberty*. All he had heard was that there were some survivors, but he hadn't known their identities. He apologized profusely for the trouble the two French six-pounders had caused.

"I know I could have confided in you, Mr. Jones," said the empresario. "But I had given Travis my word I would tell no one."

"I was under the impression those cannon were for you," said Christopher.

"No, no. For Travis all along. He is a rabble-rouser, that one. I fully expect that when the revolution starts it will be in Anahuac. There are no hard feelings then? Would you have sailed anyway, had you known about the cannon?"

"Probably," said Nathaniel. "No hard feelings."

Robertson had brought the thoroughbreds safely across the border. He described an incident with a Mexican patrol, and was of the opinion that had he not been so well-known and in such good standing with the government the soldiers would have made off with the horses.

"Your reputation may be somewhat sullied," warned Nathaniel. "The soldiers down in Anahuac know that there is some connection between you and the *Liberty*."

"I am not concerned about that. Listen. The Mexicans

aren't any more prepared for war than we. They're having problems of their own south of the Río Bravo. The government is in political turmoil. But you two have a care with those thoroughbreds. Any troops you come across will like as not try to spirit them away from you. The soldiers here have grown accustomed to plundering Americans with impunity."

The loss of the brigantine guaranteed a hard winter for Robertson's people. Nathaniel promised to return after the first snow and do what he could to help.

Robertson gave him heartfelt thanks. "A hunter of your skill will make all the difference in the world. I take it you have decided to settle elsewhere."

Nathaniel glanced at Christopher. "There's a place a few days downriver we've taken a shine to."

"Yes," said Christopher. "Arcadia. I think that's where we'll be."

Robertson wished them well, and they began their journey back to Anahuac.

Arriving in Arcadia without mishap, they decided to linger there for a while. Ingram was delighted to offer them the hospitality of his home. After several days of roaming the countryside, they found a very appealing spot in some rolling hills several miles northwest of town. There was plenty of good timber and excellent graze, as well as several springs and a year-round creek. Nathaniel liked it, too, because the nearest established farm was almost two miles away. The woods were chock full of game. Wild cattle were prolific, and a *manada* of mustangs frequented the area as well.

Informing Colonel Ingram of their intentions regarding the land, Nathaniel inquired after the means by which they might lay claim to the property.

"Land is cheap enough in Texas," said Ingram. "A half-decent pony would buy you ten leagues. The problem lies in the fact that the Mexicans are not eager to have any more Americans settle here. You have three options, far as I can see. You can just stake your claim and build your cabins and not worry about the title. We are seldom bothered by the authorities here. Of course, you would have no legal right to the land if someone cared to challenge your possession of it. Or, you could try your luck in San Antonio de Bexar, with the land commissioner, but I believe your chances there would be slim indeed."

"You said there were three options. What is the third?"

Ingram grimaced. "You could deal with Billy Parker and his bunch of rogues. Last year the land commissioner came out this way to survey and make title to the claims of settlers outside the colonies. He carried with him blank certificates of title stamped with the seal of the Republic of Mexico. All they lacked were a description of the land and the signature of the commissioner. Unfortunately for the commissioner, he lusted after the wife of one of his attaches, who soon turned up dead. Of course, the commissioner was the prime suspect in the murder, and he was arrested. He has since bought himself out of that dilemma. But his blank certificates fell into the hands of several enterprising and, may I say unscrupulous, gentlemen. They bribed an old Spaniard who had once worked as a government clerk to forge the commissioner's signature on the blanks, and now they are doing a brisk business in the counterfeits. Billy Parker is one of the men involved. A pure scapegrace, that fellow. A scoundrel of the first water. But you could acquire a certificate for that property. I have no doubt on that score."

Christopher knew his grandfather was as honest as the day was long, and fully expected Nathaniel to discard that third option out of hand. But he was surprised when Nathaniel asked Ingram what such a transaction would cost.

"Do you possess any hard money?"

"None to speak of."

"I daresay it will cost you one of those splendid thoroughbreds, then, and that regardless of whether you deal with Billy Parker or the land commissioner. You see, when you deal with a government official you must have something of value with which to bribe him. The land itself will cost you nothing. The title to it *will* cost you, if you catch my meaning."

Nathaniel and Christopher talked it over. The next day the frontiersman showed Ingram a letter which Christopher had penned.

"Bowie!" exclaimed Ingram. "You are acquainted with Jim Bowie?"

"We've never met," said Nathaniel. "But Sam Houston suggested we look Bowie up if we were ever in need."

"Good heavens, yes! Bowie knows all the right people. If anyone can get it done for you, he's the man. Here, I will see to it that this letter reaches him."

"Thank you. In the meantime, Christopher and I will return to Anahuac to get my daughter. I was wondering if we could leave the horses in your care."

"A wise decision," said Ingram with a vigorous nod. "Piedras and his bunch, eh?"

"Yes."

They left that very day, taking passage down the river aboard the same sidewheeler which had transported them north from Anahuac a fortnight before. Christopher was enthusiastic about the future, and dreaming big dreams. They would build his mother a cabin, and then one for him and Greta a mile or two away atop those rolling hills. As for Nathaniel, the frontiersman made it clear he did not require a cabin of his own. He would be away most of the time, hunting and exploring. If he had a cabin it would always seem empty to him without Amanda. It came home to Christopher then—and it was a sobering thought indeed—that one day his grandfather would disappear into the wilderness and never return. No headstone for Nathaniel Jones. That wasn't his style.

Night had fallen when they arrived in Anahuac, two days after leaving Arcadia. When they reached the borrowed cabin they found Rebecca crying quietly but inconsolably. Travis was there, looking downright grim.

"They've got your friend, Klesko," said Travis. "Captain Piedras has him locked up tight in the presidio, along with Strom and his eldest son."

"What?" Christopher could scarcely believe his ear. "How?"

"I'm afraid it's my fault," confessed Travis.

"You must save them," said Rebecca.

His mother's tears shocked Christopher. She was such a strong, dauntless woman. But then he realized that maybe she cared for Klesko as much as Klesko cared for her.

"Of course we will," he said.

"What happened?" asked Nathaniel.

Travis opened his mouth to speak, but at that moment the door swung open and O'Connor stepped in out of the night.

"O'Connor!" cried Christopher, delighted. "You're back! And just in time, it seems, for that fight you've been wanting."

"Yes, I'm back." O'Connor's face was a stony mask. "And I've brought Noelle with me."

Chapter 27

That night, storm clouds rolled in off the Gulf of Mexico, and by morning the rains had come, producing a day that was gray and dismal. In that respect it matched Christopher's mood perfectly. Nathaniel had advised him to get some sleep—there was nothing they could do for Klesko before tomorrow—but Christopher hadn't managed to sleep a wink. He was angry. Angry at the Mexican soldiers, of course, but angrier still at Travis, because it was Travis who had unwittingly betrayed Klesko.

Travis was determined to make a public confession. That morning the entire population of Anahuac showed up at the meetinghouse—everyone but O'Connor and Noelle, as far as Christopher could tell. There wasn't enough room inside to accommodate everyone, so the door and windows were thrown open, despite the inclement weather, in order that those who stood outside in the downpour could hear. Many of the men had brought their families, and Christopher deemed it only right that they did so. This was the most severe crisis Anahuac had ever faced. And some of the men, like Tucker and Lucas, were armed. They had been longing for a fight, and hoped that this business would be the catalyst for starting one.

When Travis mounted the platform at the rear of the room the crowd fell silent. He scanned the somber, upturned faces of his neighbors, cleared his throat, and plunged resolutely ahead.

"Yesterday; the soldiers took the man Klesko, one of the survivors of the *Liberty,* into custody. They also arrested Joshua Strom and his eldest son. For those of you who didn't know, the Stroms were hiding Mr. Klesko, who had been accused of smuggling in connection with the two cannon. Later, I received a message from Captain Piedras. He has made an offer—the lives of those three men in exchange for the six-pounders."

A murmur of excitement rippled through the congregation. Travis killed it with the wave of a hand.

"You may be wondering how Piedras found Klesko. That was my doing. I made the mistake of telling a young woman with whom I ... with whom I am acquainted. She happens to be the wife of Lieutenant Riaz. I was bragging to her about how we had outsmarted her husband and the captain. I had too much to drink. Not that that is any excuse. My foolish behavior has placed all of you in jeopardy. The only consolation is that I never spoke to her about where we had hidden the cannon."

Travis paused. Pale and expressionless, he waited for the explosion of outrage which he fully expected from these people who had put their trust in him. But no one made a sound. Outside, thunder rolled across the sky and the wind whipped the trees and the rain hammered against the shingles of the meetinghouse roof, but inside it was deathly silent, and as the silence extended and became even more uncomfortable someone finally coughed and someone else shuffled his feet.

"You have looked to me for leadership," said Travis, "and I have always had the best interests of Anahuac at heart. But now I have betrayed your faith. I suggest you find someone else to lead you. That is about all I have to say. I cannot ask for your forgiveness. What I have done is unforgivable. In my vanity I tried to impress a woman with how clever I was." Travis shook his head bitterly. "I deserve to be shot. I can only hope that one day I will have an opportunity to make amends, to you, and to Texas."

From the back of the room Tucker called out, "What if we don't give 'em those cannon, Will?"

"Then Klesko and Strom and Strom's boy will be executed by firing squad. The execution will take place tomorrow at dawn."

"What happens if we give up them cannon?" asked another man.

"Captain Piedras gives his solemn word that the men will not be shot. Instead, they will be taken to Saltillo in chains and imprisoned there."

"That's the same as bein' dead, if you ask me," said Tucker. "Never heard of nobody comin' out of those Mescan prisons alive."

Sitting with Nathaniel and Rebecca in the front row, Christopher glanced across at Mrs. Strom and her other two sons, who were seated on the other side of the center aisle. Mrs. Strom was dry-eyed, her head held high and proud.

"What do you think we should do, Will?" asked someone else.

"I have forfeited the right to even venture an opinion."

"Shucks, Will," said Tucker, "we all make mistakes."

Voices were raised in agreement. Clearly the people of Anahuac were still behind Travis. Overwhelmed with gratitude and relief, Travis had to work to maintain his composure.

"Very well, then," he said. "If you want my opinion, here it is. We cannot surrender the cannon. We cannot even admit that we have them in our possession. God only knows what would happen to this town. I firmly believe Piedras would make an example of Anahuac, and it would not be pleasant, I can assure you."

"What could he do?" asked Tucker.

"He could put Anahuac to the torch, and march us

all back across the Sabine. I think he would like nothing better."

Dead silence followed this dire prediction. Looking around, Christopher could read on the faces of the crowd that everyone believed Travis. He was inclined to believe it, too. Having seen Klesko and the three *Liberty* crewmen dragging a heavy timber by a rope around their necks, slowly strangling themselves with every step, he knew that Piedras was capable of anything.

"I say we march in there and take our people back by force," said Tucker.

A dozen men jumped to their feet and shouted approval of this plan.

"We might be able to whip Piedras and his lancers," conceded Travis, "but some of us, maybe a lot of us, will perish in the attempt. And then what? They'll send an army against us."

Would all of Texas rally to the defense of Anahuac in that event? This was the unspoken question foremost in everyone's mind. Christopher didn't think so. It wasn't time. That was what everyone said. The revolution would come, but not now, not yet, not over two six-pounders and the lives of three men.

"So what do we do?" asked Tucker. "Let 'em shoot those three men?"

Travis glanced at Mrs. Strom. She rose, turned to face the others.

"My husband would not want you to risk your lives to save his. We knew the risks, and accepted them. I have no regrets. We did what we thought was right."

Christopher shot to his feet.

"You can't let them die," he said, glancing at Travis.

"What do you suggest?" asked Travis.

Christopher turned to face the Anahuacans. "I say we fight. Now. What are we waiting for? What better reason to fight than the lives of three men? The Stroms took risks in doing what they thought was right, offering shelter to an innocent man. Can we do any less? So what if they burn this town to the ground. Towns can be rebuilt. So what if they march us all back to Louisiana in chains? We'll march right back again. For months now all I've heard about Texans is that they're ready to fight for their rights—tomorrow. Well, tomorrow three men die. Here's your chance. What are you going to do about it?"

"Groves is right!" cried Tucker. "I say we lick them Mescans!"

A dozen men raised a cheer.

"Piedras and his men are professional soldiers," said a farmer, rising from the pew where he had been sitting with his wife and three children. "What chance do we have against them?"

"A very good chance," replied Christopher. "They are cavalry, and cavalry has seldom won a battle by itself. Beside, their training has not prepared them for the kind of tactics we will use. Then, too, you mustn't forget that we have artillery."

"We have no ammunition for those six-pounders," said Travis.

"No, we don't. Nor do we have time to make molds for round shot. But we can make grapeshot."

"Even if we can whip the lancers, what about the army Will was talking about?" queried the farmer.

"We'll deal with that when and if it happens. The government is in turmoil. That army might not come. I have a hunch the Mexicans aren't ready for a war with us. Listen. I can tell you from personal experience that it does no good to run away from trouble. It follows you wherever you go. You may not like it, but you've got to stand and fight. Napoleon himself said that retreat always cost more in men and matériel and especially morale than the bloodiest engagement, with the difference that in battle you inflict loss upon your enemy, while in retreat only you will lose. So what do you say? Stand your ground, risk everything, because if you don't you will lose it anyway."

The farmer glanced at his wife. Eyes shining brightly, she nodded. "He's right," said the farmer. "It's now or never, boys. Let's fight!"

Suddenly everyone was on their feet, and the cheer that rose up inside and out of the meetinghouse was so loud it drowned out the crack of thunder from the gray and turbulent sky.

There was much to be done, and precious little time. By virtue of his inspiring words in the meetinghouse that morning, Christopher became the de facto leader of the Anahuacans, with Travis his able lieutenant. For the first time since his discharge from the United States Military Academy Christopher felt as though the two years he had spent at West Point had not been wasted after all.

The first order of business was to render the French six-pounders effective. While a crew of a dozen men took a wagon out to the edge of the swamp to disinter the cannon, Christopher instructed another group on how to make grapeshot. Necessity was the mother of invention—horseshoe nails, small stones, bits and pieces of iron and tinware were stuffed into bags made from hemp grain sacks. As for powder charges, Christopher put more men to work making these. One thing Anahuac wasn't short of was gunpowder. A pair of ramrods were devised by securing two tightly wrapped linsey-woolsey shirts around one end of stout, straight hickory limbs.

The question arose regarding how to transport the cannon. A wagon was dismantled and a six-pounder lashed to each of the axles. Christopher wanted the artillery to be as mobile as possible, so several farmers were dispatched to bring in their mules. Each cannon would have a hitch of four knob heads.

Men were selected to man the six-pounders, and

Christopher devoted much of his time to teaching them the rudiments of loading and firing the guns. Kindling and Spanish moss was collected, dried out, and placed in buckets covered with a makeshift leather flap. Christopher demonstrated how the powder charge was to be rammed into the barrel with the ramrods, where it was pricked by inserting a thin piece of iron—provided by the blacksmith—through the vent. The bag of grapeshot followed. Powder was then poured from a horn into the quick-match vent tube. The kindling in the buckets were set alight using flints. Then a stick dipped in coal oil was lighted and used to ignite the powder in the tube, which in turn fired the charge, which propelled the grapeshot. Each cannon was fired once, out on the edge of town, in the pouring rain, and Christopher was satsified with the results of the experiment.

He was impressed, too, by the spirit of the people of Anahuac. Everyone pitched in. The children collected the kindling for the fire buckets. The women sewed the powder charges and bags of grapeshot together; they also provided over seventy men with food. The only persons Christopher didn't see were O'Connor and Noelle. Finally he could stand it no longer. He went to Peyton's boarding house, where according to Travis his friend and the mulatto woman were staying. He wasn't too sure if O'Connor was still his friend, so he approached the meeting with some trepidation, not knowing what to expect. The look on O'Connor's face when he opened the door was far from friendly.

"What do you want?"

"Among other things, to let you know there's going to be a fight tomorrow. I remember you saying you didn't want to miss it."

"I've got more important things to do."

Christopher glanced past O'Connor. The room was small—he could see all of it from the doorway. Noelle was standing by the window, her back to him, looking out at the rain. She wore a thin white muslin wrapper, and he could see her body through it—she might as well have worn nothing at all—and he felt the old desire stir within him. The bed was unmade, and Christopher felt a pang of jealousy in spite of himself.

"Look," he said, "don't let her do this to you."

"She hasn't done anything to me."

"We're talking about Klesko's life."

"I don't care."

Christopher controlled his anger, telling himself that O'Connor was under her spell and perhaps not entirely responsible for his words. "You're confused about what's important."

O'Connor was furious. "Get out of here."

"Why did you come back?"

"I didn't want to. She did."

Christopher shook his head. "She doesn't care about you, O'Connor. She's just using you. Can't you see that?"

O'Connor knew in his heart it was so—Christopher could see it in his eyes. But the Irishman was stubbornly refusing to admit it to himself.

"I told you to get out," he snarled. "Just leave us alone."

"I want to talk to Noelle."

"You've got a lot of gall."

"Noelle."

She didn't turn from the window. Though he couldn't see her face, Christopher knew somehow that she was smiling.

"Stay away from us," warned O'Connor, almost spitting out the words. "Noelle's with me now. You're the one who uses people. You used her and then just threw her away. It's too late for you."

"I hope it's not too late for you."

O'Connor slammed the door in his face.

*   *   *

Captain Piedras was accustomed to being awakened at dawn by his orderly. But this morning Lieutenant Riaz was the one to wake him. Piedras took one look at his subordinate's face and knew something had happened.

"They have come," said Riaz.

"Travis?"

"He has brought the cannon."

Piedras was dressed in record time. His orderly always had his uniform ready, brushed out and immaculately clean, the boots polished to a high sheen. Buckling on his sword, Piedras strode out into the presidio yard.

"Have your company of lancers mounted and ready," he told Riaz, and strode across the hard-packed ground to the gate, where he climbed a ladder to an earthen parapet and gazed out over the hewn logs of the stockade wall.

A lone rider was approaching down the road from Anahuac, which skirted a salt marsh at the base of a low, brush-covered ridge. Beyond the marsh lay the bay. The dawn's early light silvered the tranquil surface of the water.

All Piedras could see of the rider at this distance was the flag of truce he was carrying, a strip of white cloth tied to the end of a crooked stick. The captain held out his hand. The orderly was ready as always, and something of a mind reader when it came to the captain's wishes. He promptly handed Piedras a field glass.

"It is Groves," said Piedras, focusing the glass on the lone rider.

He swept the glass further along the road to a collection of men, mules, and a wagon two hundred yards behind the horsemen. There were the brace of six-pounders. There, too, were Travis and Nathaniel Jones. Travis was sitting a dappled gray. The frontiersman stood in the back of a wagon, leaning on his long rifle. Piedras counted ten other men around the cannon. Next he scanned the brush on the ridge, but saw nothing out of the ordinary there. He paid no attention to the salt marsh. There was no cover to be had there. Even a coyote could not have concealed itself in the salt marsh, assuming it did not sink out of sight in that soggy and treacherous ground.

With a smile he lowered the field glass and descended the parapet, where Riaz was watching his lancers form up.

"It would appear they have accepted my offer," said Piedras. "Orderly, bring my horse at once. Lieutenant, you and I will ride out to see what Señor Groves has to say for himself."

Christopher halted his horse a hundred yards from the presidio and waited until Piedras and the lieutenant emerged through the gate and rode up to him.

"Señor Groves," said Piedras, looking smug, "I take it you have come to surrender the cannon."

"No, sir. I've come to request that you release your prisoners."

Piedras was taken aback.

"Do you know about my grandfather?" asked Christopher. "In case you don't, let me tell you, he is one of the best shots there ever was. I wouldn't try anything, if I were you. At this range he couldn't possibly miss."

"Insolent fool!" muttered Riaz.

Piedras gestured sharply to silence the lieutenant.

"You should reconsider," he said coldly. "I will order the prisoners shot immediately if you do not bring those cannon to me this instant."

"Let them go unharmed or you'll regret it, Captain."

"How dare you threaten me! Surrender the cannon."

"Come and take them."

Riaz couldn't restrain himself any longer. Steel rasped against steel as he brandished his saber. With a shout he raised it to strike.

The bullet caught him dead center. Christopher clearly heard the impact. An instant later the report of Nathan-

Jason Manning

iel's flintlock rifle reached him. The saber fell from the lieutenant's hand as Riaz pitched backward off the horses.

Sitting his horse between the two six-pounders, Travis was watching Christopher and the two Mexican officers through his own field glass. "Splendid!" he exclaimed. "Right through the heart, Mr. Jones. A very commendable shot."

Reloading, Nathaniel said, "There's nothing very commendable about being a widow-maker, Mr. Travis."

Sawing on the reins to still his prancing horse, Christopher hurled the flag of truce into the dust of the road, glowering at Piedras. The captain, disconcerted, spared the body of Lieutenant Riaz a quick glance, then wheeled his horse and galloped back to the presidio. Christopher made haste up the road in the direction of the cannon.

"Think they'll come out?" asked Travis as Christopher checked his horse beside the wagon.

Christopher turned to look. This was the moment of truth. If Piedras remained behind those walls, all was lost. The minutes crawled like hours. Christopher had to remind himself to breathe. The tension was unbearable. The only man who seemed unaffected was Nathaniel. He was standing in the back of the wagon, leaning on the rifle again, completely calm and composed, watching the stockade like a hawk. Christopher's admiring gaze lingered on the tall, straight, buckskin-clad figure of the old leatherstocking. His very presence gave Christopher a much-needed dose of confidence.

"Here they come!" yelled Travis.

Piedras and his lancers were boiling out of the gate, charging down the road at full gallop, their lances flashing in the soft golden light of the just-risen sun.

Chapter 28

"Christopher, you were right about Piedras!" said Travis with a laugh. "He had to attack. It is his nature."

In stark contrast to Travis, who was flush and edgy with excitement, Christopher sat pale and rigid as a statue in the saddle. His voice was quite calm and steady as he reminded the gun crews to hold their fire until he gave the order. He knew that what he was asking of these untried and untrained men was exceedingly difficult. The lancers were a fearsome sight as they thundered up the road. Yet the farmers kept their nerve and stood their ground.

When the lancers were a mere fifty yards away Christopher shouted the order. "Fire!" The six-pounders spat flame and smoke. The carnage was terrible to behold as the grapeshot ripped through the horsemen. Men and mounts went down screaming. The blast stopped the charge cold and threw the Mexicans into disarray.

At that moment the rest of the men from Anahuac emerged from their places of concealment in the brush along the ridge and fired a ragged but highly effective volley into the lancer formation strung out along the road. The result was devastating. In a matter of seconds thirty lancers were killed or wounded—half the men Piedras had led out of the presidio. The captain himself was miraculously unscathed. He tried to rally his command. But a second blast of grapeshot from the six-pounders finished the job. The remnants of the lancers fled into the salt marsh. The men pouring down off the ridge blocked their escape down the road.

The mounts of the lancers were immediately bogged down—some sank up to their bellies in the soggy ground. The Anahuacans swept forward across the road, yelling and shooting, an inexorable tide of buckskin and homespun. Through the white pall of powder smoke which hung heavy and acrid in the still morning air, Christopher saw Piedras slump forward in the saddle, wounded. Then he rose up and slashed at a nearby Texan with his sword. The Texan jumped back out of the way and fired his squirrel gun at near point-blank range. Piedras toppled off his horse to lie dead in the marsh, his once impeccable uniform splattered with blood and muck.

The lancers stood no chance. Their horses were immobilized in the salt marsh, and their lances were practically useless against the rifles and shotguns of the Anahuacans. It was just as Christopher had planned it. Though he had not seen the field with his own eyes, Travis had described it down to the last detail, and Christopher had made his dispositions accordingly. Yet he felt no satisfaction in seeing such brave men as these Mexican lancers fall.

In a matter of minutes the firing died down. The handful of lancers who were left threw down their weapons and raised their hands.

"By God, it worked!" said Travis. "Christopher, it worked perfectly!"

"Take charge of the prisoners," said Christopher. "Make certain no harm comes to them. And care for the wounded. Our *and* theirs." He glanced at Nathaniel. "Ready, Grandpa?"

"Ready as I'll ever be, lad."

Christopher dismounted, climbed into the wagon seat, and gathered up the leathers. Glancing over his shoulder at the six powder kegs in the wagon bed, he

gave the reins a hard flick to motivate the mules in
the hitch. Nathaniel knelt behind the seat as the wagon
trundled down the road. Up ahead, a dozen Anahuacans were engaged in a shooting match with about
the same number of soldiers on the parapets. The gate
had been closed. Christopher had expected that. He
urged the mules into a reluctant gallop. As he barreled
past the Texans he yelled, "Keep their heads down,
boys!" The men gave a cheer and advanced in the
wake of the wagon, firing as they came. A bullet splintered the weathered wood of the seat beside Christopher. Nathaniel's rifle spoke, and a soldier cartwheeled
off the top of the wall.

Reaching the gate, Christopher turned the wagon
sharply as he checked the mules. Now the Mexicans
above had to lean out to fire directly down at them. A
few tried, but the Anahuacans made them pay dearly
for the attempt. As Christopher detached the hitch from
the wagon and sent the mules on their way, Nathaniel
broke open all six of the casks with the stock of his rifle.
Working fast, they stacked the casks as the foot of the
gate. Three men, one of them Tucker, ran up to help
them tip the wagon over onto its side. Christopher
hoped this would contain the blast.

A powder trail was made using one of the open casks.
Christopher told the others to run for it. Drawing a pistol from his belt, he fired point-blank into the powder
trail. The powder flared. He turned and ran. Ahead of
him he saw one of the Texans go down, hit in the leg.
Tucker and Nathaniel helped the wounded man up.
They all took a few more strides and then the casks
exploded and the blast hurled them to the ground.

When the rain of wood splinters ceased falling, Christopher got up and checked the damage, his vision
blurred, his eyes burning in the smoke. There wasn't
much left of the gate. Drawing the cutlass, he motioned
for the Texans to follow him. He led the charge, clam-

bering over the debris of wagon and gate, bursting into the yard of the presidio. A soldier materialized out of the smoke and almost ran him through with a bayonet. Christopher struck the man's rifle aside with a downward stroke of the cutlass. One of the Anahuacans shot the soldier down. Christopher felt the man's hot blood spray his face. There were a few more shots fired, but the fight had gone out of the garrison. The Mexicans who were still standing surrendered.

It was over. Christopher felt suddenly listless and tired and a little nauseated. He just stood there, not seeing or hearing anything, looking at the body of the dead soldier at his feet. Nathaniel shook him out of it. They went to find Klesko and the Stroms.

Travis met them at the gate, looking solemn.

"You had better come with me, Christopher."

They walked up the road a hundred yards. Christopher saw the gray Travis had been riding, cropping at a clump of grass a few feet off the road. Lucas was standing near the horse. Then Christopher saw the body Lucas was standing over.

"We only lost three men," said Travis. "But I regret to inform you that one of them was your friend."

Christopher stared at O'Connor. The Irishman lay sprawled on his back, sightless eyes as blue as the Texas sky. A gaping bloody wound caused by a lance.

"He joined us up on the ridge," drawled Lucas. "Guess he didn't want to miss the shivaree. Fought like a devil."

"I wonder what made him change his mind," mumbled Christopher.

"We have won a great victory today," said Travis. "The men who fell on this field will be forever honored."

The words rang hollow to Christopher.

"I'll dance a jig . . ." he whispered, but couldn't finish.

*   *   *

Two days later, Christopher found Travis in his law office, packing books and papers into a small parfleche valise.

"I heard you were leaving," said Christopher.

"As should you, my friend. As should you. I wouldn't be surprised if we both had a price on our heads after what happened."

Christopher shrugged. "Who knows what the future holds in store. But that's not why you're leaving."

"No." Travis smiled like a boy caught with his hand in the cookie jar. He took a half-empty bottle of sour mash from a desk drawer and held it up. "Care to join me?"

"Don't mind if I do."

Travis poured two glasses and offered a toast. "To Texas. May she one day be a republic of free men."

Christopher drank to that. "You know, Will, the people here don't hold it against you."

"Perhaps not. If they have forgiven me, fine. But I cannot forgive myself. Someday, somehow, I will make it up to them."

"Know where you're going?"

Travis shook his head. "But we will meet again, Christopher. I feel it in my bones. Like you said, the Mexicans may not come tomorrow or next week or even next year. But they *will* come. And I will be there to meet them. As will you. I must admit, I have learned some important things from you. One has to do with running away. This is the last time you will see me turn tail and run, I promise you that." He grinned as though he was joking, but Christopher knew he wasn't.

Filling up the glasses, Travis knocked back another shot and gasped at the liquid fire exploding in his belly.

"So," he said, "your mother is on her way to Arcadia?"

"Yes. With my grandfather and Klesko. I'm waiting here."

"Waiting for what?"

"A ship to come in."

Travis corked the bottle and dropped it into the valise. He threw a quick, pensive look around the room. "You know, I never thought I liked this place—until today. Now I'm rather sorry to leave it." He sighed. "Funny, but I never have really felt as though I belonged, no matter where I went. And I just don't think being a lawyer is my true calling. But I know that somewhere out there is the answer. Do you belive in destiny, Christopher?"

"In the past few months I've come to."

"I wish I knew mine. It is the great mystery, your *raison d'être*—your reason for being. Yet the day will dawn when you will know that it is the right time and the right place, and you will leave your mark." Travis put out his hand. "Best of luck to you."

Christopher shook the proffered hand. "And to you. I hope you find what you're looking for."

The town of Anahuac seemed to be holding its breath, expecting a storm of Mexican retribution, but not knowing when it would come. The wounded Mexican soldiers had been well cared for, and the prisoners released. Christopher made it clear to the only surviving officer, a Lieutenant Herrera, that they had not fought in order to start a war, but rather to save the lives of three innocent men. Herrera was a reasonable man. He assured Christopher that he understood, and would pass the word along. But they both agreed it probably would make no difference in the long run.

The Anahuacans kept their guns loaded and their eyes peeled and their fingers crossed. Armed patrols roamed in the vicinity of the presidio, but Herrera and the remnant of the garrison were not inclined to start any trouble. A sentry was on duty around the clock on the docks, for there were some who said the attack would come from the sea.

Christopher kept his own vigil on the docks. He had very little else to do. Nathaniel, Klesko, and his mother were gone. So was Noelle. She had simply vanished on the day of the battle. Christopher had wanted to talk to her, to find out why O'Connor had joined the fight after all, and to tell her that he was truly sorry about what had happened, because he didn't love her, but loved another with all his heart and soul.

Yet no one could tell him what had happened to her. As far as he could tell she had not taken passage on a ship. She had not departed Anahuac on a horse or in a wagon. Perhaps she had gone up the river. Perhaps she had just walked into the woods. Not knowing preyed on Christopher's mind. His conscience bothered him. He tried to persuade himself that he wasn't responsible. Noelle's vanishing act left a part of his life unresolved, and he couldn't help feeling as though it never would be, because he doubted he would ever see her again, or even know what had become of her. In this way she would always be with him, and he wondered if she had planned it that way.

Two weeks after the battle Nathaniel returned to Anahuac. He went to Sam Fulshear's place, where he knew Christopher was staying, and he brought the old man some venison steaks. Fulshear directed the frontiersman to the docks.

"He's out there from dawn until well after dark," said the old-timer. "Day in and day out, rain or shine. What's he waitin' for?"

"His future," said Nathaniel.

He found Christopher sitting on the end of a pier with his legs dangling, reading Napoleon's *Maxims*.

"Getting ready for the next one?" asked the old leatherstocking.

Christopher was happy to see him, and asked after his mother.

"I think Becky's going to like it up there," said Nathaniel. "The folks thereabouts have all pitched in to help build her a cabin. I reckon it'll be finished by the time we get back."

"And Klesko?"

"Happy as a lark. I thought I'd come down and see how you were doing. Any word?"

Christopher took a folded sheet of good heavy vellum from the book and handed it to the frontiersman.

"Came on a coastal schooner day before yesterday," he said, beaming.

Nathaniel unfolded the letter and read:

Dearest Christopher,
   I have gone to Texas.
              Love, Greta

Grinning, Nathaniel gave the letter back to Christopher, who held it as though it were the most precious thing in the world.

"Short and sweet," said Nathaniel.

Christopher nodded. In his emotional state, he did not trust himself to speak.

Tucker came along the pier to join them. "There's a ship out yonder."

They turned to look, squinting against the glare of the afternoon sun on the gray mirror of the sea.

"There she is," said Nathaniel. "I can just make her out on the horizon."

"Wonder if she's carryin' soldiers," said Tucker, gripping his shotgun tightly.

"I wonder," said Christopher, and he was smiling.

Read all of
Jason Manning's
historical novels of the
American frontier,
available from
Signet Books.

Battle of the Teton Basin

All Zach Hannah wants is to be left alone, high in the mountains, with his Indian bride. But as long as Sean Michael Devlin lives, Zach can find no peace. Now, Zach must track down this man—the former friend who stole his wife and left him to die at the hands of the Blackfeet. It is an odyssey of vengeance that will lead him from the Yellowstone to St. Louis along the Santa Fe Trail, and back to the high country— where the mountains echo with the gunfire and blood cries of a cataclysmic war. As mountain men and Blackfoot braves clash in an epic battle that will change the course of history in the American West, Zach and Devlin square off in a final reckoning . . . that only one of them will survive.

Flintlock

In 1806, the ambitious and charismatic Aaron Burr is plotting treason against the U.S. Ruined as a politician, he devises a scandalous plan to carve his own private empire from the heart of the young republic and detach the western states from the Union.

President Thomas Jefferson suspects Burr, but he needs evidence. Surrounded by political enemies, he turns to Flintlock Jones, a legendary Kentucky frontierman and peerless marksman. Enlisting the help of young naval officer, Lieutenant Jonathan Groves, Jones embarks on a suicide mission of epic proportions as he pursues Burr and his army of ruffians across the dark and bloody ground of Kentucky and down the deadly Natchez Trace. But before the two patriots can stop Burr, Flintlock will have to face a ghost from his past whose personal mission is to destroy the United States.

112

…n Ma…

to him ase that. "Sh… ma… …. …s ugly as warmed

The Border Captains

The fledgling United States has survived
the Revolutionary War. And with the
turn of the new century, settlers are
poised to continue their westward thrust
through the dark and bloody killing
grounds of Kentucky. But in their path
stands the British military's might, and
an even more menacing and worthy
foe—the brilliant, brave, and legendary
Native American chief Tecumseh.

The war of 1812 is about to begin. And
in the hands of such American heroes as
"Mad" Anthony Wayne, William Henry
Harrison, Henry Clay, and Daniel Boone
. . . with the trigger fingers of a buckskin-
clad army . . . and in the courage, daring,
and determination of frontiersman Nathaniel "Flintlock" Jones, history is to
be made, a wilderness to be won, and a
spellbinding saga of the American past
is to be brought to pulse-pounding, un-
forgettable life . . .

Green River Rendezvous

Zach Hannah was a legend of courage, skill, and strength, even among fellow mountain men. To the Crow Indians he was a favored friend, to the Blackfeet he was a hated foe, to former friend Sean Devlin he was a rival to be destroyed, and to the American Fur Company he stood tall in the way of their scheme to rob the Rockies of the fabulous wealth in pelts. With his beloved wife Morning Sky at his side, a hardbitten team under his command, a Hawken rifle and a hunting knife in his hands and treacherous enemies shadowing his every move, Zach Hannah faced the most deadly native tribe in the West and the most brutal brigade of trappers ever to make the high country a killing ground ...

High Country

Zach Hannah was a raw youth when he left the hill country of Tennessee to seek his fortune in the West. In the year 1825, the distant Rockies offered all the wealth a man could want. The mad demand for beaver pelts spawned a booming fur trade that sent men to battle against the fury of nature and hostile Indian tribes, where they found themselves in an adventure that only the strongest could survive. Zach Hannah took the challenge ... to learn the ways of the wild and those who lived in it ... to discover that white treachery could be as deadly as Blackfoot terror ... and to find passionate love with a beautiful Indian woman—and a fight to the death to protect her ...